SPELLSWORDS

Allen Snell

DEDICATION

To my parents,

It's been a wonderful creative journey so far, and many people have helped me carry the torch. But you lit the imaginative spark that started it all.

I will forever be grateful for the love and stories you instilled in me from the beginning.

SPELLSAGA

Book One

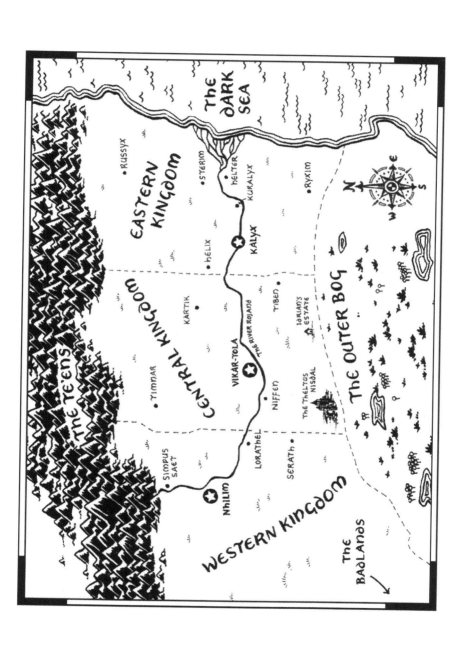

CHAPTER

"So, what's my cut exactly?" Garen made his way through the sculpted passages of the cave and into the Espen storeroom. He dropped his heavy pack onto the sorting table in the center. It rattled with the clank of trinkets, jewelry, and sheer Jundux coin, all the sounds of a successful night's work. Garen looked around to the other men. Three of the four wore a tense, awkward expression.

The fourth was Okso, leader of the Espen clan. Or rather "organization." They preferred organization. Past the bald, wrinkled skin, Okso's beady green eyes held an unpleasant stare. He took a deep breath and broke the silence. "It's been some time since we've managed to walk away with much of value. Our own come first. Seeing as how you're not one of us, I'm afraid there's no cut for you this time."

"Of course you haven't walked away with much of value." Garen raised his voice slightly. "If it wasn't for me, you wouldn't have walked away at all. You'd still be surrounded by a dozen city guards, who'd likely have your necks on the boards by sunrise." He looked around to the other men hoping he might find a trace of gratitude in them. He saw none. "So, I'm thinking I must have misheard you. I'll ask again. What's my cut exactly?"

Another Espen spoke up. "You heard right. He said you're not one of us. Maybe stick around and you'll get paid next time."

"No, I'll get paid this time." On instinct Garen reached for his sword. He stopped the impulse, leaving his fist clenched at his side.

Okso did not miss the movement and took a step toward Garen. "Listen, you want to run wild and live under your own banner, that's fine. But this is Espen coin now. And I can't spare any for a drifter."

"Well, you should have thought about that before you agreed to hire one."

1

Okso turned away and walked toward the vault locker in the back. He raised his arm and the other three men each took a step toward Garen. "Sorry, kid. Situation's changed."

"It really has."

Garen had no illusions of walking away with his even share, but at least he came prepared to bargain. These men had not. Garen even considered offering to take half his share and be gone. The evening had grown late in their journey back from Timnar, and he wouldn't mind an easy out for once. But even if he thought they'd take the deal, he couldn't bring himself to offer it. Refusing to pay him at all was more than a shot at his earnings. They had insulted his worth. Garen could walk away easier if they had reached straight into his pockets.

Instinct brought his hand to the hilt of his katana, and this time he did not stop it. "I'll make you one last offer," Garen said, sizing up the men in front of him. "You give me what's mine, and I walk out of here having saved all of your lives."

"Saved?" the youngest of the group laughed. "Saved from what?"

"Saved, spared, it's all the same really."

They offered him no verbal response, only readying their own weapons in reply. Garen knew the feeling of being outnumbered all too well. Experience taught him it came down to control more than force. And that meant his opponents would need to be careless enough to let him do so. Thankfully, one of the Espen grunts in plated armor had ignored his advice earlier in the night, but would take it more seriously in a moment.

Garen unsheathed his katana and sliced upward through the air, releasing a thin jet of flame from the arc of his blade. The tight, blue stream was not impressive in size, but he needed a focused heat more than flare. As soon as it reached the armored chest-piece, the man's arms flailed in panic, reaching for the metal plating too scalding to remove. He fell backward to the ground howling. The tunic beneath his armor provided little insulation from the searing plate he could not escape.

Garen shuddered and turned his focus toward the other two. The youngest of them stood paralyzed by the screams of his ally. Garen decided to confine him to that position for now. With another quick swing of his sword, the cave floor crept over the young bandit's feet. When he finally snapped from his horrified state, he fell forward just at the waist, unaware of the stone wrapped up to his ankles.

The third man sprinted across the room with his blade drawn. Garen raised his own sword to block the incoming strike, but the man had momentum to aid him in parrying the blade down. Garen commonly found himself outmatched when it came to strict melee. He considered himself better than most, but the man he was up against now clearly had the advantage when blades met. He imagined he'd be dead a hundred times over if not for a single asset, something he could only describe as *awareness*.

The man stepped into the parry with his left foot, and Garen could see his hips following the same line of momentum. Guessing at the shoulder that would plow into him once their blades were turned down, Garen released unexpectedly and slid to the right. Dangerous as it was to turn his blade loose in such close proximity, he guessed correctly, and the shift in balance left his foe lunging forward at nothing. Garen swept his blade around and delivered a deep slice to his side as he barreled past.

Garen didn't expect any difficulties from the last enemy trapped in his stance. An opponent with no footwork was no opponent at all. But instead of finding the youngest of the Espen rooted where he left him, Garen turned just in time to notice him a stride away with long-sword drawn. Evidently, he had some magical prowess to free himself, but the clumsy manner in which he held his weapon negated those concerns. He delivered an early thrust. Garen sidestepped the blow and knocked it aside. The position left Garen clean to twirl his katana back and slice his striking arm. But before he could bring his blade down, however, a piercing sting bit into his right shoulder, forcing the sword out of his grip. Garen watched the katana release mid-swing and bounce across the floor.

He looked up to his opponent to see how he managed the attack, but he was still off balance, unprepared to have done anything of the sort. Instead, Garen followed the haze in the air to its unpleasant source. Across the room stood Okso, a towering mass of disappointment and fury. The man was in good shape for his size and age, but the elderly titan hadn't reached it on physical prowess alone. The rumors of his magic's depth spread far and wide among the Te'en Mountains, and Garen knew enough to take them seriously. In this region, rumors were not spread by idle boredom but by active fear.

Okso raised his arms and summoned another lance of wind. Garen rolled to the side, already trying to decide the best way to close the gap between them. He did not care to evade these invisible projectiles for any longer than he had to.

One more dodge. Then straight at him.

Okso swung his arms forward again. Garen bounced to the left, but overestimated his own speed. The crippling bolt caught him on the heel, ripping through his leather boot and twisting his tumble. Garen's head smacked against the stone floor and slid against the center-room table. He lay still, dazed for the moment.

Footsteps approached him. "Should I kill him now, Master Okso?" the young bandit's voice echoed in his head.

"I think you've already proven how useless you are today."

The ringing in Garen's ears finally stopped, but he did not open his eyes or bounce back into the fight yet.

"I was simply offering to help."

"You can help by staying out of my way," Garen heard Okso mutter a string of curses under his breath, but more importantly, he heard the labored footsteps moving toward him. "Doesn't matter how many of you idiots I take on, still seems like if you want something done right, you have to do it—"

"Quicker." Garen rolled to his feet, unsheathing the short sword against his thigh. Okso did not hesitate to release another spear of wind. Prepared this time, Garen popped up a square of the stone floor under one of the table legs. The bags dropped to the floor as the table spun into the air in front of him. The blast tore through the wood, splintering the furniture to pieces and filling the air between them with debris. Before the dust could settle, Garen lunged forward through the cloud and caught Okso against his jaw with the pommel of his sword. Garen watched his jowls ripple and heard the crack of brittle bones, first from the impact, and again as he fell back against the cave floor. Garen stood over him, and he could see the look of pleading in the man's eyes already, begging for his life before he'd even spoken a word. Would he have spared Garen's life? Or more compelling, would the Te'ens be any worse off with one less clan among them?

Garen brought his sword to his enemy's throat and looked him in the eye. The silent pleading for mercy was already slowing him. He knew he had to finish the deed before that pitiful gaze froze him entirely. Garen reminded himself that Okso was no different a man than before, only in a different position. The moment Garen left the Espen storeroom, Okso would come after him or send more of these goons. Garen came to the Te'ens for privacy's sake. He had enough people looking for him. Could he really afford to keep adding to that list?

Garen pulled the sword back from Okso's throat, and the man closed his eyes and winced for the executing blow. Instead, he heard only the sound of metal entering its sheath. Garen offered a sigh of frustration and walked past him to their unsorted packs of stolen goods.

"If you don't mind, I think I'll take twice what we agreed on. After all, you were only paying me to steal from one person, and now I've had to go and steal from two."

Garen reached for the bags but froze as he felt the pair of eyes staring at him. He looked over to the young bandit, still standing with sword drawn. Whether for the fear Garen had inspired in him, or obeying his leader's command to stay out of his way, he slowly sheathed his sword as well. Garen smiled and slung both sacks over his shoulder.

He stepped out of the Epsen cave into the first hint of sunrise. Scattered patches of light seeped through the jagged horizon, but the sunlight did not invigorate him. If anything, it wrung the last drop of restfulness out of him. He tried to ignore the fatigue and started toward his own home.

The journey gave him time to wonder why he even bothered to associate with a clan again. He certainly didn't need them. Garen and his father managed to live rather comfortably off his petty thievery alone. Every now and then he could make just a few small break-ins to acquire his needed supplies, and they would be set. But that lifestyle grew old quickly. He usually worked in the smaller, scattered farming settlements south of the mountain range, but tonight Garen had ventured his first robbery into the much better guarded city of Timnar. He assumed he would need support, and agreed to work with a nearby clan. Tonight had reminded him just how costly that support could be.

Garen peeked into the bags as he walked, wondering exactly what he had taken. Most of their choices seemed to reflect "shiny equals valuable," and he would merely have to fence them to a nearby clan. Or he could journey back into Timnar and sell their merchants the exact goods he'd taken from their city.

Probably better melt some of these down first. I'd hate for anyone to recognize them.

He excitedly noticed a pair of silver-cast goblets. They were a little gaudy for his intentions, but usable nonetheless. His father had broken the last of their glassware, and Garen was tired of drinking straight from the water jug. Even boiled, he swore it still tasted like clay.

Garen retied the bags, strapped them to his waist, and continued his long journey home. He wanted to simply forget the evening's events and walk in peace, but his mind wouldn't leave the matter alone.

Why didn't I just kill him?

Garen had never hesitated to deliver a fatal blow in the heat of a fight. So, why did he find himself freezing up once he'd earned the right to finish it? What kind of thief can't take something because it's too easy?

Garen shrugged the blame off to his father. Still, he felt like three years scraping by as a thief and a mercenary should be enough to erase the few seasons of moralistic do-gooder training.

He wondered, now closing in on his eighteenth birthday, how much longer he would have the luxury of childishness.

These mountains were not the first place Garen had called home. They were, however, the first place he felt safe. And to Garen, safe meant hidden. They had moved countless times, fleeing farther and farther north with each escape. Someone was looking for them. No, it had to be more than just someone. They found Garen and his father in the most secluded stretches of forest, farmlands, and trading towns. Finally, buried deep within the maze of mountains beyond the Jundux Empire's northern border, they had disappeared. Even if their pursuers knew to look among the Te'ens, they would spend an eternity searching the stretches of intricate caves. And they would find countless other dangerous clans sheltered throughout. This fact appealed to him specifically for how well it kept wanderers from passing through.

It did not, however, scare Garen in the slightest. On numerous occasions his Te'en neighbors had ambushed him while returning home. Each time matters ended the same: each and every bandit lying in pain and Garen happy to take anything of value his assailants had with them. Just the past week, a man from some clan he didn't recognize stopped him on his way up the mountain and asked if he wanted in on a job. Garen politely let the man know that he wasn't looking for work at the time. When the man got a little pushy, Garen dislocated his shoulder and went on his way.

Surprises like those tended to spice up otherwise boring trips to town, though they seemed to happen less frequently. The clans were slowly learning that you cannot ambush someone whose rare gift of awareness lets him know you're coming. For such stubborn, aggressive neighbors, they learned this lesson quickly. Even then as Garen passed through the mountains, he felt eyes upon him. He didn't let it affect his casual stride in plain sight. On some days Garen would even wave in their direction. Today did not feeling like a "waving" day. Exhaustion had taken its toll, and now that the sun was up, he knew he could expect little sleep during the day with his father making a constant commotion.

Garen finally reached the outer entrance to his dwelling. The cave opened small and plain, and in a minute's travel the path split cleanly into two narrow tunnels. Garen walked to the fork and stopped there. He held his palm open in front of him and watched the tattoo on his forearm begin to glow. The emblem was canvassed against his tanned skin, where small, curved lines stretched out from a circle, and in the center of the circle, an eye. He had never been able to shake the image from his head, and after spending so much time with the picture in mind, he chose to have it etched into his arm and imbued it with a locking spell.

He looked behind him and listened carefully, making sure none of the more ambitious bandits had followed him. Only the steady drip of water echoed deep within the caverns. He searched the wall to his left, running his hands along the cool, damp rock until he found it.

He pressed his forearm to a particularly smooth patch on the wall. The symbol on his arm changed from black ink to a glowing bright red, and he clenched his teeth. After a few seconds, the glowing stopped. Several feet thick of dirt and rocks in front of him slowly faded into transparency until finally revealing the cleanly cut doorway. Garen unfurled his sleeve and stepped inside. Almost as soon as he had passed through, the doorway began to blur and darken until it returned to an ordinary stone wall behind him.

Garen smiled at the sight of the humble dwelling he'd forged in the mountain. He had carved nearly every piece of furnishing from the rock itself, enjoying the chance to create a home while practicing his earth-shaping spells. Every table, countertop, and even the surrounding barrier of stone had been carved by his magic. The spells of that precision and size took a heavy drain on his soul, but as it refilled, he could feel his depth growing. He made certain never to strain his soul anywhere near the dangers of an empty vessel. Still, the constant practice even on casual matters did wonders for his gifts. He had seen the power of a man fully attuned with earth spells once, and he would never let someone hold that kind of advantage over him ever again.

Garen activated the lighting geonodes in the entry room and started to call out that he had returned. He stopped himself when he realized the time. With any luck, his father might still be asleep, and Garen could slip into his room without having to deal with him just yet. Their interchanges never went well when either of them was tired. In response to his hopes, a loud crash echoed down the hall.

Oh he's up. And starting early by the sounds of it.

A whisper from Garen's father broke the brief silence. "Who, who's there?"

"It's me, Dad. I'm back from—" he stopped as his father turned the corner with the shattered half of a porcelain plate in hand. He charged at Garen, screaming an unintelligible war-cry. Garen almost let the image frighten him in the surprise of the moment. The deranged man over forty years of age wore a tattered blue tunic below his dirty, brown and gray mess of a beard. Ancient-looking scars lined his body anywhere the leathery skin was exposed. In contrast to it all, he moved with the utmost of grace while closing the distance between them. Beneath his confused mental state was the agility and fitness of a once-revered master.

Garen let his father come within a few feet before moving to intercept him. In the gentlest way he could, Garen stepped to the side and grabbed his father's wrist. The hold kept him from swinging the makeshift weapon.

"How many times have I told you never to call me Dad in public? You are to refer to me as Master unless I say otherwise." Garen could see the intensity in his eyes, reminding him just how real this was to his father. Yet Garen's own calm features reflected more than just a lack of sleep.

"Dad, we're not in public and you're not my master anymore. We're alone out here, and...is that one of the new plate sets I brought back last week?" Garen continued to hold his father back while leaning in to examine the remains of his fancy stolen dinnerware. *Note to self: no more stealing dishes that turn into deadly weapons. Wow, I'm actually child-proofing the house from my fath—*

Movement interrupted the thought. As his father squirmed, Garen quickly reached for the dish. He saw his father's leg rise to push him back. Garen kept one step ahead. Instead of wrestling for the plate, he touched a quick imbuement of fire into the dish. The burning sensation forced the plate loose into the air. Garen let go of his father's wrist to drop under the incoming kick. As soon as he touched the ground, Garen swept his father's other leg out from beneath him and sprung back to his feet. He could feel the plate dropping, threatening to only increase the mess he would have to clean up. He stumbled backward, clumsily tripping over the edge of the stoneforged table. His arm stretched back beyond his view, but he managed to snag the plate from the air just before it shattered against the ground.

Garen stood back up and shook the cave floor dirt off. *Perhaps the floors could use a good cleaning anyway.* He strode over to his father still lying on the ground, his eyes darting about in desperate confusion.

"This is why we don't get nice things," Garen scolded while shaking the broken plate in his father's face. Garen might have recognized the absurdity if he wasn't too tired and frustrated to care. He loved his father, insanity and all, but the relationship left little room for politeness.

His father stood and brushed the dirt off his increasingly frayed tunic. The wild expression on his face had faded into a much more solemn display of tragedy. "Your mother will be very angry with you when I tell her about this."

Garen's demeanor took a sudden change as well. Where he once swayed with his eyes half-open, anxious to get to bed, he now froze in stunned disbelief. Sane or not, his father would rarely speak of his mother. Stranger still, he had made the comment as if she slept down the hall, as if she would have a stern lecture for him when she woke. He never knew how to respond in moments like these. He knew none of it would matter. Instead, he seized the opportunity to walk to his own room before his father's madness took a turn for the violent again.

Garen untied the sacks from his waist and kicked them against the edge of his bed. He would show his father the success of the mission later that day after an abundance of sleep and his patience had returned to him. He removed the leather armor, noticing he would need to make some repairs after that mess. He reached to remove his swords and realized he had left his katana on the Espen storeroom floor.

I liked that sword. Oh well, I have others. Better it than...

He pulled his short sword from its sheath and weighed it in his hand. The blade was nearly a foot shorter than a katana's. His mother called it a wakizashi. It was her weapon of choice. Now, after years of running, it was all he had left of hers.

Garen set the sword down and fell back onto his bed. The patch-hide-cover didn't soften the stone platform much, but he managed to close his eyes and breathe deeply. Garen wanted to drift into a well-earned sleep, but another thought troubled him now beyond his unexplained mercy on Okso.

Why did he bring up Mom? He refused to talk about her when he was sane, why make ridiculous comments now?

The memory carried the chill of an early spring day, just like today. In fact, his last moments with her came right where the seasons stood now.

There's no way he remembers the exact day. He barely remembers me some days. Not possible. Right? Garen stared at the cavern ceiling and slowly lost an argument with himself. Today marked the four-year anniversary of her passing. Rather than lay awake in remembrance, Garen let his grieving blend into his exhaustion. He drifted off to a place where memories took their cruelest form.

CHAPTER
TWO

"I'm not going to fight you, Mom!"

"Don't tell me you're afraid?"

Of course I'm afraid. I've seen you destroy guys twice my size. "Seriously, you'd kill me."

"I'm not so sure," she replied with a grin. "Seriously, let's go, right now. Micah can even be our third to watch out for us." A startled expression lay across Micah's face as he peered from around the corner. The young pupil nervously wiped the long, dark hair from his face and stumbled out into the open field, amazed at how she even saw him. Garen had to remind himself that even though Micah's shyness made him seem young, he was in his late teens, and a full five years older than him.

"Well, I mean, I could," Micah stuttered. "But I'm not sure I understand why, Master Layna. Are you trying to make a point or something?"

"No, I just want to see what my son is capable of. He's watched us fight since before he was old enough to know his fist from his face. His father may want to shelter him, but I'm just curious if he's picked up anything from his parents." Her focus turned and met Garen's still shocked gaze. "So, have you?"

I think so. But that doesn't mean I can stand up to you. Or do I even have a choice? "Alright," Garen said with obvious hesitation. "I'll do it."

"Yes!" Garen's mom shouted, reminding Garen of a girl his own age, not in her mid-thirties. "No swords, and I won't use magic on you since that wouldn't be fair. Sound good?"

It sounds insane. Garen, however, didn't wish to ruin his mother's excitement. "Sounds great." He simply had to keep her from killing him, and that didn't sound too terrible. He hoped she'd realize after a few minutes that the few tricks he'd practiced in the privacy of his room weren't impressive enough to continue the beating and let him go.

13

Micah dropped his things and ran over to the grassy field where they stood. "This I've gotta see."

Garen didn't understand why anyone would want to witness the beating about to take place. Garen had watched his parents and their students spar for the last several years, but he had never taken part in anything. His father strictly forbade it. He wondered if agreeing to this was obedience or disobedience. It seemed like both, and there would be consequences regardless.

"Alright, now go ahead and hit me before I bury you in the dirt."

Okay, how necessary is it to taunt me? She apparently wanted him to make the first move. He would need to think of something. As Garen looked to the right and saw Micah, he decided to steal a move of his. If nothing else, it would impress Micah, and Garen loved approval from his parents' students.

"You asked for it," Garen said and ran at her. Before plowing into her, he pushed off his right foot and raised his left knee to make impact. She shifted her guard toward it. Garen snapped his right foot up to drive into her unprotected side, but she still managed to casually block the kick. He pushed off her guard and gracefully rolled out of his fall, bouncing back to his feet as if he had practiced the tumble for years, and not for the first time in his life.

Garen dropped into a defensive stance, still just mimicking what he'd seen. He couldn't believe he just tried to kick his own mother. But Garen's surprise at how well that first pass went was dwarfed by Micah's shocked expression. His secret was out. Years of watching had taught Garen more than a few tricks. Somehow, she knew and was bent on forcing them out into the open.

"Garen...you're incredible!" Micah shouted.

"He's fast, isn't he?" She said.

"Yeah, I mean, I do that little move all the time, but I could barely follow you two with my own eyes." Garen was pretty sure Micah hadn't blinked since they'd begun.

"So, you're fast on the offensive. But how are your reflexes?" Even before the last syllable left her lips, she stepped forward and swung a kick at Garen's head. Instinctively, Garen ducked to his right under the swing of it. While standing back up he deflected a punch coming for his chest. Garen let his momentum carry him into a handspring that dodged his mother's second kick. As Garen landed back on his feet after successfully dodging three rapid attacks, he began to take some confidence in himself. Garen had watched his mother fight seriously before, and this didn't feel like her going easy on him. Even still, Garen understood what one punch could do to a man. Students talked about the things they had seen her do during missions, even unarmed, like punch a man's chest so hard that his heart stops beating or kick someone's rib cage clear into their lungs.

All these legends seemed peculiar, though. The woman standing in front of him wore a baggy blue tunic that gave no indication of her toned muscles. She was fairly tall with long brown hair pulled up for the occasion. She did not bear the image of a hardened warrior. Garen believed she looked much like an average mom should look: loving, kind, and somewhat delicate. At the notion of the last image Garen let down his guard.

In his mind, the fight was over. They'd traded blows, and his parents could continue to ignore it or train him with the rest of their students. Either way, there was nothing left to prove. His mother did not feel the same. Perhaps she wanted to teach him a lesson about dropping out of stance, or maybe she honestly thought he could snap to and defend himself. Whatever the purpose, she lunged at him. Her fist struck fast and deep into Garen's stomach. Words ran through Garen's mind but never had a chance to form in his mouth. The pain rang in his mind until he was deaf to it. As he doubled over, darkness closed in on his vision, and all Garen's senses blurred into numbness.

* * * * *

Garen screamed and sprang forward in bed, immersed in darkness and his own sweat. He sat perfectly still for a moment, waiting to hear some noise, but no sound came. Finally, Garen reached down to his stomach to feel the bruise he'd just received, but no mark existed. He put his hands to his face and felt the coarse texture of his skin. In the four years since that dream, his fractured ribs had healed and his body matured. The memories of that day, however, made Garen feel thirteen again.

Though he hardly considered the dream uncommon, it had never felt so real before. The details of it began to slip from his memory by the second, and an array of emotions rushed with it. Garen felt his anguish surge that an image of his mother lunging at him became the last memory he would have of her. When he regained consciousness, he found his father and their other two students standing over his bed—all except for his mother and Micah.

Micah, that…that…Agh! The mere thought of him pulled a dustless rage from Garen's mind too profound for simple name-calling. Any other memory besides that depicted Micah as an honest friend. But an ocean of redeeming qualities couldn't make Garen forgive him for his failure that day. Micah's sole purpose during that spar had been to watch their backs and protect the two of them. When Garen woke up, however, his father tearfully informed him that his mother had been ambushed and killed, that "Micah did all he could, but the man overpowered him."

Except Micah didn't have a scratch on him. He didn't even try. He just stood there and watched. She was probably too busy making sure I was okay after that punch to notice anything else. The frustration boiled in him until it formed an audible fury. "It's his fault!" Garen searched beside his bed for something to throw and vent his anger. Pulling the first thing his hands grasped out of the bag, Garen let the goblet fly across the room, and it rang against the stone wall.

The irony consumed Garen as he began to understand his father a little more than before. Part of him had to laugh as he empathized with his mad father, but a deeper fear whispered its frequent chills. He was one step closer to becoming just like the man. It was only a matter of time until the series of pain and losses drove him to the same brink of sanity.

A more immediate concern replaced the distant fear. The house had been silent too long. He knew that if he could not hear his father, he had reason to worry. Garen jumped out of bed and stumbled into the main living area. "Dad?" Nothing but silence returned his call.

Garen turned the corner to take a quick glance at the time geonode on the wall. The magical ore had been imbued with a simple spell to change colors in regular intervals so he could tell the time of the day. More exact, expensive devices existed, but the simple fixture was enough to make life easier living in a hollowed-out mountain with no windows. Right now, the stone emitted a light purple glow, telling Garen he had slept through the entire day and back into the early evening.

Still seeing no sign of his father, Garen had no choice but to venture out. With any luck, he might find him catching a breath of fresh air in a lucid moment. Garen found the smooth spot along the stone door identical to the one on the other side. He and his father had the same tattoo, and either could touch the emblem on their forearm to fade out the stone wall. Instead, Garen placed his hand against it.

Still warm.

The heat generated from the locking spell told him his father must not have left long ago. Garen pressed his shoulder to the stone and after a brief tinge of pain, watched the wall disappear. He hoped to find his father simply standing there, staring blankly at the rock wall. He did, after all, forget quite regularly how to use the lock. Garen wouldn't even have minded to see the plain cave walls that usually greeted him as he left his home.

Instead, he released a small orb of light to examine the new craters and debris that stretched across the entryway. Patches of blood layered the walls, mostly above and around where the two dead bodies lay. The picture seemed clear. Some number of men greater than two had ambushed his father. Garen imagined that all of them paid for their actions in some way just based on the sheer volume of blood he saw. But without the presence of his father in the room, Garen knew who won.

He took a moment to study the corpses. They wore a similarly plain garb and bore a matching tattoo along their necks.

Even though he had no clue as to their clan identity, he was somewhat relieved to confirm it was a local vendetta. These mountain thugs he could deal with.

Still, a lack of fear did not prevent his rising anger. Overwhelmed by the sight in front of him and unconcerned with honor at the moment, Garen grabbed one of the bodies by a leg and dragged it out of the cave into the dim light of the setting sun. He had a few questions to ask and having an example of the clan he was looking for couldn't hurt. He pulled the body along the cliff paths, setting out for some neighbors that he wouldn't purposefully call friends, but they would suffice. He only needed answers, and he knew how to use stronger motivational tools than friendship.

Garen tried to remember the name of their clan, but his apathy toward their territorial disputes had dissolved that memory. He approached the massive wooden door that sealed his neighbor's cavern and looked around. He could feel the customary sets of eyes upon him, but none from the hideout in front of him. Apparently, after a certain time of night, trespassers had to knock.

Garen grabbed the corpse by the ankle and put all his strength into heaving it at the door. An echoing "thud" resounded through the mountains as the limp body smacked against the wood. With the anger and impatience compounding in his mind, Garen knew that tapping with a fist just wouldn't send the message he wanted.

A few seconds later a small wooden panel swung open, and two weary eyes appeared in the slit. Both blinked rapidly trying to focus on the violent image in front of them. Garen wore an impatient grimace, still dangling the body in the air by its foot. Blood covered his hands, and the moonlight only emphasized the disturbing shade of red. Garen watched both eyes snap wide open in fear. The small wooden panel slid shut just in time to muffle a frightened shout of profanity.

So much for the friendly way. Garen dropped the corpse and pressed both hands against the massive wooden door. He began to saturate the wooden beams with water, freezing them down. He thawed the grains with a touch of fire and just as quickly froze them back down. As he repeated the process, the beams began to warp and splinter, bowing under the increased strain. The air pressure surrounding them began to spike, and Garen channeled it into an wind-driven impact. The series of diverse elemental spells consumed more of his soul's depth than he preferred, but he always enjoyed the result. The air ripped into the damaged planks, shattering the doorway and sending the wreckage inward.

Garen picked up his lifeless doorknocker and dragged him through the wooden shrapnel. As he entered, three men stumbled into the entry room with him, all clearly still waking up yet carrying swords and axes as if they'd slept with them. At that moment Garen realized he had not planned well enough to grab any weapons before setting off on his search. He had to hope that either he could gain some answers without fighting or that these three men fought as sloppily as they looked.

"I'm not looking for a fight. All I want is some info, then I'll be on my way. That simple."

The largest of the three men stepped forward holding out his oversized axe. "Well, what if we don't want to tell you nothing? Maybe we haven't forgiven you for how you treated us the other week, roughing up one of our men and all. Not much of a thanks for sending you someone to offer you a job."

Just my luck. He was one of these guys...whoever these guys are.

Generally, Garen didn't think twice about drawing lines against his neighbors. In the thieving world, enemies could be just as profitable as friends. This moment was the exception. Still, he knew that his leverage did not hinge on a kind reputation, but on fear.

"It doesn't matter what happened then. This is now. And if you want to get rid of me now, you just have to answer my one question."

"And why would we do that for you?" another chimed in.

"Like I just said, you'll get rid of me. And then I don't have to use one of *your* dead bodies to knock on the next door I find tonight." Garen flashed a menacing grin to sell the threat. He had no intention of murdering these three men simply for information, but they didn't know that.

Their reply came with hesitancy, but finally the stocky leader holding the axe responded. "What's your question?"

"I'm glad you asked." Garen's smile faded. "Do you recognize this man?"

"Tough luck, kid. We don't know him."

"Just so we're clear, I have no problem killing all of you," Garen bluffed again, remembering just how much of a problem he seemed to have.

"Wait, hold on." One of them stepped forward, carefully inspecting the markings along his neck. "I don't know him, but I recognize the arrowhead tattoo. It's the symbol of the Sanstric clan."

"Good so far, now where might I find these Sanstric?"

Garen listened as the nervous man described their location. The directions consisted mostly of pointing and a few notable landmarks, but Garen was happy to make haste in the general direction rather than waste any more time to let them draw a map.

"Thanks for your help. Now, if you'll just dispose of the dead guy for me, you can all go back to sleep." Leaving the body in the mess of splinters he'd created, Garen turned and walked out the door. He would find these Sanstric, and with any luck, his last living family member.

CHAPTER
THREE

Whoever these Sanstric were, they lived a bit further north than Garen had ever needed to travel. He carefully crossed another crude rope bridge and turned a sharp corner, edging along the side of the mountain. The peaks and canyons tilted sharper, making for an unpleasant balancing act along the tight pathways above the chasm below.

Beyond the eerie atmosphere of the Te'ens at twilight, another presence set him at unease. Garen still felt like he was being watched from behind. Distant eyes usually preferred to watch from a safely hidden alcove, but this time the feeling hung with him instead of fading.

Occasionally he would pause, trying to determine if he could trust his instincts or if the tall shadows were simply playing tricks on him. He had the glow of a full moon to work with, lighting up the browns, grays, and scarce greens around him enough to convince himself that he had full control of his surroundings. If they were real, he should be able to see them.

While he struggled with the presence following him, Garen had no doubts about who waited in front of him. He kept his eyes locked on the narrow path, never looking up to give any indication that he could feel both men staring at him. They crouched in a window carved out of the side of a cave wall ahead. They had weapons, and Garen was grateful. He had a second chance to arm himself with more than his soul's depth before going deeper into the fray. Still, even as he heard them shift their weight and prepare to jump down, Garen did not flinch. A powerful lesson from Garen's brief training stayed with him through the years: the only thing more dangerous than the element of surprise is tricking someone into believing they have it.

As Garen passed under them, one of the men dropped down, his sword on course to slice through him. Garen sprung forward to dodge the blade's arc. He twisted in the air and swung his left foot into the side of his assailant's skull. The blow would have sent the man over the cliff's edge, but Garen grabbed him by the wrist. Unfortunately, his other hand failed to snatch the weapon before it tumbled into the black void. The loss frustrated Garen, but not enough to let his enemy follow it down into the depths. He pulled the man up and slammed his knuckles into the bridge of his nose. The man rolled back, out cold.

Garen looked up in anticipation of the next man to jump down at him, but no one came. He shrugged his shoulders and started forward again, hoping to lure the second out. Sure enough, just a few steps later, Garen heard feet hit the ground running toward his back. Garen turned around just in time to see the foot soar toward his head. Surprised by his speed, Garen ducked somewhat frantically to barely miss his kick.

Now's no time for getting sloppy. He's the underestimating idiot, not you.

Garen stepped forward as he rose to his feet, and put his fist into the man's side. The blow turned him sideways, and Garen's elbow cracked into his chin. The second impact knocked him into the air and towards the ledge. The man made no reflex to catch himself.

It would have been no tragedy to let this man fall either, but with the utmost need for a weapon, he reached out a hand and caught him by the neck of his tunic. "Not yet." Garen felt along the man's side for any weapons, but found only a pair of sai.

"Wonderful. I lose the impressive long sword and now I'm stuck with a couple of blunt forks. Do I look like I know how to use these ridiculous things?" Garen tossed the bandit onto the dirt path behind him and glared down with an honest expression of disappointment on his face. "You are officially worthless." An image caught his attention before he left. Along the side of his neck laid a distinct arrowhead tattoo. "Never mind," Garen muttered. "Apparently I'm getting close."

Garen walked away while tossing the twin sai around in his hands, trying to get a feel for them. *These things can't be too hard to use.* He ran his hands along the disappointingly smooth tips. *Doesn't look like I'll be stabbing anyone today. But I guess the weight of these things could really leave a bruise if I connect...* Garen thrust an arm up, picturing the blow against an imaginary jaw and smiled. *Actually, that might just be a good plan to start with.*

With his new experimental weapons tucked into his belt, Garen continued the tedious march down the trail. The longer the path grew, the higher his worries rose. He tried to calm the fear with stories he'd been told about his father. Whether they were exaggerated or not, he'd survived impossible odds much worse than this. Garen only hoped his captors had some purpose in all this. So long as they didn't just want to murder an old man out of spite, Garen could take back what was his and everything would work out in the end.

With his fears at rest, Garen still had to question who would have the motive to go through this. He still suspected revenge at play, though he couldn't remember ever crossing these Sanstric. Another possibility tugged at his mind, but he refused to consider it. The Te'ens hid them well, and nobody outside its peaks would find him or his father up here. They simply couldn't.

Garen passed under the final landmark his neighbors had described. A thick arch loomed over the path. The stone had been cut away smoothly enough that Garen considered it could be a magically formed feature, but the placement was just random enough to suggest nature's own hand at work. Just past the arch stood another massive wooden door constructed in the wide cavern entrance. With an abundance of silence already, Garen began voicing his thoughts aloud.

"What is it with the big doors today? I don't know who you think you're keeping out." Garen thought for a moment about the ridiculousness of knocking with this many eyes watching him. The thought also crossed Garen's mind that he should jump and climb into one of the high windows where his onlookers sat.

"No, I think I'm just in a front-door-mood today." Garen

politely tapped his knuckle three times on the door, and though the sound was soft, it echoed heavy and deep into the caves. Still, no other sounds responded.

"Someone really needs to teach you people some hospitality," Garen said as if actually offended. The silence continued. "Fine, I'll clue you in. Hospitality is you opening your door so I don't have to tear it into shreds. Make sense? One way or another, I'm getting in. This way saves you a door."

The doors swung open. Whether they had taken his advice or planned it from the start, a figure lunged at him from the darkness inside. Garen pulled out the pair of sai, still undecided on how to make use of them. The shadow emerged with a sword drawn, giving Garen some incentive to try using his new weapons correctly.

He reached Garen's ground and lashed down at him. Garen knocked the blade aside and stepped past him. The man turned to face Garen, gripped his sword tightly, and lunged for another pass. This time, Garen stood his ground. He caught the blade between prongs on its horizontal swing. He had never tried it personally, but Garen had seen a few sai-wielders break swords from this stance. He attempted to flick his wrists and snap the metal, but did little more than strain his own joints. Ignoring the pain, Garen watched his opponent pull his sword from the sai trap, confused about what he had just tried to do.

"Hey, don't give me that look. I've never used these things before. Besides, you're just lucky your sword is thick enough I didn't snap it in two." Garen looked at the man's thin blade and regretted his choice of excuse.

"You know what? Not worth it." Garen stepped toward his enemy and chucked a sai at his head. The Sanstric fighter made the mistake of knocking it away with his sword, unaware how quickly Garen could close the distance between them. Garen planted his foot beneath the man's guard and knocked him off balance. Garen stepped back and threw the second sai. One of the tines cracked against the side of his head as he hit the ground.

Garen changed his mind about the usefulness of these

24

new weapons, and retrieved one of them from the dirt. However, nothing would rival the comfort of a well-balanced sword in his hand. Garen reached down to borrow the weapon when he noticed signs of another struggle. Near the doorway, more blood and charred rocks were scattered across the ground, and Garen wondered how much his father might have caused. Surely the flame magic his father was renowned for could have overpowered as many thugs as they had escorting him. Perhaps he had escaped here, shown them who they were messing with and made his way back to their home.

Garen looked around for any other clues leading away from the scene. Instead, he saw only one clue leading inward to their cavern. The scattered patches of blood thinned into a trail and led into the darkness. A few torches shed light further down the passage, but Garen needed a closer look at the shadows right in front of him. He conjured his own orb of light, but as he witnessed the sight in front of him, he lost his focus and the light vanished. In the brief glimpse, he had seen the source of the blood. A dismembered arm. The limb would have been meaningless, impossible to identify save for one feature. Across the forearm was an emblem of the sun with an eye in its center.

The serenity Garen clung to shattered. He realized everything might not return to normal. He had placed so much confidence in his own abilities. They were his only foundation. Now he had to face the truth that no amount of talent could bring his father back from the dead.

Garen did not have time to stop and wallow in remorse. He could still feel distant onlookers, the same eerie sense of being followed as before. They were slowly growing closer. He couldn't keep letting these fights slow him down. If any chance remained of saving his father, he understood time was not on his side.

Trap or not, Garen took off in a sprint down the cave, blindly racing through the stretches of darkness between torches. With each step, Garen expected to feel something sharp connect with him from below or beside, but the farther he ran, the more he understood that they didn't seem interested in ambushing him anymore. Blind corner after corner, Garen witnessed perfect spots to hit him from. Perhaps he had finally convinced them to save their men for one large group instead of these faulty ambush attempts. He did not like the idea that his enemies could adapt and learn.

Finally, he saw light streaming in from around the next corner. He would at least find someone. Garen's feet slid as he turned the corner and stopped to witness the display in front of him. A well-lit, monstrously large chamber lay before him. Some twenty to thirty Sanstric men and women lined the outer wall, all wearing similar white and brown rags and armed for a fight. In the very center of the barbaric assembly stood two men whose attire did not match the common dress of the room. The first stood tall and ominous. His red tunic projected a distinct image of refinement, even royalty, among savages.

The man to his left could not stand at all. He knelt half-naked and bleeding from the countless open wounds lining his body. The few strands of gray in the bushy brown beard highlighted the blood-soaked tangle. As Garen dared to stare deeper into the man's gruesome appearance, he saw they had lacerated and possibly broken his left arm. More noticeably, they had torn off his right. He looked straight down at the ground, hiding his face from the world, but Garen could still recognize his father.

"Garen Renyld, it's been quite a while, hasn't it?" the man in red spoke. The voice struck a note deep in his memory, and his whole head shook with the rush of his past trying to surface. He couldn't move his eyes off his father to place it.

"Can you believe he couldn't remember me? After all the time we spent training, he didn't even recognize me. You were right for looking after him. He really is unstable."

Garen could feel his grip tightening as his pity gave way to rage. Still unable to move his eyes from his dying father, he felt his vision blurring with hatred. He wanted to do to them what they had done to his father, to show them what that kind of pain felt like. They had tortured him to the threshold of death without empathy. Garen would personally let them experience that same level of agony.

Emotion continued to overtake the logic that he didn't stand a chance against even half the people in the room, but at that moment, Garen didn't have the calm rationale to fear death. With common sense fully blinded by emotion, he clung onto the one empty hope he had in the room: he could still save his father. Garen finally turned to his father's captor, standing patiently in his royal garb, just waiting for a response.

As Garen looked into the dark, cold eyes, the cloud of memories circling his mind came crashing down on him. But they did not crash in unison. At first he assumed it was Micah, who would have aged several years since he'd seen him last. But while the face bore a resemblance, it was clearly not Micah. The second wave of memory hit, triggered by the first.

His younger brother. Pyralis.

The confusion in Garen's mind replaced the rising fury and left him speechless. Pyralis had been his parent's youngest student among the three brothers. He was still a few years older than Garen, but he was the closest thing Garen had to a friend his own age growing up. Though in all their years, Pyralis had always been the one to play the victim. No matter how unrelated the circumstance, it was always the world versus Pyralis in his mind. Garen never much cared for that side of him, and in time they grew further apart. He still remembered a phrase he'd heard Pyralis mutter time and again toward the end of their training together. *This world is broken.* Garen assumed it was his way of coping, still setting himself up as the victim. But in this moment Pyralis had found a new role to cast himself in. He had taken his own victim in his broken world.

Garen didn't have the presence of mind to ask why. He had no grace to give. He burst forward with his sword and sai ready to strike. Two Sanstric stepped out in front and blocked the swing, leaving Garen no more than a foot from the betraying face.

"I must admit, I hate for us to be meeting again like this. I had always thought you and I shared an understanding of the greater evils around us."

27

"Greater evils," Garen whispered through the anguish in his voice. "I can't imagine there's still anyone above you after this."

"I gather how wrong this must look. But Garen, come on, certainly you have seen with your own eyes the horrors the Dawn of Magic has brought into this world. Surely you understand that this world is *broken*. Well, I've found a way to fix it. A way to restore everything to its proper state. But we're all going to have to make sacrifices. Surely you can let go of what's left of your father for the sake of this entire world."

Garen heard the words, but his mind raced in another direction. Did they need his father three years ago? Was Pyralis the one chasing them, forcing them deeper and deeper into hiding? He didn't even need to ask. He responded without words, only the resolute stare of hatred at the man who had stolen every drop of peace from his life and still had the nerve to ask for more.

Pyralis understood the nonverbal answer and let out a frustrated sigh. "I don't know why I thought you'd understand. I guess I'd hoped you'd have grown into a man after all those years on your own. What a waste." He turned and walked away from Garen. "You can kill him. He's as useless as I'd feared. It's time for the last part of our agreement. Get my old master out of here and you'll have your payment then."

The sight of his father being dragged away released a new level of rage. Garen pushed all his energy forward on the two men holding him back. The metal of his weapons glowed white until their swords snapped. He'd never seen magic like that before, but he'd never been this close to losing his father either. Garen proceeded to run them through, even with the blunted, glowing sai.

The remaining Sanstric charged forward at Garen. He swung wildly into the mass of them, drawing blood at each pass. Bodies began to fall around him, but the flow of death did not slow his rampage. The gruesome melee ensued until Garen felt a blunt force crack against the back of his neck. The pain flooded into his brain, and he felt one of his legs twist and collapse.

Just before he blacked out completely, Garen saw a sight

so strange he assumed it was a hallucination. Here in a central cavern, high among the arid Te'en Mountains, Garen watched a tidal wave of the purest blue water crash through the entrance and immerse them all.

CHAPTER
FOUR

Light filtered through Garen's swollen eyelids, but as he tried to open them further, pain quickly overtook his curiosity. "Am I dead?"

He spoke the words to himself, but two voices responded to his question, both feminine, and neither kind enough to answer him directly. The first gave a confident laugh with the airs of an "I-told-you-so," and the second a sigh of frustration.

"Oh, let it go. We both knew he'd wake up eventually."

"Yes, but a girl can hope, can't she?"

Still unwilling to fight the pain in his eyes, Garen began to feel around at his unknown surroundings. "Seriously, because excruciating pain aside, this still kind of feels like living. And I was kind of hoping for something a little more...different."

"Oh shut up already. You're alive enough." Going solely on pitch, this one had a higher, sharper, and noticeably more annoying ring.

"Tell me Garen, can you open your eyes?" He drew the contrast from this soothing tone, lower and less shrill than the one before it. He couldn't even remember the last time he'd heard his name not followed by a curse.

"You know, I thought about it, but I've grown pretty accustomed to the back of these eyelids. I can't imagine giving that up just to figure out where I am or who I'm talking to."

The higher pitched, and clearly younger, let out a rather forced laugh. "Oh joy, he's as much fun to talk to as he is to carry."

Garen furrowed his eyebrows, trying to figure out how to scowl at someone with closed eyes. "Oh joy, a second voice of sarcasm in the room." Turning his head toward the other, he added, "Is that how I sound? Because if it is, I promise I'll never do it again."

"How about you leave my younger sister alone." Her

response both confirmed the guess on the ages and made a connection he probably should have seen coming. "She's not here to harm you, and in fact, she saved you from an unseemly death. You owe her your life."

"Yes, well, my deepest thanks. Sorry my life isn't worth more. At least this way I don't owe you much, do I?"

"Convenient."

"Don't be so sure of that," the older sister said. "I can tell you we didn't follow you through the mountains and bring you here for our own amusement. I wish I could tell you more, but Kiron has asked to speak with you himself first thing when you woke up. You should really save any questions for him."

"Oh, there's a few rolling around in my mind. But right now I'm not feeling too terribly threatened by this cozy bed, and the most dangerous threat I can imagine is that mouthy sister of yours, whom you seem to have under control." An offended sigh came from the intended source, but Garen continued, "So, I think the question and answer session is going to have to wait. As much as I'd like to know where I am, why I'm here, and how in the miserable world you found me, I don't quite feel up to wandering around to play meet and greet just yet."

"And I imagine you shouldn't, on a broken leg." The heavier footsteps and the male voice told Garen of a new entrant to the room. He sounded young, possibly near Garen's age, but with the certainty and authority in his voice of a man twenty years older. Whatever the status or position, he carried some weight in both word and burdens. Garen considered toning down the rudeness until he had a better grip on his circumstance.

"Forgive me, sir, if I can't quite greet you properly. My eyes seem to be experiencing some difficulties at the moment. But if you came to explain the situation to me, I am very much all ears…and not much else."

"I would if you had an urgent need to know. But you aren't furious for answers like I'd feared you might be. I'm not going anywhere, and I don't guess you'll make it too far. This conversation can wait until you're at least well enough to sit up."

Garen let his silence cue them to leave, and he heard only

the closing door. Garen didn't much care for the chore of regular conversation, and the splitting headache that crept in a few minutes back didn't help the transition. Along with the physical pain came the more crippling recollection of his father, and the gruesome image Garen last saw of him. He would have liked to call them back just to ask if they had "rescued" his father too. This blur of reality made no sense to him, but Garen had to quiet the impulse for answers. They would come soon enough, and Garen couldn't hear much else over the sound of the pillow calling his name.

* * * * *

Garen snapped from the dream and tried to catch his breath. He reached up to wipe a thick layer of sweat from his forehead. The memory of his mother's death had rattled him a little more than usual again, but he knew he'd survive. The flood of memories brought him back to his present location. He noticed his eyes were no longer swollen shut, and he blinked a few times in disbelief. Garen ran his hands across his previously battered face and found that his nose still tinged with pain as he touched it. It was evidence he hadn't imagined the pain, but proof of its rapid retreat. Though a little greasy and covered with stubble, his skin felt smoother than he could believe, given the series of cuts and scrapes from just the other day.

Was it just the other day? How long have I been out?

The same held true for the rest of his body. Where Garen distinctly remembered lacerations across his chest and arms from the carnage, now unblemished skin covered him. A subtle grin swept across his face, amazed by the healing his rescuers afforded for him. Even if he had slept for a week solid in that bed, none of these wounds should have sealed so perfectly. Not that he had ever been injured to that degree, but he'd inflicted his share of it. No one looked this clean afterwards.

Garen threw off the sheets of the oversized feather bed. The more he began to move, the stranger his skin felt. Finally, he realized they changed him out of his tattered clothes and dressed him in a soft silk gown. The fabric had no use in the mountains, being neither warm nor durable. No matter how smooth the texture, at this moment he'd have felt far more comfortable in sackcloth than these threads.

The plush surroundings definitely had a calming effect, but this much luxury made him nervous to the core. Garen didn't have friends. He knew people that wouldn't cut his throat on first sight, but not many. Most of them he had worked with on an occasional organized mission, protecting their backs, saving their lives. But he didn't belong to their clans, a fact they were always quick to remind him of. Eventually, he grew so tired of the charade he learned to find work on his own, work that usually made more enemies than friends. His run-in with the Espen was no revelation. It was a reminder of a lesson he should have learned long ago. He was better off making honest enemies than dishonest friends.

Yet here Garen sat, staring out from the edge of the bed at a high-arching window on the opposite wall. Even with the lavender curtains drawn, enough sunlight flooded the room to reveal the marble floor lined with ornately patterned rugs, a series of framed landscapes along the walls, and an elegant mirror adorning the space above a grand chest of drawers. Once again, Garen returned to the only answer that made any sense. They had the wrong guy.

The time had come to find out for sure. Garen slid off the bed, remembering the broken leg just as his feet touched the ground. Strangely, it didn't recoil as he expected. The leg still wouldn't support his full weight, but with a slight hobble, he made his way over to the window, admiring the elaborate décor. With a quick toss of the curtains, he could see down into the city of Vikar-Tola stretching out beneath him in all its hectic glory. The merchants' carts and artisans' shops had a healthy flow of customers rushing through the streets.

He visited the city a few times as a kid, but back then it was the capital of the entire Jundux Empire. The Division of Thrones reduced it to the humbler status as capital of the Central Kingdom, and the city had certainly diminished in a few regards.

Still, he would recognize this restless heart of commerce anywhere. There wasn't another city in the three kingdoms that saw such a lively degree of trade. Being squeezed between the other two had its upsides.

From the high vantage point of his window, Garen could only assume he had landed his way into Vikar-Tola's luxurious palace. A good bit had changed since he'd last visited, but beyond his door he imagined a wide hallway carrying servants racing in every direction. He didn't need anything in particular, but he wanted to try to order a few around, just to see what it felt like. Excitedly, he flung open the door to explore his fancy new surroundings.

Instead, plain walls and a narrow, lifeless passageway stretched out before him. Half a dozen other doors lined the hall ending in a descending spiral staircase at the end. He hobbled his way toward it, the floor strangely warm on his bare feet for such an empty passageway. He could only hope his leg would hold out on him for the trip down. Bracing himself against the rail, he struggled through the first couple of steps.

A door squeaked from the hallway behind, and Garen turned to see the source. A thin, dignified man stood looking his way, hand frozen on the knob and mouth gaping.

"Garen Renyld. He told me you would heal quickly. I assumed he was reassuring us, not prophesying a miracle."

"No, a miracle would be getting down these steps in one piece." Garen winced in pain as he pointed to his aching leg.

He laughed and walked toward Garen. "Yes, though most people are not inclined to be walking at all on bones they shattered the night before last."

Garen had to abandon his theory that time alone had closed his wounds. As the tall figure came closer, the dim geonodes cast enough light to reveal the details of the man. From the first image, Garen felt like a peasant stumbling into noble presence. He wore a finer tunic striped with pale greens and brown, far from beggarly, but it by itself didn't suggest a royal nature. Garen guessed at his status from his posture and the manner in which he carried himself. The graceful strides he took didn't scream importance, but they whispered prestige to anyone paying attention. His hair fell to his shoulders, perfectly straight with a light brown hue. His skin, though lighter than Garen's, had just enough shade and grit to keep anyone from mistaking him for sheltered.

"Then you wouldn't mind just picking me up and hauling me down this flight, would you?"

"I believe this way is easier on both of us." Garen felt a gentle gust circle his legs and looked down to find a visible ring of wind forming on the floor around him. Gently, the force took his weight off his feet and lifted him inches above the stair he stood on. He looked up to see the man at the top of the step behind him, smiling at Garen's amazement. "The platform will follow you as you walk. Try it."

Garen wished he had level ground to test the spell first, but with reasonable faith he stepped down to the next step and stopped there. The transparent, spinning circle followed his movement, leaving Garen still levitating and putting no pressure on the bad leg. "That's a handy little trick. It's not going to fade out on me anytime soon, is it?"

"It will stop when I tell it to. Now, let's get you to Kiron."

At the bottom of the stairs lay another hall, equally plain and quiet. He wanted to take another look out his window just to prove he hadn't dreamed his vision of Vikar-Tola. The blank corridors looked nothing like his bright, elaborate room. This hall had only a few doors along the way before they arrived at the final one. Garen's mysterious guide opened the door and gestured him inside. The room had no windows, but a few geonodes along the wall gave the space a warm glow. A few trinkets and baubles sat along the back wall with a sizable table in the center. At it sat three complete strangers: two females and a cloaked figure. Though he had never seen them, Garen guessed he might recognize their voices.

"Master Kiron," the voice came from behind him. "I found him up and wandering even on that leg. I thought you would want to speak with him."

"Yes, thank you, Drake. You're welcome to stay and join

us if you would like." The voice matched the authoritative young man from the day prior, but with the cloak and hood he wore, Garen still could not get a glimpse at his face. The concealing attire puzzled him, but he didn't know how to ask, "Why the hood?" on first introductions. That question would have to wait.

"Thank you, but unfortunately this surprise caught me on the way out. I've been requested at my family's estate." Drake turned his focus to Garen. "I need to end the spell. It will be easiest if you sit down, please."

Garen looked over to the group at the table, where one of the girls motioned with her head toward an empty chair. He watched Drake as he sat, and without so much as a twitch of his hand, the swirling platform disappeared.

"Don't stay too long. We're likely to need you here shortly," the hooded voice spoke. Garen looked back to Drake and saw a distinct emotion sweep over the noble's face. He recognized the feeling immediately: disgust.

"No need to worry. I won't be staying any longer than my obligations would have me."

The powerfully proper man took his leave, and Garen turned to face the three across from him.

The cloaked figure spoke up once more. "We met briefly, but I did not get a chance to tell you my name: Kiron. I believe you'll remember these two, but I don't think you've been properly introduced either. These are the Talia sisters, Naia and Morgan."

The two sat next to each other, sharing a resemblance in their eyes and little else. The girl on the left, Naia, had a petite figure, a cute face, and long jet-black hair. She wore a stern grimace and crossed her tiny arms on the table to complete the expression. Garen couldn't remember the last time he'd seen such a frightening yet frail creature. All of this stood in contrast to the girl beside her. Morgan must have been several years older than her sister, probably mid-twenties compared to late teens. Her expression carried a warmth her sister's lacked, though her build told a different story. The gray sleeveless tunic revealed coarse skin and toned muscles lining her arms. She was a head taller than her sister even while sitting, but Garen realized at least half of that was a difference in posture. Sadly, Morgan had nothing cute about her, and behind the smile was the visage of a dedicated warrior. Her hair had the same dark hue, but the close-cropped style conveyed more pragmatism than beauty.

Garen knew before they spoke how to match up the voices. He had hoped for the intolerable one to have a correspondingly ugly exterior, but instead took some delight in the mismatch.

Garen had bigger questions circling his mind, and he hoped he had not stared for too long. "Well, I'd introduce myself, but it seems everyone around here already knows my name. Can we start this discussion with how I became famous without my knowing? Because most people that know my name just want me dead, so this attention is all beginning to rattle me."

"Famous is a strange position for you," Kiron said. "You could walk the streets of this city for an hour before you found a soul who hadn't heard your name. But you'd spend twice as long looking for a single person who actually believed you were still alive."

"So, what gave you enough suspicion to hunt me and my father down?"

"Oh, *we* knew you were alive. We knew your father was alive. Three years we've spent searching for you two with no luck."

"Until now?"

Kiron let out a quiet laugh. "The Te'ens were a good choice for you. But you have a habit of leaving your name dripping from tongues like a curse in blood. It took us some time, but we just had to follow the trail. Are you sure you were really trying to stay hidden?"

Garen rolled his eyes at the question. He was trying. But to the best of his knowledge, it was just some vengeful creature from his past hunting them. How could he have known he had the better part of the three kingdoms on his trail? Garen did not feel comfortable sitting here answering to people he owed nothing. "Well, you found me. Much appreciated. But you caught me at a rather bad time. So, if you'll excuse me, I have a father to find."

Garen stood from the chair and turned to leave, trying not to wince too noticeably from the shock wave of pain up his thigh. "Garen," Morgan said firmly. Her voice carried enough sorrow to freeze him, but he didn't dare turn for fear of the news that would follow. "Your father is dead. I'm sorry. But it took all we had just to get you out alive. We saw the same thing you did. No one could have survived those wounds."

He spun to face her. "You don't know that! And who are you to come riding in and take me away from him when he needed me most? Then you just sit there and assume the worst and expect me to do nothing?" Morgan tilted her head down, not knowing what to say. Even Naia for all her smug demeanor became visibly grieved by the weight of their words. Garen waited a second for anyone to say something, then turned back to the door, face flushed with as much rage as anguish welling up in his eyes.

As soon as he stepped through the doorway and cleared their line of sight, Garen frantically scanned for an escape from this nightmare. The stairs that brought him down went no further. Unless one of these plain doors was an exit, the whole place he'd seen so far was partitioned off from the rest of the palace. At this point, he'd have taken a locked room to break down behind in peace. After years of invulnerable isolation, he did not have the fortitude to cry in front of strangers, and he could feel despair setting in. His right leg finally buckled under the strain he had ignored, and he fell to the floor. He took one look at his shaking hands and began to sob.

The door opened, and Garen lifted his head to see Kiron emerge into the hall. The embarrassment only worsened his state and the tears began to burn. Kiron stood and waited patiently, not saying a word. Several minutes passed before Garen found the strength to just close his eyes and breathe deeply.

Kiron broke the silence. "I can't imagine what it must be like to have your world ripped from under you and experience this kind of loss all at once. But that world outside these walls will offer you no sympathy. I have found you to offer so much more, the first of which being a place to rest. Please, let us take you back to your room, and once you've had all the time you need to recover, then we can discuss your situation. I assure you we have many a similar interest."

It was the second time someone had told him they were similar. Pyralis believed that Garen could share his understanding as he stood next to his maimed father. Now these people wanted to rip him away from it all and just assume he'd be fine. Garen sat there for a second considering his options. He had none. Though it damaged his pride greatly, he had no choice but to accept their hospitality for the moment. He nodded in assent. Kiron called the girls out to help him upstairs. Garen awaited a snide remark once more from Naia on the difficulty of carrying him, but none came. They took him to his room and left him in silence. Garen lay wide-awake, torn on how long he should wait before finding a way out. He imagined that day would come as soon as his leg could handle it. One way or another, Garen would find those responsible for this.

Pyralis.

Revenge blanketed over his natural grieving as he imagined all the horrible things he might do. And the darkness soothed Garen.

CHAPTER
FIVE

Garen wondered if he might end up staring a hole through the ceiling. He had no idea at what part of the day he had woken up, but the dim light filtering through the curtains suggested a quickly setting sun. Garen had slept more in the last few days than he could remember sleeping in most weeks. Much to his dismay, however, he couldn't quiet his screaming thoughts. Finally, the hours of stillness gave way to action. Garen's mind would not stop spinning, his eyelids would not stay closed, and the ceiling refused to crumble at his piercing gaze. Once again, he slid off the bed and onto the ground, forgetting the pain that would follow. He felt the expected sting, but he could handle the strain. Even since earlier that day, he had healed tremendously. Garen didn't normally incur that many injuries. Thieving tended to involve more running than dangerous confrontations. Still, even he knew bones didn't piece themselves back together this quickly. Primal spells could cauterize wounds and brace fractures, but this was the work of something else entirely.

Time for answers.

Garen made his way toward the door but stopped upon catching his own eyes in the mirror. He stood frozen for a moment, analyzing the strange creature he saw there. His wavy brown hair had grown longer than he usually let it. Patches of dark stubble lined his chin, and although Garen didn't care enough to shave daily, he wouldn't normally let himself reach this unkempt of an appearance. Years of living alone with his father made him appreciate the little nuances of dignity all the more, if for no other reason than to remind Garen of his own sanity.

Yet what truly held his stare had nothing to do with the details of his grooming habits. The fierce glare seemed to search him for deeper truths.

Are answers really what have you so worked up? Would it make any difference if he told you this was the Theltus Nisdal or the middle of the desert? Or if he claimed to be a murderer rather than a savior? Do you really boil with curiosity, or do you just fee! helpless?

"Knock it off, Garen," he said to himself. Then, with eyes fixed on his own dark stare, he forced a weak smile through the grief and added, "You're the sane one, remember?"

A knock at the door broke his train of thought along with the imaginary confidence it bolstered. "Are you awake, Garen?" The voice belonged to Kiron. "I have a few things for you."

Garen opened the door to see the man's face still shrouded behind the low-hanging hood. He held a satchel of considerable size. "I had Drake travel out to your shelter in the mountains. It should help with the shock of being thrown into new surroundings."

He eyed the seemingly sincere man for a moment, still finding it difficult to read his intentions without a clear glimpse at his eyes. He took the package and motioned him inside. "You picked a good time. I think I'm in the mood for a dose of that understanding you keep promising."

Garen took a seat on the bed, dropped the satchel next to him, and took a quick glance at what they had retrieved for him. Taking only a few steps in, Kiron leaned stiffly against the near wall. After rummaging through his belongings, Garen closed the bag and looked quizzically into the shadow beneath Kiron's hood. "So, your lackey Drake made it there and back by sundown, did he? I didn't think we were that close to the Te'ens."

"We aren't. My fastest horse would take days to reach it. Drake just has a talent for racing through those long distances."

"And he broke into my house—"

"Easily. No insult to the locking spell you devised. I've never seen anything like it. But rocks are rocks, and nothing is immovable anymore. You'll find rather quickly that the people you're surrounded by are no amateurs. They are some of the finest minds and hearts the kingdom has to offer this."

"Alright, then. Time for the big question. What is 'this'?"

Garen could practically feel the smile glow through the darkness. "Finally, a question worth answering. Though I imagine

42

you already know quite a bit about us. How familiar are you with the Spellswords?"

The word triggered a memory. He needed a second for it to surface naturally. His mind raced with the rare instances his father shared of his past.

"My parents," Garen finally responded, too distracted to give the question a proper answer.

"Yes, Seth and Layna Renyld, two of the most impressive Spellswords to ever carry the title. Of course, they didn't start this journey together, which makes them the first to take a spouse from within the trade. I don't suppose I have to tell you how unique that makes you?"

Garen rolled the question around in his head for a moment. He was tempted to snap back with a snide bit of sarcasm, but the intrigue of their topic kept him serious for the moment. "I honestly think you might, since my father never cared to talk much about his former employment as one of your special soldiers. You could start with what a Spellsword really is."

"I'm amazed at how safe and sheltered they kept you." Kiron paused, possibly letting Garen feel the sting of the backhanded compliment, or perhaps deciding where to begin.

"Your father taught you the basics of magic, so you understand how and where you draw the power from?"

Garen gave this comment another due pause, wondering where this question might take them. "Yeah, he always referred to it as a soul's depth. It's what you feel draining as you manipulate nature."

"Did he tell you it wasn't always that way?"

"No, I think he was saving magic history for when I turned fourteen." Garen only spoke the words in instinctive defense, but it reminded them both at what an early age he began his training and how briefly it lasted.

However Kiron took it, he gave no indication of concern. "I see. Less than a couple hundred years ago, the depth of any man's soul was much smaller, certainly not enough to cast magic from. All we had was a spark of life at the pit of our souls, just enough to sustain us in a material realm. Do you know where that 'spark' came from?"

"The Theltus Nisdal, gate to the Spirit Realm." Garen dryly confirmed, understanding the history lesson but unsure of its significance.

"Right. It took five scholars a lifetime of study just to find that physical junction between that realm and ours. Back then it was just a pinhole of an opening."

"So, you're saying it's not anymore?"

"Not a pinhole, anyway," Kiron said. "They stretched it. A flood of energy poured through the gap, but the only containers in this world capable of storing such power were the human soul. That's why anyone can use magic, Garen. Just about anyone who can find their depth and let it loose."

"If everyone has that depth, then why don't I see a parade of earthquakes and firestorms on the streets each day?" He didn't like the tangent their conversation was taking, but he wouldn't pass up a chance at an honest question that bothered him. Even when he started his training, spells weren't hard to conjure. But his encounters with others showed him just how rare his gifts were. His father had deflected the question when Garen was young. Hopefully, Kiron would be more forthcoming.

"Some never find their depth. It doesn't help that almost everyone describes it differently. I've heard some people tell me they feel it in the pit of their stomach, and spending that fullness creates an ache, or a hunger in them. To me, releasing that depth feels more like exhaling, but with a heavier and heavier weight on my chest."

Garen knew how hard the feeling was to describe. Neither example resonated with him exactly, but if you took away the hunger part, aching was a good way to put it. It was the kind of fatigue that slowly builds while running. You can't always tell how much fight is left in you, but your body screams louder and louder when to stop.

"Alright," Garen said, "so what about those that do find it? I see a lot of small magic everywhere I go. Lighting a hearth. Conjuring clean water. Even shaping a home from stone can take people weeks. I'm seventeen, and I could build something with

44

two stories in a day. Explain that."

Kiron laughed. "I do enjoy your confidence. The answer is complicated, though. Some of that depth I'm sure you've earned. The years on your own had to test your soul in ways that a safe training regimen can't duplicate. And the untested soul runs very shallow. There is a second way to deepen it, however."

"That being?"

"Inheritance. A child's soul is forged of the combined depth of his or her parents. Curiously, though, most enlightened masters of the arts don't spend their time in..." Kiron showed his decorum in the carefulness of his words, "sensual activity."

"So, that's my story?" Garen said, less than thrilled with his answer. "Two unstoppable forces stop fighting your battles long enough to make a kid, and now I'm some asset for your group?"

"Not another word of that," Kiron reminded him the authority his voice could carry. "Your parents loved each other, and they loved you. That's actually why they left the Spellswords. Seth and Layna wanted a reprieve from the madness, to keep from raising a child by day and putting down rebellions by night. They struck a deal with Emperor Tibalt. The crown would soon pass to one of his sons, and Seth offered that in exchange for a secluded piece of land to themselves, he would train his three sons into honorable warriors. Even the emperor couldn't refuse."

"Okay, so my parents didn't want to exploit my innate abilities. Isn't that what you're asking me to do for you?"

Kiron sighed. "Garen, we aren't just another interest group or clan or some self-serving gang. We are the defenders of peace within the three kingdoms. This world is wrecked with the people that have used their depth to torment others, some so terrifying that I cannot simply send in unprepared soldiers. The balance of justice requires even greater skilled individuals to stand against them. Yes, I admit that we have sought you with great interest to your potential, but not to exploit for our own gain. Forces are surging around us," Garen flinched, expecting to hear the same bitter words Pyralis used. *Greater evils.* Instead, Kiron continued, "a persistent darkness, and we cannot hope to endure without the efforts of those equally devoted to light."

Garen had to admire the unexpected rhetoric, even if it offered him little appeal. Three years prior, he would have fallen for every word in that speech. Three years, however, taught him just how far and deep that darkness stretched. All of life became a struggle just to survive, and Kiron's belief that light might actually overcome seemed like a fable. It was the kind of nonsense like a few rabbits teaming up to defeat a fox. Somewhere deep inside the thought, Garen wanted to cling to the hope, but that nature lay buried under years of pain, shoveled on by how little pity the world had for idealism.

"So, you're the good guys, even heroes of sorts. I have yet to see why you'd want me corrupting a pure team like yourselves."

Another lengthy pause followed the response, this one unnerving even to Garen.

Kiron raised his head from the bowed posture in which he stood. Enough light spilt under the hood to reveal just his mouth as he spoke the haunting words, "No such thing as good people. Just decent ones, willing to serve more than themselves."

Garen had no chance to toy around with the notion. The words pierced him on impact. They did not ring with the arrogance of a perfect world like before. They just told of a man who honestly believed that a few dedicated individuals could make this world a more livable place. That much, Garen could respect. Whether he believed it or not.

Kiron tucked his chin to his chest once more and spoke in a quieter voice. "We're also willing to pay you an absurd amount of gold."

The comment shattered the gravity of his thoughts, and Garen let out a genuine laugh like he had not felt in ages. "Master Kiron, I believe you may have managed to appeal to both my limited good nature and my lust for wealth in one blow." Garen took a second, letting the laughter wear off before he could bring himself to delve back into the weight of the situation. "I've lost both my parents to this darkness you're up against, whatever it is. These Spellswords of yours, they take down guys like that?"

46

"More than just 'like that.' Those responsible for your losses are some of our primary concerns. The attacker that took your mother's life, and now Pyr—"

"Wait," Garen stood, eyes gaping. "Are you saying you know who killed my mother?" Comparatively, Garen couldn't care less about Pyralis. Dreams of revenge that once seemed distant suddenly felt within his grasp. He could find and destroy Pyralis on his own, but the long-forgotten hope of avenging his mother struck a deeper chord.

Garen had investigated the matter during his first few years on his own but with no success. He considered just finding Micah and killing him to settle the matter. After all, Micah's negligence allowed the assailant to strike his mother from behind in the heat of the moment. Garen ultimately decided against the misdirected revenge. Even after Emperor Tibalt's passing, the murder of his treasured, middle son would have messy consequences.

Kiron's voice shook his thoughts back to the question he'd asked. "We do. Of course, we're far more than just assassins. Mostly, we protect the innocent rather than hunt the wicked. But we've been known to accomplish one with the other."

Garen sat back on the bed and let his mind reel at the possibilities. He still had no intention of joining ranks with these people, regardless of whether his parents had been Spellswords themselves. But they had strung him along in another way. They had information that was of use, and Garen was happy to saddle up next to anyone he could profit from, especially when they made it this easy to steal it. "I'll need the night to sleep on it."

"Right, of course. I didn't come to get a contract, only to offer understanding. If you're content, I'll leave you to your thoughts."

Garen stood to see Kiron leave, then suddenly remembered one last question, stopping him before he closed the door behind him. "I have to know one last thing before I go making any firm decisions."

"Go ahead."

Garen concentrated for a moment, toying around with a

few phrasings. Finally, he blurted, "Why the hood?"

Kiron froze as well, then let out a casual laugh. "Let's just say you might not like what's underneath. One day I'll show you."

Garen shrugged off the weak response. "Fair enough. Oh, and, thank you for," he turned to motion to the luxurious suite behind him, "all of this."

Kiron beamed another smile through the shadow. "No need to thank me. It's been yours all along."

"I'm sorry, what?"

"This room belonged to your parents. As far as I can tell, it's all rightfully yours." The space around Garen suddenly shifted, taking on an entirely different feeling than the strange setting he felt at first. The details came alive to him, now living relics of his parents' taste and style, every nuance of design a testimony to their character. The headboard and curtains and rugs all rambled on about the life of his parents he never knew. For just a moment, Garen felt an absurd jealousy surge in him, sincerely envious of the furniture's lives above his own.

Kiron gave him a moment to glance about the room, but did not wait for a reply. "Get some sleep, and rest that mind of yours."

"Will do," he barely stammered.

"Good night, Garen."

With the door closed and privacy restored, Garen hopped back onto the bed. It felt entirely new. He was both at home and intruding on his parents. The entire tangle of emotions made him feel very childish. Still, he had not forgotten the more pressing matters of his stay here. Even without a formal offer, Garen understood their intentions well enough to give the idea serious thought. He never had the lofty dream of becoming a hero as a kid. Maybe it had to do with the sheltered life his parents worked so hard to give him. The more he thought about it, the more Garen found he couldn't remember any dreams of grandeur from his youth. And at this point, the idea of anything but merely fighting to survive felt foreign to him. This opportunity gave him the chance to keep fighting, but after years of unstructured freedom, he wasn't sure if putting on a leash just for security and a mountain of gold would be worth the cost.

Maybe it's just pride.

Garen certainly understood his streak of arrogance, but something more than his ego held him back. His parents trusted this group, and the promise of wealth and respect had its own lures. Yet even with generous profits accounted for, a voice inside him screamed to shove the offer back in Kiron's dimly-lit face and run. In all of Garen's years on his own, not once had the world tried to offer him any relief. Given his talents, survival didn't require much effort, but the leap from survival to something more gave him pangs of unease deep in his stomach. Even more unsettling was the truth that life never divided smoothly into the pure against the corrupt. Yet aside from the mild annoyance of Naia, these people had all the signs of an unpolluted cause. No matter how tempting the offer, he couldn't imagine joining ranks in a group where he didn't feel like he belonged.

* * * * *

A loud, vibrating hum woke Garen. He sat up and saw the noise's source sitting on the chest of drawers, now pulsating with a rich blue glow. He slid off the bed, taking just a moment to appreciate the complete lack of pain in his right leg, and made his way over to the device. The vibrant blue geonode had a smooth, cylindrical shape, of which he had seen only once before in his life. His father owned such an item, and though Garen had no clue to how the magic was crafted, he understood the purpose. The geonode ore had a sound transmission spell imbued in its core, and when pressed against the side of the face between his ear and mouth, it could send and receive sound. His father frequently warned him not to play with the expensive toy, but Garen wouldn't have known how to use it to reach someone on purpose anyway. Fortunately, answering seemed an easier task.

Garen placed the glowing stone against his cheek and uttered the most awkward, unconfident "Hello" of his life.

"Garen, you're awake." The deep feminine voice belonged to Morgan.

"Yes, well, slowly but surely. What can I do for you?" Garen scratched the back of his neck and stretched a little, trying to wake himself up quickly in case he had to follow through on the offer.

"Nothing needed, just extending an invitation. Kiron said you were thinking things over, but I know I can't think while I'm cooped up. Make it down to the meeting room quickly, and maybe you can talk Kiron into letting you accompany us."

"So, I could be your shadow for the day? It doesn't exactly sound like you need my help."

"We don't. But you'll see what kind of work we do. And you'll gauge how much stronger than us you think you are."

Garen paused to make it seem like he was still thinking it over. Her persuasion, however, had immediately convinced him.

"Alright, I'm in." Garen looked down, remembering the fragile linens that covered him. "I don't suppose you could spare something more battle appropriate? I'd hate to fight crime in my pajamas on my first day."

Morgan gave a quick laugh. "The satchel Drake brought should have your basics. Can you handle that much, or should I come up and dress you myself?"

"If I stick to one leg at a time, I should be fine." Garen did his best to return the verbal jest, but the embarrassment of forgetting his own pack seemed to have won.

"Hurry." The glowing stopped, and Garen took a brief second to once again evaluate himself in the mirror. He still looked like trash, but he knew some fresh air would at least make him feel better. He could tag along for now, and if all else failed, easily slip out of their grasp if he felt the need. He clenched his fists at the promise of adventure, and he felt his recently neglected muscles ripple up his arms and across his chest.

Maybe they'll end up needing my help, and I'll get to hit someone.

The thought scared Garen for a moment, wondering if he had become as violent as the intention left him feeling. He dismissed the concern. Every sane human has the need to wreck a man's face every now and then.

CHAPTER
SIX

Garen found Kiron in the large meeting room from the day prior and easily persuaded him. He mostly just repeated back some of the same baiting words Morgan used to pull him into the excursion. Drake, Naia, Morgan, and one new face, a burly colossus of a man, huddled into the dimly lit room to sit down at the table alongside the two. Garen noticed the group now filled all six chairs. He wondered if they set the number on purpose. He had no way of knowing, but the placement felt intentional with its symmetry. He wondered if in their apparent years of searching for him, if that chair had always been there, empty and waiting.

Garen tried to listen in as the two sisters bickered over something the other had promised, while the loud stranger he didn't recognize pried into the details of Drake's trip east. As Garen took a seat, the booming voice trailed off, and he looked up to see the man's eyes wide with curiosity above a friendly smile. Garen smiled awkwardly back and wondered whether he needed to introduce himself. Before he could attempt it, Kiron cleared his throat to gather their attention off of Garen.

"As I mentioned, we received word this morning about the theft of some rather valuable property last night in a residence east of Tiben. Normally, I'd just let the local authorities handle the matter, but the description of the incident has all the marks of the Rendhills."

"About time," Drake sighed in relief.

"I know." Kiron continued. "We've all waited patiently since Drake's discovery of what we're hoping is their base of operations. Now we have a chance to catch them with dirty hands and put an end to their break-ins."

The unfamiliar face in the group spoke up. "What if they gotten rid of it already? If we bust up the place and don't find what we're looking for, they're just gonna get vengeful, and it ain't right leaving the surrounding folk with a spiteful bunch of

Rendhills, scheming and all."

"A possibility, but the artifacts they lifted will take some time to fence. Plus they've become fairly competent at giving our local guards the slip and getting back to their hideaway. They might be a step ahead of the night-watch, but they won't expect us. My guess is most of them will be tired from the job last night. You all know they aren't renowned for their fighting anyway, but don't underestimate the tools of their craft. Keep your eyes peeled for traps. Still, I don't expect any real threats you four can't spit on."

Morgan coughed unconvincingly.

"Yes Morgan, I'm well aware. You have five today. Garen Renyld wants a first-hand look at what we do, so feel free to show off a bit. Try not to make it look simple, will you? I'd love to plan more of it out, but given their barrier over the base, it looks like you'll be coordinating as you go. You have my full confidence. Stay safe."

The others stood even before he uttered the word confidence. Kiron led the group into the hallway, and Garen ran up beside Drake. "So, I finally get to see where I'm at in the palace. I'm guessing this whole corridor has some kind of magic seal over it. I tried to come up with my own locking spell, but you guys must be ages ahead of my first attempt."

"That was a first attempt? I emptied half my depth just carving my way through the rock around it." Drake laughed and shook his head. "Actually, though, we don't need any of that." Garen watched as Kiron stopped at one of the doors on the hallway, turned the bolt, and opened it politely for them. "It turns out, in a palace this size, the least conspicuous thing is one more locked door."

As they stepped out, Garen's embarrassment was quickly dwarfed by a sense of awe at the ornate world around him. Marble, gold, and granite seemed to swirl together creating their elaborate surroundings. He was too lost in the carvings worked into every arch and column of the palace to have counted, but he must have descended six or seven stories down the crystal staircase.

The main floor made even the other passages look cheap, bouncing with life and noise within the domed-ceiling hall. Drake led them away from the grand entrance to a much smaller hall down the east wing. They eventually arrived at a courtyard exit, where at the sight of the group, two guards immediately stepped out of the way and opened the door. They emerged into the fresh spring air around them and the manicured grass beneath their feet. Garen had never nursed any tender sentiments about nature before, but the glow of the sunlight felt strangely soothing after days without it. He looked around to find the others pausing momentarily with the same contemplative grin.

Drake stepped out from the group, and Garen instinctively followed. He stopped as he felt a small but firm grip on his shoulder and turned to see Naia.

She cocked her head sideways and gave him an insulting glare. "No need to smother the boy. He just needs a second to focus."

Garen looked to find the whole group awkwardly glancing in his direction. "Oh, my apologies. How could I forget after all the times I've been through this? Are you guys always this accepting to your new recruits?"

The hulking unknown in the group stepped toward Garen and wrapped an arm around him. Standing this close to the larger-than-life warrior, Garen didn't focus on how big the man was, only on how small he felt. He shifted uneasily within his giant grip as he spoke, practically shaking him with each word. "Don't mind no attention to the little girl. She's just all twisted up cause she's afraid she's not the strongest in the group no more." Garen watched the seven-foot, ox-like man release each syllable from his leathery lips. He spoke the words with a carefree spirit, entirely unconcerned with how he sounded. It gave a pleasant contrast from the prim and proper tones of the others, but no matter how amusing, did not make Garen forget his grievance with the snotty one.

"Well then, why don't we have it out right here? We can turn that fear into terror." Garen felt the grip around him tighten, and his feet left the ground. He landed on his back a second later, several feet from where he once stood. The lumbering man looked down with a woeful scowl, wholly different from the welcoming smile a moment ago.

"I said pay no attention to, not pick a fight with. You two come to blows, and I'll be the first to knock the both of ya out. That ain't how we work."

"Noted." Garen stood and walked back toward the group, rubbing his shoulder. It didn't pain him that badly, but the sympathy couldn't hurt his case. "So, Mr. People-throwing monstrosity, you have a name?"

The odd title elicited a grinning response. "Name's Argus Ashling, Spellsword aide."

Garen squinted his eyes inquisitively. "An aide, you say? So, you protect these three?"

"Nah, I'm not the only aide. Morgan here's not a full-fledged Spellsword neither."

"Argus!" both sisters roared.

Morgan delivered enough judgment in her eyes to frighten them all. She added harshly, "I don't think that's a conversation we need to have just yet."

Garen made eye contact with her to try to read the situation. She simply rolled her eyes and turned away. "Fair enough," Garen said. "That's just one more question for Kiron when I get back. I'm rather curious now what makes Naia and Drake so special, and more importantly, if I'm special too."

Naia gave a serious nod too sudden to be genuine. "Very special. I've seen you fight two whole bandits and live. Not at the same time, of course, but still. Two of 'em. Whew."

Garen had his own sarcastic comeback picked out, but he bit his tongue at the image of Argus pounding him waist-deep into the ground. Still, he could not silence the antagonist in him. "Well, maybe with a—"

"I'm ready." All eyes turned to face Drake, now consumed within a thin vortex of wind. The group filed into place behind him. Morgan positioned Garen into the back right of the square, about five feet to the right of Naia and an equal distance behind herself. The wind drifted behind Drake and wrapped firmly around each of them. The pressure squeezed Garen even tighter than the embrace from Argus, crushing his arms and legs in place. Garen could only turn his neck, and the image he caught to his left held that pretty little brat sticking her tongue out at him. He laughed at the sight, unsure how to respond. They were probably close enough in years, but he was used to dealing with people twice his age, not ones who acted half of it.

Without warning, the five of them shot into the sky, keeping perfect form from where they stood. Garen closed his eyes on instinct, but opened them when he realized he could feel no rush of wind on his skin.

Here's an interesting sensation.

The invisible chains that held them together shielded them from the piercing chill they would face at these speeds. Garen could no longer even move his head, but he could see the ground beneath him just fine. From this height he could see the full city, more than just the sliver in view from his window. The unmatched expanse of it all reminded him of the Vikar-Tola he knew as a child, when it was still the capital city of the Jundux Empire.

Garen was still on the run north with his father when the Division of Thrones took place, but word traveled quickly, and he knew the aftermath well enough. With Emperor Tibalt's passing, his advising council appointed each son to rule a portion of the empire. The rumors and gossip spoke of murder. In most stories, it was a poisoning. In others, dark and terrible magics. Regardless, the empire was in no position to choose a new emperor from among the three sons. Garen had his own suspicions that Micah could be behind the whole ordeal. He shouldn't have a problem causing the death of yet another innocent person. But no fingers were pointed. Instead, Pyralis was appointed over the Western Province, Micah remained in Vikar-Tola to govern the Central, and Amiri, their oldest brother, received a throne in the Eastern Province.

The whole mess seemed like a terrible mistake from the outside. After all, the three provinces split into separate kingdoms within the first year of their joint rule, but Garen had a reasonable guess at its purpose. The Jundux Empire had been united for barely a hundred years since the Dawn of Magic. Under the rallying cry of Lord Jundux, the people banded together out of fear of the powers now surrounding them. It was only a matter of time before they realized the real powers to be afraid of were among themselves, and the same fear that pulled them together began to rip them apart. In recent years, hostility continued to boil over geonode trade between the east and west. But none of that directly concerned Garen. Most of the sources he acquired his goods from weren't exactly "selling" them in the technical sense.

Their race through the clouds slowed, pulling Garen's thoughts along with his body back down to earth. They had crossed an immense amount of farmland in the short travel and arrived just outside of Tiben.

Drake closed his eyes. "I can feel it right up ahead there. It interferes with the natural wind currents."

In an eerily synchronized fashion, Drake, Naia, Morgan, and Argus drew their weapons. Drake held a thin longsword, nearly four feet in length, but with both hands he twirled it with grace. Naia and Morgan both drew matching shortswords from their sheathes, but held different weapons to complement. Morgan gripped a hand-axe, somewhat blunted enough for Garen to guess the weapon served a more defensive purpose, probably for trapping an oncoming blade. Naia's left hand held an elaborate blue dagger, the more likely defensive choice for parrying. Yet, she clutched the knife with a violent grip that left him unsure about her intentions with it.

Though all the members seemed to have chosen weapons suited to their image and style, none fit as perfectly as Argus' instruments of destruction. He had slung the massive bronze shield off his back and into his left hand. The face of the shield had seven sizable genonodes embedded into it, each carrying the spells of powerful mages he could draw from in an instant. His right hand gripped a massive war hammer, the head of which was larger than Argus' own. Rather than the traditional spike on the back end, both sides were blunted. The unusual design made no difference, though. Someone on the wrong end of that swing was doomed no matter what shape struck him. It was certainly less barbaric than the spiked clubs and hammers he'd grown accustomed to in the Te'ens.

That might be the most dignified dealer of blunt-force trauma I've ever seen.

With a smile on his face, Garen drew his own weapon of choice, a spare katana from the satchel Drake retrieved from the Te'ens. He had to admire his own choice in combat. The blade was long and slender enough to stay agile, keep his enemies at a fair distance, and use magic to even the odds. If they should ever come in close, he had another means of assault strapped more closely to his side. Garen checked that the wakizashi was in place and firmly gripped his katana in anticipation.

He noticed Morgan giving him an obvious look of concern. "You look a little tense, Garen. Maybe you should keep that sheathed and just watch. After all, you've never encountered a Rendhill nest before. They can catch you off guard if you don't know their tricks."

"Hey, as long as I'll have time to explain that before they take a swing at me, I should be fine then." Garen knew he could probably get by without the sword, but he took particular pleasure in proving himself right.

"Fair enough," Drake said. "But Morgan is right. You're just here for a breath of fresh air, and I don't want to have to look out for you if traps start flying. Naia, would you care to do the honors?"

"I'd be delighted. Did you say it was that way?" She pointed into the center of the open field.

"A little to the left and you have it."

A thin jet of water shot from the tip of her blade as fast as his eyes could follow into the open space. But as the stream hit a certain point, it vanished entirely. Naia tensed a little and concentrated. The line of water expanded into a cylinder. The water blurred the image, but he could see a building on the other side of the violent water portal.

Argus responded to the obvious look of confusion across

Garen's face. "It's some kind of big old force shield device. Keeps the whole place unseeable, and it don't let nothing through that ain't as fluid and piercing as Naia here's water blast."

The group stood watching for a few more seconds until Naia broke the silence, her voice full of tension from the strain of the spell. "That should be plenty big enough, even for Argus. Get your lazy rears in there."

The group ran toward the opening and dove straight through the hole into the now flooded grass on the other side. Garen followed the group, diving through the wall of water and into the opening it created, then dodging the gush of water that poured through. The passage through already soaked him, but it wasn't the wetness that bothered him. The water had an icy sting to it, and Garen wondered if she just couldn't control the temperature or if she set the chill intentionally.

The flow through the opening began to slow, and Naia stepped through the portal herself. She didn't have a drop on her, and smiled as she watched the others rub their arms from the cold.

"A little warmer next time, if you don't mind," Drake said.

"Oops."

They shook it off and walked up to the main door of the sizable warehouse in front of them. Naia and Drake looked at each other and nodded. "My favorite part," she whispered.

Garen watched their eyes lock on the door ahead and their grips tighten. The door froze solid and exploded inward, the crystallized debris flying into the open chamber. The combination of elements reminded Garen of his own method. Only rather than applying simple heating and freezing spells, the display took place on a much grander scale. The frost left each beam brittle enough that a light breeze could have crumbled it to pieces. Drake's force of wind did not simply crack it. It obliterated every fragment into dust. The intensity of the spell spoke of their confidence just as much as their method of entry. Garen followed in behind the others, swords drawn, with very little effort given to stealth.

Clearly, these Rendhills had put too much faith in their outer shield. Not a single guard waited within the first hall. As they came to the end of it, two men, half-dressed and clumsily holding their weapons, charged at the group. Drake engaged the one on the right. Swords met, and Drake quickly dropped his enemy with a forceful knee to the stomach. Naia effortlessly dodged her assailant's swing and delivered a crushing elbow to the side of his face. The blow spun him around completely. She caught his chin on its next pass with the pommel of her dagger, tossing him onto his back.

Garen stood in awe for a number of reasons. To start, they moved with an art he had not witnessed in quite some time. But more curiously, they did not simply slice their enemies down as they could have. Showing mercy at their level of competence was an odd sign. Though he wasn't sure why, Garen was glad to see them intent on the purpose of their mission and not creating a body count.

They turned the corner into a central area, a sort of storage room with stairs connecting to the open upper level. Another disheveled guard appeared at the ledge of the upper floor's railing and pointed a crossbow down at the group. Argus leaped to the front with shield raised and deflected the bolt to the side. From behind him, Naia conjured a simple icicle in the air, and with a swing of Drake's sword, the projectile sped through the air into the shoulder of the man before he could reload another bolt.

Garen snapped out of his child-like entertainment at the action and focused on his surroundings. As he took in the adjacent corridors, Garen sensed another pair of guards about to come out behind them. He stepped to the hall's entrance and waited. As the first turned the corner, Garen lowered his sword and cut a deep slice into the tendons above his knee. The man screamed and fell backward onto his friend, knocking them both over. The one in back scrambled to his feet and readied a sword, unconfidently stepping toward the fearsome intruder. Garen realized how untrained these thieves were and sheathed his sword. The Rendhill bandit finally charged him with all the courage he could muster. When the man finally swung, Garen stepped to the side of the vertical slice and sent his fist into his throat. The bandit dropped his sword and fell to his knees gasping for air. Garen closed his eyes and whispered the word, "Illumine."

An immeasurably radiant light emitted from the whole of his body and sent both Rendhills from clutching at their knee and throat into a terrified howl, scratching at their miserable eyes.

"What in the soulless city was that?" Argus screamed. Garen turned to remember he actually had allies for once, and even from around the corner they felt the stun of the blinding light.

"Sorry, just, uh, showing off like the rest of you." Garen didn't feel like admitting he had forgotten about them entirely.

"Well, next time give us a warning or something," Naia fumed.

"Right, right, my apologies. Anyway, what's the policy on a couple of helpless guys? Do I have to kill them?" Garen asked the question as if he didn't care either way, but was as uncomfortable playing executioner in public as he was in private.

"No, that won't be necessary," Drake replied. "We're just here to recover the goods and shake them up a bit. It isn't like we could exterminate them anyway. Looks like most have already abandoned the place." Drake tossed another Rendhill against a wall with a gust of wind and turned to Garen. "We try to avoid casualties if possible. Unless, you know, they deserve it."

Garen liked the answer. These Spellswords weren't quite the naïve idealists he'd figured them for. They actually matched the humble description Kiron offered.

No such thing as good people. Just decent ones, willing to serve more than themselves.

Garen wondered if they could solve more problems in life by paying morally neutral individuals to do the right thing. He concluded that it might help, but in all the kingdoms they wouldn't find enough gold, and probably not enough morally neutral people either.

The group made light work of the few bandits remaining. One particularly unfortunate Rendhill made the mistake of lunging at Argus head on. The one-man-army took all the time he needed to pull back his hammer and deliver a full swing. Garen cringed at the sound of impact with the man's shoulder, sending him clear through the wooden beams of a walled-off chamber.

Naia stepped first into the room glowing with the hues of countless stolen geonodes. Garen admired the hoarder's nest a little, but remained attuned to the commotion taking place much deeper in the building. Past the hall where the two men had rushed him from, a few more were frantically working on something. Garen imagined a vault of priceless treasures too rare to keep even in the first sealed room. Without a thought to the others, Garen slid away from the group. He crept down the hall and up to the door. Behind it, two men argued. Leaning against the wood, Garen heard a loud click like a metal lock unbolting. With a little helping from a conjured force of wind, Garen kicked the door open and drew his sword. If he made quick enough work of these men, he'd have a chance to pocket anything of value before the others even found him.

The Rendhills spun around in shock, but not so stunned as to forget their defenses. One of the men held a glowing yellow geonode. He shrieked and held it out in front of him. Garen slid to a stop, prepared to dodge whatever barrage of spells would come flying from the gem. The space in front of him remained clear. Instead, a square of the floor under him began to emit a matching yellow glow. He looked up to notice the same strange tile above him on the ceiling. Before he could step out of it, the squares connected, walling him behind a thick pane of the cloudy yellow barrier. He slammed a fist against it, but the surface was as solid as stone. Garen tried shouting as he continued to bang against the wall, but given the silence on the outside, he knew neither his enemies nor allies could hear him.

The Rendhills turned back to the large safe they had opened, but Garen did not have a chance to peer inside to see for himself. He focused on the rear wall of his cage, which he could swear was closer than when it started. Within a moment, his fears were confirmed, and he watched the back wall slowly shrink in on him. He recklessly began to throw waves of fire and wind against the surface in front of him, even as the backlash burned and stung him. The barrier shrugged off the assault, showing no signs of damage. The back wall pressed up against his heels, solid as ever, and slid him forward. His back flattened against it, and he knew the pressure would start any second. He closed his eyes and braced himself for the torture. The tightness in his legs and chest grew. The walls began to squeeze past the point of comfort. He could feel it in his bones.

Anything but this. No... please, anything else.

Suddenly the pressure released. The unexpected change in force knocked Garen forward to his knees. He looked up to see Morgan clutching the same yellow geonode that sprung the trap. Beside her laid one fallen Rendhill, and the other slicing toward Naia. She bounced back out of reach and released another gush of water from her blade into his face. The water sizzled and popped as it touched his skin, and Garen realized she had full control over the conjured water's temperature.

"What were you thinking?" Morgan yelled.

"I was just—"

"Just what? Being a reckless little idiot?" Naia chimed in as she silenced the screaming Rendhill with her pommel to the back of his neck.

Garen turned to her, his gratitude in the moment erased by her smug attitude. He had no violent intentions, but his body only knew one response to insults like those. He reached for his sword.

Drake saw the situation taking a turn for the worse and announced his presence in the room. "Calm down. That's why we're all here." Drake stood just inside the doorway and motioned that they come back outside. "Guards from Tiben are here to clean up the rest."

Garen filed out of the room between the two sisters. Though he held his tongue, Naia could not help but get in one more comment. "You got lucky," she whispered harshly. Garen wanted to fire back and tell her how wrong she was. But the truth was no insult to her. It would have been a compliment. Garen knew what lucky felt like. He had just experienced it in the Sanstric caves with Pyralis. Luck was all a person could hope for when they were outmatched and alone. For once, luck hadn't saved him. Allies had. The deck was stacked in Garen's favor, and the people with him, not pure luck, came through. He still didn't appreciate being made to feel the fool, but given the circumstance, and the possibility he might deserve it, he could tolerate them saving his life one more time.

On their way out they located the source powering the barrier spell and smashed the massive purple geonode to pieces. Garen assumed none of them had the tolerance to leap through another of Naia's freezing water hoops.

They departed via the same windy blur they arrived in. The entire return trip Garen considered some of the final questions he had compiled, but he liked what he saw. Kicking down doors and seeing the looks on petrified faces had a certain appeal to his style. He actually enjoyed the thought of honest work for once, especially if he could still have his fun. Obviously, there was some merit to having other people watch his back, even if they did want to rub his face in it. If Kiron was serious about his mother, and crazy enough to take the fight to Pyralis, this Spellsword thing might be worth a brief try.

One of the last aspects Garen couldn't wrap his mind around hung in the left corner of his eye. Naia had all the signs of a spoiled girl whose sheltered world revolved around her. Yet watching her in action made Garen question it all. She fought with skill and grace. Her affinity for water magic was astounding. And her age implied the talents were out of necessity rather than discipline. Perhaps she'd been through a bit of her own trouble. He wouldn't find out by running away. Garen decided he might stick around to pry deeper. If they had any common ground, it intrigued Garen to find out how two young fighters could live such different lives.

CHAPTER
SEVEN

The group made their way back into the palace, discussing the rest of their day. Morgan and Naia planned to wander the market district for a while, then come back for some rest before patrolling that night. Drake had a banquet back east he was obligated to attend. Argus grinned and told them about a bet he had to settle with a she-devil named Carla.

The group stopped at the plain door and Drake proceeded to unlock it. As he did, all eyes turned to Garen. "Oh, me? Well, I haven't exactly been here long enough to start making plans."

A look of excitement flashed across Argus' face. "Oh, I can't no way let you stay here by your own self. You're coming with me. I mean, Carla's a tricky one, and I can make use of another honest man. Plus, I'm thinking she might have a friend for you."

Being referred to as an "honest" man certainly piqued Garen's interest, but Morgan leaned out from behind Argus' towering shoulders and emphatically shook her head side to side, mouthing the word "no."

Garen caught the signal and looked up into Argus' inviting smile. "Sorry, I think I'm going to take another day to myself. You know, figure out some more details of my situation here."

Drake opened the door and held it for the group to file through. As Garen passed by, Drake whispered, "Good decision." Garen followed the crowd all heading up the stairs to their chambers.

"In case you're interested," Morgan offered, "Naia and I have patrolling duty tonight. It's nothing quite as exciting as today, but fresh air is fresh air. I just hate to see you locked up here while you work through what's on your mind. Nothing worse than being trapped in a room with yourself." Garen let his mind trail off at the notion and his eyes stared blankly over her shoulder. "...that, and I could show you the city a little."

Garen noticed her awkward smile, expecting a response from him. The years of solitude had done little to reinforce his active listening skills. He snapped back to their conversation, replaying the words in his head until he found the topic at hand. "I used to visit here a lot."

"No need to put the kid to work so quickly," Drake teased as he parted ways to his own room.

Morgan nodded. "I'd forgotten that you grew up here. Then neverm—"

"No, it's fine," Garen said. "Besides, I was just a kid, and I don't remember much. It could be nice, seeing what's new and all. So, it's just you and Naia?"

"We're typically scheduled in pairs. But we could always use the extra company, and I'm sure you have stories to pass the time."

Garen leaned against the doorframe, trying to think of any reason to back out, but he knew he'd already lost. "You don't think Naia would mind?" He looked behind them to gauge her reaction, but realized she'd already stepped into her room.

"She'd better not. You two are going to have to forget whatever imaginary rivalry you have against each other."

Garen lowered his head and let out a noticeable grin. "I'll do what I can."

"So, tonight then?" Morgan asked.

"Maybe. Check with me when you're about to leave. You know where to find me."

"That I do. Rest easy, Garen."

"Thanks." He closed the door and unstrapped the swords from his waist.

Rest is getting old.

Once again Garen looked up to find himself in the mirror. *No, this time I really do want answers.* The confident smirk on his own face comforted him, and he made his way out into the hall.

Now, if I were a creepy little man who likes to hide behind a hood, where would I be? Garen wandered down to the general meeting room where he usually found Kiron, but the space lay empty. There were still a number of doors in the main hall that Garen had never seen opened. He thought about trying a few handles. Life as a thief left him no reserves about peeking behind strange doors. The problem with barging in was the equal chance of being seen. Before he would resort to blatant snooping, he had another tool at his disposal.

He stood still and pulled in the surrounding light to scan the floor and pick out all the other people on it. The first attempt gathered too broad of a field, and the input nearly blinded him. Whatever gift he had that could let him see beyond the limitations of his eyes, it could not take in a hundred servants, guards, and nobles all at once. He tried once more, focusing on just his immediate vicinity. All four Spellswords drifted about on the floor above him, but in the same floor as him, two doors down, two individuals stood talking. The first was a frail, old man and the second a familiarly cloaked figure.

Garen would love if this spell of his extended to pick up sound. He crept down the stairs and walked over to the door, but even now with his ear almost touching it, he couldn't distinguish a word they said. The dignified elder bowed low to Kiron, beyond that of a polite gesture.

Interesting. Apparently our hooded friend carries some kind of rank.

Kiron simply nodded as his friend walked to a corner of the room. A glowing white disc appeared beneath the older gentleman, and in an instant he vanished completely. The rarity and value of such a geonode spoke volumes on its own.

Garen heard footsteps approaching the door and snapped out of the trance, recognizing he needed to do something less suspicious than just stand there whistling when the door opened. He preempted the problem by knocking. Kiron opened the door with a surprised jolt to see Garen standing there.

"Garen, I'm glad someone showed you which door was mine."

"Yes, well, yeah. Can we talk?"

Kiron looked back over his shoulder into the room. Garen

tried to get a quick glimpse too, but Kiron quickly closed the door behind him. "Yes, I think now would be an excellent time to talk." He led the way into the meeting room where they both took a seat at a table far too large for just the two of them.

Kiron eased into the conversation as casually as he could. "Drake briefly mentioned when he came in that all went as planned."

Garen considered mentioning the crushing trap he wound up in, assuming the sisters hadn't told him already. He saw no reason to. "That it did."

"Good. I was hoping this was a smooth trip for you, and that you got to witness some of the more impressive attributes of the group."

"Yes, that's kind of what I need to ask you about."

"Probably the same question I knew I would have to answer by the end of the day. Let me guess, 'What separates Drake and Naia from the others, and what exactly is a Spellsword?'"

Garen marveled at his accuracy, but did not wish to surrender his calm composure just yet. "More or less."

"Well then," Kiron fidgeted for a moment, then took a deep breath and began. "Garen, do you remember an event I referenced in our last conversation? The stretching of the Theltus Nisdal?"

"I do." Again, the unrelated questions forced Garen to play along in order to see how it connected.

"When those five stretched the gateway, they let out more than just spells and sparkles. Five spirits, living entities from the other realm, crossed the gate into ours. As the legend tells it, they quickly found out they could not exist without form in a world of shapes and substance. So, they took the form of five elements: water, earth, fire, wind, and light."

Garen stared blankly into the shadow of Kiron's hood. He wanted to start putting the pieces together, but too much still didn't make sense. Kiron checked to make sure he followed, and with a nod from Garen, he continued.

"Those elements, however, did not have the ability to

sustain these ethereal creatures. Though it dances, fire has no life, and though it howls, wind has no breath. They found the same clever hiding spot as the rest of their realm's energy: the soul. But rather than spread themselves across this world, they each chose specific vessels. Five human souls became their hosts, each embodied with a direct link to the Spirit Realm and a frightening mastery of manipulating their element. When they realized the power they had, it was only a matter of time before they understood the tools at their disposal, and their value to the empire. Those five became the first Spellswords. And since the masses had not yet learned how to train their own depth, those men were like gods."

Garen sat in silence, trying as quickly as his mind could manage to connect the dots to the current day. "You said my parents were two of these people...but this all took place over a hundred years back, right? How old were my parents?"

An involuntary laugh cut Kiron off as he tried to respond. "No, no, your parents were not among the first. Neither were Drake or Naia. They all inherited their gift from someone who carried it before them."

"Did I inherit," Garen paused to phrase the fragile question correctly. "Am I...?"

"No."

"Oh." He tried to wipe the stunned look off his face from the unexpected response. "I guess I just thought after you tracked me down—"

"What I mean is that you aren't yet. Garen, you have an untold potential, depth of soul like few have ever seen. But the passing of these spirits is not a voluntary gift. These elemental creatures are not as selfless as the humans they first found a home in. All they desire is power. When the host dies, the spirit does not seek a well-intentioned soul to take up residency in. They seek power. And who is the one person certain to be at least as powerful as you?"

The implication hit him like a brick to the chest. His breathing fell shallow, and every muscle went limp. "The person that kills you." Garen closed his eyes and asked in quiet, muffled words, "So my parents were murdered for this power?"

"Most likely."

"And now the killers are running free with the destructive spirits they stole?" The words pained him, but he choked them out as well as he could.

"They are, but that's where you come in."

Garen raised his head with a look of hopeful curiosity in his eyes. It vanished in a moment's time and the more accustomed cynicism took its place. "What do you need me for? You've got your Spellswords and aides in order. Why don't you take care of it yourself?"

"We've been waiting for you, Garen. Nearly a year ago we found your mother's killer, but we clung to the hope that we'd find you. This is your fight. You were not meant to fade into obscurity as a thief."

Garen opened his mouth to object. He wanted to remind Kiron that he had a greater purpose than just petty thievery, that he was protecting and providing for someone. Kiron continued without giving him the chance. "You're right. We could have strung him up and passed the gift on to Argus or Morgan. But for all you've had stolen from you, it's time for you to take something back worth stealing."

Garen sat in silence for a moment, letting the words resonate in his head. Finally, a difficult grin crept its way onto his face and a strained chuckle escaped his throat. "Awful generous of you to look after me like that."

"Well, I didn't mention the part where I wanted you on our side so we never end up crossing swords."

"Heh. So, let's say I was interested in this Spellsword deal. What do you need from me? Is there some oath I need to swear? You don't need any of my blood, do you?" He tried to make light of it, but Garen realized he was in uncharted territory.

"Garen, you offer the world more gifts than you can know, but your oath would not be one of them. I trust your sworn word about as much as I trust Argus with something fragile. None of the others are bound here by contract. They stick around because this is home, because they love what they do, because they recognize a higher calling on their lives. Some have their personal reasons. You'll find Drake to be highly concerned over the balance between the kingdoms. The Talia sisters may only seem to care about each other, but I can assure you, the cruelties of this world have burned a deep sense of justice into them."

"And most importantly, the absurd amount of gold," Garen added to lighten the conversation.

"Yes, I'm sure that doesn't hurt either. So, all I need is an open mind from you. If you commit to our cause tonight, we leave for your destiny tomorrow. That is, unless you have plans."

"I should be free."

Kiron rose to his feet and Garen followed, both put at ease by the outcome of the conversation. "Oh, one other thing that I don't think has come up. When the group is stationed overnight here in Vikar-Tola, we try to keep a pair of Spellswords in the city to patrol. It's good to have a quick response in case a situation arises, and I think you'll find it helps keep us all humble. Spellswords have had a terrible history of at some point believing they are above the common law."

"Makes sense."

"Naia and Morgan are on duty tonight. Why don't you see if they mind you accompanying them?"

Garen politely nodded and suppressed his smile. "Are they? I'll check and see if they care." He made it a few steps toward the stairs before the question on his mind nagged him persistently enough to turn and ask.

"Kiron...my mother," Garen paused, unsure how to ask without sounding childish. "She had the Light Spirit, didn't she?"

Kiron nodded. "You'll enjoy hearing stories of her. Idle minds can spend the next century exaggerating her gifts, and they'll probably still underestimate her. They say she could disappear and reform anywhere. The light she commanded could pierce stone. And beyond the elements, she could access deeper magics. I've seen her close her eyes and watch something happen on the other side of the kingdom. She knew how her enemies would strike before they knew. I don't believe your father ever bested her, though he tried."

"I know a little more of his stories. Fire, right?"

"Seems odd, doesn't it? Such a gentle man with such a destructive power flowing through him? But it was his focus that made him unstoppable. He was the anchor for them all. Garen, I hope you don't feel betrayed that they kept all this from you. They only wanted to protect you. They were the two most devout, peace-seeking fighters I have ever known. Harmony was always plan A."

"Looks like that fell to pieces. What's plan B?"

Kiron raised his head just enough to let the light expose his jaw and reveal a sinister grin. "We punish the baseborn mongrels responsible. We throw a blood-soaked tantrum until order is restored. It'll take us some time to confront Pyralis, complications of dealing with a king and all. But your mother's killer is operating a slave-trade ring just across the Western border. His life is forfeit. Plan to leave tomorrow at noonday."

Every word he spoke further endeared Garen to the cloaked zealot, yet no words seemed appropriate for a response. With a somber nod, he turned and made his way up the stairs to his chamber. Thinking back to a few childhood memories, his parents' elemental affinity made sense. Garen could never understand why his mother always seemed to know when he'd done something he shouldn't, and a rare time or two he thought he remembered his father so frustrated that tiny cones of flame pulsated from his fingertips. He had seen enough of Drake's wind manipulation to peg him as such. He had witnessed less of Naia, but water seemed a fair guess.

Now he understood why Pyralis had taken his father. Garen wondered if there was someone out there with an Earth Spirit too, and whose side he would be on. Still, the biggest confusion in their discussion concerned himself. Garen knew how adept he had become at seeing around corners and using light to a number of advantages. From the moment Kiron listed the elements, light made perfect sense to explain his particular gifts. Garen reveled in the irony that by enacting his vengeance, he would acquire what he thought he already had.

He shut off that stream of emotion and fell back on the

still-foreign cushion of his mattress.

How do people who own beds this soft get anything done? I think I would just sleep all day. The idea of a brief nap had a certain desirable side to it, so he let himself relax a little. His face bore a smile of untold serenity. Beneath that face, however, lay a mind too ashamed to admit his anguish at the mere mention of his mother.

* * * * *

"I'm not going to fight you, Mom!"

"Oh, come on! Don't tell me you're afraid."

Garen felt his lips move, but no sound came out. His mother spoke a silent reply, and Micah shrugged. Despite a strong sense of reluctance, Garen stepped forward to spar.

His mother turned, mouthing words to Micah. She looked back at Garen and audible sounds finally echoed. "So, have you?"

Have I? What's the question? Oh, learned, have I learned. Have I learned? I think so. Do I even have a choice?

"Alright," Garen muttered with a sense of hesitation. "I'll do it."

The scene fell silent once more. Their lips moved, but remained mute. Garen looked over as Micah dropped his bag and ran closer to them. Disgust consumed Garen's mind at the vision of the would-be-king, but his face would not acknowledge the feeling. His body belonged to a thirteen-year-old Garen who was far too nervous to think about anything else.

Sound returned at just the opportune moment to hear his mother taunt him, "Alright, now go ahead and hit me before I bury you in the dirt."

Garen stood in confusion for a moment until his muscles took action and lunged at his mother. Just before he reached her, he leaped off his right foot. He raised his left knee for the impact. He watched as she crouched low, just as he anticipated. At the last second, Garen snapped his right foot up to drive into her unprotected side. She diverted her guard to the side and casually blocked the kick. He pushed off her guard and gracefully rolled out of his fall, as if he had practiced the tumble for years.

Did I just try to kick my own mother?

Micah's eyes grew wide. "Garen...you're incredible!" The volume had returned, and the ringing it caused nearly deafened him.

"He's fast, isn't he? But how are your reflexes?" Even before the last syllable left her lips, she stepped forward and swung a high kick at Garen's head. The moment slowed, and he watched the attack come at him with all the time in the world to contemplate a response. He chose to duck under it. While standing back up, a punch casually sailed toward his chest, which he knocked down instinctively. He let his momentum continue to carry him back into a handspring that dodged his mother's second kick. Garen landed proudly on his feet after successfully dodging all three rapid jabs.

Confusion took the place of his confidence. The woman standing in front of him did not look like a hardened warrior. She was short, thin, her long brown hair pulled up for the occasion. Garen saw the loving, kind, even delicate side. He felt his guard drop.

The fear returned in a flash as his mother pivoted forward to strike him. The fist came in even slower than the barrage preceding it, but he could only helplessly watch it draw nearer. Her hand sunk deep into his gut, replacing coherent thoughts with guttural screams. He doubled over. Darkness closed in on his vision. All Garen's senses blurred together as he felt his face make contact with the cold, wet grass beneath him.

The frequent nightmare had run its course, and now Garen, who became strangely aware of the dream itself, would wake up mid-gasp in his usual puddle of sweat. Only he didn't.

The setting reappeared. Through quick blinks and red-tinted vision he watched his mother and Micah run to his body. He tried to stand, but couldn't move off his back. He reached his hands out to stop the ambusher. His body convulsed. They did not understand until too late. The blast tore into her. A woman's scream filled his ears, and the darkness returned.

CHAPTER
EIGHT

"Thanks for going out with us tonight."

"You're welcome. It was, eh, fun. I guess."

Morgan laughed at the response. "Sorry again about the prank. I swear it was Naia's idea."

"No, that was quite the joke. And you two were right about one thing at least. That town drunk really did look like the murdering type. Next time just stop me before I implicate half the bar."

"Perhaps. Just think of it as a welcoming present. That and having to reorient your days correctly. You'll get used to waking up at various times as needed before long, I promise."

"Thanks, though I've actually got some experience with that. Taking care of a crazy father doesn't let you keep a standard schedule."

Morgan's eyes grew wide, and Garen realized how awkward it must be to hear him talk about it so casually. Even with the calluses of their years living through it, he felt guilty for even bringing it up, especially when he'd blamed her for his death just a few days ago. "Sorry."

"No, it's fine," she said. "Have a good night."

He closed the door to his room behind him and stood in uneasy stillness trying to unravel his thoughts. His lengthy nap had begun to wear off, and he knew if he laid down on that cozy bed, he couldn't keep from dozing off for a bit. Yet behind those heavy eyelids, his mind spun uncontrollably at the agenda for the day.

Stay out all night, take a nap, avenge your mother, inherit an unstoppable power, then what? Any chance I'll save the world before night falls again?

Garen paced aimlessly throughout the room, tracing the same circuit from the far corner by the bed to the opposite side near the closet, looking up only as he passed the mirror, never failing to take a curious glance at himself. Nothing troublesome plagued his thoughts. Nothing profound really needed to work itself through in his head. Mere anxiousness crawled under his skin so intensely that he could only keep on pacing, stopping occasionally to sit on the side of his bed, then resume the track as soon as his mind and legs grew fidgety.

His pacing led him to the window eventually, and he opened the curtains to glimpse the city in its early hustle. Merchants rolled carts into the street. He saw a few drawn by horses, most likely farmers from the nearby settlements bringing livestock to butcher and market. The greatest surprise for Garen came from each levitrans he saw skimming over the city. The air transports were not cheap. A costly sum of wind geonodes powered the flying rig. For a time, it was a rare sight to see one even in the Eastern Kingdom where the geonode ore was freshly mined and at its cheapest. By now, he'd heard, the Eastern skies were full of them and apparently had begun making their way into Vikar-Tola. From what he understood about the geonode imbuing process, it took quite the depth of wind magic to keep these transports airborne for as many seasons as their customers were promised.

The idea didn't sound too strange for most Central citizens. The popular caricature of the Eastern Kingdom was a glass fortress of robe-wearing wizards, all just confined to their own business and magic. But Garen had seen its capital city Kalyx with his own eyes, and while it was a sight to behold of magic-forged architecture, the people there were still just people. That kind of labor-intensive magic for these geonodes had to come from somewhere. The concept of "industrial magi" didn't exactly seem plausible.

The Western Kingdom had their own theories on the matter. The boom in the magic trade nearly crushed the economy of the west, which lacked any deposits of geonode ore in its iron and copper mines. The poverty led countless numbers of their people into slavery, and they began to question why the East suddenly needed so many slaves. Rumors spread of sweatshops used to drain the depth out of a person imbuing stones for sale, and as soon as they had replenished, sucking them dry again and again.

Garen knew that both countries were likely reacting out of selfishness and prejudice, and the truth was somewhere in-between. There had always been a high demand for cheap slaves, even within the Central Kingdom. The poverty of the west could have generated that need on its own.

Unfortunately, their king did not seem to be taking any direct actions to deal with his people's suffering. Instead, Pyralis was busy spouting nonsense about a broken world and betraying the friends of his youth to steal some powerful spirit. If miraculously Garen's father showed up, unharmed at his door, Garen would let any other criminal off the hook. But to earn their trust and abuse it made Pyralis more than just an enemy. He was vile in a sense his own contempt couldn't fully explain. And where Garen could stand to let all kinds of evil carry on so long as they were out of sight, out of mind, and out of his way, Pyralis was different. He would love to see that man fall over dead watering flowers no less than on the end of his blade.

Today, however, was not about Pyralis. Today he would right another wrong. If this world really was broken, then it was Garen, not Pyralis, who would be one step closer to setting it right.

* * * * *

Garen gave himself one last glance in the mirror. Somewhere in the painful morning of anticipation, he had decided to finally clean up a bit and lose the appearance of a man stranded at sea. The wavy brown hair still had enough length to bother him, but it looked infinitely better without the shimmer of caked-on grease and with a clean-shaven smile. He wore his leather jerkin along with lightweight cloth trousers. Gazing into the mirror, he noticed just how much he looked like the others.

Funny I'm one of them now. Well, almost.

He rested his hands on his sword belt, then drew both weapons, twirling them in a blur. He smiled and sheathed his katana, but clung to the wakizashi, appreciating the weight of the blade. The grip seemed to burn in his hand as he examined the ornate design. Garen occasionally crossed swords with someone who preferred the Western craftsmanship of a fine katana. But his accompanying wakizashi was far less common. His father told him the sword belonged to his mother, that she visited a city in the far northwest famed for its steel production and had to buy the finest of such an oddly named weapon.

Funny it became her favorite. Funny it's actually mine now.

The thought made him increasingly aware of just how much he had inherited over the years, but now more than ever he stood prepared to earn something by his own doing. The fear and retreating stops today. They won't claim my mind. Not like my father's.

He sheathed the sword and gave himself one last affirming nod in the mirror.

Garen was the first into the debriefing room, but the others arrived soon enough. Finally, Kiron strode in, dressed in his usual full cloak, just absurdly mysterious enough to make Garen want to laugh. He restrained the urge as he noticed the solemn expressions around him. Kiron noticed the serious demeanor as well and began without small talk.

"It's a big day for every person in this room, not just Garen. We do not take assassinations lightly, but for this occasion we have no doubt of its necessity. I think most of you are at least familiar with the target, Sustek Nash. He's been running a slave-trade ring from the slums in the west all the way to his Eastern buyers. His base of operations, however, is right on the Western border. Now, you know my aversion to tinkering with the many problems in that waste-ridden land, but Sustek's identity makes this the exception. If you need any more incentive than the murder of Layna Renyld, I can tell you that his dealings are far from legitimate. We knew for a fact he cuts deals for families, usually in the form of fathers selling their wife or kids to pay off their own debts."

Garen looked around to see how the others were

reacting, and though the Talia sisters listened in somber fashion, both Drake and Argus wore scowls darker than his own. Argus let his contempt drip from his words as he spoke. "So, how much are you wanting us to bang up the place? Cause if these creeps are in league with Layna's murdering piece of rot, I got no problem dismembering a few of them."

The mention of her name suddenly connected dots Garen couldn't believe he didn't see coming. Studying the dark, worn lines on Argus' face, Garen realized the age of the brute. More than likely, the two fought alongside each other.

"I would prefer you stick to smashing in walls rather than faces," Kiron answered. "Those above us are likely to catch some trouble for our interfering across the border. I'd like to keep it as minimal as possible." He walked over to the shelf along the far wall, picking up a box-shaped trinket with a colorless geonode embedded into the front. The stone projected the face of a man against the wall. "That's your target, and you know the mission imperative: Garen gets the kill. Garen, make it clean. Don't leave without checking his pulse to confirm the job's done. Unfortunately, I can't prepare you for the difficulty of this encounter. He may have picked up any number of tricks with the Light Spirit inside him, or he could just be an elevated thug without a clue as to what he's holding. The best we can tell is that Nash was given a death sentence, sent on a suicide mission to raid your home. When he returned successful, he received a god-like status among his peers. Whether he deserves that title, or if he got one-in-a-million lucky, I think it's time for those odds to catch up with him. You have my full confidence. Stay safe."

The group wasted no time. Drake assembled their wind transport in the courtyard, and though the journey lasted three or four times as long as their previous flight, for Garen the travel passed too quickly to enjoy it. If not for the dramatically different landscape, he might not have noticed the incredible distance they travelled. Garen had only briefly ventured into the Western Kingdom during his years on the run, but he'd heard more than enough stories to accurately paint the scene.

Before the Division of Thrones, Micah and Pyralis' father

Emperor Tibalt ruled the Jundux Empire. He helped establish a strong economy blending the limited sale of magic in the east with the industrial advancements of the west. They built vast craft-houses in the barren plateau of the Western Province, making use of the flow of ore from their mines. Still, the east always remained somewhat more prosperous. The magic trade simply paid better than metalworking and manufacturing. The strict limits of the production of geonodes were the only force keeping them in relative balance. The west did make some breakthroughs, including a few smelting advancements and a device that harnessed steam into a usable force. The machine could do little more than pump water, but it gave the people hope.

Then came the Division of Thrones. That hope quickly faded as Emperor Tibalt's oldest son Amiri took hold of the Eastern Province and repealed every limitation he could on the magic trade. The Western Province couldn't compete with the abundance of magic stones flooding the market. No available technology could match them. Their creation was simple too. The material could hold onto a spell for later use. Then anyone could cast it using the depth already stored. A stone imbued with fire magic could glow for seasons-on-end. What mechanical innovation could compete? Within a matter of years, most craft-houses shut down, and when the Jundux Empire split into separate kingdoms, Western cities either vacated or crowded together to endure what soon became an inescapable poverty.

Garen could already see the tangle of rust and rocks the people of Serath called their homes. The city was unique in ways that belied its meek appearance. Given the abundance of ore from the nearby mines, the city was nearly covered in slanted patches of sheet-iron roofs. If not for any of the other features, the city might have looked beautifully advanced. However, the mud bricks that lay beneath the metal told another story. The shacks comprising most of the city were crammed together, clumsily smashed into rows and clusters. They leaned in any direction they chose. In the narrow roads between them, children chased each other through the dirt and laundry flapped in the dusty wind.

Drake did not want to draw any more attention than necessary by flying straight into the slums, but even the short view from the distance painted the life of humble survival. Garen could empathize with such a situation, especially having it forced upon them.

"Ugh, now I remember why I hate coming out here," Naia groaned in frustration. "How do these people even breathe?"

Ah, such a soft heart, that one.

Drake took charge once again and addressed the group. "Alright, we stand out bad enough as it is. Keep close together and move quickly through the town. Argus, bring up the rear and make sure no one follows us. This time, no distractions."

Argus gave an offended huff. "Hey, ain't my fault these peoples are so weird. You don't ever forget anything, do ya?"

The five passed through the city as quickly and quietly as they could, but still heads turned at every corner to examine their strange presence. A couple alleys later Drake stopped in front of an estate unlike anything around it. The building was fenced off from its surroundings. It stood tall and straight, seeming to mock the misshapen shacks surrounding it. The siding had been paneled in the sheets of iron, and possibly braced with imported lumber for the wooden frame supporting it. Even more noticeable than the contrast in luxury was the surrounding atmosphere. Most of the city was alive with noise and commotion. The air in this place was heavy and stale, and the only sounds could be heard much farther in the distance. The owners of this house had more than just gold. They had a reputation, and the people of Serath knew better than to wander too close.

"This is the place, Sustek's base of operations and private living quarters. Let's hope he's home."

Garen knew they couldn't see inside well enough to know for certain. He chose to use his gift for scanning the place, but the moment he focused, he realized something just as valuable.

If he has this Light Spirit, he can do what I can, but better. He knows we're here.

"Hurry, they're all running out the back!" Garen sprinted around the edge of the house with the rest of the group following. As he turned the corner, the last of six frightened men bolted out the back door and fled into the street.

Of the six, the most disgustingly overweight of the bandits quickly fell behind, probably not even a fighter but a bookkeeper or something. As Garen approached him he grabbed his shoulder. Garen spun him around to identify his face, but it obviously didn't match the image Kiron had shown them. Garen pushed him away and stepped back into his stride. He followed the gang down a few alleys and turns until he reached the next slowest of the bunch.

This would be a lot quicker if I didn't have to stop each time.

Garen ran up alongside the man and looked into his flushed red face. "Sustek Nash, you know the guy?" The bandit repressed his look of terror and tried to throw a sloppy punch on the run. Garen ducked under the incoming fist. Rather than return the blow, Garen stepped just in front of him. His heel barely clipped the man's foot and flipped him onto Garen's back. Then, with a lunge upward, he tossed his assailant across his back into the side of a building in the narrow alley, all without breaking stride.

I think that's a yes.

Garen looked up just in time to watch the remaining four turn a quick left into an open door. Garen followed in blindly without thought to what trap might wait for him. Luckily, the bandits merely cut through the house and raced out the front door. One of them, however, stayed behind, standing between Garen and the door.

Oh how I wish I wasn't in a hurry. I'd love to open that doorknob with your jaw.

Garen leapt head-first through the window beside the door, tumbling onto the dirt in front of the house and back into his sprint. Garen picked up his pace even more, intent on keeping the last three in view. They cut left at the next alley, but recoiled back and ran the opposite direction. Garen thought the path might have been a dead-end, but he understood the true reason as Drake emerged from the alley. He had his arms back and body horizontal, quite literally flying down the road. Argus followed behind him with his feet strapped to the floating shield and carrying both girls. Garen smiled at the sight of his allies and quickly caught up with them.

The road stretched out into barren flatlands. With no hope of urban shelter to lose their pursuers in, the three stopped and turned to face the Spellswords, trying to hide their frantic gasping for air. Drake landed back on his feet. Argus set Naia and Morgan down. Garen stepped to the front of the group to take a good look at the three remaining, hoping they had chased the right man.

"The one on the right," Naia whispered.

On any other occasion at such an obvious statement, Garen might have turned and rolled his eyes or given a sarcastic "you think?" Instead, he could not turn away from his mother's killer, lost in the strange emotion of the moment. He wondered how different his life might have turned out if only this frail little man never came into the world.

About four years too late for that. Of course, I don't suppose that'll stop me now.

The two beside Sustek looked at each other, then charged the group. Argus and Morgan stepped in front of Garen to clear the distractions. Argus waved his shield along the ground and a dim blue light shot out from it. The first bandit, only a few feet from him, stumbled forward as his legs buckled. Argus swung low with his hammer, catching the man's jaw and flipping him back the other way. The other drew a sword and clashed it against Morgan's. Garen turned his head from their struggle and looked again at the man who had stolen so much from him. At the moment of that intense glare, Sustek turned and ran aimlessly into the expanse of desert.

Garen clenched his fists in a frustrated rage. He did not have the patience to endure another footrace. A flash of light took Garen by surprise, and when he opened his eyes, Sustek Nash slid to a panicked stop in front of him. He saw the

Spellswords standing in the distance where he'd been a moment ago. It didn't make the slightest sense to him, but his attention was too focused on Sustek to care.

"Whatever you want you can have it. Just don't kill me." The man fell to his knees and began to sob.

"Pathetic. You get your status from killing my mother, and I'm supposed to take pity on you?"

Sustek looked up in confusion. "I've done a lot of horrible things, I know it. But I swear, I never killed no woman."

The sincere terror in his voice shook Garen's confidence. In that moment, he realized how little evidence he had of this man's guilt. He had the word of a man without the honesty to show his own face, and little else. Of course, his parents had trusted this group. Now Garen wondered if these were the sort of blind orders they were given to follow.

"Layna Renyld, four years ago! Did you murder her in front of her son and one of her students?"

"I'm telling you, I don't know what you're talking about," he pleaded.

In his years learning whom he could trust, Garen had to nearly make a living off of reading people. The skill went to waste once he realized that no one was worth trusting in that environment, but the talent remained. Garen looked into Sustek's eyes and he saw a killer. But it was the kind of low-life that would stab a friend in the back or make a deal that eventually led to their death. Anything, as long as it didn't put the blood on his hands. Garen couldn't be sure if this man had the raw courage to assault his home and take a life.

He needed more time. Unfortunately, the problem with imprisoning anyone since the Dawn of Magic remained. Those who had the slightest depth could bend and break their way out of ropes or chains. Those without the gift suddenly had the time and motivation to learn. Judgment had to be immediate in order to be effective, but that didn't make decisions like this any easier. Garen held his piercing stare at the trembling thug in front of him, and then coldly replied, "I'm not sure if I believe you, but I'm not going to kill you just yet."

Garen took a step past Sustek toward the others, hoping to explain his predicament. He simply couldn't execute a man like this without some deeper proof of his guilt. Garen never had the chance to explain. Their mouths opened and Garen knew what was happening behind him. He could feel the dagger racing for his back. Garen was too close to pull his katana, but he never planned on using that blade in the first place. He spun to the side of the dagger's thrust and plunged the wakizashi into Sustek's chest. The movement happened too quickly for Garen to realize what he'd done until he heard the final, labored breath.

"You idiot, what were you thinking?" His blank expression showed no response. "You can't die! Tell me, what happened? Who sent you to kill her?"

His shouts meant nothing. Sustek's body went limp and fell forward, deeper onto his blade. Garen let go of the sword and the body attached to it and looked down at his shaking hands.

Why would he do that? I had just promised to let him live.

Garen steadied his hands by burying his face in them. His palms muffled the string of curses that followed. His eyes peered out above his fingers at the body in front of him. "But I guess that makes both of us liars."

Garen pulled the sword from Sustek's chest and raised it to clean the blade against the sleeve of his tunic. Another instinct took over, and instead, he struck the wakizashi into the ground next to him, still coated in blood. Garen turned to catch the darting glances of the group. He walked back to where they stood alongside the two groaning bandits. Argus placed a heavy, comforting hand on his back.

"It's done," Garen choked out. "But you can check his pulse if you'd like. I'm not walking back over there." Morgan stepped past him silently and confirmed it.

Drake offered a gentle smile. "You did what you had to." Drake looked around, but no one else dared to offer any words of comfort. "This expanse is wide enough. In just a moment we can leave. There's nothing left for us here."

Garen endured the travel back on their wind chariot, only

this time the trip seemed to last an eternity. Earlier that day a thousand thoughts cluttered his mind. Now he felt nothing. He wouldn't even describe it as a lifted burden. It was more like a void. He assumed he'd feel relieved or perhaps still furious. He expected at least some tinge of energy with this new Light Spirit inside him. But there was no glowing ceremony to signal the transfer. Instead, the numbness encased him.

I'm just tired from these backward days. I'll feel better once I have time to adjust.

Still something else troubled him, and he searched his mind trying to uncover the source of his unease.

Should I have left my mother's sword there like that?

The decision came on impulse, but Garen did not regret it. He had clutched that blade for plenty of years, desperately hanging on to the last remnant of her. That was the first moment he felt the freedom to let go. His white knuckles were tired, but something deeper than fatigue pried his fingers from that weapon. Beneath the fears and the uncertainty of his new environment, he found the simple truth that gave him release. He had a much greater part of her to carry into battle from now on.

CHAPTER

Garen adjusted to his new home much easier than he expected. Days went by with simple tasks and missions to keep him occupied, but also gave him the rest and isolation he needed to refuel. Patrol nights messed with his body's sleeping habits, but he was well underway mastering the art of flexible slumber. Just looking at the big picture, Garen knew he had sacrificed a thousand freedoms to make the transition. These freedoms, however, were the ones he couldn't care less about. Living life by his own agenda might have seemed appealing at some point, but freedoms like not having to talk to anyone sane or never having to share a meal with an honest friend, those were miserable freedoms.

Garen adapted the best he could. Moments passed that made him wish he had more control of his days, but the majority of the time he appreciated not having to make all the calls. The freedom of deciding for himself what to do each moment was a valuable one. It was also one of the heaviest liberties imaginable. He felt strange without that burden on his shoulders, simply taking orders for once. But he could not deny it was lighter. Garen wondered if he would ever miss the freedoms of his mountain home or if this new community would ever grow old. So far, he felt neither.

One thing Garen remembered quickly: surrounding himself with talented people did wonders for his own rusty skill-set. One of the first values his father ever instilled into him was that everyone has something to teach. Sometimes Garen would try to practice the proverb, but most of his encounters in the Te'ens had little to offer. The Spellswords, on the other hand, practically oozed with innovations. The more he fought alongside them, the more determined he became to copy their tricks and talents and add them to his own arsenal. Envy consumed him every time he watched Drake fly off on a disc of wind, or Naia fight with weapons of water that could change from whip to spear to sword at her command. The concept of a team was still foreign, but learning from his teammates was practically thievery, and he was well versed in that trade.

After weeks of sparring against the others, Kiron finally had time for a training session with him. Perhaps he'd get to train the new light spells he was supposed to be a master of. He made his way down to their training room. The space looked like their meeting room across the hall, but without the giant table or any trinkets along the back wall. The floor, walls, and high ceiling were cut of the same gray stone. A few racks of equipment lined the wall nearest the door, but otherwise, the space lay naked beyond the eight or nine scattered geonodes embedded into the wall, giving off a steady orange glow.

Garen had an appreciation for the blank, hard floor beneath his feet. His early training taught him never to practice on a cushioned surface if he could help it. *You won't be fighting out there in a padded room*, he grew up hearing his father muse. *I'm not going to mess up your feet by training you like that in here.*

The door opened, and he spun to see the predictably cloaked figure step in. "Oh, you can't be serious," Garen said. "Do you really plan on training me wearing that absurd drapery of yours?"

"I'd wager I can see better than you. Besides, we need to work on some fundamentals with you. I don't expect any full-on sparring sessions just yet. Of course, if it happens, it happens…" Kiron's voice trailed off as he spoke the last few words, and Garen could hear the grin he couldn't see.

"That's fair. After all, what if I bested you flat out on our first meeting? No way would I listen to a word you said after that." Garen had a smirk of his own emerging.

"I won't say you're wrong. Though I think we can both agree it's a little sad that you'd settle for overpowering a simple man like myself." The mirth had dropped out of his voice. "Garen, you've been the biggest fish in your sad, little pond for a long time. It's all but ruined you."

"So, what's my new Standard? Naia? Drake?"

"Not at all," Kiron replied. "Of course, they may happen along the way. But they will never be your aim."

"Then, if you don't mind, what is my 'aim'? Do you have someone else here for me to measure up against?"

"Not a person, Garen. Perfection." An involuntary chuckle came from Garen as the words reached him. The notion seemed as impractical as it did absurd. "Yes, I know," Kiron added, "it strikes you as one of those sentiments people say but can't possibly mean. Well, I mean it. Sometimes there really is one best block to use, one best spell to cast, or one best moment to turn and run. The options seem limitless, but they are not. A sword coming at you offers only the choices to block, parry, or preempt."

"Or get stabbed."

Kiron ignored the comment. "I don't care if what you choose puts you on top at the end. You may win a fight, but did you allow for moments of uncertainty? You may disarm them in ten seconds, but could you have done it in five?" Garen's drumming against the side of his leg reached a distracting volume. "You aren't much for theory, are you?"

"I guess not. You see, I thought it might actually be useful to figure out how to harness this new spirit friend I'm sharing a body with." Garen stepped back into a low stance and began flailing his arms around, visualizing bolts of light or energy or whatever he'd be able to shoot out of his palms.

"Actually," Kiron began with a sigh, "That's exactly what we can't do just yet."

"Oh wonderful, more lecture. Should I find something to write this down on?"

Kiron's tone took an unexpected turn for the upset and urgent. "Stop it. This is more important than you can imagine. More Spellswords have met their death because they failed to grasp this simple concept than any other fault you could think of."

"When you put it in terms like that, you have my interest. I happen to be in the business of not dying."

"Then understand this. You can cast spells of unimaginable power using the Light Spirit. Spells based in light will not draw from your own depth. Instead, you'll be using the direct connection across the realm that your spirit affords you. The only part your depth will play is simply how wide the gate is to draw from that light. The more depth, the more you can pull out at once. As you master it, you'll go beyond simply blinding your foes. You'll see beyond what your eyes can take in, move at speeds that defy nature, and, with time, focus beams so intense they can cleave stone. No one will be able to do the things you do."

Garen's smile grew, but he knew these boasts were only the preface. Kiron's voice took a harsher tone to prove just that.

"But if you rely on light alone as your strength in battle, you'll be dead in a season. Overplayed strengths become weaknesses. They make you predictable. They cut down on your options. Not every problem can be solved by a single element, and no tool is appropriate for every task. As wise men say, if all you have is a hammer, everything starts to look like a nail."

"So, what do you want me to do about it?" Garen followed his logic for the most part, though he didn't understand how to practice everything *but*.

"We'll be practicing your resourcefulness with the remaining four elements," Kiron said. "Everything in this realm can be broken into the five base elements, but they are not random forces. There is an order to their existence." Kiron looked to the ground, and Garen watched a fine layer of sand spread across the floor between them. Kiron bent down to draw on his new canvas and scribbled out a crude pentagon with a symbol at each corner.

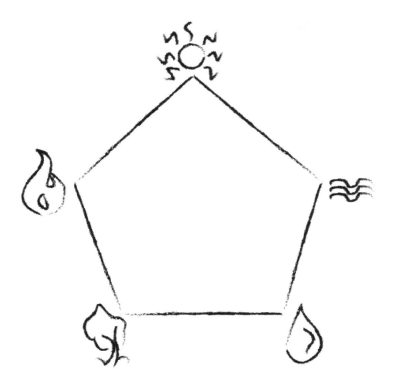

"These are the symbols of the elements. You are familiar with them all, yes?" Kiron asked.

Most of the shapes were obvious enough to determine on his own. A tiny flame on the left, a few curved lines on the right. A tree and a drop of water lined the bottom of the shape. The symbol at the top might have been a bit more difficult, except he had seen it before, or at least part of it. He had the same circle and outward lines tattooed into his arm. This version, however, did not have an eye in the center. Given the simple design, Garen tried not to read too much into the connection, but he couldn't ignore the obvious. Both the symbol on his arm and the one in front of him had something to do with light.

Garen nodded for Kiron to continue. "This is the balance of life. Some elements work together in harmony. Other elements across from each other work in contrast, and they hold this world in balance. The more you respond to an element with its natural opposite, the more effective you will be at balancing. Of course, you see that every element has two others across from it, so the options are still plenty."

Garen felt himself zoning out again. His attention snapped back to witness Kiron's disapproving frown. A long strand of fire began to grow from Kiron's right hand, stretching out across the ground. Garen stepped back from the growing coils of flame near his feet, deeply confused once more.

"I guess we won't be able to talk through it. Test one then," Kiron said. "Fire, possibly the simplest element in its pure destructive power, as well as its necessity for all living systems. Your task is simple. Stop it." Kiron snapped his arm, and what Garen now recognized as a whip of fire rushed at him. He rolled to his left, barely missing the crack, but still feeling the heat burrow into his shoulder.

"Acrobatics won't save you from an inferno, Garen. Take a stand."

Rising to his feet, Garen glanced over to Kiron's diagram, his eyes bouncing across from the fire emblem. *Wind and water, wind and water. Okay, simple enough.* He looked up just in time to see the whip curling down at him again, and instinctively released a jet of icy water from the palm of his hand. It reached the fiery strand and evaporated on contact, leaving Garen standing directly under its unchanged arc. Once again, he tried to roll out of the way, but with less success this time. The whip's crack released an oppressive heat over the right half of his body and he could instantly detect the smell of his own burnt hair.

"Thanks, friend," Garen said. "I've been meaning to get that trimmed." Kiron offered no response, but sent the whip racing for Garen's head once more. Garen summoned a small disc of wind under his feet and rode it into the air, making use of the room's spacious height.

"I thought you'd learned that running won't help. The fire will always be faster than you!" As Kiron pulled back the whip for another swing, he also released two fireballs large enough to swallow him entirely.

Garen stood confidently in his place, hovering near the ceiling in preparation for a few soul-intensive spells. He knew Kiron was right. Light would not stop the onslaught of fire. The years on his own, however, taught Garen plenty of other responses.

Garen swung his left arm across his body, followed by his right. Each hand released a thick wall of ice and hurled it toward the incoming flames. The ice dripped and thinned instantly, but the frigid barrier held up long enough to crash into their targets and knock them off course. Garen's attention then turned to the braid of flame soaring toward him. The water and ice spells had used a generous portion of his soul, but he didn't have much else to use his depth on today.

He reached out with hands clenched, forming rings of wind around the whip. As more formed, they began to connect until a miniature cyclone surrounded it. With only a fraction of a second until impact, Garen pulled his arms back to his chest. As he did, the column of wind tightened around the cord of fire. He stared directly into the arc racing for his face. The cyclone tightened one last bit and the flame suffocated, extinguishing it from end to end. Instead of the searing trauma, a warm gust cascaded over him.

"Well played."

"Oh, we were playing?" Garen lowered himself back to the ground, but kept a reasonable distance in case his trainer had more challenges to present. "If that was playing, I'd hate to see what it looks like when you want someone dead."

"Oh, anyone can tell the difference. It's written all over my face."

Garen laughed and took a few steps toward Kiron. "So, I'm done almost dying. What's next?"

"For one, that little display of yours showed me an area that needs work. Do me a favor and toss another of those ice-sheets against that wall."

Garen shrugged and performed the task. He reached back with his arm, slung it across his body, and sent a near replica of his previous creations racing through the air.

"Excellent. I assume you have the depth for a few more?"

"That's why you keep me around."

"Good. Now do it again, but don't move your arms."

"Excuse me?"

"That's right. I want you to do exactly the same as before but with your arms tucked at your side. You're casting from your center, Garen, not from an appendage. You don't honestly believe your soul is in your fingertips, do you?"

Garen found himself once again unable to argue, but equally unsure how to make them a reality.

"You've been trained to let your body flow with the nature of the spell because it aids your imagination," Kiron said. "You're pretending your movements are mimicking the action of the spell. But they aren't. It's a crutch.

"It's understandable. That's how anyone starts learning, but you aren't just anyone. You're a Spellsword now, and that means more than having a powerful spirit at your command. After all, Argus and Morgan have no such gift but they live up to the title of Spellsword in full. If you want to do the same, your hands need to be focused on the physical side of the fight, not waiting for a moment to let go of your weapon and cast. You can channel through your sword to focus the origin of a spell, but you should not be dependent upon its movement. Now, try again, but motionless."

Garen prepared for the spell, trying to focus himself as best he could. He let loose the intention of the spell, but what came out was a sad disappointment. A thin sheet of ice only half as wide as its predecessors appeared in the air. It sailed only a few feet before falling to the ground and shattering.

Garen turned back to Kiron, unable to hide his look of embarrassment.

"Now you have something to practice in your spare time."

"Lucky me."

"I understand, it is a difficult way to cast, but you know it isn't the only. For our purposes, which will usually be spent fighting several foes at the same time, it will be the most effective. You may find for duels that letting your body move with the intention of the spell does help. There are others that rely on verbal or written sources for their power. But spoken incantations are for those who can only hear with their ears, and written symbols serve those who can only see with their eyes. You will need neither. You must hear the silent and perceive the invisible. Then, while their tongues stammer and fingers draw idly, your hands are free to carry a weapon and your mind is free to clutch your wit."

"My wit, eh? This is the first I've heard it used as a good thing. My father seemed insistent it would be the death of me."

"Well, your father was a very different man than you. For a warrior as calm and controlled as your father, taunting had no effect on him and if he tried it, it would only serve to distract him. You on the other hand," Kiron paused to laugh. "I think it actually focuses you. Correct me if I'm wrong, but fighting is a sort of game to you. The more you banter, the more game-like it remains. And if it's just a show, then there's no fear."

"You're not wrong," Garen grinned.

"There is a downside, of course. Fear can be a good thing. It keeps you alive by telling you to avoid certain risks. You know, certain risks like standing your ground under a crashing whip, pushing all your focus into the cyclone meant to suffocate the fire instead of dodging to buy yourself more time. But it worked, so I supposed some risks do pay off."

"Ha, it is a good thing. I knew it," Garen said in triumph.

"No, it'll probably be the death of you."

"What? I thought you just said—"

"I said that some risks do pay off. That's the kind of mentality you take when you're the underdog, hoping to find an advantage against a stronger foe. Garen, you are the stronger foe. Or at least you will be. You don't need those risks because the natural order will put the fight in your favor. Still, you fight like some low-life bandit, struggling to get by. You aren't. With a little more training, you'll be one of the sharpest fighters the world has ever seen. Risks are not your friend."

"So, you're telling me to play it safe?"

"I'm saying you don't have to create all-or-nothing scenarios. I'm saying that fear is sometimes a good thing and, if you can keep a level head, you don't have to try so hard to stay immune from it. But mostly I'm saying you need to stop being *you,* which we both know is a waste of time. Thus, I'm going to hold my tongue now and remind myself I can't make you into any fighter, just a better version of yourself. You're going to taunt and poke fun mid-swing, and if your father couldn't break you of the habit, I'd be a fool to try. Just do me one favor, will you?"

"I'll try."

"Be careful. I've worked too hard to find you only to lose you to one of your many glaring flaws."

"Certainly. With confidence like that in me, I don't see how I could fail," Garen said.

"That's how it goes, I guess. You're overconfident. I tend to worry. Care to share?"

"Sure, next time I'll do the training. Do I get to throw fireballs at you?"

"In time, Garen, in time. But I have no more today, fireballs or time." Kiron stepped toward a case mounted by the door. "I do have one thing for you. Drake tells me you left your mother's sword at the scene of her reckoning. I can't say I understand, but now I worry about that dull katana you're left clinging to."

"Well, it's better than nothing."

Kiron sighed. "I did not bring it up to offer you nothing." He opened the wooden case and carefully removed a sword from it. As Kiron walked closer carrying it, Garen recognized the shape of the blade. It was a katana just the same as the worn-down weapon he carried, but somehow more. Garen could tell its significance just from the careful posture that Kiron carried it to him. He reached for it, unsure what he was accepting. The sheath was made of rough, dry wood with scorched sections scattered throughout. To the casual collector, such signs might have taken away from its value. Garen knew the opposite was true. This weapon was trustworthy enough to carry into battle, not some ceremonial piece. He removed the blade and felt the perfect balance of the sword in his hand. Kiron took a step back. Garen could not help but spin the sword a few times just to feel the incredible lightness.

"Not bad," Garen said, now closely eyeing the blade itself. He couldn't imagine how many times the metal had been folded over and over to create such a well-forged edge. "So, where did you get it?" Garen's eyes fixated at the base of the blade. The bronze guard answered his question for him. The face of a tiger had been crafted into it. Eyes peered up at him from one side. Etchings in the bronze displayed the stripes. He rotated the guard and saw the tiger's detailed nose along the bottom. The braided wrap beneath it was redder than any flower or piece of nature. It was the color of red that only a fire can produce. He had never seen the sword before, but he knew one person they'd called "The Red Tiger."

"That sword belonged to your father, Seth Renyld," Kiron confirmed for him. "If I'm not mistaken, it was hand-crafted for him. That's Western steel, forged by Jundux's arms-master himself. I was reluctant to give this to you at first. In all honesty, I wasn't sure I'd ever see you again once you'd taken care of Nash. But if you truly intend to walk in your father's shoes, best we give you a weapon suited for the role."

Garen still wasn't sure how long he intended stay with these Spellswords. As such, the gift made him uncomfortable. If the sword had belonged to anyone other than his family, he would have refused it outright. Instead, he sheathed it and smiled awkwardly.

"Thank you."

"Just like the room, it really was yours to begin with. I apologize for holding it back this long." Garen shrugged and Kiron did not push the apology any further. "Practice on that motionless casting, will you?" Kiron stepped out of the room. Garen set the sword aside and sat down in the middle of the cold floor. The task seemed simple enough. All he needed to do was learn how to move a mountain without lifting a finger.

CHAPTER

Garen ran out of patience long before he ran out of depth. The stillness was maddening, and he couldn't think of a better way to shake it off than a jog through the city. Shortly after Serath, Kiron suggested the practice of trying to channel the Light Spirit while he ran, but Garen preferred the exercise for the rush of imagination he felt. A small part of him missed the feeling of living on the run. Maybe not the short nights and panicked dreams, but definitely the chases. There were glorious moments, entire posts of guards at his heels as he escaped a city. Sometimes he could lose them in the shadowy maze of buildings. Sometimes he would sprint into the woods and let the terrain separate them. Either way, he couldn't help but grin the entire time. And as he passed a guard post running down the Riverside district, he imagined the man bolting after him. Instead, he waved politely and Garen was left with only disappointment.

I wonder what Kiron would do if they caught me robbing someone.

It was an interesting scenario, but ultimately unexciting. He was pretty sure he could beat the hooded man in a footrace easiest of all. But even that thought reminded him of Kiron's advice to stop comparing himself to others. Maybe his spirit training would satisfy him. Garen stepped his jog into a full run for a while and eventually a sprint. It didn't feel like magic. It felt like hard work, and he was already growing short of breath. He stared at his aching feet as he pushed himself up the stone road leading away from Riverside. He cast a simple light spell on his legs, but having glowy trousers wasn't appearing to help.

He knew he couldn't keep the pace of his sprint for much longer, but he just wanted to feel that thrill again, even if he wasn't being chased. He grunted as he reached the top of the hill and saw where the road took a sharp descent to his left. This was his spot. He barreled down the road, screaming as he went.

Several locals stopped to stare at the crazed man running past them. He was nearly going too fast downhill to keep from falling forward, but he pushed against the pavement in long strides as hard as he could. He looked down at his feet just in time to watch his right ankle flicker between skin and pure light as he pushed off it. Garen lifted his head and let out a shout of triumph. He'd done it. He hadn't even realized how much he needed to prove it until he saw it for himself. But now there was no room for doubt. He was the Light Spellsword, and no one would ever be able to keep up with him ever again.

The moment of celebration ended as Garen's left foot failed to land when he expected it. He looked down in a panic to notice he was still a foot off the ground and soaring faster above it than he imagined. The steep decline of the path leveled off and Garen tried to land in stride. When that failed, he took the fall as cleanly as he could, tumbling over his shoulder and eventually rolling to a graceless stop once the stone road had claimed all the exposed skin it wanted. There were only half a dozen onlookers. Most were too stunned to move toward him or help. Garen stumbled to his feet, succeeding the second attempt, and gave a casual wave with his bloody, scraped palm. He limped his way back toward the palace, wondering if he'd pass another of those helpful guard posts. He wouldn't be dreaming of a chase this time, though.

A few palace servants gave him funny looks on his way toward the Spellsword annex, but thankfully none of the others were there to ask questions.

Oh, do I feel bad for these sheets.

Garen fell forward and relaxed his body. He was on patrol with Drake this evening and could use a little rest first. Not that he found Drake boring, but tonight made his fourth night this week on patrol. The inclusion of Garen into the group's rotation for patrol complicated things, going from four to five. Kiron, however, solved the problem instantly by scheduling Garen with each other individual once a week. The idea didn't exactly thrill him, but he had nothing better to do with his time. Plus, he took great satisfaction watching Naia groan and complain at the prospect of spending an entire evening together alone. She had mostly ignored him this past week, but Garen knew she couldn't keep the silent treatment up forever. One of these nights, she would be too tired to put up her walls, and he would figure her out.

A loud knock woke Garen.

Did I really fall asleep? What time is it?

"Garen, are you ready?" Drake called politely from the other side of his door. "It's time to go."

Oh, that time.

"Well, no, but..." Garen sat still for a second and focused himself. "I'll be out in a minute."

They left the palace gates and made their usual patrol passes through the more troubled portions of town, simply as a reminder of their nightly presence. The hours passed uneventfully, and eventually they found their way into the Thirsty Soul. From the outside, Garen first assumed it was a necessary stop on their patrol. The slurred insults and arguments could be heard from a block away, all shouted over a near-empty music geonode, barely churning out tunes that should have run dry seasons ago.

Perhaps at one time, it was a haven for the outlaws and miscreants of Vikar-Tola. Instead, the nightly presence of the Spellswords transformed it into an entirely new phenomenon. Every night owl who simply wanted to play the thug charade without actually risking their safety found their way to the Thirsty Soul. As it turned out, the Spellswords were only too happy to allow it from a few noisy tables away. The general ruckus kept to such a chaotic level that they could talk about whatever they wanted in complete privacy. You could barely hear what the person across from you had to say, let alone eavesdrop on someone else.

They entered to find a number of the usual commotions. A few men shouted and threatened one another violently, but they had yet to start a fight that Garen had seen, and tonight would most likely continue that trend.

"Slow night tonight, is it Iosif?" Drake asked the man

behind the old, dry-rotted bar.

The greasy, balding gentleman turned around and stood as tall as his hunch-back allowed. He flashed an eerie smile, revealing the few crooked, yellow teeth he still had. "A little bit, but night's young, Drake. Can I get you two anything?"

"We're okay for now. You just let us know if anything out of the normal comes up."

"Normal?" Iosif laughed and wiped away the involuntary spit that ran down the side of his face. "I haven't seen normal in here in years. How's about I let you know if I see anything that *is* normal. That ought to terrify the likes of us all."

Drake gave the conciliatory laugh, nodded his head, and walked with Garen over to a secluded table in the corner.

"Does he say that…?"

"Most nights? Yes." Drake said. "I'm not sure if he has some sort of memory loss or if he actually finds the line that amusing. But I don't see the harm in permitting him a good laugh each time. If I ran a place like this, I'd probably end up a lot crazier than he has."

"Yeah." Garen leaned back in the fragile wooden chair and yawned.

Even amidst the shouting match taking place across the room and the creak and groan of every shoddy chair, table, and floorboard, they still found themselves caught in an awkward silence. Finally, Drake broke the ice. "You've been with us for the better part of a season. What do you think? Are you getting used to this life yet?"

"It's not too bad. Beats sleeping on a rock."

"I can imagine. What about community meals in the evening? I won't pretend to know you too well, but it seems like you're a little quieter there than usual."

Garen didn't like the feeling of being interviewed and sat forward with a look of contempt on his face. "So, what, you're saying I'm usually a loud-mouth rambler?"

"No, no," Drake replied immediately. "I didn't mean to offend."

The chair squeaked as Garen leaned back again and gave

a smug grin. "No, I'm kidding. You're probably right. I'm still not used to a bunch of people in a room where nobody has their weapons drawn. I mean, I tend to just get fascinated watching Argus eat. I'm waiting for the day he swallows a spoon."

They laughed at an image of Argus with his mouth full, suddenly confused and searching both sides of his hands. It was amusing, but the comment covered up the truth more than he cared to admit. Frankly, those evening suppers were a constant reminder to Garen how estranged he had become to social environments. His first attempts at contributing to the group were always long winded and forced. He could feel the bitter taste in his mouth after relating some pointless thought or inappropriate story. Lately, as Drake had noticed, he began trying a more reserved approach, trying to find that balance. Apparently, he hadn't yet.

"Not to mention," Garen added, trying to keep in the conversation and leave his insecure thoughts behind, "I have to say the food is breathtaking. The palace chefs really put to shame what I'd gotten used to in the Te'ens. Mountain goat isn't exactly 'tender.'"

"Of that I'm certain. We are a spoiled bunch." Drake paused and stared intently down at the table, clearly something on his mind. "What was it like?" Vagueness and all, Garen knew exactly what he was asking.

"It's quiet, mostly. Unless you count the wind. Or my father. You know looking after him at all hours I wasn't out working," Garen stopped to smile at what he used to consider an honest day's work. "It took most of my time and energy, but there isn't much to take from that kind of life. You're really not even living half as much as surviving. Why? You're not thinking about taking any vacations to a local barren, bandit-infested region near you?"

"No, not at all. I wouldn't know the first thing about that kind of life. And I'm not sure I'm half the man you were to take care of your father, even after…" Drake trailed off, wanting to say or ask more, but holding himself back. Garen assumed it was a restriction of proper etiquette.

"You can ask about it. I did live with the man for three years. I can't say I have all the answers to his state, but I've certainly learned how to deal with him."

"If you say so. Then I have to ask, and you're more than welcome to refuse an answer. What happened to your father?"

The question caught Garen off guard. He couldn't remember a moment yet where the people around him didn't already know his own story better than himself.

Drake misinterpreted Garen look of shock as one of distress. "I'm very sorry, there's no need to talk about that now."

"No, it's actually quite fine. I just didn't know that wasn't already common knowledge. Here you guys knew so much about me, I just assumed you knew as much about my father."

"As I recall, Kiron knows about the day of the ambush. But you two supposedly just disappeared from that day forward. He cleared up rather quickly that you weren't to blame for the incident, but no one knew for certain if you two were even alive. Kiron says he always knew, but even for him it was a glorified hunch. No one else honestly believed you'd both be alive. And no one was more shocked than us to find out the condition your father had survived in."

"Well," Garen let his mind slowly travel back. He found the memory he had no choice but to carry with him. "It was a standard escort mission, just another royal nobody passing toward the east onto Kalyx. The forested area had a bad reputation for bandits that like to rob rich caravans, so we agreed to accompany the party through the thicket. Dad always liked to combine good practice with good deeds.

"Pyralis and I had something of a falling out the week prior. We were on a mission when Amiri was struck from behind, and Pyralis just watched him go down. If I hadn't been with the two of them, the emperor would have lost his eldest son that day. He made it out with just a broken arm."

"Wow."

"Yeah, so on that day I was still pretty furious at Pyralis. I spent all my focus and time monitoring his every move that when the ambush struck, it caught me off guard as much as anyone else. The ground exploded around us, sending all of us, horses, carts just soaring through the air. At least a dozen men emerged from the woods and charged us. My first thought was to go protect our escort.

"It didn't take me long to notice that in all the directions the ambush came, none charged for the carriage. Micah, Amiri, and my father all had three or more men rushing toward them, and I had a handful myself. Our team held up like we were trained, dropping a bandit with every chance we could until the numbers seemed manageable. Except Amiri. I remembered he was fighting with one arm tied up in that sling. I knocked back the last guy on me and raced to help him. He had been relying exclusively on magic and I could tell he was all but drained. I stepped in front of him and cut down two bandits as quickly as I could.

"That's when I saw him. This tall, stocky man stepped out into the clearing and stared me down. I'll never forget that look he gave me. It was menacing, but somehow sadder. He raised an arm toward us, and the ground separated under me. As I dropped, he buried me right up to my neck. Then he closed his eyes and lifted both hands. I swear the entire landscape behind him rose from the ground and swirled in the air. He brought his hands together and the spinning mass of dirt, rocks, and trees merged together. He opened his eyes one last time and gave an unmistakable glimpse of regret."

Drake watched in honest suspense. Garen could hardly believe the Spellswords had no knowledge of the attack. But it needed to be told, and Garen forced himself to spell out the more difficult part.

"His arms moved forward and the avalanche of earth soared down where I was trapped. I would have died right there...had my father not entered the tragedy. He raced in front of me and unleashed a fiery wind so intense it managed to hold it back. The standoff lasted only a few seconds, but as I watched helplessly from the ground. I remember bouncing between terror and hope at each nudge of the stalemate. Finally, it all began to slide downward, slowly winning out against the torrent of flame.

That was the last memory of my father as I knew him. He turned to me, gave me a smile, and dove to my side, putting up a barrier with every last drop of depth he had in him.

"I heard the avalanche fall around me and press into the shield. As it crushed the barrier, it drained him, and he screamed while easing that sphere down around us. He wasn't a loud man. I'd never heard him like that before."

Garen stopped himself on the verge of tears. He had retold the story to himself a hundred times and never became emotional anymore. It seemed opening up to someone else brought him back to the pain more than ever.

"You don't have to say anymore if you don't want to."

Garen took another deep breath and forced back any of the signs of weakness in his eyes. "No, there's only one thing more. I watched the smile fade from his face, and his eyes closed. But the barrier held even after he was gone, and I waited in that shell as long as I had air before blasting my way out."

The two sat in the silent chaos of the room for some time after those words. Garen needed time to calm down from the detailed memories, and Drake, so he guessed, needed time to process the story.

"Thank you, Garen. I know that wasn't easy."

"Yeah, but it would probably be easier if I wasn't a giant baby about it."

"Nonsense, I'd be more concerned if you could recount a story like that without it affecting you in some way. It just," Drake paused, looking uncertain.

"What is it?" Garen asked with a sniffle. "I think after that last question you should be able to ask anything."

"It just doesn't explain how your father went mad. If he really did empty his soul in that spell, he should have died on the spot. The body can't sustain life with an empty soul."

"I know," Garen said. "That's the crazy part." Garen bit his lip, hating himself for the choice of words. "When I came out, the emperor's sons were gone, along with the ambushers. I pulled my father out, and that's when I realized he was still breathing. I got him most of the way back home just using my depth, but when he woke up, he wasn't himself anymore. I couldn't then, and I still haven't figured out today, why."

"And when you arrived home, strangers were waiting for you. Thus, you ran," Drake tried to fill in the story.

"A lot of good that did."

"What other choice did you have? It wasn't like you knew about us then. And we weren't nearly organized enough to find you at that point."

"Oh really," Garen said with genuine surprise. "So, you haven't always been this pristine little unit?"

"Goodness, no. You said all of this happened in the fall three years ago? I think Kiron was appointed as the Spellsword director shortly after that. I don't believe he recruited the Talia sisters until that following spring. Argus and I carried the title at the time, but he was the only one to serve alongside your parents. For me that was just a formality. I was still trapped in far too many obligations back east."

"I've heard you mention that before. How exactly did you end up out here if you're something like third cousin to the king?" Garen realized the change in focus was as abrupt as it was awkward, but he didn't mind so long as he could keep from having to talk about himself again.

Drake looked down with a somber shake of his head. "I'm afraid I don't have any grand tale that brings me here. Noble households make for a rather sheltered life. From as early as I can remember, I was trained to fight and cast because one day I was going to inherit a great gift. And now here I am, spoiled with talents I barely had to work for. Kiron and my family back east take extraordinary care of me. I can't begin to understand the path you've had to endure to bring you here today. I feel a bit like I've coasted the whole way."

Garen tried to imagine what that kind of life would even feel like. He could look back at the road behind him and trace every movement. Even though the memories were less than joyful, the idea of arriving in this place without them seemed somehow worse. Garen wasn't sure whether to envy or pity the predicament.

"Well, don't be so hard on yourself. Life in the Eastern Kingdom isn't all I hear it's cracked up to be." Garen said, trying to keep their conversation from going to a darker, heavier place again. Instead, Drake's eyes focused on the table in front of him and a new flush of emotions consumed his face.

"It's true. King Amiri doesn't realize what he's doing to the kingdom by repealing the geonode trade laws. The rumors I hear about their geonode workshops make me sick. The vagrants, and worst of all, children sold off to work in these labor houses. They teach them marketable spells and then force them to imbue the geonode ore to the brink of their soul's depth. Naturally, Baron Ambersong swears the child-snatching stories are just Western gossip and nonsense, and he's shown me the guild halls personally. But I know when I'm being shown what they want me to see. I know the bodies they would sacrifice to build an empire on top of them." Drake's voice had reached an uncomfortable volume even for their choice of surroundings, but Garen knew better than to interrupt his thoughts. The convictions in Drake were bottled to an uncontrollable level, and trying to cap it now would only guarantee an explosion later.

Thankfully, Drake noticed his own volume and lowered his voice. But as he looked up from the table into Garen's eyes, he knew the conviction had not faded in the slightest. "I hate what my home is becoming. I hate that I am still tied to it by my name and crest. But worse than that is being so goffing helpless, having all this power but not enough influence to do something about it."

Garen saw the tension in his eyes. He clearly hated the chains of his Eastern lineage, and yet he still did not have enough to be of use. He despised it, and yet he needed more.

"Emperor Tibalt was brilliant in how he ran all three provinces. Amiri, however, can't seem to keep from running a third of that territory into the ground. You can read history scrolls and listen to stories of the regional warlords before the Dawn of Magic, and it makes you wonder why there are never two great rulers in a row. Just once, just once I want to see a wise king work wonders, and then the next leader take over and be even better."

"I guess the arrogant moron trait skips a generation."

"That's a theory." Drake thought for a moment. Then finally he added, "Though I was considering that perhaps good fathers are harder to come by than good kings."

They both sat in silence for a while, scanning the bar and wanting to keep from starting any new conversations. Garen considered mentioning he had a good father and that it didn't seem to matter. But that felt ungrateful, even if he couldn't explain why.

Their attention turned just in time to catch the shouting match reach its apex. The red-faced runt that had been screaming up at the other finally cocked back and swung his fist into the man's jaw. Though the weight of the alcohol did most of the heavy lifting, the impact was enough to stagger the man, both tripping over the chair behind him and shattering it beneath him. Drake stood immediately and strode toward them. Garen quickly followed, unsure how to respond. The knock-out champion stood disbelieving and breathing heavily until he felt Drake's hand on his shoulder. He turned around, eyes wide with fear.

"About time," Drake said with a gentle pat and walked away. Garen followed him out of the bar, the only one not too shocked to be laughing the whole way.

CHAPTER
ELEVEN

Spring gave way to summer in Vikar-Tola. As the weeks passed, Garen settled into a casual routine. Garen hated routines. Not that his life offered many chances to form them, but on the rare occasion they did, he always found a way to squirm out. He'd made plenty of poor decisions and partnered with many an unsavory ally simply in the name of changing things up. This time, however, Garen was not in complete control to simply "change things up." His training sessions with the others went well enough. Drake and Naia could both devastate him in a fair fight, but he was learning how to adapt. Kiron still refused to offer any direct training with his Light Spirit.

They took occasional missions to handle matters beyond the scope of the common guard. Garen enjoyed his part in keeping the Central Kingdom safe, but he could see no progress in their plans regarding Pyralis. While Garen tried to wait with patience for his day, the monotony was starting to get to him. He felt restless, and doubts crept their way in. Did they really plan to kill a king? Why was Kiron so reluctant to develop his gifts with light? He still had too many unanswered questions about Sustek Nash, and their avoidance of the topic was not setting his mind at ease. Why did no one want to talk about how he gained his spirit? Had he done something wrong? Was there more he should be doing? Every worry lined the most mundane conversations. It spoiled what should have been peaceful moments.

Word of a new mission reached Garen, and he tried to anticipate it positively. Even if the journey turned out to be, yet again, unrelated to his interest in these Spellswords, he wouldn't mind a break from the palace and patrols. Missions were at least the most unpredictable bit of his routine. He strapped his father's katana to his side and headed toward their meeting room.

"Alright everybody, I have some good news and some bad news," Kiron began.

"Bad news first, please," Naia interrupted in a frustrated tone. "We're not so fond of your usual 'get-their-hopes-up-so-I-can-smash-them' routine."

"Good news first it is," Kiron said. "We've had reports of unnatural sounds and unauthorized access into a highly dangerous, restricted area." Garen had nearly begun to salivate with excitement.

"And the bad news is," Kiron continued as the room held their breath. "That place is the Theltus Nisdal."

Groans and disappointed sighs filled the room.

"Sorry, I don't understand," Garen said over the still grumbling table. "I thought this place was supposed to be wild with danger. Why are we suddenly upset about some legitimate thrill and action?"

Morgan turned in her chair to face Garen. "There are a couple of guards posted around the outside of the closed-off temple, and once a season or so we get report from them that they saw someone entering or leaving the area."

"Only problem is," Argus jumped in, "them guards are scared witless by the eerie whatnots going on in the temple grounds. Elements firing off randomly would scramble any man's mind. So, we go on out every time they report intruders, but we never found a soul there."

"Argus is right," Morgan turned her attention to Kiron. "It's a guaranteed waste of time and unnecessary risk for us all. I know we're all a little hungry for adventure, but that doesn't mean I'd sign up to walk through fire."

Garen anticipated the customary sigh from Kiron, and he delivered. "I understand your concerns with the place, Morgan. We all do. But we can't just brush it off and pretend it doesn't exist. Besides, the guard who made the claim actually swears he saw two distinct figures of very different heights and weights entering the west gate. That's a little precise for paranoia."

With a much softer, complacent groan than before, the group sighed in agreement and made their way to the courtyard. "So, you're really not fond of this place, are you?" Garen asked Morgan as casually as he could.

"Oh, I guarantee after a few minutes there, you'll understand exactly why." With those words, she stopped to pull up the right leg of her trousers and exposed a vicious scar, one burned into her skin.

"Did you find someone there?"

"No, not someone. It's the whole place that's trying to kill you. Or maybe it doesn't care what kind of damage it causes, but it causes quite a bit. The earth can shift and swallow you whole. Crystals can cover your body and freeze you where you stand. Or if you're lucky like me, without warning, you look down to realize your leg is on fire."

"The elements just fire off randomly? Do you think the connecting point between two realms is causing it?" Garen wasn't entirely familiar with the terrain, but he knew his history well enough.

"That's about the only theory that makes sense," Morgan sighed. "Whatever it is, just be careful."

Garen shrugged the words off, but when he looked back, she still held the eye contact, reinforcing her request. "I will be on my highest guard," he assured her with a smile. "And on top of that, I'll even pause every few steps to make sure none of my appendages have burst into flames."

Morgan eyed him intently for a moment, just long enough to make him uncomfortable. "You'd think after all these years with my sister I'd have warmed up to that sarcastic sense of humor."

"Well, she's not as smooth as me."

Morgan laughed, a gesture that told Garen more about what she found absurd rather than her honest amusement. "Are you seriously going to compete with her about everything?"

Garen had never considered sarcasm as a battleground, but he wasn't about to back down now. "I just might. Tell her it's on."

Morgan sighed and rolled her eyes as she walked away. "No. I won't."

* * * * *

113

Once outside, each Spellsword took their places for another travel on Drake's chariot of wind. The trip south showed Garen a few sights he had never seen, mostly flat and plain farmland stretching as far as his eyes could see. Eventually, the southern horizon dotted itself with trees, and the lush field beneath them took a turn for the soggier. Farmlands became wetlands, and then stagnant wetlands became an outright swamp. Even this high in the air, Garen could smell and practically taste the moldy stench of the ponds beneath him.

Finally, they approached a break in the dying trees revealing a spectacle Garen could not have imagined in all his life. This temple they had referred to had nothing in common with the tiny shrines set up in border towns for spirit worship. If those were temples, this was a monument. Though the stonework lay covered in ages of moss, the elaborate craftsmanship flaunted itself through the crumbling decay. Inside the massive outer walls laid an array of chambers, smaller rooms, and courtyards, all connecting up to a looming central tower. The purpose of such an ornate structure remained a mystery to him, but of all the things he knew for certain, this place was built by magic.

Drake set the five of them down in a comparatively dry field of grass and turned to face them. "Alright, no one wants to be here less than I do, well, except for Morgan maybe." She gave an exasperated nod. "I think two groups would cut our time in half. I'll take Argus. Garen, would you please accompany the Talia sisters?"

"Wait just a second," Naia said. "Are you saying we need his help?"

"My apologies," Drake sighed. "Talia sisters, would you please accompany Garen?"

"We would be delighted," Naia said, mocking Drake's mannerly tone.

"Wonderful. You three move through the eastern complex. We'll cover the western end and meet by the south gate to search the tower together. Sound fair?"

"Fair enough," Garen added and followed after the girls,

whom he hoped had a better idea of where they were going than he did.

Most of the ground within the walls was completely submerged. Thankfully, thin stone pathways connected the chambers. They passed courtyards of dancing fire and muddy whirlpools. Garen had no idea if they were ever meant to serve a purpose, but the layout was at least entertaining. With his sense of smell in protest, it was nice to appreciate something.

Morgan pulled back a large wooden door to the first enclosed chamber they'd seen. She held it for them as they stepped into the dark room. Garen summoned a small orb of light just to see what mysteries it had to offer. The carvings along the wall immediately drew his attention. Thick lines, circles, and half-circles formed an intricate pattern covering the full interior of the room.

They looked carved rather than painted, and Garen reached a hand out to touch the stone. At the instant of contact, a blue-green light filled the engraved lines and spread throughout the chamber, illuminating every last connected shape. The room came to life under the turquoise glow, and Garen put out his own magical source of light.

"That's new," Morgan whispered in awe. Garen wasn't the only person wide-eyed by the sights in front of him anymore. Naia and Morgan moved around the room, curiously investigating every little trinket and artifact that had seemed dull and uninteresting before. Garen, however, felt a pull from an object near the back of the room.

"Hey ladies, what do you make of this?"

They set down their own preoccupations and walked over to where Garen stood. Before them lay a giant stone table, perfectly smooth save one small symbol in the center.

Morgan squinted at the emblem chiseled out of the center. "Each of these courtyards has a table like this, but I've never noticed the mark in the center before." She and Garen both leaned in closer, and then pulled back and stared curiously at Naia.

"What?" Naia leaned in over the stone table and saw the

sign for herself. The emblem had been worn away a bit, but an unmistakable droplet of water laid etched into the stone. "Interesting," she shrugged. "Well, what do you want me to do? Hit it with a water jet?"

"Actually, no." Morgan said. Let's just pretend it was some gutsy vandalism and move on."

"Agreed," Garen and Naia said aloud together in a rare moment of similarity. Both looked to the other, and then away.

"Oh, and one other thing," Morgan added, looking at Garen. "Don't touch anything."

They continued their sweep of the eastern complex, and Garen quickly understood why a guard posted outside the walls here would be unnerved by this place. He could frequently hear the ground shift in the distance and an occasional flash of light made him guess that fire-spouts were flaring up elsewhere. Above one of the more flooded patches they'd avoided was a tiny waterfall without a source. The water just appeared in mid-air and poured onto the ground.

"Hey look, Naia. Another infinite source of water that can't shut its mouth."

"And those were his last words," Naia said as she reached for her sword. "But he died as he lived: a joke."

Naia tried to turn around to face him, but before she could, Morgan spun her sister's shoulders back forward and they kept walking ahead of him without a word.

They had to stop and wait as the water surged up and covered the walkway in front of them, and then slowly dissipated. This place had plenty of reasons to make a person skittish, and it gave him an idea.

"What was that?" Garen shouted, pointing off into the distance. Both sisters spun and tried searching in that direction.

"What did you see?" Morgan asked, ready to spring into pursuit.

"Not sure, but I don't think it could have been an element. It moved like a person darting between rooms."

"So which way did he go?" Naia clamored in the equal excitement of a chase.

"Not sure…" Garen said as he finished the spell. A tidal wave of the foul swamp-water rose behind them. He was afraid one of the girls might turn around simply because of the rancid odor churned up in the swelling liquid. Thankfully, their eyes stayed fixed in the opposite direction. Garen took a step to the side and guided the wave directly down onto the unsuspecting Naia, to which he offered a last second "Look out!"

The water struck, and all he heard was her shriek. The wave cut it short as it engulfed her, carrying her into the neighboring pool of filth. Naia's head surfaced, and she saw Garen cackling. Whether she understood his guilt or just wanted someone to blame, her eyes screamed revenge.

The water rose from underneath her and she rode on top of it like a beast at her command. The water picked up speed and charged right for him. With a wall of water this wide coming at him, Garen had no choice but to jump above it. Naia was ready, and the still laughing Garen stood no match for a full-fury Water Spellsword. She leapt off the tidal wave and lunged straight at him. He raised his arms to defend himself, but it was no use against the speed Naia was coming.

She tackled him and drove them into the water. The impact with the mud was surprisingly painful. Garen couldn't exactly take in all that was happening to him, but he felt Naia's hands grip his throat and the back of his head. He seemed to be getting pushed and smeared into the grime. When she finally let him go and he came up for air, Garen found himself covered in the foul stench of the swamp water and its muddy under-layer.

They climbed back onto the stone pathway to find Morgan simply shaking her head in disapproval. "Next time Drake splits me off with you two," she scolded, "I'm going to make Kiron pay me double. First as Spellsword aide and second as babysitter."

The three continued their sweep of the remaining eastern complex and met Drake and Argus at the south gate.

"What took you guys so…" Drake began, but changed questions when he saw their state. "Better yet, what happened?" It was obvious to anyone more than a simple accident took place, and not because Naia was covered in swamp-water, or even because Garen was covered in mud. It was because Morgan was covered in embarrassment to be seen with the two of them.

CHAPTER

TWELVE

Garen kept to the rear of the group as they entered the central tower. He reasoned that since he knew his way around the least, he had no excuse for taking any pointless risks at the lead. Also, with Naia up ahead, he didn't mind staying as far away as possible from her. The cold southern air had picked up, and each brush of wind made the shivers worse. With Naia experiencing the same soaking-wet consequences, Garen didn't expect forgiveness anytime soon. He kept his distance accordingly.

The lower levels of the tower had a subtle grandeur about them. Massive windows lined the outer walls, carved right out of the jet-black stone. The group took no interest in the architecture and went about their routine for each room they examined. Walk in. Spread out. Look for any signs of disturbance. Head upstairs to the next tier. No one said much of anything. They just silently searched for what they had already decided didn't exist and moved on.

Curiously, each floor really did look disturbed. Tables and trinkets and books and baubles covered the place in random disarray. Anywhere else, he'd have believed that the world's messiest scholars lived here. In a place where the ground shifted every few hours, tsunami swamp waves crashed against the tower, and miniature whirlwinds could rearrange anything not fastened to the floor, a little chaos seemed understandable. Any of them would have instantly gone into high alert if they found a single fragile relic intact or a room without singe-marks along the floors and ceilings. Garen quickly discovered the source of the group's cynicism toward the mission. How do you determine something is out of order in a place that intentionally defies all such order?

Just when the monotony begun to wear heavy on Garen, they emerged into a level of the tower laid out differently than the others. A small glimmer of light came from an ascending stairway across the room, but none other to speak of.

"One day I'm gonna figure out why this madhouse has got one goffing floor without any goffing windows."

"Argus, language," Morgan scolded in the breath of a whisper, but clearly loud enough for all to hear.

"Sorry there, Morgan," he apologized. "Just a little tired of the same old chase."

Drake's voice called back from darkness ahead. "We're all a little tired and frustrated, but we'll be done soon. Garen, we seem to be missing a healthy dose of lighting. Think you can remedy that for us?"

Garen took a step toward the wall and noticed the same pattern of connecting semi-circles etched in the stone. "I think I can do one better than that," Garen announced, cracking his fingers in preparation to awe his crowd.

Just as before, he placed his palm flat against the dark face of the wall and watched as the gentle blue-green glow spread instantly, filling every last crevasse of the pattern. The room laid emptier than any of the others, save for a small raised platform in the center of the room. Just like before, the dark stone took on an entirely new texture coated in the vibrant color.

"Ta-da!" Garen announced, spinning around to see the looks of amazement on their faces. For a moment, he witnessed just that. Each eye darted along the walls and ceiling, taking in the grandeur expansion of lights. The expression, however, disappeared as the floor swayed beneath them. Debris poured out from the trembling walls and filled the air. Naia snapped her head down from gazing at the quivering ceiling and shot Garen a look of contempt.

"What part of 'don't touch anything' did you need repeating?" Naia screamed over the sound of the shaking tower.

"Hey, I got you your light, didn't I?" Garen shouted back, meanwhile more intent on looking for the fastest way out of the one floor without windows.

"Good call! Now they can find our corpses easier!" She had barely finished the sentence when the bulky arms of Argus lifted her off her feet.

"Soon as we're done not dying, you two can kill each other all you want," Argus growled while barreling forward. Garen followed alongside Argus as they sprinted directly toward the nearest wall. Argus screamed and the orange geonode on his shield flared brightly, shattering the two feet of stone like breaking a thin wooden board. Argus never stopped, leaping out his newly formed window without any hesitation.

Garen stood at the edge, eyes fixated on a structure in the middle of the room. The wide stone table was just like the one he saw earlier. This one, however, had a different engraving in the center. Curved lines emerged from a circle, like a childhood depiction of the sun. In the center of that circle laid an open eye. He had seen it countless times before in his dreams and in the quiet moments of his mind. He could turn over his forearm and reveal the same image he'd sown into his skin. More than just a simple recognition, he felt a link between them. He stood lost in his gaze at the eerie extension of his identity.

A chunk of ceiling landed a few feet in front of Garen, snapping him back to his less-than-stable environment. With one last curious glance, Garen leapt out and gave himself a current of wind underneath to slow his fall. On the way down, he watched one of the windowed floors of the tower collapse on itself, followed by another. Eventually, the whole column gave way, and the structure topped over, landing on top of the eastern complex with an echoing crash and a skyward surge of swamp water.

Garen spotted the others watching the same destructive spectacle from the south gate and floated their way. He still hadn't mastered his wind control enough to soar in any direction as fast as he pleased, but slow, gradual movements became easier with time.

Before he even touched the ground, he could feel the comment coming. "Garen, we were starting to get worried," Drake said. "I thought making a quick escape was your specialty."

"Sorry about that," Garen muttered without thinking, his mind still picturing the stone platform. "I saw something that, eh, distracted me."

Argus let out a booming laugh and wrapped an arm around Garen's shoulders. "Still got the eyes of a thief, do you?"

Garen paused to make the connection, then gave a humble grin. He had no desire to share what he saw with the group before he picked Kiron's brain in private. "Yeah, I guess I still do."

* * * * *

"Let me confirm. You blew up...the Theltus Nisdal?" Kiron asked.

"Well, you know," Garen paused to consider just how much trouble he could be in for causing the collapse of a historical and spiritual relic. "Not on purpose."

"And how exactly did this happen again?"

"I touched a wall," Garen said, also wondering whether it really seemed fair to put the blame on his shoulders.

"Did no one tell you not to touch anything?"

"It was mentioned." Garen cringed at the shrill voice of Naia still ringing in his head. "I really am sorry. Do you think the king will be angry?"

"Oh, I expect he'll be livid. But unless Micah plans to go down and rebuild it brick by brick himself, he will get over it...eventually." Garen breathed a deep sigh of relief. He knew he would have to face Micah at some point, but he preferred when he did, he wouldn't already require mercy from the man he despised. Years alone taught Garen quickly that there weren't many fates worse than owing a debt to an enemy.

"Anyway, I didn't bring you down here to interrogate you. It's time to start your light training. Part of me wants to wait longer, but you need to understand your spirit and its gifts now. I recognize some of these exercises may seem basic, but trust me. They're good both for your technical mastery and just for me to know where you're at."

Garen didn't care if the first task would be reciting the alphabet. If it had to do with his mother's spirit and how to use it, he would go along. He'd begun doubting what he'd seen on his run that day, and some training would finally let him prove that he did have the spirit, which meant Sustek was guilty after all. That peace of mind would be worth more than any new skills and tricks. "Teach away."

"The first exercise should be simple. I have some drawings and I want you to describe them the best that you can."

"Uh, okay, but how is that supposed to help me with...?"

"Because I'm not going to show them to you."

"Oh."

Kiron picked up a thick piece of parchment and held it up with the picture toward himself, away from Garen. "Now concentrate and tell me everything you can distinguish."

Garen squinted his eyes and tried to feel the light coming off the picture. The spell was more detailed than how he usually searched an area for people. But the light bent toward him in the same way. The process disoriented Garen quite a bit at first, giving the sensation of moving while standing still. But he had worked past that long before he had the spirit's help. By now the spell had become a simple manipulation of light, and he could now see the sketch right in front of his eyes.

"It's a little blurry, and by the looks of it very poorly drawn," Garen began.

"I had Morgan draft it for me. I'll be sure to pass on the compliment."

"Alright, I'm pretty sure it's a flock of birds overtop what looks like trees."

"Good, good," Kiron said, reaching for another piece of parchment. "Now how about this one?"

"Looks like a horse. Or maybe a cow."

"Yeah, I'm looking at it right here and frankly I can't decide myself. Good enough. One more."

"Okay, it's a person. Kind of an angry, short little guy. He's got a long sword and some armor and—hey, wait a second. Is that supposed to be me?"

Kiron laughed and set down the drawing. "Yes, I do believe so. You've gotten pretty skilled at bending light to your own eyes. Now I want to test how you are at bending it into another's."

The concept seemed delightfully simple but with only one problem. In all of his resourcefulness, Garen never once considered he could do the same trick for someone else.

Garen had to pause and laugh. "You know, I've never quite tried that."

"Really?" He didn't need to see Kiron's face to imagine the look of shock. "Well, it's probably for the better. I'm not sure any of us could have found you if you'd have gotten this down."

"What exactly would I use it for?"

"It has friendly applications. Instead of just peering around a corner yourself, you can share that same gift with a friend."

"And the more devious application?"

"You can disappear. Bend the light around yourself so you don't even exist to that person. Or for a more disastrous effect, project that image somewhere else and leave your enemy swinging at the air while you strike from the blind-spot you gave them."

Garen smiled. He was starting to see the uses of having this spirit more than ever.

"Can you do it?" Garen inquired.

"Actually, neither myself nor any of the Spellswords can do this in particular. And perhaps we should talk about that first."

"What, about others using light magic?"

"Sort of. You've certainly noticed that some spells take a much heavier toll on your depth than others. Creating stone from nothing is far costlier than reshaping a brick into a spear. And the deeper magics, those beyond manipulating the elements, have enormous costs. The relay geonodes that let us communicate between cities. The magic that lets one mind control another. Some of these require the depth of a dozen souls working together to accomplish."

"Okay, so from cheap magic to deep magic, where does light rank?" Garen asked.

Kiron chuckled. "Somewhere between the two. We may treat light as one of the elements, but there is quite the difference between hurling a stone and crafting an image. One is a single force. And the other is a thousand unseen, skilled hands at work. Even the simplest of light spells take an enormous toll on the soul. Of course, there's no way for you to experience that now. For the rest of your life, the Light Spirit will provide you with all the depth you need to shape light. But it was a testament to your own depth that you were able to use those skills at all before the spirit. The rest of us have to resort to imitation. Surely you've noticed all lighting geonodes glow with the flicker of fire through the stone, not the white orb of light you can summon."

Garen had wondered why he was the only one that ever seemed to use his particular tricks with light, but he had always credited his own cleverness. He'd never imagined that the others weren't capable.

Kiron tapped his hands together as he thought. He snapped his fingers in epiphany. "There is, I believe, a better way to show you. Do you remember the five elements I showed you some time ago?"

Garen recalled the crude diagram scratched into the floor of this very chamber. "I do, but light was just a part of the shape."

"Well, that was one depiction."

"So, there's another?"

"Indeed. And now that you've seen the Theltus Nisdal in person, it will be easier to explain." Kiron created the same layer of sand and etched the same quick diagram. Only this time he continued by drawing a line from each element to the symbol at the top. The added lines turned the flat pentagon into a crude model of a pyramid, with light rising above the others.

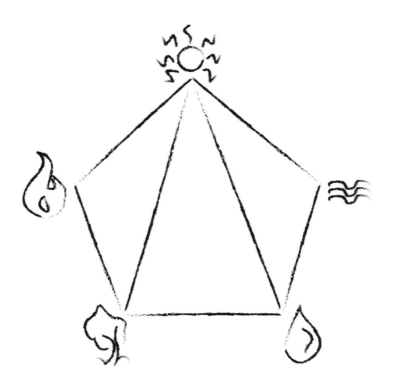

"So, what does that make me at the top of the pyramid?"

"By the organization of the elements, their leader. The ancients believed light was central and revered by all other elements. Fire is but a cheap, passing form of light. The plants of the Earth cannot grow without light. Water is clear to allow passage of the element, and wind is its cousin, trying to imitate on a physical level its grace and flow. Light to them was more than just the ability to see. It governed knowledge and authority. When the elements are shown in this fashion, the sun is generally drawn with an eye in its center." Kiron drew the missing part of the symbol. Now the same image he'd stared down in his mind and in the temple had now followed him to the floor of their training room.

Kiron made sure to cut Garen off before he could say a word. "But I do not organize this team as nature tells me. I organize it as I see fit. You are the newest recruit and nearly the youngest. Do not think for a moment that you get to pull rank with any of the others. I will have them knock you off your feet for even implying your superiority. However, it is important that you know just how special your gift is, and why you aren't likely to see any of the others imitating your specialties."

The words both humbled Garen and filled him with pride. They also made sense of previous mysteries. The general unease in the group at his first appearance seemed far more understandable now. And Naia hadn't just lashed out at a random target. Garen was a measuring post, the level of skill and ability she could never possess. Her bratty actions did not come from petty disdain, but of an unfair imbalance. For the first time since he met Naia, he actually felt sorry for misjudging her.

"Understood," Garen said in a low voice and bowed his head. "Thank you."

"Oh, don't thank me just yet," Garen raised his eyes just in time to see Kiron in full charge at him. Before Garen could ready himself, Kiron's fist made contact with the bridge of his nose.

CHAPTER
THIRTEEN

Garen stumbled back awkwardly, trying to stay on his feet. The impact from the blow, however, hit too hard and disoriented every sense. Finally, he felt his weight tilting to the side and couldn't coordinate his legs quickly enough to balance. He fell over onto the hard floor, only worsening his state of disarray.

Still, even as his eyes remained closed, Garen instinctively asked the obvious question, words muffled by his cheek still pressed against the ground. "What was that for?"

"It was for disappointing me."

Garen slowly rose to his feet, still shaking the dizzy feeling in his head. "Come again?" His eyes finally focused on the man he could have sworn a moment ago was his ally. He had taken two swords from the training rack by the wall and now began to walk toward Garen. It was luck he saw Kiron when he did. Not a moment later he threw the sword to him. Despite the grace which Garen plucked the weapon from the air, he stood awkwardly and unsure how to react in the moment.

"You're a disappointment to all of us, really. All the spoken confidence of an arrogant mastermind, and none of the living performance to back it up."

"Hey, now," Garen said, backpedaling as Kiron approached striking range. "No need to make this personal."

"But that's exactly what this is. It's not a matter of skill or natural talent. You've those by the shiploads. It's a matter of person, and you're just not man enough to live up to it all."

Finally, Kiron brought his blade in, swinging from the shoulder. Garen met his sword and parried it down, still slowly retreating.

"If you've got a problem with what this life's made me, you put down that sword and let's chat. Otherwise, I need you to back off." Garen ended his last few words with more emotion than he anticipated, and he realized the fading confusing had given way to frustration.

"Now why would I do that?" Kiron shouted, taking the volume of Garen's command to the next level. "We've already got one coward in the room."

By Kiron's initiative, their swords met again, then quickly once more. Garen intended to make the same parry and step away, but his feet lost balance as the floor crumbled beneath him. Garen realized his opponent had caused the disruption, but without solid ground to push off of, he could only summon a small gust of wind to slide him away from the conflict.

"Nothing ever changes, does it Garen? Always running. You know, you've become quite adept at surviving. But surviving and fighting are two different things. I'm beginning to wonder, do you even know how to fight?"

"Keep pushing me, and I think you'll find out."

Once more Garen felt the ground under him shift, shooting upward. Prepared this time, he lunged from the front edge of the platform toward his taunting adversary. Garen unleashed a sizable fireball from the tip of his blade. He followed it with a half-hearted thrust. A simple wind spell pulled the fire apart. Kiron casually stepped to the side of Garen's blade. Embarrassed by the weak attempt on his part, Garen spun to face Kiron and took a step back of his own.

The insulting string of his laugh damaged Garen's remaining calm enough on its own. Kiron, however, chose to add more. "You're like a child playing a game he doesn't know the rules to. Playing it safe, trying not to stand out. Maybe I'm crazy, Garen, but when I see talent, I expect to be shown brilliance. Same as when I see lightning strike, I expect the roar of thunder. So, here I stand, looking at a radiant bolt in the night sky, but I'm not getting much more than a dull thud from you. Would your parents—"

"Choose your next words carefully," Garen interrupted, breathing heavily, but not from exertion, "because you're about to cross a line."

"Oh no, we wouldn't want that," Kiron shouted. "My

goodness we don't want to be crossing lines. Because your parents didn't die trying to grow and shape you into a confident man. They died so that we could all play it safe, to keep us from crossing lines."

The fury inside him boiled over and he charged forward, putting everything he had into a beam of piercing light. Forced by the move, Kiron stepped to the right of the blast. Then, with Kiron's guard open, Garen swung fast and low, aiming to cripple a foot at the least.

Kiron stepped down on the swinging blade. The metal snapped at half length. Before Garen could even assess the change in momentum, the pommel of Kiron's sword struck him directly on the temple. The impact knocked him to the ground. Just when Garen could feel his own consciousness slipping, a rush of icy water came crashing over his body.

"Anger is a funny thing," Kiron mused, now standing several feet away. Garen tried to block out the voice to refocus himself. Though Kiron spoke with a tone of importance, Garen had to reorient himself first. The room finally stopped spinning, and he tried to find his way back into the conversation.

"—a distinct purpose. You squint, narrow your vision, and focus on one thing. Anger can lead to tremendous strength, but it also blinds you. That beam of light could have cut right through me, but it left you clueless to how easily I would counter your strike. All the strength in the world means nothing if it steals the knowledge of how best to use it."

Garen tried to take in his words and the wisdom that seemed to follow, but his mind was still on their fight. Kiron, however, continued to teach as though poisonous insults hadn't flown across the training room or they hadn't just tried to kill the other.

"You may be tempted to let rage focus your energy into a narrower, intense strength, but I guarantee it will take just as much away. Your greatest advantage will always be to keep your eyes wide, absorbing every last detail of the fight. You will never find a resourceful victory with your eyes half-shut in fury."

Garen decided to play his game, pushing the questions of

their spar to the back of his mind. "So, I'm not supposed to get mad? How exactly do you just turn an emotion off? Should I fight with my ears plugged?"

"I'm afraid that would only further impair your senses. The solution, I believe, is not in how you prepare for a battle, but how you respond in the moment. If I took another swing at you right now, would you let it strike you?"

"No," Garen said, trying to follow the sudden change in thought. He couldn't help but feel that in every conversation with Kiron the man had two personalities, and each liked to change the topic on the other. With a passive aggressive air Garen replied, "Assuming you weren't just stabbing me in the back this time, I'm sure I'd block."

Kiron ignored any of the intended sting. "Exactly. When an opponent attacks your calm and tries to swing at you with an emotional blow, wouldn't it be much wiser to block than let it draw blood?"

"Alright, but I'm not too adept in the art of blocking words and feelings. Do they make a shield for that?"

"In a strange sort of way, yes. You remember a saying your father used to utter in frustration? 'That tongue is going to be the death of you'"

Garen smiled at the memory of his father's tiresome reply to Garen's mid-spar banter. However, even though Kiron has brought it up before, he couldn't help but feel this time that Kiron mimicked the very tone of the saying with incredible accuracy. He wondered how, even if Kiron knew his father quite well, he could possibly have caught the nuance of speech his father used with him personally. Garen pushed the conundrum to the back of his mind and answered the question at hand. "I do."

"Well, I am going to speak words at this moment that I may never again have the audacity to say. Your father was wrong."

"Go on."

"You and your father were very different men. Your father, quite like the Fire Spirit he possessed, had a deep need for focus. Flames require a central point, not spread throughout. But light is another story. The most useful light is one that covers all direction, and though a little focus may be required to shine on a given point, too much focus leaves you blind and vulnerable. I believe that tongue of yours is the best tool you have to keep yourself as emotionally distant as you need to be."

"I think the rest of the group might need that in writing." Garen laughed, noticing as he did how calm he had become in just a matter of minutes. "As crazy as I still think you are, I have to admit that makes some pretty strong sense. I would call today quite the success."

"Who said anything about calling it a day? I've still got a grudge to settle with you." Though Garen's sword had snapped in two, Kiron still held his blade at the ready. Garen caught the movement of his sword hand just time to roll back under the swing and tumble a few feet away.

"Not this again," Garen said to himself, barely loud enough for Kiron to hear. He knew the stubborn nature of his teacher and didn't plan to waste his breath talking him out of it.

"Of course 'this again.' Do you think I could just let you walk away after that miserable demonstration? I think you need to learn a painful lesson for falling so short after we've heard so much about you."

"What a shame," Garen said, staring at the ground. He slowly tilted his face upward and revealed his grin. "Because no one's heard of you at all."

Kiron offered the shortest of laughs to confirm his approval and charged with sword raised. Without a weapon of his own, Garen resorted to simple impact spells, blocking each swing of his opponent's blade with a barrier as strong as stone. He had not, however, practiced enough motionless casting, and with his arms flailing to block each swing with a spell, he knew his wild thrashing would leave himself open for a magic counter. Garen had the concern just as he felt the rush of wind on his back. He leapt into the air. He hung for a split-second above the current intended to throw him into the reach of Kiron's sword. Instead, the gust followed through and required Kiron to divert his attention to stopping his own spell. In that moment, Garen seized the opportunity and launched himself in the air toward Kiron. With a flip mid-air to build speed, he brought his foot down. His heel connected with the side of Kiron's neck, knocking him forward and onto his face from the blunt strike.

Garen pushed off from the kick and landed behind Kiron, waiting to see if the successful gambit would convince him to back off. Instead, he heard the rumble of laughter as Kiron lifted his face from the ground. "I leave you my guard open, and you choose to stun me with a flashy, amateur stunt like that. At this point, I can't count how many times you've embarrassed yourself."

Garen could feel his blood boil again. They both knew the blow had the intention of mercy. Rather than argue, he followed his teacher's instructions.

"Really? You can't count to two?"

This time without the consoling laugher, Kiron raised his weapon again and sprinted toward him. As he ran, spouts of water and fire surged from the air beside him. The fountain of each raced not directly at Garen, but closely along his sides. They locked him where he stood without any space to maneuver a sidestep of the incoming blade. He considered using more force spells to block the attack, but the tight conditions didn't leave him much space to move his arms. His motionless casting still needed far more practice. With only a moment before the blade would force Garen to decide, he had an idea. One riskier than ever, but for his own curiosity, worth trying.

Kiron continued his lunge and swung without any hesitation at the defenseless target. To Kiron's horror, the blade passed clean through the image. He realized his student had learned more than just one lesson from the day. Masking the true fear that came with that thought, Kiron spun around with his sword, hoping to catch Garen in a vulnerable state. He shouted to continue the façade even as he swung blindly. "You're unbelievably—"

"Oh, believe this!" Kiron had guessed correctly about his location, but not his unprepared state. With a staff of stone conjured from the floor, Garen easily blocked the swing. He followed by swinging one end of the rod to his adversary's cloaked face and cracked hard against it.

Kiron slid along the ground, and Garen wasted no time retrieving the dropped sword at his side. He stood over Kiron with the tip to his throat. "Now, for the soulless city's sake, are we done?" Garen tossed the weapons to the side of the chamber and stepped away from his pinned teacher.

Kiron coughed, which slowly turned into a laugh. From his humble position on the ground, he began to offer a soft applause. "Yes, I believe so. You've learned more today than I could have hoped. Also, I believe both of our faces are in need of some repair."

Kiron stood and wrapped an arm around Garen, walking with him out of the training chamber and into the hallway. Garen felt a sense of relief cascade over him as they left, glad he could call Kiron a friend once more. Still, one issue plagued his mind.

"So, all those comments about me being a coward and a disappointment. Those were all just an attempt to get me riled up, right?

"If you say so."

"No, wait," Garen insisted as Kiron tried to enter his chambers and close the door. "Were they or weren't they?"

Kiron stopped with the door open just a crack, and even without seeing his face, Garen could not miss the smirk.

"I believe you're on patrol this evening, are you not? Better get some rest first."

CHAPTER
FOURTEEN

Drake and Garen made their usual passes through the city, neither much for small talk on a humid night. It didn't take long for them to find their way to the Thirsty Soul, and Iosif greeted them with an accustomed yellow smile. A short conversation later, the greasy tavern keeper had explained the regularity of the evening and, per usual, promised to inform the two if anything normal should occur. Drake and Garen sat at a table against the wall, casually keeping an eye on their surroundings but more intent on just sitting for a while.

"I can't help but notice you and Naia seem to be getting along better. Or at least, there's less flagrant name-calling around the table."

"Ha, I'll admit, it is nice not having to answer to rat-face," Garen said, "but I wouldn't say we're 'getting along.' More like we're agreeing to ignore the other's presence."

"And is that working?"

"It could be worse. And since Naia begged Kiron to stop putting the two of us on patrol together, it hasn't been that hard."

"Alright, I have to ask. Is there a reason for the instant feud you two developed?"

Garen leaned back and sighed. "I've wondered that myself every now and then, and I honestly can't say. I mean, at first I just thought she was snotty and obnoxious toward everyone, and I was happy to play along. When I realized it was pretty much just me, it became a sort of game. You know, to see if I could provoke her, maybe find out why. At this point, I don't think I'd know how to respond to her any other way. And truth be told, I don't mind it."

Drake gave an observant grin, silently screaming the implication, *Oh really?*

Garen caught the look and laughed. "Fine, fine, maybe it's

more than that. Maybe I've lived too long taking care of crazy. Maybe I have a thing for crazy."

Drake's smile grew. "She's a beautiful girl. I think it's perfectly natural that you'd—"

"If you finish that sentence, I will kill you. Right here. In front of everyone. Messy too."

"Fair enough," Drake replied with a smirk. "Your secret is safe with me."

"No, wait a second, there's no secret. It's not like—" Drake raised his hand to stop the defensive ramble. Garen knew he had no chance of convincing Drake otherwise, and so he chose to let it go. They sat through a measure of awkward silence until Garen felt a strange chill sweep over him.

"Okay, I know this might sound a little odd, but something's off. Mind if we go and check around outside?"

"By all means," Drake offered, standing to leave. "If you've got even the slightest hunch that would add some action to the evening, take the lead." Garen left the tavern and stared at the vacant streets. He wasn't sure what could mess with his mind like this, but he couldn't ignore the feeling. It seemed to intensify as Garen wandered off on a back street. Garen felt himself slip into a different state of consciousness. Light bent down alley after alley as Garen began to take in the vast surroundings of nearly half the city.

An explosion in the far west of the city nearly overwhelmed Garen's senses, knocking him off his feet. Sitting in the middle of the road, he took in the multitude of light from the location of the blast. A man stood alone in the center of the road there, motionless despite the swirl of smoke and debris surrounding him. It cleared enough to let one image enter Garen's mind, a face he had never expected and would never forget: Pyralis.

Without a word, Garen dropped into a dead sprint toward the blast. He heard Drake's footsteps follow behind, but Garen raced with the enhancement of light that not even wind could keep up with.

"Garen, wait up!" Drake cried from the distance behind

him, but Garen had no intentions of waiting an extra second to get to the man who killed his father. The traitor had the nerve to show his face in Garen's city. He would not hesitate to punish him for the arrogant gesture. Garen approached the site of the explosion and started to funnel in light from the area. The blast gave him a direction but he still needed to locate his prey exactly. Garen turned the final corner and arrived at the scene. Pyralis didn't seem to have targeted anything in particular, just sent up the flare as a sign.

Or worse, a trap.

Garen spun around, ready for the ambush. None came. He tried to channel the surrounding light again, but in the dark of night, the gift had its limitations. If Pyralis found a dark enough alleyway, Garen wouldn't find him without using his own eyes.

"Coward! Come out here and die." Garen shouted in frustration. A few heads poked out of open windows and cracked doors from the commotion. At the sight of his innocent audience, Garen's rage began to swirl with confusion and doubt. He realized how much confidence he'd put in his abilities, and how misleading they could be. He'd only envisioned Pyralis' face. Was it real? Was his own mind filling in the blanks? The frightened stares from every direction worried him all the more.

Is this how it starts? Am I going to imagine made-up enemies before I lose my mind?

"As a point of reference, promising death is a poor motivational tool." Pyralis' unmistakable voice made it all real again, and the confident rage resumed control. Garen sprinted down the alley toward the sound of the voice. An unexpected sight came into view. Pyralis leaned against the stone wall as nonchalant as ever. In that moment, Garen saw no trace of the unreachable king he anticipated, fortified behind a palace of walls and soldiers. He still dressed the part. A pristine white arming jacket covered all but the sleeves of his red tunic. He had the casual posture of a common thug, as though he'd grown up on an alley just like this. Garen might have admired the humble nature coming from any other man of royalty, but it only stoked his fury in this moment. This man was both king and criminal, using resources to lead this misguided assault against Garen and his family. Only Pyralis had no walls, no imperial guards to hide behind in this moment. Garen unsheathed his katana and charged in at full speed.

Pyralis unsheathed a pair of thin-bladed scimitars. He parried the violent swing, letting Garen barrel past him. Garen spun as quickly as he could to strike again, but Pyralis moved out of reach. A gust of air carried him onto the roof's edge overlooking the alleyway.

Pyralis shouted loud enough for every neighboring soul to hear. "Have you heard the news lately? Garen Renyld, son of the legendary warriors Seth and Layna, previously thought to be lost to this world, now emerges from hiding as the defender of the people. You can imagine how surprised I, of all people, was when I heard such an impossible report."

Garen imitated the wind spell and leapt up onto the building after him. Pyralis did not stick around to chat. He quickly darted across the rooftops. Garen was certain he could catch him in a footrace, but as the chase began, leaping between buildings left Garen falling farther and farther behind. What gifts he had in raw speed, Pyralis matched in agility. The chaotic path of gaps and leaps favored the latter skill-set immensely. Garen sent a variety of elemental assaults on the run to slow Pyralis down, but he maneuvered every rock-bomb and icicle-storm Garen could put in front of him.

The mere thought of letting him get away sent a new level of fury through Garen's body. Mid-air between rooftops, Garen closed his eyes for a brief second and clenched his fists. He opened them only a second later to find himself standing in front of his rapidly fleeing enemy. Pyralis ran with his head turned back, looking for where his pursuer could have disappeared, unaware he was running straight at him. Garen was equally caught off guard by the involuntary shift. Had he stayed frozen any longer, Pyralis might have plowed right into him. Just before the collision, Garen swung his katana awkwardly from the hip. Pyralis turned at the last second to witness the danger. He turned his blade in time to shield himself. Still, the block had no footing to brace from, and Pyralis quickly crumbled under the pressure of Garen's katana. Pyralis rolled backward, barely missing Garen's next swing, but leaving him in a weakened stance. Garen knew that as long as he did not relent, the tide of this battle had turned. He would soon find his opening.

"That was a curious little move you just pulled," Pyralis said.

"Keep talking. Just make sure you're comfortable with each word being your last." Garen brought in another quick slice of his blade from the side. Pyralis struggled to maintain the speed to react in time, barely bracing his sword, but not well enough to keep from losing his footing again. Pyralis bounced back to his feet, once more dodging a fatal swing.

Nimble little freak. This must be how I make Kiron feel.

Oblivious to his own musings, Pyralis resumed his words. "No, Garen, I meant it as quite the compliment. Since you have no interest in fixing this world, I assumed you were worthless, that I would just have to dispose of you. But now it seems you've found what I was unable to: Layna's killer. And that makes you so very..." Garen knocked aside a failed thrust and kicked him onto his back. To his surprise, Pyralis grinned and whispered the haunting word, "valuable."

"Shut it," Garen shouted, still relentlessly hacking away. "I have no need for the flattery of a dead man."

"Hmm, then perhaps you'd pay more attention to the screams of a dead man."

"What, resorting to begging alre—"

"Garen!" Drake's voice echoed over the crashing mortar to the east. Garen spun to look at the dust rising from the direction, then back at the menacing grin on Pyralis' face.

"You might be moments away from finally settling your grudge with me, Garen. But I guarantee I can weasel my way into staying alive longer than your friend Drake can."

Garen stared down at Pyralis and let his hate surge like it never had before. The vision of a beaten man giving the smirk of victory nearly sent Garen over the edge, waves of liquid rage begging for a chance to wipe it off his face forever. But beneath those waves laid a foundation that would not let Garen sacrifice the life of a friend to take the life of an enemy. If it had presented itself as a surface choice, Garen would have chosen revenge. He wanted it more than a chance to save his own life. Instead, it was a question of identity rather than desire, and it offered him no say in the matter.

With a look of disgust, Garen swung his blade and released a violent shockwave, crumbling the rooftop beneath Pyralis. Just as quickly, he turned and raced in the direction of Drake's shout. Even though he heard Pyralis scream as he fell, Garen knew he would survive. He always survived. Garen had seen Pyralis bested in a dozen different ways, but he had a wit that could hold onto life in the center of a hurricane. And every time, he would always wear the same indomitable smirk. But not forever.

Garen didn't have a hard time finding Drake, but he wasn't the only one. The sounds of metal plating clanked loudly as the city guards rushed from their outer posts to the commotion in the market district. Even louder than their heavy footsteps, however, were the sounds of the struggle. Just from the chaos, Garen imagined they were throwing the whole city back and forth at each other. Moments from turning the last corner, however, the violent crashes fell silent. Garen sprinted into the clearing to find the stone road torn and molded in every direction, as if a hundred landslides collided, many of them uphill. The entire fronts of buildings had been ripped off, and now those inside the houses huddled, shaking in the corners. Those farther away poked their heads into the streets. When they saw the devastation in front of them, their looks changed from curiosity to terror. But the thick cloud of dust that hung in the air kept anyone from seeing the source of the madness shrouded in the center. Garen tried to bend the light in and back to see what he was up against, but even he couldn't begin to navigate his way around the cloud.

Several of the guards had gathered around the edge of the dust, and Garen knew with numbers on his side that his best choice was to see and be seen. He released a massive gust of wind into the debris. The cloud parted and left two figures standing in the clear. He recognized the limp body of Drake slung over the shoulder of a burly, older man. Having felt the wind, the man turned and looked Garen in the eyes. He had the same beaten, tired look from many years ago, and without a moment's hesitation Garen recognized him. This was the same man that launched the ambush on his family, the man that tried to crush him into the ground. He wore an unmistakable grimace of regret, but it was hardened by the years. The lines of sorrow were nearly etched into his face.

Without a word, he turned and disappeared into the ground. The earth opened and closed behind him in an instant, leaving no trace of the two and no indication of the direction they fled. Garen had seen this man manipulate the rocks around him before, and knew that he had no chance to find him, let alone catch him. Garen fell to his knees, reminded of the last time he saw the man. And even though his life was not in danger from this encounter, he felt just as helpless.

CHAPTER

FIFTEEN

A cloud of silence thick enough to choke on hung over the Spellsword dining table. Garen had woken everyone up and given them the news of Drake's capture immediately the night before, but they all agreed, much to their grief, that they could do nothing at the present. Kiron assured him that they would find a way to handle the matters once their minds were clear and better rested. Now, with so many unanswered questions about his disappearance, everyone's mind raced trying to answer the mystery. The busy thoughts and awkward glances left their usually relaxed atmosphere coated in fearful silence. Every set of eyes tried to avoid Drake's empty chair, and yet its haunting void kept drawing their glances, building the tension as they ate.

Garen could see the concern for Drake stamped on everyone else's faces. Still, he could not stop his mind from wandering elsewhere. He kept thinking back on his duel with Pyralis, if he could even call the sick game of cat-and-mouse a duel. If Pyralis' intention had only been to distract and delay Garen, why did he not use any fire-based spells? From all the years growing up and training with Pyralis, a distracting flicker or a full-fledged torrent of flame had always been a signature of the aggressive fighting style he employed. That very fact had left Garen so instantly despaired when he found out how the spirits chose their next host. Garen knew that Pyralis would gladly kill any man to acquire that kind of power. And as ruler of his Western Kingdom, who would have the authority to take the spirit over their king? If anyone took the life of Seth Renyld, Pyralis would, and yet Garen saw no new power. If he could stake his life on anything, Pyralis could not possess a power and choose not to abuse it.

What was it he said to me? He was planning on killing me, but when he understood I had this spirit, he changed his mind and said I was "valuable." Which means...

An excitement in Garen began to build, and his words of joy overflowed out loud. "They're alive!"

Morgan and Argus each gave their own uniquely confused look toward Garen. Even Kiron's head raised in a manner to question the outburst.

"Optimism from Garen?" Argus said, sounding as startled as he looked. He covered his ears and mumbled, "Next thing I know my goffing head's gonna explode."

Morgan looked over to Garen, her eyes much redder than he expected. He saw the sadness and rage welled up in her eyes, but her proper posture and smile tried to tell a different story. He knew which one was lying. She started to say something, but her sister interrupted.

"Ignore him, Morgan," Naia said, still refusing to direct her bitter scowl in Garen's direction. "This spineless wretch just left his partner to die, and now he'll say anything to escape the blame. Though I have to say," she sighed, now clearly addressing Garen without eye contact, "the false hopes bit is probably crueler to us than you imagine."

"No, I mean it," Garen persisted. He tried to formulate his thought process that lead him there, but the sting of Naia's words distracted him. "And for the record, I didn't leave him to die. We were both chasing Pyralis, and Drake, somehow, got left behind. He's a Spellsword...I didn't imagine he'd need babysitting."

Naia faced Garen and slammed her hands down on the table. Above the shaking of their plates, her wild blue eyes stared coldly into his own. "And that's how you've chosen to remember Drake in his absence, a helpless child that only the mighty Garen could protect." Every ounce of loathing she felt nuanced her tone as she unleashed her aggression. "Wake up. We're all just people, and we watch each other's backs." Naia turned her gaze down to the floor, distraught between an apparent swirl of emotions. "What you did was brash and arrogant, and your inability to think about anyone but yourself just killed a good man."

Naia turned and walked toward the door, but Garen had a hard time letting anyone take the last word, especially words like those. He knew, somehow deeply, that he should let the moment pass. The downcast faces of his friends at the table told him that stirring things up worse would only deepen their wounds. But that brash side of Garen that Naia had just mocked would not sit idly and take it.

Garen stood up and let his retaliation pour out. "Well now, listen to who's talking. It's miss 'I don't need anyone,' here to lecture me on watching people's backs. You're just so eager to take the high ground, dying to look down on someone else. I don't care where you stand. I know who you are. And you'd have done the same thing."

"Oh, you know me?" Naia laughed, turning again to face Garen. The laughter brought out a rage-infused smile, and she began her march across the room toward him.

Morgan's eyes filled with worry for the unfolding scene and stood to intervene. "Naia, there's no need to—" she announced, but the sound of crackling at her feet cut her off. She tried to take a step toward her sister, but found her feet solidly frozen to the ground. A look of panic filled her eyes, the way anyone would react to an unexpected state of paralysis. When she realized its cause, she sat down. She could have easily broken through it, but apparently conceded to her sister's stubborn nature.

"Fine, Naia. Just tear us even further apart," Morgan whispered. Even as Argus stood to try the same, Morgan shook her head, and Argus stayed put as well.

"How could you possibly know me?" Naia continued, unfazed by the attempted intervention. "Every waking second since you've been here your life has been devoted to yourself."

"So that's what this is about. Poor little Naia doesn't get all the attention anymore." Garen watched as her teeth clenched, realizing he had found a vulnerable spot to prod a little. "I'm sure it was just a peaceful little bubble where everyone worshipped you until someone came along and stole some glory."

The fury of her expressions turned to action as she materialized a perfectly sharpened icicle and held it mid-air. "This isn't about glory! It's about a friend's life. You are the most infuriating person I have ever met," Naia boiled, launching the projectile straight for Garen's head.

He brushed the icicle away with a simple burst of wind and stood his ground. "So, you're saying I was right about you living a sheltered life?"

"Shut up. You don't know anything about what I've gone through." With her words Garen felt the tone back away from pure rage and toward feelings of remorse. If Garen paid closer attention to the subtle shift, he might have stopped. But he had already formed his next volley and couldn't bear to let such well-crafted words go to waste.

"Oh, but I *do* know your story, ice princess. It's written all over your face. Daughter of some fabulously wealthy nobleman, probably Eastern Kingdom. Wait, who am I kidding, definitely Eastern Kingdom. You had every little wish your spoiled heart desired. And you were gifted, they said, even a prodigy. And now, as if you didn't already have enough reasons to believe you were better than everyone else, you inherited a tremendous power and a charge to protect the world, yet another pedestal you could put yourself on and look down at the rest of us."

"Are you done?" Naia replied, still surging with anger. "Or would you like to hear the real story?"

"Regale me, your royal spoiled-ness."

Naia snapped into a frenzy and summoned dozens of ice shards in the air surrounding Garen, each pointed directly at his skull. The spell was as unfocused and volatile as she was, and the pieces shook no less than her own hands. For a brief moment, Garen wondered if he had gone too far, gotten himself into a mess that he would actually have to fight his way out of. Naia stood posed with arms raised, her whole body tense and shaking. He stared into her fearsome blue eyes, and in that instant saw the pain masked by the explosion of her temper. He could not determine entirely why, either by the loss of Drake or the assumptions he had just made, but she could hardly keep in the anguish ready to overflow. Garen watched the dam break. As the tears came out, Naia whipped her head away and ran silently out of the room. The icy blades melted in the air and poured onto the ground around him.

Garen stood in the center of the soaked floor, looking around for any clue of what just happened.

"I think it's time you learned a little about the hornets' nest you keep poking," Kiron offered, motioning with his hand for Garen to have a seat back at the table.

Argus stood and announced, "If you're planning on just sitting here, I'd best make sure Naia's okay." Kiron nodded and Argus made his way out the door.

Garen nervously took his seat. Slowly, cautiously, their eyes shifted to Morgan. Without a spoken request, she began the story, knowing that Kiron wouldn't try to recount the narrative in front of her.

"It isn't exactly a day I like to remember. But it's not like I can forget it either." She closed her eyes and took a deep breath.

"Naia didn't grow up in the spoiled life you think, Garen. Not Eastern Kingdom either. It was a small farming village a bit southwest of Vikar-Tola. And back then, you'd have been right about a few things. She was sheltered. And she was gifted. Our parents barely made ends meet until Naia came into this world. Then a funny thing happened when she was only about eight. Naia found out that she could use her magic to manipulate the weather. And I don't mean the elements of weather. She actually brought rain or storms at a command."

Garen looked to Kiron in shock. He'd never even heard of magic that could do such a thing.

"It's true," Kiron added. "Rare, and very advanced, but like most gifts, some have an affinity to it."

"Well, Naia certainly had it. And it's amazing how successful your harvest gets when you control the frequency of rain."

"I can imagine," Garen said. "But how does that lead to you getting mixed up in all this?"

"It all happened in a day. I was twenty, so Naia would have only been about fourteen. The two of us were off to our usual mischief, exploring around the woods just outside of town. We heard some noise in the distance, unbelievable crashes like whole buildings crumbling to the ground. We raced back toward the village, and we began to hear the screams. What used to be a thriving community was leveled to the ground. It was the kind of devastation only natural disasters should be able to produce. There was no purpose, no material gain from the assault. Just destruction for destruction's sake.

"Our house sat on a hill just outside the center of the village, and we looked over to find it still standing. And that's when we saw the creature responsible, a man sick and twisted enough to enjoy this kind of massacre. He rode on top of a tsunami wave larger than the house itself. Naia and I watched as he rode that wave straight through our home, leaving only the crumbled traces in its wake."

The connection struck Garen and he blurted out, "A Water Spellsword?"

"No, we have only used Spellswords to refer to our specific collective. When another takes a spirit from us, they are Rogues," Kiron said. "For countless years the Water Spirit rested within the faithful Spellsword Nereus. But Nereus was in his elder years, and one lucky bandit took his life and ran wild with his powers. The new Water Rogue leveled a couple other communities before he came to theirs. As you might guess, his recklessness caught up with him."

Kiron looked to Morgan, nodding for her to continue.

"That's where his short-lived reign of terror ended. After the shock of what I witnessed, I wanted to charge in and take him on myself. I wasn't exactly a warrior back then, but I was raised learning how to protect myself. I would have thrown my life at him, another senseless death. But instead I felt Naia's hand grip my shoulder. She had a cold stare, eyes fixed on the horizon. When I turned to see what she was so focused on, I saw the storm clouds form above the man and his chariot of water. I wasn't even sure if Naia could be causing it. She'd never done anything on this scale before. In just a matter of seconds the entire sky was a sheet of dark clouds. Then lightning struck. But it wasn't the simple kind, not some crooked line that flashes and disappears. I watched a dozen bolts arc down into the water. They branched off in every direction, and I swear that image hung in the sky long enough to sear into my mind."

"And it killed him?" Garen realized he was sitting on the literal edge of his seat.

"Instantly. The Water Rogue's strength became his undoing. There was nothing more than charred bones to identify him by. Everything else just washed away."

"Except for the Water Spirit, which chose Naia as the next host," Garen said.

"Yeah. We raced over to the house, but we both knew what we saw. After clearing away the wreckage, we found our parents' bodies."

"I found the Talia sisters shortly thereafter," Kiron continued, wanting to take the strain from Morgan momentarily. The strong warrior would not be reduced to tears, but the compounding anguish on her face was no less for it. "I offered Naia the same choice I gave you, Garen. She said yes, but with one condition. She wouldn't leave her sister."

"It is strange how that all worked out." Morgan turned to Kiron. "After what happened that day, I vowed I would protect Naia with my life. Then just a few days later, you come along and offer me a job doing just that. Hard to believe it's been over two years, huh?"

"Hard indeed." Kiron revealed the smallest of grins beneath his darkened hood.

"Garen, I'm sorry my sister has been such a pain. I know you've been through a lot lately, and apparently Naia has forgotten how much it hurts. I'll talk to her about that. But you need to back off a bit. Apologize for that little stunt, and if you really think she seems sheltered, then understand that's just the last shard of innocence she has left. Don't take it from her, okay?"

"Yeah, I'll uh...I'll do that." Garen watched Morgan stand and leave the room, and he could not have felt any smaller. He and Kiron sat in silence for a moment to take in the gravity of the story. Garen owed much of his success in life to his ability to read a person, and in this case, he had missed the mark entirely. He had a lot of reexamining to do now that he had the proper context. But his thoughts would have to wait. Kiron interrupted them with a question.

"So, Drake's alive, huh?"

CHAPTER
SIXTEEN

Kiron stood at the head of the table. The three orange geonodes in the room cast the same number of distinct shadows against the oversized map hanging on the wall behind him. He carefully explained the details of their conversation prior, articulating his reasoning far better than Garen had.

"If the man who took Drake is the Earth Rogue, and I think he is, that means they would now have control of three spirits. The level of strength we've employed for the last while, with only three Spellswords, they could now unleash themselves. But Garen's logic follows. That doesn't seem to be their goal. This Earth Rogue sounds more like a puppet than anything, with no sign of the other two. It's as if they're deliberately keeping these spirits out of important hands. And that means there's a very good chance both Drake and Seth are still alive."

They exchanged hopeful glances, looking for a group consensus that they could believe such a wild hunch.

Noticing their reluctance, Kiron continued. "I was already on the fence whether this was a reasonable conclusion or just our hopes playing tricks on us. Then we received a rather telling piece of information. One of my contacts in the northern flats reported a man matching Garen's description of the Earth Rogue. He said to me, and I quote, 'Man popped up out of the ground like a turnip,' and he was seen carrying a full-grown man over his shoulder as he entered the caverns behind the Crystal Falls."

"Well, that's a stroke of luck," Argus said, first to climb on board with the optimism. "Naia's a force of nature in a place like that."

"Exactly," Kiron replied. "And that's why it's a trap."

"He's right," Naia said, the realization hitting her as well. "It's a dream location for me to flail around in, but it bottlenecks going down to the base of the falls and there's more places to hide than I'd know what to do with." With each stroke of understanding, her fury rose. "That sick freak is trying to lure me in on a rescue attempt. He's going for the whole set of us!"

Kiron nodded with a slight shutter at the notion. "It was a clever move, but a little impatient. I think Garen really stumbled onto something. As for why they would keep trying to thin out our numbers, or what delayed purpose they could have in mind for these spirits, I can't begin to tell you. But I do have a plan for how we might be able to turn this nightmare around."

"Then let's hear it," Argus said.

"There's one thing I have to make clear before I propose the idea." Kiron stopped and let the silence of the room set his tone. "What I'm suggesting will go beyond anything I have ever asked of you before. I think you've all heard me say at one time or another that there's no such thing as good people, only decent people willing to—you know the rest. Let me say now, I sincerely hope I've been wrong. What this is going to take from each of you, some more than others, is more than I can fairly compensate in gold. I can't pay you for your life, and you'll be risking it more than ever before. Especially you, Morgan."

"Uh, me?"

"What does Morgan have to do with this?" Naia asked, caught equally off guard, and clearly feeling someone else at the table should be risking their life first.

"Because Morgan is our only hope of finding where they're keeping Drake and Seth without losing Naia to their trap."

"I get it," Morgan stated in a soft voice, still perfectly audible over the silence of the table. "We have to give them bait to know where the trap leads."

"Exactly. And I can't think of any other way to find out where they might actually be keeping the others. All we can guess is that it has to be near the palace. Pyralis has his hands too dirty in all of this to keep it very far from his throne. But that isn't enough."

"I don't like this at all." Naia spouted. "What if they find out it's not me? Whatever purpose they're keeping the others alive, they won't have for her. They'll just kill her! If you're going to do it, you have to send me."

154

"I'm sorry, Naia, but I can't," Kiron interrupted, the harsh tone exposing the sleepless strain in his voice. "We need you if there's any chance of saving the others, once we find out where they're being kept."

Naia folded her arms, still brimming with disapproval. "I don't like it."

"That's why I knew I would need to handle this differently. This plan is not an order. It is a request and the best hope I can put together. Morgan, I've asked the most of you, so let me ask you first."

Morgan responded without hesitation. "Drake would do the same for any one of us. I'm in." Naia looked away and swore under her breath.

"Thank you, Morgan. Garen, you'll need to accompany her down into the Crystal Falls for a variety of reasons. Whatever this ambush is, you'll be putting yourself near the center of it too."

Garen thought for a moment, not just about the question, but of Kiron's words a moment ago. He had no doubt in his mind that he would say yes, but did that really make him selfless? Perhaps Garen didn't understand all the risk, or he simply underestimated his own mortality. Whatever the cause, he wouldn't even blink at a chance like this.

"No gall, no glory, right?"

"I figured as much. Argus, Naia, you'll mostly help monitor this first stage with me, but the following mission to retrieve them is going to put us all in deep. This is your chance to back out now."

"Not a chance." Argus cracked a sly grin.

Naia clenched the edge of the table. "You know, if this whole mess blows up in our faces, I'm not even going to get the pleasure of saying I told you so." She paused and swallowed her regret. "But I won't stop you. I'll do what's needed." If she had raised her head, she would have seen her sister smiling at her with an unmistakable pride.

"Thank you." Kiron paused, giving a moment of respect to their decisions. "Still, I don't have to tell you that time isn't on our side. Morgan and Garen, please ready yourselves and meet us in the courtyard."

The group silently wandered out of the room, the weight of this mission weighing heavy on everyone. Garen, however, had another thought on his mind. As they poured out of the room, he motioned for Naia to step aside for a private word. Though she rolled her eyes in reluctance, she followed.

"Hey, listen," Garen began, unsure how to form the words he needed to say.

"Oh, I'm listening."

"I just, well, I didn't know the whole story, and I want to say I'm sorry about the other night."

"So what, now that Morgan told you what happened you feel bad for me?"

"No...actually, I mostly just feel like an idiot," Garen pleaded, scratching the back of his neck sheepishly.

"I guess the good news is your keen powers of perception are improving." Both of them laughed. It was only a tiny, fleeting laugh, but Garen realized its significance. They had never shared such before, and though it had a heavy coating of awkward, he recognized the milestone for what it was. And strangest of all, Garen let slide a joke at his expense.

CHAPTER
SEVENTEEN

"Just so we're clear, I think you're crazy for agreeing to this." Garen poked his head into Morgan's room. She sat on the edge of her bed, silently staring at the ground. A torn strip of pale green cloth dropped from her grip and she covertly slid it under the bed with her foot.

"Coming from you, that's a compliment, is it not?" She raised her head and revealed the remains of her smile, crumbled ruins of the dauntless grin she gave earlier.

"The highest." Garen paused, realizing he might be interrupting something. "Do you need a minute?"

"No, I've said my goodbyes." She rose to her feet, still holding onto the painful smile.

"Cut that out right now." He spoke the words with confidence, but the outburst came from a place of scared surprise, uneasy with seeing the hardened warrior in a vulnerable place. He believed they were the right words to say, but they were also the only ones that came to mind. Garen had little experience dealing with any female in a fragile situation.

"Relax, I didn't say forever. It just might be a while before I get to come back here and rest." Garen nodded and headed down to meet the others.

They made their way into the open courtyard where Kiron, alongside an impressive new levitrans, awaited them.

"I thought about making you walk," Kiron said, "so you could appreciate Drake's gifts the whole way there. But I'd also like you to get there by summer's end."

Garen heard the words, but he gave no indication. The vehicle's blue shimmer entranced him. The entire contraption hung nearly motionless in the air, no more than a foot off the ground. Garen had seen the flying transports from a far distance away, and he'd heard stories of East Kingdom city skies full of them, but he had never actually gotten this close. The glimmering metal curved smoothly around the edges, but widened out into a rectangle. Within the metal shell were four seats arranged two by two. The air was open above them, but a large pane of glass stretched up from the front of the rig, likely to shield the wind at those speeds.

Even more so, the magic that made it run left Garen in awe. With a quick bend of light, he peeked under the bottom. He'd expected countless dozens of geonodes to line the bottom. Instead he found six massive chunks of the magical ore, mostly enclosed in the metal flooring. Each protruded just enough to emit a green glow that covered the ground beneath it.

"Please, Garen, if you can bottle your recklessness for a day..." Kiron pleaded.

"Wait, are you saying I actually get to drive this thing?" The joy in Garen's voice made him sound five years younger.

"Truthfully, you'd probably be my last choice. Well, maybe in front of Argus now that I think about it."

"Why am I hearing my name?" Argus called out, entering into the courtyard in front of a noticeably reserved Naia.

"Mi—" Morgan's eyes grew wide for a second. An unmistakable look consumed her as though she'd made a terrible mistake. That image of panic, however, turned quickly into a cough. Garen recognized more had just happened than a syllable caught in her throat, but he didn't figure that now would be a good time to press her about such a thing.

She finished her fake cough and continued, "Kiron was just saying you're the least qualified person to drive the new levitrans."

"Agh," Argus grunted and spat, a common response for him after walking outside. "Don't much care for them flying hunks a garbage myself. Don't feel right, and don't sit right neither."

Morgan raised an eyebrow at him. "Uh huh, and I'm sure that's the levitrans' fault." Garen felt at ease to see Morgan maintaining her strong front, but he couldn't help notice the opposite reaction from Naia, hiding quietly beside Argus.

"Final briefing, Spellswords," Kiron motioned them closer. "Morgan, I trust our physicians were able to hide the tracking geonode securely."

She grimaced. "They cut a little deeper than I'd prefer," she patted her hip. "But there's no chance of it falling out. I'm just glad I don't have to fight hard enough to win anything."

Kiron nodded. "Just enough to survive. Your more demanding challenge will be conjuring enough watery destruction to make them assume you're Naia. Do you think you can manage?"

"Oh, I've let my sister beat up on me enough over the years to learn a few tricks."

"Good. Now Garen, we're putting a lot of trust in you for this as well. Make sure they take her alive and don't get caught yourself. You should be able to assess everything going on and stay in control, trap or not."

"Yeah, sounds good. So, do I really get to drive this thing?"

"Garen!" Kiron shouted, his tone more serious than any of his training sessions had even shown him. Garen's body tensed and his eyes snapped from the levitrans to the source of the anger. "People's lives are at stake here, and I will smash this transport to shimmery pieces before I let you drive Morgan into a trap unprepared."

Garen lowered his head in shame, but raised it when he heard Kiron sigh deeply. "But I appreciate the confidence, and yes, you really do get to drive it. I figure you'll have to get back to us somehow after they take Morgan, and I'd much rather you get some practice time sitting next to a responsible human first. But other than that, you're all set to go."

Garen didn't hesitate to jump into the levitrans, but as he climbed up front, he realized both seats looked identical. He didn't even know which side to drive from. He turned to ask for help, but wisely chose not to interrupt them.

"Naia..." Morgan said softly, walking toward her sister.

"I'm not saying goodbye! And you're not either. We'll be there to get you out before you know it."

"Yeah, I know you will." Morgan smiled and turned to leave. "Left side, pal."

"Oh I know," Garen said, casually sliding over. "Just watching you two. Never can be sure if someone's going to cry or get punched. Or both."

"Alright, just strap in and let's see if you can take us out of here without making any holes in the palace."

Garen clasped the harness across both shoulders and looked back to see the others leaving the courtyard. "Alright, listen well," Morgan snapped her fingers in his face. "You've got six geonodes working for you, one for each direction. See these?" Morgan leaned over and pointed down at Garen's feet to the two pedals and to his right a large lever with a knob on top. "There are smaller geonodes attuned to the drive controls. Four directions you can push this lever and two pedals—think you can figure out the rest?"

"Pretty sure I can. The lever is the directions around me and the pedals take me up and down, right?" Garen didn't wait for an affirmation, and stepped on the right pedal to take them up.

Unfortunately, his calm composure shattered as Morgan screamed, "NO, THE PEDALS TAKE YOU FORWARD AND BACK PRESS THE LEFT PEDAL NOW!" Garen slammed on the left pedal, stopping them mere feet from the massive statue of Emperor Tibalt. He kept his foot down, and the levitrans accelerated backwards toward the palace doors. Again, Garen put all his weight the other pedal to stop them until it started forward. After two more alternations, he finally brought it to a complete stop.

"Why would you think the pedals raise and lower? That doesn't even make sense."

"Oh, sorry, I guess not," Garen choked out, too embarrassed to explain that his initial assumption really did seem better than having to keep his foot down once they were in the sky.

"Now, forward and back on the drive stick will lift and lower, left and right uses those front two geonodes, which turns it. Think you can handle it now that you have a clue what you're doing?"

"Yeah, I think that'll help."

* * * * *

When their paths crossed, Garen seemed to get along rather well with Morgan. Few men would consider her "attractive," and she tended to live above his attempts at humor, but he respected her stronger focus in watching over Naia. Even personally, she was a confident pillar in a new environment for him. In many ways, he admired her, or at the very least had no problems with her company. At this moment, however, he did not much appreciate her disdain for small talk. In a group setting, she said what she needed to and contributed to any discussion. But in a more closed setting, such as, perhaps, a quarter-day's journey in a levitrans, Garen realized that she didn't have a chatty bone in her body. Every now and then one of them would find a topic to toss out, but just as quickly as it began, the conversation would drop off. Garen would be left wondering if it rested on his shoulders this time to bridge the awkward gap. Morgan, on the other hand, seemed perfectly at ease in her stillness.

Toward the end of the trip, Garen decided to feign an acute focus on the controls of the levitrans. Even as they sailed straight through open skies, he pretended the task of flying required his extreme concentration, and he could in no way afford the distraction to speak freely. Whether Morgan picked up on this or not, Garen had no idea, but at least he relieved his own conscience of blame for the silence.

"There it is," Morgan said, much calmer than expected after the tedious drive. "That's the tip of the Crystal Falls."

"Better park this thing now. We have a covert mission to fake. I'm guessing it might trigger a few suspicions if we just flew in and dropped you out in the open for the taking."

"How about we just focus on getting this thing out of the sky with our lives intact?"

Morgan coached him down, but the process didn't provide much challenge. Morgan was right with her earlier assessment. Flying is much easier when you know what all the controls do.

Garen brought the levitrans down into a secluded field and tried to park it near a few trees, hopefully concealing it with a bit of the brush. Unfortunately, as they got out, Garen could see how much it still stuck out against a purely natural landscape.

"Here, I suppose you should probably be carrying this." Morgan tossed him a small, disc-shaped geonode. Garen caught it and noticed its green glow. It matched the shade beneath the levitrans.

"This spell locks the flight geonodes," she said, "and it'll unlock them for you later. It's the only thing that keeps some random farmhand from finding this thing and flying his way to Kalyx." Garen peered around the edges of the vehicle for a few seconds, looking for any kind of place to tap or matching socket. "What are you looking for? Just activate it like any other geonode."

"Oh, I guess that makes sense too." Garen accessed the depth stored within the stone, and the levitrans slowly drifted down until resting on the tall grass. Fairly pleased now with the degree it blended in, Garen pocketed the stone and walked in the direction he'd seen the Crystal Falls from the sky. Even though the trees in the field were spaced apart, they stretched far and high enough to blanket the view of anything beyond them. Knowing what awaited them beyond the grove, Garen found the tranquil scenery and chirping birds rather creepy.

As they walked Garen continued to bend in light from all directions ahead of him, but not another soul appeared.

"Morgan, you know what I'm looking forward to?"

"Hmm, I'm going to guess the part where you don't let yourself get captured by vicious enemies who may or may not kill you."

"Well, yeah, but besides that."

"Then I don't know."

"I'm looking forward to making it down to the bottom of the falls, finding out that it's not a trap, and walking out of here with my father and Drake all without having to unsheathe my sword."

Morgan laughed. "Wouldn't that be something? Maybe

we can take a quick swim in the lake before we head back too."

"Oh, I wouldn't have it any other way. My father hated getting wet when he still had his sane mind. Can't imagine what he'd do if I threw him under the falls now." Despite the darkness of the situation, both of them trotted through the trees with honest smiles on their faces.

Finally, they reached the end of the grove and out beneath them stretched an image Garen could hardly take in. The relatively level ground they had traveled over dropped steeply. A narrow trail descended down into the valley, allowing a clear view of the falls. Garen had only seen the tip from the sky, but standing this close, he could witness the full performance. The show began at the peak, where water spilled over the cliff as smooth as if poured from a bucket. The water fell almost sheet-like, with a few clumps and wrinkles where it flowed thickest. The soft and gentle, nearly threadlike quality ended in a violent crash at its base, whipping up a thick mist. The foam concealed the point of collision, as if providing a shroud for the cold trauma relentlessly taking place.

Garen took his eyes off the magnitude of the falls and took in the scene as a whole. The valley lay covered in a natural overgrowth, bursting with greens of every hue. All of this lay against the sharp contrast of the Te'en cave wall, pushing dark browns and grays through the lush greens and blues of the valley.

"Wow," Garen said, more lost in this trance than his experience with the levitrans. "Pyralis sure does know how to pick a scenic choice for his ambushes."

"Yeah, he's a real sweetheart. I'll be sure to thank him."

Garen gasped, causing Morgan to pivot forward and unsheathe her sword. "Where?"

"You're actually turning into Naia. That was *sarcasm!*"

Morgan lowered the weapon and rolled her eyes. "Any useful information?"

"Well, let me check." Naia was right earlier. There were endless places to hide and ambush from. In a scan this broad, he had no way to account for every possible person, but he could certainly figure out the basics of their plan of attack. Sure enough, soldiers lay scattered around the bottom of the path near the lake. They made sure the ambush would be difficult to flee from, but sitting right next to a body of water like that, Garen wondered what would have happened had they sent Naia with him. She really might have wrecked them all. Then again, he had no idea what secrets Pyralis had in reserve for a stunt like this.

A dozen or more men and women armed with crossbows waited in a cave obscured by the waterfall, but they could solve that problem easily. What worried Garen most was the last pocket of ambushers he found tucked away in a well-hidden cave closer to the lake. Very few had any weapons, an obvious sign of their depth. He knew that a small troop of mages would add any number of unpredictable challenges to their mission.

Most frustrating of all was the element of surprise. Garen could rip it from them easily. A few dozen fireballs with precise targets could rout the ambushers and send them into a panic without having to take a single step down that trail. It would keep them from being trapped. But this mission required just the opposite. He had to be sure his attackers kept that advantage from the start.

As a whole, this objective had little in common with his usual tactics: take down those in your way, run from those who aren't, don't get killed, and take whatever you came for. And it frequently played out just that simply. Kiron had given Garen, for the first time in his life, a mission that required him to create a "controlled loss." He had very little experience on the losing side. He didn't much care to start. But he could not afford to ruin this mission, either by actually winning this fight, or pressing them so hard that they take more drastic measures. He would defend himself, set Morgan up with the best chances, and flee.

"Mind if I have a look?" Morgan asked. Garen was still new to bending light into someone else's eyes, but he wouldn't turn down the practice outside of their training sessions. He worked back through each of the spots he'd noted and watched her eyes grow wide at the stream of illumination coming in.

"Wow, they sure sent them out," Morgan sighed at the massive force awaiting them.

"I know, right? I just wish they'd sent more *here*. I honestly don't know how we're going to make this look like a convincing win for them."

Morgan smiled and narrowed her eyes at Garen. "Yes, obviously that's what I meant."

"See, there you are again with the sarcasm. Are we really going to role-play this whole mess?"

"We'll find out. If at some point down there a random sheet of ice cracks you over the head, it was Naia, not me."

Garen had to laugh at the truth of it. If he really were on such a mission with Naia, she would definitely find a way to get her shots in during the commotion as "payback." "Alright, I'm thinking we need to make a pretty sharp entrance to make it clear who you are, or uh, supposed to be."

"Say no more." Morgan stepped forward and stared intently down the trail. The lake at its base began to ripple, then quiver as if the ground beneath it was shaking. But the surroundings remained motionless. Finally, a stream of water, just like the threads he had seen in the waterfall, erupted out of the lake and spread its way up the path. The flow left a thick sheet of ice in its wake, covering the path. The feat would have been merely notable from Naia, but coming from anyone else, the magic astounded Garen. He watched in wide-eyed amazement, but as he stared Morgan down he could see the toll such a spell was taking on her.

The spreading ice reached them. Morgan ignored the sweat that had beaded on her forehead and grabbed Garen's wrist, pulling him onto the ice.

"Let's do this," she shouted, and the two of them began to slide their way down. Garen was glad she quickly let go of his hand. It took every ounce of agility to keep his balance on the ice slide. He considered dropping to his back and finishing the descent in a way that didn't risk an unsightly fall. But he couldn't argue with how cool the pair of them must look sliding down, showcasing themselves to the ambushers.

"I'd hate to spend all my time dodging and deflecting arrows," Garen shouted, now having to compete with the sound of the raging waterfall they approached. "Could you use that gift of yours to buy us some time from that cave behind the falls?"

"Don't mind if I do." With the same confident mastery, Morgan focused ahead. Garen, who had slid ahead of her, whipped his head around toward the falls to see what she might conjure up to further prove her identity. This spell had no warning signs or tremors to raise suspicion. In the blink of an eye, the entire waterfall redirected and funneled into the cave. Garen wished he could have seen the looks on their faces as the torrent of water crashed in on them, but he imagined they probably didn't even have time to react. The waterfall returned to the normal course that nature had given it. Still, those few seconds it flooded into the cave led him to believe they wouldn't have to worry about deadly crossbow bolts anytime soon.

By this point, Garen and Morgan had reached as far down the trail as they needed. They weren't quite up against the rocks, but the path had leveled out and Garen had a lurking suspicion that the trap would likely spring after an entrance like that.

As predicted, the hidden warriors leapt from beneath bushes and behind trees, charging in on the two. Morgan melted the ice beneath them, preferring not to slide around uncontrollably. Thankfully, the rest of the trail remained frozen over to slow their attackers. Some had no problem getting straight to them, while others slid clumsily, barely moving forward at all. The result was perfect for the outnumbered pair. What should have been a converged, simultaneous assault thinned down into a steady trickle. The flow kept coming but never in overwhelming odds. Garen and Morgan met their blades as the ambushers charged at them, both in an entirely different league of swordsmanship.

"Garen, I don't think you're going to get your easy rescue wish. This is starting to look a bit like a trap." Morgan had to shout at the top of her lungs just to be heard over the waterfall.

"I know. I had to unsheathe my sword and everything."

"You think we could still go for that swim?"

"Let me check," he shouted out, trying to lean his head over his shoulder to be heard, but still keep his focus on the axe wielder bearing down on him. Garen stepped to the side of the next downward swing of the axe, which lodged itself into the dirt. "Say, you wouldn't mind waiting here while we go for a quick dip, would you?"

The brutish man furrowed his eyes under the darkest, angriest eyebrows Garen had ever seen. The warrior then ripped the axe from the ground and swung it around in a clean slice for Garen's head. He narrowly ducked under the lethal arc, meanwhile turning back to shout his reply.

"No, they seem pretty set on fighting us."

"Typical."

Garen laughed as he spun back around, his sword taking the abundant opening in his enemy's guard. He really needed to start looking for his opportunity to leave Morgan safely before he'd cleaned out their entire ambushing force.

The ice surrounding the rest of the path melted away, and Garen remembered the group of mages he'd seen.

"Naia, brace for some incoming spells."

A fair of fireballs tore between them, followed by a few ice spears. Having to dodge projectiles made their footwork a little fancier, but the real difficulty came from fighting people who could melt their icy surroundings. The ambushers caught trying to fight through the foliage or slide down the path were now free to charge in unison.

"I think I can take about thirty of them, how about you?" Garen shouted, still trying to keep an eye on Morgan.

"I think you should save your jokes until we're out of this."

The smile faded from Garen's face. He couldn't help but notice how strange the ambushing forces had been placed. Nearly all of the assault came from the waterfall front. Even those hidden up the trail would rush around them and hit from the same angle. Garen would always prefer to fight three foes to his front than one on either side. Their formation let him do just that, all while facing the waterfall. Even with their superior and now highly mobile numbers, the attacking strategy kept the fight on even ground, and Garen could not figure out why they would choose to crash at them like a wave rather than surround and choke. This was a trap, after all.

"A trap," Garen muttered to himself. He released a blast of wind into his attackers. They staggered back, and the spell bought him enough time to spin and find what he feared. Two men lay hidden in the brush up the hill. They held long bamboo shoots up to their mouth. Had he guessed their presence a second later, they would have sent a dart into his back just the same as Morgan's. He couldn't react quickly enough to warn her, but if the dart had a substance to knock her out rather than sheer poison, this might be his best chance he had to hand her over safely. Garen sidestepped his incoming dart and watched the other pierce the back of her neck.

She continued to swing her sword for a few more seconds, but the toxin worked quickly. He could see the sluggish nature of her movements. Finally, she stumbled backward and dropped her sword. Her eyes met his for a moment. In a final moment of consciousness, she looked utterly confused. Garen considered running. He had done the best he could imagine for his objective. He knew there was no shame in leaving at that instant.

He watched her fall and knew his job was done. But he felt something entirely different. An impulse took over, the same drive that kept him going year after year with his father. The sight of a helpless friend was more than he could handle, or least more than he could ignore. Garen sheathed his sword and raced over to Morgan's body, scooping her off the ground. He turned and sprinted as quickly as he could up the hill.

What was that? And what are you going to do now, accidentally drop her? Trade her for a clean getaway? As strange as it might look, Garen realized he would need to turn around and reengage the fight. He never had the chance. The ground opened up in front of him. As he slid to a stop in front of the chasm, a body emerged from the ground, rising up and meeting him face to face. Garen stared into the dark brown eyes of an unforgettable expression. He wore a solemn grimace, never seeming to take joy in the incredible power the Earth Spirit granted him. But whenever Garen had seen him, whether next to his father or with Drake, it always accompanied a terrible loss.

His fear shifted from Morgan's safety to his own survival. He'd imagined this encounter might come sooner or later, and came prepared with a few ways to keep the advantages in his favor. Garen had no choice but to drop Morgan into the grass beside the trail, meanwhile summoning a disc of wind to ride on. He knew the quickest way to lose this fight would be to trust the ground beneath him.

"It didn't work for him either." The Earth Rogue spoke slowly, his tone matching the remorseful expression. Though normally Garen's feelings of pity echoed the man's gloomy demeanor, in this case it fueled a rage inside of him.

"You're going to wish it did." Garen pulled his sword and swung wildly. Pillars rose from the ground to block each slice. Garen unleashed a wave of blinding light from his body, halting the other charging warriors and leaving the Earth Rogue momentarily dazed. Before he could get in another slash with his katana, the ground rolled over the Earth Rogue and shielded him from anything else Garen could throw at him.

Still, he was glad to have him on the defensive for once and continued the assault. Garen looked back to see if Morgan was still safe. Instead, he saw two men pulling her away. The vision gave a sure sign of success, but Garen felt another reckless surge to stop them. The emotion did not prompt any more foolish actions, but it did occupy his focus for longer than it should have. A chunk of rock cracked against his head. The blow knocked him off the disc of air and flat onto his back. He looked up at the spinning sky in half focus and tried to regain his composure. Before he could, the ground opened beneath him, and he felt it swallow him up to his neck.

Even with a ringing sound in his head and a few additional, blurry images of the stocky man in front of him, Garen knew his predicament. "You think you can hold me like this again? We'll I've got news for you. I'm not the same helpless kid I was then." It was true. Garen had reshaped his entire home on numerous occasions just to practice his earth-based spells and expand his own depth. That moment of helplessness all those years ago had fueled the fire of his training. He was determined it would never happen again. Garen took his grip of the dirt and rocks around him and began to push them out. The ground remained solid, giving no more than a light tremor as evidence of his struggle.

"I'm sorry, but you could empty your soul on that spell and still not break free."

"I'm glad you have so much practice crushing people," Garen shouted back, but knew it was hopeless fury. Instead, the words shook the Earth Rogue's resolve, and a more panicked remorse washed over his face.

"It's not me, it's him. It's not me, it's him. It's not me..."

"What are you mumbling?" Garen realized the grip around him had loosened. Garen tried moving the ground again, and it budged enough for him to squirm a little.

"It's not me it's him..." He covered his ears and closed his eyes as he chanted the nonsense phrase.

Garen pressed the ground out a little more, and he thought it could be enough. He summoned a current of wind under him and he felt his legs dislodge slightly and scrape upward against the rocks. The speed of his ascent was too gradual to notice. A few more seconds and he would have his arms free. His motionless casting was still on an amateur's level, but with full range of motion, Garen felt he could shape the rest of his way out.

The Earth Rogue's voice stopped and another replaced it. "It's not you, it's me." Instantly, the ground sealed back around Garen, locking him in around his elbows. He pushed even harder into the spell, desperate to use any depth he had left just to free his arms. The ground felt like iron against his impulses, gripping him tighter than ever before. Garen looked up to see what had refocused his enemy and saw another man standing in his shadow.

He did not recognize the face, but it made a strong enough impression to make him feel like he should. Even in a cold stare, he radiated an eccentric aura. His hair interchanged black and gray at will, short yet still managing to jut in every direction. Stony green eyes peered out under thick, dark eyebrows. His face was cleanly shaven except for a cord of dark hair emerging from his chin and coming to a sharp point.

Meanwhile, Garen could not turn his head to see what was coming behind him, but with a little bending of the sunset light, he had no problem detecting the blow-dart carrying pair coming up behind him. Even with the knowledge of their presence, it wouldn't help him dodge this time.

Garen let his focus fall back to the Earth Rogue and what looked like his puppet-master standing behind him. He felt the piercing sensation on the back of his neck, one after the other. His body was locked in too solid to shiver, but it did not stop the chills from going up his spine. He would have preferred a moment of blunt force to the skull over the eerie sting of the needles.

A swell of competing emotions raged within Garen. To some extent, he felt a hopeless exhaustion. He had achieved the biggest part of their objective, and now they would be able to find him with Morgan. But that exact notion of hopelessness evoked a storm of rage. He would be quitting. He would be putting the lives of his father, Drake, and now Morgan into the hands of the others. Whether for trust issues, control issues, or the sheer matter of pride, the raging storm overtook him. He closed his eyes and screamed with every ounce of anger he had in him. The war-cry continued as the toxins from the dart violated his brain, trying to take his fury away. His voice began to trail off. The soothing medicine reminded him of the allies he knew would come to his aid. In one last bit of the remaining anger, Garen squeezed out a pitiable shriek and pictured his friends.

Garen slipped into a state that felt more like dreaming than waking, but somehow neither. Suddenly, he saw them clearly, just as he imagined standing in their common room. No longer enclosed in dirt, he lost his balance and fell backward. Garen felt a set of thick, bulbous fingers catch him and lay him on the stone floor. Through half opened eyes, he looked up at Kiron, Naia, and Argus. Their stares were speechless.

"See, I knew you'd come for me." Garen sighed and

passed out happily on the ground.

CHAPTER
EIGHTEEN

Garen awoke in the warmth and comfort of his bed. He yawned and stretched, slowly sitting up to begin another day. If he had woken up in an unfamiliar environment, he would have immediately replayed his memories to find out how he had wound up there. But the common surroundings led him to think nothing of it. He continued to sit up and rub his eyes until he noticed the people standing around him. At the vision of Naia, Kiron, and Argus, an anxious panic spread over him.

"They took her! I was trapped and—"

"It's okay," Kiron said.

"But they had me too and I, and I..." Garen's eyes focused on Naia's and his frenzied hysteria transformed into a very singular confusion. "How did I get here?"

"We've actually been waiting here hoping you'd tell us that bit," Argus responded.

Garen looked over to Kiron, looking for any clues to the mystery.

"We were just sitting in the meeting room, planning the next step. Suddenly you were standing right next to us, ready to pass out. And you had a pair of darts in the back of your neck."

"Yeah, they," Garen reached up to feel them, but he felt only the tiny puncture holes in their place. At that moment, Garen realized he was no longer in his leather armor. Someone had changed him into more leisurely sleeping attire. Even though he was clothed decently, a streak of embarrassment flashed through his mind and he pulled the covers up some, looking suspiciously at the friends around him that might have disrobed him.

"Relax Garen, we had a court physician see to you. You were drugged with something those darts had been tipped with. It knocked you out for a few hours, and we had him change you out of your armor."

"Uh, thanks?"

"So, how did you get back?" The mystery of his return even had Naia anxious for some answers. "We didn't find the levitrans."

"I didn't take it back. If you need to go retrieve it, you should find it by the trees south of the falls."

"For goodness' sake, Garen. Are you telling me that you light-shifted straight from the Crystal Falls here?" Kiron asked.

"Light-shifted?" Garen remembered how it felt to transfer even a tiny part of him to light and how quickly he moved. This didn't feel anything like that. He didn't guide himself into the palace. He just arrived. But he knew there had to be an explanation, and his Light Spirit seemed like a fine choice to blame. "Maybe. Why, is that even possible?"

"Hmm. If you would have asked me yesterday, I would have said no. But I'm looking at some pressing evidence that suggests otherwise." Garen watched Kiron's hood sway and knew he was shaking his head in disbelief. "How did it happen?"

"Not sure. I remember getting angry, really angry. And then I got sleepy, and then I imagined you guys. That's about it. Wait, I don't get it. Kiron, didn't you say I'd be able to move like that one day, using the Light Spirit?"

"Potentially, but that takes years of focused training. And much smaller steps. It requires transforming your body into pure light. Your grandmother actually set the precedent, I believe, bouncing from one side of Vikar-Tola to the other."

"Wait, are you saying my gr—?"

"I am, but that's a story for another, more peaceful time."

Garen scratched the sore spot on his neck and winced with a smile. "I guess it just runs in the family." Kiron and Argus gave a small laugh, but he noticed Naia standing patiently, burdened by another question on her mind.

"Do you know if..." she hesitantly began.

"Morgan should be safe. They hit her with the same dart as me, and I even tried to carry her out of there. I messed up, just about got myself killed because I—," Garen paused to reconsider his words without sounding foolishly sentimental. "It's just strange watching a friend get taken and letting it happen. I almost blew the mission. I got lucky." Garen realized he was rambling in his tired state. "Morgan, though, she's safe."

"Thank you."

"You're welcome," he said with a modest smile. Garen caught a glance between Argus and Kiron, both surprised by Naia's politeness.

"Well," Kiron cut in, "we're very glad you're back safe. Unfortunately, even though you're probably somewhat rested, it's actually quite late and Morgan's tracker shows she's still being moved. In the meantime, we're going to rest. Don't go running off to do something stupid, and we'll see you in the morning."

All three of them slipped out of the room and left Garen alone with his thoughts. He considered what kind of stupid things Kiron was afraid of. Garen did have reason to believe his father might still be alive. But he had waited too long in this group to throw away their help now in rescuing him. The vast forces at the waterfall proved how far Pyralis would go to gather these spirits. Wherever he kept the others, it would be guarded no less. As much as it pained him to admit, this was beyond his capacity to sneak in and steal what he wanted.

His mind drifted back to the waterfall, watching Morgan fall helplessly to the ground. Neither grief nor regret had triggered the memory. Instead, he seemed to watch himself with a critical eye in that moment, wondering why he had gone against the entire mission objective to pull her away from the danger. Just a season's length ago, Garen would have left her to fend for herself, even if it had nothing to do with a goal. The very theme of his life had been survival through independence. Now he had begun violating logic and reason to save others that don't need saving, and all at the risk of his own life. His mind went back to an old friend of his, one he hadn't seen in at least two years. Panther hadn't exactly served as a mentor, but he was the closest thing Garen had after his father went mad.

Panther had a simple motto that kept life "uncomplicated," as he liked to put it. *Never invest. Always get paid.* An idea like that would turn most men into unashamed hermits, but not Panther. He was happy to work alongside and accept any manner of favors, so long as they understood not to expect anything in return. The one-sided friendship turned away any upright, decent types of men, but the work Panther dabbled in didn't exactly attract decent individuals to begin with.

Panther could not have hoped to meet a person more fitted to his life philosophy than Garen, who was fourteen at the time, a little lost in the world, and ripe with talent for exploiting. Garen learned more about surviving on his own from that man than anyone else in those days, and Panther invested enough in him that Garen wondered at times if he wasn't the exception to the rule. That all cleared up as soon as Garen found himself at the sword of a few mercenaries that did not like being lied to. For the first time, he truly needed Panther's help. And for the first time, Panther was nowhere to be found.

He hated the man for some time after escaping that mess, but it only reinforced what he learned. "You can really only rely on yourself. Anything else makes life too complicated." He wondered what Panther would think if he saw a stunt like what Garen pulled today.

Probably laugh at me. Tell me how much I still haven't learned.

Garen had a good laugh as well, if for no other reason than how distinctly he could imagine his old friend mouth the response while wagging a finger at him. For a man who called himself by the name of a beast that stalks its prey with stealth and surprise, Panther had to be the most obvious, predictable man he'd ever met.

The train of thoughts bothered Garen as he tried to close his eyes, unsure if he was still experiencing the effects of the poison. Panther was the closest image he could equate to himself in the years past, and now he was living out his life in blatant opposition. That strong-willed, independent Garen had not died quietly the way he might have guessed. He knew that some part of him hated what he did today. That kind of idiotic heroism felt like a disease to the self-reliant side of him. Yet the other half took a tranquil joy in the humble thank you Naia offered him.

Both identities waged war against the other, and Garen tossed and turned, wishing the fight could take place somewhere other than his mind. He finally buried his face in the pillow and had a thought that put the conflict to rest. Tomorrow he would set off to rescue two recent friends and a distant statue of what used to be his father. His actions would decide for him.

CHAPTER
NINETEEN

From the first glimmer of sunrise, Garen made his way down to the meeting room. He expected he would be the first to arrive. Certainly, the others would need their rest before the journey ahead. To his surprise, he found them already waiting. He felt embarrassed to be the last to show, but some part of him was glad to see their anxious dedication.

"Sorry, if I'm late."

"No rush," Kiron said. "We won't be able to do much until sunset. But we are glad to have your input."

"So, what do we know? Has she stopped moving?" Garen asked.

Kiron bent over the table and picked up a geonode trinket. It had a small metal plate with four stones sunken in. He carried it to the map covering the wall and held its flat side against the parchment. Three stones glowed a faint white, while the fourth shined purple. The trinket had more parts than Garen understood, but the purple stone was definitely a tracking geonode. It would be paired to the one inside Morgan and glow brighter as they grew closer.

Garen had seen this kind of spell used to find or follow things before, but it was only helpful to track short distances. Anything more than a city away and the change in brightness would be too miniscule to follow. But this solution was ingenious. Garen had never seen a spell complex enough that it could recognize locations on a map and let the stone glow as if it were really there. Moments like these reminded him there were always deeper magics to discover.

Kiron slid the trinket left until the purple light intensified and filled the room. He cut the spell off, but left the stone pressed against the map. Garen took a few steps toward it until he saw the name of the Western Kingdom's capital beneath it.

"Nhilim? Seriously?" Garen said.

"Yes, it seems Pyralis doesn't want his precious hostages out of sight from his throne," Kiron answered. "Or he has some other reason for keeping them under royal watch. There's a good chance they're within the palace grounds."

Garen's knowledge of Nhilim was all second-hand, but the stories were less than flattering. "How bad of news is this exactly?"

"Well, it's not all bad. Keeping them in the city instead of some hidden facility means we'll be able to approach much easier just by blending in. Unfortunately, that's about the only break we're going to catch. The Western palace was built after the empire split two years ago. As such, I haven't been able to secure any information about the layout. It's possible with time I could, but any amount of waiting is a risk. By the looks of it, we need to make our way there tonight, blind or not."

"Hold on, I thought we had the break-in wonder boy here for these kinds of missions." Naia turned to Garen. "Why don't you just do your invisible thing and slide right in?"

"It's not as simple as just turning invisible. I actually have to bend light around me and into their eyes. So, if they have scouts looking that I don't know of, they can see me. Plus, I'm still practicing the spell on multiple targets. Right now, I couldn't cloak myself against more than four people, let alone an entire palace watch. And those four would need to stand completely still. If someone starts walking, it takes all I have to keep the illusion up for one."

"Yeah, that is a bit disappointing," Naia teased.

Kiron offered Garen no chance to defend himself. "Limited as it may be, it does have some proper uses. If we can get Garen into some higher-security hallways, he won't have to bypass massive sentries, only a few well-placed guards. The problem becomes any Proximity Alarm Geonodes. Naia, Argus, you'll have the task of finding the control room for any PAGs and making sure we can slip in undetected."

"Hold on," Garen paused, looking around the room. "If Naia and Argus are taking that job, who's this 'we' you mentioned. Me and...wait, you're not—?"

"Yes, as a matter of fact, I am. We seem to be a little shy on Spellswords at the moment. And besides, I'd worry myself sick waiting here. This way I get to make sure you don't screw it up in person."

"Are you," Garen had to stop and let out a burst of laughter. "Are you serious? Do we finally get to see your mission-ready, outdoors cloak? Wait, wait, no, I've got a better one. What if we run into someone who recognizes where you bought that shroud? Won't they give away your secret?" Argus and Naia tried to resist, but both couldn't help but join in the laughter.

"Or what about," Garen began, but stopped with a blank look on his face. "Nope, that's all I've got."

"Like it or not, I am coming." Kiron did not share the same amusement as the others.

"Oh no, I'm not against the idea at all," Garen said, desperately trying to keep a straight face. "I think we'll all stay out of trouble with a responsible chaperone like you." Garen lost it once more, chaining into a snicker from Argus.

Kiron let their laughter fade, but Argus chose to break the silence first. "This is gonna be epic. We're gonna smash 'em so hard they'll know what hit em."

Both Garen's and Naia's smile took a curious twist as they looked inquisitively at Argus. Naia raised the obvious question they both had on their minds.

"Don't you mean they *won't* know what hit them?"

Argus looked back and forth between the two of them, equally confused. "You said that they will know what hit them," Garen clarified.

"Well of course I did. When Argus Ashling hits a man, that man don't mistake it for something else. He knows exactly what hit him."

Garen and Naia peered around Argus to make sure they were hearing him right, and sure enough, they both shared the same wide-eyed smile. For that solitary moment, their tired souls let loose of the fears and doubts they had clutched so tightly these past few days. Without a word, they were lost in a laughing fit of their own.

* * * * *

Kiron was right about the ease of infiltrating the city itself. The outer walls of Nhilim had been poorly maintained, sagging and crumbling in more than a few spots. Argus suggested that they cut their way through, but Kiron would not risk any suspicious activity when they did not need to. Silently, each of them was equally afraid the wall might collapse on top of them if they began opening holes in it.

Instead, Kiron had purchased a small cart and grossly underfed donkey from one of the farmers in an outlying village. The poor farmer had probably never seen that much gold in his life. Even around Nhilim, one of the more fertile regions of the west, the badlands did not allow much farming or herding. Instead, the city had to survive on its wealth of mines, smelting, and labor houses.

A high volume of traffic flooded into the city as dusk approached, and they easily slipped in among the miners. Kiron insisted that Garen and Naia were the two most recognizable, and so they had to hide inside the cart. They both shrugged in agreement, but when the moment came to actually climb under the blanket into the small, enclosed space, their expressions changed.

"Are you okay with...?" Garen asked.

"Yeah, why, are you?"

"Oh, of course. I was just, you know, checking."

"No, yeah..."

They climbed in and lay on their backs, shoulders scrunched against the sides and each other. They both tried to slide farther apart from each other, but the sleeveless tunics in the mid-summer's heat left the bare skin pressed up against the other. The contact was casual, innocent, and downright forced, and yet it felt strangely personal. Her skin was smoother than his. This girl beside him, the one that could level a city on a whim, was soft. He could feel her frailty. Though Garen could not tell why, he could feel his heart beating twice the speed at the thought. For a moment he feared in their tight quarters that she could feel the quickened pulse pressed against him. It made it worse that he had no way to find out if she could. The circumstance prevented them from talking even if they had wanted. Still, a forced silence was no less of an awkward silence.

Garen tried to turn his attention to the coarse sackcloth irritating his nose. He could hear the banter of the miners as the cart mingled in with the crowd. Most of the voices told absurd stories laced with curses and innuendos. One voice spoke louder than the others, and Garen realized he was addressing their party.

"It's a bit late to be bringing in food to market, ain't it? Mind if I snatch me some for the missus?"

Garen could hear Argus fumbling with words to stop them from reaching into the cart and finding something unexpected. No simple miner would have any clue what he was looking at if he ripped the cloth away and stared at the two of them. But the surprise might raise a little more commotion than desirable, especially approaching the city gates.

"I don't think that would be wise," Kiron spoke up. "This cart is going to the palace."

The miner gave an angry sigh. "Should've known. Seems everything goes straight to the royal table anymore." Garen gritted his teeth at the truth of their poverty, but with their disguises intact he could at least breathe easier for the moment.

"Say, what's his deal with the cloak? Hiding something?"

Just how did we have to end up next to the most curious miner in the kingdom? This time Argus' voice raised with an answer.

"Ah, he's horribly disfiggered. I'd show you, but you'd probably vomit all over yourself."

"Oh," the miner responded in shock. He looked away and the pitch of his voice lowered. "Well, uh, sorry for asking."

The remainder of the journey was far less eventful. Before long he heard the voices fade away as Kiron steered them toward a secluded part of town. The cart stopped and Argus pulled the cloth away, allowing Garen to finally scratch the burning itch on his nose. Naia seemed more focused on getting out of the cramped space pressed up against him, and he could tell something had gotten into her too. He looked over, expecting some comment about how glad she was to be free of that cart with him. She said nothing, and when she returned the look, Garen realized he had nothing to say either. Thankfully, Kiron commanded their attention.

"We're not far at all from the palace, but I don't think our little cart stunt is going to get us through the citadel gates. They might have the basic caution to inspect what foods we have."

"Alright, so we sneak in," Naia said, brushing the remaining hay from the cart off of her and then turning back to Garen. "Do you have enough sunlight left to get a good look around the palace?"

"I can try." Between the distance and quickly setting sun, what would have been a mildly difficult job became fully taxing. Still, as he pulled light from each corridor he could see the entrance to the next and pulled it his way as well. He repeated the process down several halls and into a few open rooms until he'd scanned the entire layout.

"It looks like a normal palace. Suites, guards, and everything else you'd need to survive in luxury while your people starve."

"What about alarms? Were there any vacant halls marked with PAGs, little glowing dots on ceilings or corners?"

"Not that I saw. The whole place looks like it's just under watch by the guard."

"And you're certain there aren't any corridors walled off, major sections without a door entering them?"

"Nothing more than a few separate, closed rooms. Unless Pyralis can conduct all of his mischief in that tight of a space, they aren't here."

"Or you're just looking in the wrong place." Argus knelt down to the ground and pressed a hand against it.

"Is something strange about the dirt?" Naia asked.

Kiron laughed. "I get it. Where do you hide your hostages from someone making use of light?"

Argus looked up with a toothy grin. "Where the sun don't shine."

CHAPTER
TWENTY

Garen realized in those moments how much he had underappreciated Argus' talents. The gargantuan man had trained for the better half of his life in preparation to become a full-fledged Spellsword, and he had the magic toolbox to prove it. Simple contact with the earth attuned him to its shape and composition. Argus could search for anything out of the ordinary beneath the surface, a skill even Garen couldn't comprehend without using some sort of light.

"Yeah, there's some kind of tunnel running about under here. Thing's a nightmare of a maze. I couldn't tell you where an entrance is."

"So, we dive in?" Garen asked hopefully.

"Not yet we don't. I found our missing PAGs, but they ain't in the tunnels neither." Garen and Naia shared an equal look of confusion. "It's a thick layer a dirt between here and the underground, and there's PAGs stretching out across the whole bit. You try and tunnel right now, they'll know exactly where we're at and exactly what we're doing."

This time Naia wore the clever grin. "That's assuming only one alarm goes off."

"I'm sorry, I don't quite follow you," Kiron prodded.

"So, if two alarms go off," Naia said, "they'll know we're one of two places. And if a hundred go off—"

"They won't have a clue where." Garen happily finished.

"Right, but you're forgetting one part." Kiron lacked their shared enthusiasm. "We may not be telling them where, but we're telling them when. I'd much rather take our time in the palace, find where they monitor the PAGs, and enter unannounced."

"Sorry, boss, but I got to go with Naia on this one," Argus said with a shrug. "Lurking inside some freak's fortress with not a one idea where this room is sounds even riskier."

187

"Plus," Naia added, "we don't even know that this control room is in the palace. If it's underground then we're stuck regardless."

Kiron sighed deeply. "What was I thinking, expecting a covert mission when there's a perfectly good chance to smash things and run in screaming?"

"More importantly," Garen said, "why is that not our motto?"

Naia and Argus set out to make their rounds surrounding the palace. They seemed confident that with enough anchor points between the two of them, they could rip up the dirt and set off the entire grid at once. Garen and Kiron decided to wait in the quiet stretch of Nhilim's market district and sat down between a pair of abandoned stalls. They could hear the shouts and shuffling of a tavern down the street, but at this time of day in a market this sparse, the two of them might as well have been invisible.

They sat in silence for quite some time, but the longer they sat, the more a single thought weighed heavy on Garen's mind. Eventually, sheer compulsion to break the silence pulled it out of him.

"So, you know all those years Amiri, Micah, and Pyralis spent training with my parents?"

"I'm somewhat familiar," Kiron replied, barely above a whisper.

"I can't say I remember everything, but there's one thing that keeps eating at me. How in the world did Pyralis get mixed up in this killing and kidnapping business? Seems like his brothers are content to disappear and hide behind their thrones. Is it strange to wonder why he won't just do the same?"

"Well, as I understand it, Pyralis has always been the passionate one in the family. It's a form of obsession with 'what's fair.' My best guess is he's acting out on some misguided notion related to that. He was always bent on enforcing his brand of self-serving justice."

Garen's memories brought the notion to life. Pyralis could accept any measure of undeserved gift without hesitation:

royalty, magic depth, caring friends and family. But the moment life refused what he assumed to be his, he was the victim, always playing the part in his own tragedy. He was arguably the strongest of his brothers, and yet being the youngest left him over the poorest of the three kingdoms. Now his kingdom was a part of him, and they were the hardworking miners and crafters the world had slighted. Garen still couldn't begin to sympathize with Pyralis, not ever, but he could trace some of the steps that led him there. Each of them seemed to reinforce his chilling mantra. *This world is broken.*

Kiron spoke up again. "Still, don't be so certain his brothers are saints just because they keep out of the obvious trouble. Each of Emperor Tibalt's sons has their own darkness."

"Oh really?" Garen said in surprise, but with enough sarcasm to convey his disbelief.

"It's true. Amiri looks about as polished and upright as any man could from a palace balcony. But he's an utter narcissist. Prideful to the very last drop."

Garen couldn't help but laugh at the words. He had never seen or heard anyone speak poorly of the dignified eldest, and now Kiron had unleashed a full dose of mud-slinging.

"You're laughing, but it's true. The man has all the appearance of a king and all the inner workings of a monster. He's shallow and two-faced, and just like I said, a narcissist. The more the world sees only his good side, the more prideful he gets."

"Wow, you really don't like the guy."

"It's not quite that. I look up to him in a few ways. It's just like I told you, every brother has their own weakness."

"Every brother? Even Micah?" Garen had spent most of his life hating the man for a mistake he made, the mistake that cost his mother her life. But now he could access a reason to hate the man not just for what he did, but for who he was. Kiron could finally unveil the loathsome tyrant and prove to Garen how right he had been to despise the man all along.

"Yes, even Micah."

"You're kidding, how so?" Garen tried to voice his

concern with a genuine gloom, but he was practically salivating for details.

"I find him to be something of a coward. Probably not even kingly material. It's hard to believe he's even cut from the same cloth as Amiri and Pyralis."

"You don't say!"

"I do. And it pains me to acknowledge, but the man lives in isolation, too afraid to let anyone close and too gutless to look his burdens in the eye."

"I wondered why I hadn't seen him or any sign of him around the palace all this time."

"Yes, he doesn't get out much." Kiron paused, hesitant to finish his thought. "But for your sake, I hope you get to meet him one day."

"For his sake, let's hope I don't."

They sat in silence for a while more as Garen replayed the glorious slander in his mind over and over. And the more he did, he couldn't help but wonder about the source.

"Kind of makes me curious what kind of person has a wealth of juicy details like that. I'd just as easily take a look under that hood, but for some reason I can't. Quite the powerful enchantment you have there."

"Sometimes we can't see what we can't bear to imagine."

Garen stopped to ponder the statement and eventually just started laughing. "See, that's why I like you. You're all riddles and mystery, like a shrouded little puzzle box. One of these days though..."

"We'll see."

"Hey, you kids aren't falling asleep, are you?" Argus' voice roused the two from their leisurely posture sitting against the market wall.

"We were thinking about it if you took any longer," Garen said.

Naia turned the corner, clearly hearing his jab. "We just avoided a goffing city's worth of guards and set spell anchors around the entire palace walls. I thought we'd return to a due measure of praise."

"Oh, you did that? I thought you just left to get a drink. Well, then I am impressed beyond words."

Naia rolled her eyes, but she did so with a grin. There could be no mistake that she was warming up to him, or at least didn't want to murder him quite as much.

"Alright, if everyone's ready to start the madness, I say we get a move on," Argus bellowed with enthusiasm.

"It's time," Kiron quietly affirmed.

Argus and Naia looked to each other, counting down from three on their fingers.

"Boom." Argus said the word and the entire city echoed him. Dirt flew into the sky, not enough to wreck the town, but enough to confuse anyone looking outside as much as anyone monitoring the PAGs. Garen had no time to admire the storm of dirt as a hole opened beneath them into the ground. Argus pointed his shield at the metal surface. He shouted and the shield emitted a bright red glow, tearing the metal open and letting them fall straight through into the tunnel. The metal flooring clanked as their feet hit the ground. The air underground had a crisp chill to it, and showers of dirt continued to pour down through the opening. Garen rubbed his arms for a second and tried to shake the dirt from his hair.

"Can you scan up ahead and give us a clue where they might be keeping the others?" Kiron asked.

Garen tried to pull what little light he could, but the scarce, dim glow from a few geonode fixtures didn't help much. "I really can't."

Kiron's sigh gave a clear indication of disappointment, but Garen didn't have any control over his limits. He could create light, but that required bending it down the way, bouncing it off what he wanted to see and pulling it back. He had improved the trick with practice, but it only helped when he knew what direction to look in. He really needed an abundance of light to work with for any searching this broad.

"Alright, looks like we're doing this the old-fashioned way. I'll go with Naia. Garen and Argus take the other direction. Try to work your way along the outer edge and then cut in. With any luck, we'll meet in the center."

Garen and Argus raced down the tunnel to their left and turned the corner to find their first two guards.

"Argus, when I say 'now,' you're going to want to close your eyes, and probably hide behind that shield of yours too."

"Yeah, thanks for the warn—"

"Now!" Garen screamed just as the guards turned to face them. At one point in time, the simple spell had been too bright for even Garen to witness, and he cast it with eyes closed. Now, he had no problem receiving massive amounts of light and gladly watched his blinding spell play out. The overwhelming beam filled the room, and Garen witnessed the look of pain flush the guards' faces. The spell was bright enough to blind a man already staring at the sun, and these two unfortunate souls working underground didn't have a chance. The tunnel returned to its darkened state just as quickly, but the damage had been done.

"Can I look yet?"

"Yes, now."

Argus opened his eyes moments before plowing into the first guard, who had fallen to his knees. Instead, quicker than imaginable for a weapon its size, Argus pulled the war hammer back and swung it upward, shattering the man's jaw. Garen watched the fierce impact and decided his spell was far less cruel. The man would regain his sight much easier than he could put all those teeth back in his mouth.

Meanwhile, Garen grabbed the other soldier who had fallen on his back scratching his eyes. He pinned him against the wall.

"Where are you keeping them?"

"Keeping who?" the guard choked out. Garen didn't care to waste time arguing and tossed him to the side. He continued his sprint down the corridor with Argus closely behind.

They turned corner after corner, always expecting to face another group of the patrol. Corner after corner, they found none. Either Pyralis put a little too much trust in his precious alarms, or the guards had moved very quickly to protect their prisoners. He hoped Naia and Kiron weren't having to do all the heavy lifting. He would never hear the end of it.

Even more curiously, the network of tunnels had several large rooms spread out between them. Many were locked, but this was the kind of situation where producing his own light was most efficient, weaving it in through a keyhole and back. Occasionally, he would see men cowering in the corner while alarms blared, all clearly not the fighting type. Most rooms held nothing but foreign trinkets and scattered bits of parchment with nonsense drawings on them. A few had vats of an indeterminate liquid.

"We're wasting our time along the outer ring. We need to get to the center, now," Garen shouted.

"But we need to meet with the others before—"

"No, I'm not letting them get away!"

Garen took the next fork inward, and Argus reluctantly followed. They were somewhat relieved to encounter a few more guards, and cut through them easily. A little resistance told them they were headed in the right direction. Based on how long it had taken them to sweep along the outer bit, Garen had something of an appreciation for the sheer size of the catacombs. As such, he imagined they still would have quite a stretch of tunnel before reaching any central room. Garen slid to a stop in sheer amazement as they burst into an enormous chamber. The stone ceiling reached as high as they had space underground. Unlike the passageways they had entered from, this room had more than sufficient lighting. Red geonodes lined the columns that seemed to randomly jut up from the ground. Yet the overabundance of thick pillars also cast endless shadows and made even the broad, well-lit chamber feel cramped.

Argus led them cautiously into the expanse. A slow, heavy clap began somewhere in the chamber. They spun around looking for the sound's origin, but the echo seemed to come from all directions. Garen resorted to his more attuned sense and used the glowing red light to scan the room. To his horror, he did not find Morgan, Drake, or even his father. Instead, several dozen palace guards hid in the shadows, and one familiar face stepped out to greet them. He wore a white arming jacket, though everything except his solid black trousers was tainted red by the eerie geonode lighting.

Pyralis stopped his applause and spoke. "Seems we keep running into each other. Are you following me?"

Garen's impulses took control. Before he knew it, he'd unsheathed his katana and sprinted toward him. Pyralis maintained his carefree posture as always, but this time he retrieved something from the pocket of his trousers. Pyralis slowly opened his grip, letting faint purple seep through his fingers. Garen slid to a halt.

"You came all this way, played right into an obvious trap," Pyralis paused to examine the stone in his hand closely, "just for this little thing?" He tossed the geonode at Garen. "Well, you've certainly earned it."

Garen caught it and confirmed the initial fear that froze him. This was the tracking geonode inside Morgan.

"Where is she?" Garen said, pausing to let his rage drip from each word.

"I think the only obvious answer is 'not here.' Otherwise, why would I have cut it out of her?"

Garen burst forward again. Pyralis readied his curved blades and knocked his swing to the side. Strangely, he passed up the obvious counter-attack Garen had left open to him.

"Relax, Naia is alive and well in my care. We both know I didn't kill her."

Garen pivoted as quickly as he could to compensate for the embarrassing mistake. "Of course not. That would just ruin your growing Spellsword collection, since you're clearly not interested in the spirits."

"Oh no, you've got it all wrong. These Spellswords are as worthless as any vessel. But you don't always have to smash the jar to steal the goods. Until we reach Project Theltus, I have three free containers."

The cold language pushed him over the edge again. Garen lunged in with two quick thrusts and used a spell to rattle the ground beneath them. Pyralis managed to stay on his feet to deflect the first stab, but the second gave him no choice but to fall backward. Garen tried to catch him with a low slice as he fell, but Pyralis dropped one of his swords and used the free hand to back-spring onto his feet. He barely rose above the incoming slice.

"I meant what I said, Garen. You have a chance to fix this broken world for good. You are the final piece to this puzzle. We can give it all back and restore the world. Surely you don't think your life is worth more than that, do you?"

The sheer arrogance of his voice drove Garen into another slashing frenzy, but this time the blur of his katana moved too quickly for the single, curved blade to handle. Choosing to take the fight to another level, Pyralis released a torrent of flame. Garen, however, had the advantage on the magic front. He channeled a steady gush of icy water from the tip of his blade, a handy trick he'd borrowed directly from Naia. The column of water engulfed the flame and soaked Pyralis in the process. He shivered and backed away while Garen lunged forward for the open thrust.

For the second time in two days, a surprise met Garen from the ground. The floor cracked, and stones grinded against each other. A broad-shouldered figure emerged in front of him. The Earth Rogue stared back with inexplicable grief. His actions showed no hesitation, though. Before Garen could level his sword at the man, a chunk of stone dug into Garen's side. He stumbled back in pain, once again consumed by helpless anger. It was just like the waterfall. This time, though, he did not have to face him alone. He had friends.

Argus charged with his war hammer raised and swung violently, more aggressive than Garen had ever seen the man before. The Earth Rogue raised a wall to block the strike, but Argus smashed clean through it. The stone may have absorbed most of the blow, but the erupting shrapnel knocked its creator to the ground. Argus didn't hesitate to leap over the debris and swing for a finishing blow. Garen had never seen his friend so ruthlessly engaged in a fight, though he could understand the sentiment. If Argus had trained this long to inherit that spirit, the goal was too close not to give it everything.

Unfortunately, Argus' killing swing never made its intended contact. His feet were ripped out from under him. The whip that wrapped around his legs glowed several shades of green, yellow, and red along its cord. Garen quickly realized the whip had been braided with small, spiked geonodes, and he shuddered to think what kind of spells the weapon would unleash upon its victim. Garen let go of his aching side and moved toward them. Sparks rippled through Argus as he thrashed and screamed.

Garen's eyes followed the cord until he found the twisted person attached to the cruel instrument. A tall, slender figure, unmistakably feminine, held the whip with unnerving confidence. She watched with pleasure as her victim rolled about in agony. Garen could not watch the suffering idly and rushed to wipe the smirk from her pale face.

Had Garen simply been motivated to break the connection with the spell-infused whip, he could have sliced cleanly through the cord. But after seeing the face that could inflict that kind of torture with glee, Garen had a more fitting impulse. He moved quickly and silently, bending the light around him and becoming invisible to his target. She neither saw him coming nor predicted the slice that severed her wrist. Panic swept her trembling body as she stared down at the nub on her right arm. Her lifeless hand still clutched the whip's end as it rolled along the ground. Without her activating the geonodes in the cord, Argus uncurled from his pain and ripped the tether from his legs. The Earth Rogue, however, was back on his feet as well, and he quickly put Argus on the defensive. Bits of stone from the surrounding pillars sailed toward Argus. It took his constant coordination to deflect some with his shield and blast anything else apart in midair.

Meanwhile, the recently disfigured woman beside Garen snapped from the horror of her injury. Garen had become focused enough on Argus' situation that he stopped shielding his image from her. Now her eyes were wide with rage staring at her assailant.

"You bastard!" She clumsily reached for a dagger, but Garen could easily tell she had little control without her dominant hand. She would never be able to get in a slice. Garen misjudged the weapon's purpose entirely. The short blade was lined with more geonodes, and three blue ones along its edge sparked to life. An arc of lightning caught Garen in the chest, rattling him as he fell to his knees. His leather jerkin soaked part of the surge, but he could still feel his limbs growing numb by the second. His teeth grinded so hard he thought they would crack. The tension through his body locked him in place. He tried to stand, but the muscles in his legs didn't respond. Every part of him was clenched too tightly to move from his knees. He had sheer moments before it fried something vital.

He summoned what strength he could to toss his sword at her. The throw was weak by any standard. Even though she stood less than ten feet in front of him, the blade sailed up into the air and fell at her feet. She laughed at the pitiable attempt, not realizing the purpose of the throw. His katana became a lightning rod for him while it hung in the air. In that brief moment, Garen gathered his faculties enough to leave an image of him behind, still frozen in pain. He bent the light around him once more and raced toward the woman who still believed she was in control. His fist struck the side of her neck, dropping her into a crumpled heap on the floor.

He retrieved his katana from beside her. For a moment, he considered using it to remove any chance she might come to. The sight of her severed wrist only further conflicted his feelings about executing an unconscious, maimed woman.

Garen had little time to rehash that dilemma. Pyralis had given the call for his poorly hidden guards to move and close in on them. Garen assumed the armored lackeys wouldn't overcome him in either swordplay or magic. He did, however, fear that the tangle of bodies would cloud the battle, separate him from Argus, and keep Pyralis safe. If he had any chance to gain value from this failed rescue attempt, he would need to either assist Argus in gaining the Earth Spirit, or finish his business with Pyralis for good. A dead mound of guards would accomplish neither.

Garen sidestepped the nearest incoming blade and

dodged his way along the outside of the chamber, trying to find either of the targets. In scanning the room, he saw another soldier rushing at him. Garen parried the first stab and rolled forward under the high slice that followed. Garen brought his sword up to deflect the next blow as soon as the guard turned around to face him, but the strike never came. Garen paused his search for Argus to look at his missing enemy. He found the man standing right where he left him, only Garen hadn't frozen him solid against the pillar.

"Always running, aren't you?" Naia said.

"Oh, you know, just saving some for you."

Naia and Kiron both emerged from the tunnel.

"It was another trap," Garen said. "Argus has the earth guy in his sights somewhere and Pyralis is in there too. But we were right. He is collecting them, keeping them alive, and he said something about a project."

"It's fine, we can still use this. Na—Morgan," Kiron corrected himself, looking around suspiciously. "Find Argus and assist him. Garen, you're with me. Let's settle this."

Garen raced through the columns alongside Kiron. The deep bonds of trust forged in their training sessions came to life. They turned aside guard after guard in remarkable sync, cutting a path to Pyralis. Finally, they saw him surrounded by his soldiers in the red light.

"Garen, I thought you'd run off," Pyralis shouted. "Now I see you just needed a friend to make the fight fair."

Garen looked to Kiron for some sort of response, but he remained silent and head kept low.

"Come on, let's do this," Garen whispered.

"Looks like your friend is a little shy. Fortunately, I'm not." Pyralis charged with his surrounding forces. These soldiers were more skilled than the brutes they'd faced so far. Garen very quickly realized that even two of the king's royal guards could hold him back. Garen would occasionally gain the advantage with a well-placed spell, even mimicking Naia by freezing one man against a pillar as he brushed past it. But Garen was no Water Spellsword, and the man easily broke free from the thin bonds.

He noticed Kiron was having even less luck, slowly losing ground and risking some close swings. Garen delayed one of his attackers with a burst of light and moved to help his friend. Pyralis saw the movement and stepped in his way, meeting swords. He stared into Garen's eyes with a smile.

"It looks like someone in this room isn't who they claim to be."

Garen parried his blade down and stepped back in terror. If Pyralis had figured out Naia's identity, Morgan couldn't be safe. He swung lower from the hip, again meeting his block.

"How did he do it?" Pyralis casually asked between clashes.

He? Who is he talking about?

"How did he do what?" Garen said, focusing now on the two men rushing at his back.

"How he got you to forgive him. I thought you'd go to your grave hating that man. Unless you don't—"

Pyralis disengaged, allowing Garen to turn entirely. With momentum on their side, the two royal guards kept Garen on the defensive. He couldn't risk any counter-cuts against these two. He back-pedaled their advances and sidestepped until Pyralis came into view. The king stood motionless, mouth gaping. Garen had seen a variety of emotions course through his childhood friend, but never this kind of pure shock. Pyralis had a way of playing off any measure of the unanticipated, never giving the appearance that someone had actually thought ahead of him. And yet now Pyralis stood with his jaw down, absolutely dumbfounded for all to see.

The daze in his eyes snapped into a wicked smile, even holding back laughter. "Guards, cease," Pyralis shouted. His soldiers obeyed instantly and stepped out of reach. Kiron dropped to one knee and panted heavily.

"Your associate had me curious. So, with a little fire-light, I took a peak. I hope I didn't burn you, old friend."

"Shut up," Garen screamed. "I don't care how you know him, it doesn't change a thing."

"Oh, it doesn't? I think you'll change your mind when I—"

"No, Garen, I'm sorry. I should have told you sooner," Kiron coughed out.

Garen's anger turned to an honest confusion, softened by the outright contrition in Kiron's voice.

"Oh, he's in the humbled position now," Pyralis said, "but indeed we should be bowing to him."

"Kiron?" Garen looked to his shrouded friend, searching for an answer to the mystery.

"No, I don't think 'Kiron' is right," Pyralis said with an artificial uncertainty. "At least that's not what we called him growing up."

Garen looked back at Pyralis, eyes wide and brow furrowed in horror.

It's not possible. I would have...he couldn't be.

"Garen, greet your sworn enemy, your king, and most notably, my brother," Pyralis paused, savoring the taste of words he could not wait to let flow from his grinning lips. "His Majesty, King Micah."

Garen turned to Kiron for some sort of explanation, but instead he rose to his feet and pulled back the hood. The unmasking revealed no horrific scars or burns, as Garen sometimes imagined would line his face. But Kiron, no Micah, was right when he once said, "you won't like what you see." From an outside perspective, it must have looked like Garen stared down a monster. Garen did see the monster beneath the short dark hair and remorseful brown eyes. He saw the man that his mother once trusted with her life. And now, through deception, tricked him into doing the same.

The closeness of their bond from a moment ago transformed into a scalding metal plate grafted to his skin. The contact burned inside him, too deep to remove. He stared down the king he despised, brimming with the rage of his betrayal. Yet another impulse found its way into Garen's overflowing mind: regret. Though it violated every natural emotion he felt, he had watched Micah prove his loyalty and friendship, and Garen knew that he could not dismiss him as the same uncaring villain he once did. That shimmering ray of hope had little chance of competing with the fresh and searing wound of his fraud, but it confused him just the same.

"Alright, I think he gets the point," Pyralis said, his excitement having faded. "Tranquilize him and Micah. Kill the rest."

Garen snapped from his stare and looked to his other enemy, internally torn between so much loathing. The complexity of his situation overwhelmed him. Garen found himself frozen, staring down the guards charging at him. None of it mattered. All he wanted was a life less complicated. He hated complications, and he would give anything to go back to a place without them. A place with...

CHAPTER
TWENTY-ONE

"Panther?"

"Garen? How in the lifetime of a tortoise did you get here?"

Garen spun around, trying to find the answer to the question. The dark bedchamber told him nothing.

"I don't particularly know." The sight of more uncertain surroundings did not offer Garen the escape from complications he sought. The frustration returned and he turned to look for a door. "I need to get out of here."

Panther shook his head and looked him over. His eyes stopped on Garen's katana, still unsheathed and coated in blood. Garen cleaned the blade and put it away. "You really don't know?"

"Not a clue. But I'm not staying."

"You and me both, then. But don't go empty handed. Fill this with as much shiny as you can find on the way out." Panther tossed Garen an empty sack. He felt somewhat conflicted about looting the house of a man he didn't know, but started mindlessly tossing valuables into it anyway. His full attention was not on whatever heist he'd fallen into.

"Have you been following me or something?" Panther said, poking his eye into a dusty old jewelry box.

"No, I just kind of," Garen paused, unsure why he was about to tell the truth. "I got myself into trouble, and I was longing for a time before things got complicated. I just closed my eyes and showed up next to you."

"You've got some weirdly powerful eyes then. But I'm glad that blood I saw wasn't from nearby." Panther clamped his teeth down on a gold bracelet, made a disappointed face, and tossed it in his bag anyway. "So, you got yourself mixed up in other people's business? Didn't I teach you the most important—
"

"Never invest. Always get paid. Yeah, you mentioned it."

"What did you get yourself into?"

Despite his instinct around Panther to tell the truth, he would happily avoid the specifics. "I tried to make friends and work with others for a change. They just didn't turn out to be who I thought they were."

"Uh, Garen, you're breaking my heart. You can't go working in other people's business. You've still got a lot to learn." Garen saw the contradictions of his friend's advice just as clear now as he had at a younger age. Panther claimed he was teaching the boy to never help others without personal gain, but he employed him the whole time doing just that. And if Panther did try to make it worth his time, he'd be breaking his own rule. Either way, the man kept on rummaging and pilfering, convinced he had the secrets to life figured out.

A creaking sound grabbed both of their attentions. The boards squeaked louder as the sound approached them.

"Panther, who lives here?" Garen whispered with sudden urgency.

"Not someone I'd like to face off with."

Great. At least Panther hasn't stopped robbing people that could squash him into a pulp.

"Okay, listen. Do not move, no matter what." Garen took a step closer, standing directly in front of Panther. The doorknob turned, giving Garen a fraction of a second to find the eyes of his target. He had a stunned moment when he realized the intruder was female, but the light found her eyes just the same. She peeked into the empty room, breathed a sigh of relief, and left.

Garen did not feel like risking the creaking floor to alert her again. He summoned a small disc of wind that carried them both to the window. They opened and climbed out as quickly and quietly as possible. Garen nearly jumped straight out, but Panther's hand on his shoulder told him to look down first. The house had been constructed on bamboo stilts and a thick, black swamp awaited him below. Garen recomposed the disc, helped Panther onto it, and made their way out of the area with two sacks nearly full of assorted valuables. Once he made it to a solid looking patch of dirt, he brought them down and let Panther take the lead.

Garen wanted to ask about his old friend's move to the swamp. His previously dealings had been in northern mountain villages. But the more pressing question on his mind had to come out. "So, who did we just rob exactly?"

"Oh, that would be my ex-wife."

"You're kidding me. You, *you* got married?"

"Yeah, I gave it a try. Lots of value to be had, you know?"

If laughter wasn't the furthest emotion from Garen's mind, he might have chuckled at the idea of his self-absorbed comrade promising to share his life with another human. "So, let me guess. It didn't work out?"

"That woman is greedy to the core!"

"Of course she is," Garen sighed.

"Alright, fine then, let's hear an answer from you. How exactly did you keep her from seeing us? Your new friends teach you some crazy mind control secrets?"

"No, nothing like that." Garen considered explaining the sensation of actually bending each strand of light, but even he wasn't sure of the specifics anymore. He just knew how it felt and that the spell worked. "Let's just say I can alter what people see."

"Count the feathers on a turkey, you're telling me you can make yourself invisible?"

"With its limits, sort of." Garen could see the cogs turning in his predictable friend's mind. They walked in silence for a moment until finally reaching Panther's home. The residence had a similar construction to the other wooden huts they'd passed, except for the massive tree sprouting up from the center of the building. Garen guessed the use of natural terrain aided the bamboo stilts with a little more stability, especially for a house three times the size of most huts in such an outcast territory.

A few geonodes lit the inside of the expansive living quarters. The main room was cluttered with glimmering trinkets carelessly piled around the edge, but the distinct lack of furnishings still made the room feel enormous. Beside the doorway to Panther's personal chambers, he did have a large dining table, and Garen was surprised to see two chairs pulled up to it. He had no idea whom the other chair might exist for, unless Panther found it easier to con a man out of his life savings easier if he was sitting.

"So, how did you build all this?" Garen asked, knowing well that his friend would sooner cut off his own hands than pay someone for this kind of labor.

"Goodness no. I don't know how to rig a place like this up on those bamboo poles and the like. I hired a group to build it for me."

"You're serious? Panther, I feel like I don't even know you anymore, paying honest men for their work and all."

"Never said I paid them. Seemed some troubles and debts from their past showed up right before I could give them what they earned."

Garen found an honest laugh and set his fears to rest. This was the same man as ever. They chatted for a while longer, Garen carefully keeping the topic from where he'd come from. He was much happier to let his mind escape into the stories of Panther and the mishaps that led him to the southern reaches of the Central Kingdom. Eventually, the crafty storyteller grew tired and let Garen know as much.

"Sorry I don't have an extra bed," Panther yawned, telling Garen nothing he hadn't already guessed.

Garen didn't realize how tired he was until he curled up against the hard floor. He found a sack of stolen clothes against the wall and rested his head on it. He didn't wait up for Panther to offer anything else. Garen knew he wouldn't. If things were like the old days, Garen could help himself to whatever he cared for, and Panther would merely complain about him taking all the fresh fruit or likewise.

His thoughts did not stay focused long on the simple life with Panther. He could not help but wonder how Naia and Argus fared after he left. He left so suddenly that he didn't have time to notice if Argus had overpowered the Earth Rogue. Maybe he did, and then Argus and Naia could have handled that fight. A voice nagged at him, reminding him how impossible it felt trying to fight against that level of earth magic. If Drake and Garen had each failed, what hope did Argus have?

Guilt tried to gain a foothold, but he tossed and turned, reminding himself that they weren't his problem. They were Micah's pawns and could take care of themselves. They could trust that man right up until it cost them their lives, just like his mother. But Garen wouldn't be another casualty. He'd lived the dreams of other people for too long, and though he hadn't felt the suffocation at the time, he could certainly breathe easier now. He had forgotten the novelty of absolute freedom, nothing shackling him to an absurd duty or someone else's problems. No more following ill-conceived plans and walking straight into deliberate traps. He could find his father some other way, any other way he chose. Or, Garen dared to consider, not at all. Perhaps his father wasn't alive like Pyralis kept leading them on to believe. Maybe that was his bait, trying to lure Garen in to complete his collection. Just a part of his ridiculous scheme.

What did he call it? Project Theltus?

He didn't know, and he didn't care. All those concerns were behind him. At first, he didn't expect to sleep easily that night. But with the renewed vigor of his independence, he quickly dozed off, unburdened of all his complications.

CHAPTER

TWENTY-TWO

Though he found rest, he did not hold onto it easily. Garen tossed and turned through the night. He woke repeatedly, each time haunted by the scattered details of his dreams. But he chose to blame his unrest on the hard-wooden beams supporting his spine. Eventually, a spicy aroma woke him. He looked over and found Panther sitting at his table, slurping his soup.

"Is that...?"

"Leek stew," Panther said. "With a kick."

"For breakfast?" Garen asked, rubbing his eyes.

"Better than any other time. Spice tends to rally the troops, especially as I'm getting up there in age."

Garen noticed in the morning light that the years had not worn well on him. The man seemed shorter, smaller. Whether it was Garen's own growth spurt or not, the effect was the same. He walked over, but Panther didn't bother to look up, and left Garen staring over the top of his thinning tangle of black hair. He looked down into the pot to decide if he would venture the meal, but at a closer proximity to the pungent odor, Garen took a seat without grabbing a bowl.

"So, you still moving around with your crazy father? Or you got him locked up somewhere?" Panther had never cared much for subtly. Or tact for that matter.

"No, but someone else does."

"Eh, their problem now. I told you he's not your dad anymore. It's just a statue of him. Looks like him, but it isn't."

"Yeah, you've mentioned that," Garen said.

"So, you don't owe him nothing. Besides, with him you were always investing, never getting paid. See how that's backwards from—"

"Yeah, I get it," Garen interrupted. He wondered if Panther ever had parents. "Sorry," he quickly added, careful not to offend his only source of hospitality in a strange new environment. "I've just got a lot on my mind right now."

"Well, lucky for you, I've got just the thing to take your mind off whatever's bothering you."

Garen had seen the possibilities rolling in front of Panther's eyes from the moment he learned about Garen's abilities. He knew the wild scheme would come tumbling out sooner or later, but he hadn't decided if he would take it or not. For the first time in quite a while, the world was open to his taking. He didn't mind the nostalgia or aid of his current setting. He just wasn't ready to join some new team.

"Listen, Panther, I don't want to get too deep into—"

"Say no more. I get it. You don't want any more complications."

"Yeah, something like that," Garen said.

"That's a good thing. Tells me you're learning. And you don't owe me nothing, so you have as much right as any man to tell me no. I also know that you're going to get crazier than a honey-less beehive just sitting around here. If you ever get bored..."

"You'll find an adventure to keep me busy." Garen started to smile. Panther's manipulation was obvious, but that didn't make it any less effective. "Alright, what do you have?"

Panther slurped another spoonful and slid the bowl away in excitement. "Ha, you're going to love it. I've been scoping out a place due north of here for most of the season. The home is massive and secluded, just inside the Central Kingdom's territory. Locals tell me he's some rich collector, priceless geonodes and the like."

"Yeah, I know the type. And we both know it's a suicide mission." Garen said. "I can rob clueless rich people. Geonode collectors actually know how to protect what they have."

Garen reached for the bowl Panther had left unfinished and tried some. The spice didn't counteract any of the bitterness, and it was a pitiful combination at any hour of the day. But it was better than listening to his stomach growl. He swallowed another spoonful.

"That was my first thought too. But I decided to check it

out just to see if there was any chance. Frankly, there isn't as much work as I'd hoped this far south."

"Alright, and you found an unguarded entrance with no alarms between it and the goods?"

"Better," Panther said with a grin. "I found a window of time that he turns off every PAG in the place."

Garen's eyebrows rose at the idea, but his piqued curiosity didn't dispel the obvious reservations. "Every alarm in the estate? How can you even know that?"

"I have a friend with the tools to do a full magical sweep, and I called in a favor."

"A favor?" Garen said, nearly choking in surprise. "I thought you didn't invest in people."

"Fine, not so much a favor as I blackmailed him. But it's true. Only alarms left in the place are small cage sensors on the pricier items—"

"—which I can remove—"

"—which you can remove. But guess when he turns the PAGs off?"

Garen pondered for a moment what would cause a wealthy collector to unprotect his valuables. "Special occasions? Temporary insanity?"

"Then it's a mad-man's holiday for every second he's at home."

"Wait, are you saying?"

"That he locks the place up like a freak's fortress when he's away on business, then turns the whole lot off when he's there? Yeah, I'm saying."

Garen still had his doubts, but the situation at least looked feasible. "Alright, so how many guards are we talking about?"

Panther began to laugh.

"Oh great," Garen moaned. "It's an absurd number, isn't it? Tell me it's less than ten."

"How about zero?"

Garen joined in the laughing. "What is wrong with this guy? Why haven't you just walked in there and taken it all for

211

yourself?"

"Eh, the man keeps to himself, but he does have some dogs. Noisy little critters too."

"That might explain the lack of alarms. Doesn't want them setting off his own security. Still, they're just common hounds, right? That's never stopped you before."

Panther sighed in frustration. "You want to know? He's gotten up in my brain, Garen. I rob paranoid and cautious people, and I like their insecurities because it tells me they're weak. This guy is practically welcoming a goffing invasion this close to the Outer Bog, and I bet he sleeps like a stump. It's unnerving."

Garen could empathize with the feeling. Where Panther found comfort, Garen always felt a personal justification for stealing from those who could not protect their own. Perhaps this man could rise to that challenge.

"Alright, you've sold me. So, when do we strike?"

"Ha, I knew it was your style," Panther celebrated. "If he holds to his usual routine of coming and going, he'll be back in three days."

"Three days it is then." Garen leaned back in his chair and put his hands behind his head. Life from this seat felt infinitely better. There was no one manipulating him from behind a hood to join their twisted little team. Just the thrill of a mission without being tied to their group, and best of all, not a complication in sight.

* * * * *

The three days did not pass as quickly as Garen had hoped. For all the joy he felt for the return of his freedom, he had little clue what to do with it. He felt like a man inheriting a fortune, but stranded from anywhere to spend it. Even worse, the nightmares had not disappeared along with his outer concerns. Each night they continued to gnaw at his resolve. His dreams would take him to a metal grating. Hands reached up at him. He knew the hands were his friends, but all he could do was kick them back and escape their grip. He could never seem to leave them entirely. He felt responsible, as if he had somehow put them there. The nightmare would end, and Garen would have to dispel the fears and doubts with his own truth. He would switch back and forth between igniting his hatred for Micah and telling himself his father was beyond saving. And each time it almost worked.

On the third day he woke with a relentless wet cough. He tried to move around and shake the feeling off, but his whole body felt bogged down. His joints were stiff and sluggish. Panther took one look at Garen and recognized the symptoms.

"You've got the swamp sickness."

"The what?" Garen asked, searching for a chair to fall back into.

"Well, that's what I call it anyway. Hit me too a few days after I moved here, something about the thick gunk in the air. I should have thought of that before I planned the break in. You're going to feel worse than a sunburnt naked mole rat for another day or so."

"Good to know," Garen slunk back against the wall, "but I think I can still manage." Garen had no idea if it was true or not, but he knew he wanted to. The sooner he finished this job, the sooner he could move away from it all and start his own life.

"Are you sure? Just remember, you don't owe me nothing."

Garen nodded, but something deeper in him disagreed. Panther had invested in him years ago. Contrary to the man's own teaching, it made sense he be paid for it.

"No, I want to. Besides, I never get sick. There's no way this will last until tonight."

Garen regretted those words as they hiked northward out of the swamp. While the crisp, dry air of the plains soothed the ache, Garen still wanted to fall face-first into every lush tuft of grass he stepped through. Finally, the estate appeared as a speck on the horizon and slowly grew into the impressive mansion Panther described. They found a spot to lay back and survey, and Garen was only too glad to conceal himself in the overgrown field.

Shortly before dusk, a black levitrans pulled up to the house. A tall man casually stepped out and strode his way inside.

"Not even a servant to greet him at the door. This guy really likes to keep to himself," Panther said.

Garen would normally assume the same, but something about the man's relaxed demeanor told him otherwise. "I don't know. Maybe he doesn't want to be pampered. Just because you're rich doesn't mean you want servants to do everything for you."

"I know I would. You think if I had that kind of money I'd open another door for myself in all my life?"

"Panther, I'm not sure if you'd even bother to feed yourself at that point."

He stopped and pondered the idea. "I think that might be crossing a few boundaries, but I'd sure try it. That would let me just lean back and…"

"Shhh," Garen said with a poke at his friend's side. "There's another levitrans pulling up."

"Oh great, I knew this whole no guard thing had to be a fluke. He's probably got some high dollar mercenary guarding the grounds now and I don't want to—"

"Shh already! I don't think this guy is quite the security type." Indeed, the man wore a belted blue tunic that came to his feet, and had enough Eastern-fashioned jewelry on him to suggest nobility. The owner of the estate came back outside and greeted the man with a hug, further validating the guess. "It's just a friend."

Garen stopped and imagined himself on the other side of the field, greeting a friend at his humble mansion. He had the open world in front of him and a chance to create any life he might choose. Would it look like this? A normal, friendly man faking the life of a wealthy hermit?

The hours dragged on. They had to arrive before sundown for Garen to get a clear view of the inner layout, but they couldn't make a move until the middle of the night. Garen was actually glad to lie down and try to conserve strength in his body. The noble visitor left mid-evening, but they chose to wait another few hours just to ensure he would be asleep. Garen was about ready to doze off when Panther shook him and signaled for them to move in.

They approached with caution, but felt increasingly foolish doing so. It became obvious that no one was watching or even cared about their suspicious activity. Garen found the wide glass windows he had spotted from the distance. It was rare to see them this massive. They probably had to import it from the industrial magi. Garen had no guilt ruining the expensive material as he carved into it with a precise beam of fire. The edges melted in a wide arc until it formed a circle. Garen lifted the pane of glass out, and they climbed through the opening.

Garen conjured a tiny orb of light in his hand and led them to a curious room he'd spotted earlier. The faint light revealed display case after case of geonode-enhanced weapons. Some were clearly antiques of first design. Some looked fearsome enough to use on the spot. He saw a dozen swords with the magical ore inlaid in the handle or along the blade. The imbued spells made the weapons sharper or lighter, and most men would pay handsomely for the craftsmanship. Garen never cared much for the feel of them. He trusted the weight and blade of his katana as it was forged. These enhancements usually deceived their wielders as much as they helped them.

Garen brought his focus back to their objective and again felt at unease. Considering the number of traps he had walked into lately, the ease of this mission did not sit well with him.

"I'm starting to think this was a bad idea," Garen whispered.

Panther gave no response, only made his way to the first display case. They both froze at the distant clicking sound against the marble floor. The quick, faint steps clearly belonged to an animal rather than human, but he didn't feel like meeting either right now. He was just getting the hang of bending light around two people. Trying to do so at a dog's eye level would provide another unwelcome challenge.

He had no time to complain and quickly sent the illusion into the mastiff's eyes as it turned the corner. The dog looked up and around for a second and returned its focus to the ground. Garen breathed a sigh of relief. It had worked. The animal looked right through them without a peep. Garen watched as the dog sniffed the ground and continued toward them.

Oh, right. That.

His eyes filled with panic at the sense he could not control. What would happen when the creature followed the scent and bumped into an invisible leg? If Garen could smell Panther's unique odor, this thing wouldn't have a problem.

Without any other options available to them, the two intruders stood in perfect stillness, hoping the animal might trust his eyes over his nose. The dog continued sniffing its way toward them, still oblivious to what scent he was following. Unfortunately, Garen's congestion added some difficulties to his stealth. He could hold back the aching cough in his throat, but the overload of mucus presented another problem. His eyes squinted and mouth opened. In turn, Panther's eyes bulged as he shook his head side to side. His disapproval could not stop the inevitable. Garen sneezed. The mastiff erupted in alarm, and his barking echoed through the entire house. Garen wasted no time to sprint for the exit, but Panther turned instead to the display cases.

"What are you doing?" Garen shouted.

"He knows we're here. Might as well make our exit with a few treasures, right?"

There were a hundred reasons not to. Every second counted in this moment. And nothing in those cases could be worth his life. They were lucky enough the dog kept his distance, howling his alarm through the house instead of tearing into them. A second animal barked from deeper within the home too and Garen heard sounds of it moving toward them. It was outrageous to do anything other than run. Unfortunately, that meant no time to argue with Panther either, and he wouldn't abandon someone in a moment like this.

A vision of himself under Nhilim flashed into his mind. He saw the faces of Naia and Argus reaching through the metal grating of his nightmares. He abandoned them. Suddenly his flight stood in clear contrast to his identity. If he had the common sense not to abandon Panther, why did he think it was okay to abandon the others?

He ran to his friend and smashed open the glass case in front of him. Garen's panic and haste overrode any common-sense for what traps it could trigger. He reached in to remove the jewel-encrusted axe, and a quick burst of gas hit him in the face. Garen stumbled and fell backward. His eyes and throat burned. His vision fogged over. He saw Panther staring down at him.

"Get us out of here," Garen choked out through the haze. Panther looked down in pity, the wheels turning once again in his companion's predictable mind. Self-preservation overtook any human concern. The first few steps away spoke of regret, but he eventually turned and sprinted out of the room.

Abandoned. So, this is what it feels like.

His consciousness faded without any anger toward Panther's desertion. His disappointment turned inward for becoming just like him.

CHAPTER
TWENTY-THREE

Garen's eyes opened slowly, a feeling he couldn't say he ever expected to feel again. Even more strangely, he was not bound or restrained in any way. Instead, he laid freely on a remarkably soft surface. He sat up and looked around, thinking from the soft feel of a bed that he had wound up once more in Vikar-Tola. Instantly, the foreign surroundings told him this was not his chamber.

"Oh, good. You're up."

Garen turned to the unfamiliar voice entering the room. The movement sent pain coursing through his stomach and reminded him of his current illness.

"Who are you?" Garen asked through the discomfort. He vaguely recognized him as the owner of the estate, a tall, middle-aged man with short brown hair. Garen noticed a kindness in his eyes and a warm smile spread between the edges of his sharply-lined face. For someone talking to the thief he'd just caught, his entire expression seemed out of place.

"I take it you don't bother to learn names before you cart off a person's most valuable possessions. That's very inconsiderate, don't you think?"

Garen raised an eyebrow, but decided to play along. "Yes, not learning your name was the most inconsiderate thing I did to you today."

"It was, but no matter now. My name is Idrian. May I ask yours?"

"Not if you intend to put my head on display. I think I'd prefer the placard to read 'Stupid, Nameless Thief.'"

"A thief who uses the word placard? No, I don't think 'stupid' will do. Regardless, I'm not going to kill you."

"Oh, a live exhibit? You know, I've always been something of a performer." Garen expected a frustrated response, but Idrian held his calm posture.

"I'm not joking. If you're well enough to move, you're free to go. I have no intention to pursue you. I asked merely out of politeness."

Politeness?

The man was either insane or from an entirely different world. Garen searched Idrian's aged smile for the catch. Finally, Garen shook his head and stood up from the bed. His joints still felt sluggish, but it would take a good deal more pain to keep him in an awkward setting like this any longer. He made it halfway to the door when the mystery overwhelmed him. Idrian's mercy stood in perfect contrast with Panther's philosophy, which wouldn't do a favor even on a promised reward. Garen was familiar with the greedy ideal to receive without giving. He knew very little of men who could give without receiving. It intrigued him, but he'd walked away from curiosities before. This was different. It called into question the very assumptions he could make of a man. He walked to the door, and more than anything he wanted to exit without saying a word. Idrian stood perfectly still behind him, not saying a word. Garen clenched the sides of the doorframe, infuriated by this man's confidence that he couldn't leave without asking. And equally frustrated at how correct he was.

Garen turned back. "Why?"

Idrian smiled. "Because I used to live just like you. I'd pick challenging marks and rob them blind. I'd like to think I was quite good. But one day I broke into a house I had no business in. A very wise man caught me and sat me down. You might have even heard of the Fire Spellsword. His name was Seth Renyld."

Garen swallowed hard and tried to hide the surprise on his face.

"So, you do know the man?" Idrian asked. Garen did not like the feeling that he was being read.

"Only in myth," Garen replied. He wasn't sure how his father would tie into this story, and would prefer to keep his own relation a secret at the moment.

"Yes, and there are plenty of those. But he was very much a real man, the kind neither street-gossip nor fireside

220

exaggerations seem to capture. He caught me breaking in. The man was half-asleep and still he bested me without effort. I could tell how angry he was with me, but instead of finishing me off, he sat down next to me. He told me he had a son on the way. He said he couldn't stand to raise a child where everyone took as they pleased. He said he'd let me go if I made him a promise. He wanted a better world for his son, and he asked if I'd help. It began a very unlikely friendship between us. But that night he taught me a truth that I have never forgotten in all these years."

Garen knew the phrase the man taught him because his father instilled it deeply within him as well. He had buried the sentiment along with all the other moralistic, irrelevant teachings of his youth. In this moment, however, the ancient memory raced to the surface and that irrelevance dissolved. If Garen cared to expose his identity, he could have mouthed the words along with him.

"The greatest life is lived in true community, where everyone gets because everyone gives."

Garen's eyes welled up. His father had told this man one thing, and Idrian found a better way to live. How many years had his father dedicated to raising his son, and Garen still failed to learn that simple concept? He marveled that even though they had taken his father's mind and enslaved his body, his legacy could not be caged. Garen spent so many years imagining that he was the one trying to rescue his father. Now he understood the true order of it all. Even in this moment, his father was fighting for him. He feared he might break down in front of this stranger, but the flooding memories of patient lessons brought him greater peace than anguish.

"I have somewhere I need to be," Garen choked out. The clarity of the moment made him wonder how he ever gave up on his father before.

Idrian simply nodded his head. "I have a spare horse if you need to get there quickly."

Garen did not accept gifts easily. In light of their conversation, however, he knew that he could, and he did.

* * * * *

It had been years since he'd saddled a horse. They were easy enough to steal, but they weren't worth the extra mouth to feed for long. It was especially true during the year he fled north with his father and found himself venturing in and out of the mountainous Te'ens. Thankfully, his childhood education had centered on useful skills such as those in place of martial training. Even once his mother passed and his father began taking him on escort missions, learning how to judge a horse and keep them from spooking was occasionally valuable.

Idrian's stable was a meager outcropping of his home, but it had all Garen needed to tack up. The horse itself was exceptional, far livelier than he expected. He wasn't sure exactly how far from Vikar-Tola they were, but Idrian assured him he could make it well before nightfall if he rode hard enough. Garen assumed it meant they were closer than he realized. Once he set out, it became clear Idrian's confidence was in his steed rather than the distance.

It ran faster than any man's spare should. Still, the ride stretched on for an eternity in his mind. It started with an optimistic joy, the kind of serenity from knowing he was on the right path. The longer he rode, however, traces of shame began to haunt him. If the Spellswords were back in the palace, then they would know he left them to die. And that was his luckiest possibility. For all he knew, none of them made it out alive. The idea turned his stomach, and he refused to imagine what that would mean for him. Somewhere buried in his mind, he knew he might be the last free Spellsword, the only person between Pyralis and his selfish ambitions.

Garen arrived late in the afternoon as predicted. He followed Idrian's instruction to leave the horse with the guard's stable, and they responded to Idrian's name with surprising deference. Garen considered asking why, but he had more pressing questions. His route to the palace took him through the market district. The city had calmed from the height of its morning bustle, and most of the remaining commotion was spent

222

tearing down shop. He stopped the first person he saw gossiping with a customer and asked her what had everyone so riled up.

"You haven't heard?" the large woman dropped her previous conversation and stared at him with wide eyes. "It's King Micah. He was supposed to give his mid-summer address today but he never showed."

"So what?" the other woman picked lazily through the apples on the cart. "You know he's not much on public appearance. Maybe he just decided not to."

"Yes, but he's never missed an address before. And why would the officials gather the city and prepare for his speech if they knew he wasn't going to do it, huh? Oh, and another thing," she turned back to Garen, "I have it on good word from a friend that works in the palace kitchen that she hasn't prepared anything for the King in almost a week! Shy or not, King has to eat, right?"

"Bah, you and your friends are always making up stories out of nothing."

Garen did not stick around to hear them argue any further. Micah might have to disappear from one life rather often to live a second, but Garen knew where to find them both. As much as he dreaded entering into their halls, he could not waste any more time on second-hand guesses. He had to find out for himself.

Still, the gut-wrenching possibilities twisted into him as the guards let him pass into the palace. If Micah really was missing, he could not imagine a scenario where Naia and Argus would flee without their king, leader, and mentor. Before he even stepped foot on their private halls, he could feel the empty chill of their rooms, the blank stare of the meeting table. The vacant space would scream, "Why?" and Garen had no answer. He wanted to blame it on his hatred for Micah, but true as it was, he could no longer pretend that justified his actions. He took a deep breath and held it, as if the choking fumes of regret beyond the door would suffocate him. Slowly, he turned his key in the unmarked door leading to their hall. He didn't want to push it open, but it had to be done. He stepped inside.

223

"Argus? Tell me that's you!"

The mammoth of a man strode his way over to him, and Garen couldn't remember the last time he was this happy to see his bulbous fingers outstretched for him. Garen hated the backbreaking force of a hug from the man, but he had found no way to avoid them thus far, and for the first time, ran intentionally into the heavy embrace.

The arms closed around him tighter than even he remembered, pushing the air right out of his lungs. "Ok big guy, happy to see you too. But you're about to pop me," Garen choked out with the last of his air. Argus did not release the grip. Without any air left to squeak another protest, Garen flailed his legs to deliver the obvious message. Still, the bear hug did not relent, and Garen began to worry less about his breathing and more about his spine. He continued to kick and squirm, but the grip only tightened. He craned his head to the side as much as he could at the sound of footsteps approaching.

Naia walked steadily toward them with a blank expression on her face, her eyes glazed over and lifeless. Garen tried to squeeze another plea for help, but nothing came out. Her steady march continued until she stood directly beside him. He knew she would be furious with him, but she showed no emotion at all. Garen searched her dead stare for any desire of revenge. Her glassy eyes showed no trace. She reached up and stabbed a small needle into his neck. He couldn't tell whether the lack of air or the needle's poison took effect first, but the corners of his vision grew dark and then faded away completely.

CHAPTER
TWENTY-FOUR

The grass stretched between his toes, a lush and comforting feeling for such uncalloused feet. Garen stared out at the flat horizon, fields of perfect, waving grass just like the patch between his toes. Except this spot was sacred. He didn't even have to look down to know it. The exact positioning of the massive stone house to his left. The battered storage shed of sparring equipment to his right. And the exact spot his mother died directly beneath him. A new kind of curiosity pulled his vision downward. The grass was unstained, and the usual dotting of craters and dirt-mounds absent. Where shouts, screams, and laughter should have echoed at all times, only the quiet breeze surrounded him. Everything was too perfect, and Garen understood where he really was.

"You aren't dreaming." The hard, feminine voice did not come from a distinct location. He couldn't turn and face. It hit him from all angles, even from inside his own head a little.

"Alright," Garen said with uncertainty in his voice. "Then where am I?"

"Don't you recognize your own mind?"

"Sorry, I'm usually on the outside of it."

"So you think."

Garen paused to unravel the cryptic response, but eventually dismissed it. "Yes, this is definitely a dream." He turned to make his way into the house, but found himself frozen in his spot. He could step, but the house stayed just as far away.

"Then understand this dream has a purpose. I do not frequently aid my host, but both of our lives are in danger."

At the word "host," a guess entered Garen mind to whom he might be addressing, but he had to know for sure. He gave up on his struggle to get away. "Who are you?"

"My name has long since been forgotten. But you may know me by the role I serve. I span the Gate of Truth. I am the spirit tethered between your soul and the Spirit Realm."

Garen never imagined a chance to meet the spirit inside himself, but he imagined a lot of things weren't covered in the short lessons he'd received. Most noticeably, Micah failed to teach him the proper nature.

"My apologies," Garen said, surprised by his mannerly tone, but unsure how else to address it. "I was taught you were a spirit of light."

"You may think of me as the Light Spirit if it suits you, but that is merely a facet of this Gate. What I must now teach you, if we are to survive this day, is that light is only the physical dimension of my gifts. You draw your depth from the Gate of Truth. With it you can search the very confines of the mind and soul. Knowledge is its true strength, and only with its power can you heal your allies and blind your foes."

Garen put the puzzle of saving his friends on hold for the moment and skipped back to an earlier notion. "Wait, how is your life in danger? If I die, you'll just move to the next host."

"Not this time. They have taken you to the place where I was first tethered, the Theltus Nisdal."

Garen actually had to laugh at the mention of the old shrine. "Oh, then you've got nothing to worry about. You see, I kind of accidentally destroyed that place last time I was there."

"Actually, it is I who must apologize. That was my doing. I activated the altars without all five of us present, and the ancient rite could not be performed. It caused the collapse. I feared this day was coming soon, and hoped to deter anyone from finding the Theltus Nisdal's true use. But the magic remains intact, and they have used the man you call the Earth Rogue to rebuild the structure."

So, this is Project Theltus. Garen stopped his thoughts for a moment, wondering if she could hear them just the same.

"What happens if they do have all five spirits?"

For the first time in their conversation, he felt hesitancy in her reply, an unusual break in conversation for a being of sheer power. The human reluctance of her response hinted at the mortality in question.

Despite her pause, she spoke bluntly. "They will kill you and trap us in the altars. There is no escape. Without a host, we will wither and die, and without our presence in your realm, all five Gates will close."

The looming death for them both Garen had guessed, but the rest hadn't crossed his mind. "You're saying there will be no more magic?"

"If the spell is precise enough to leave the opening exactly as it once was, yes. This realm will return as it was before. The only magic seeping through will be the spark that generates life among the material, as it once was."

"And if they're off by a little?"

"If the opening between our realms is closed all the way, the spark of life at the bottom of every human soul cannot be sustained. Like flames, each will slowly suffocate and die. Yours would be the last generation to inhabit it."

The sun arced across the sky into a vibrant sunset. The endless fields turned a ghastly white. The sky went dark. Her voice began again, and it grew more and more distant.

"I can remove the drug from your body that is keeping you from waking, but I cannot work in your friends without your control. Remember that you command more than light. I span the Gate of Truth. Only this can heal them. Only this can set them free."

* * * * *

Garen's eyes flew open as he emerged from the dream or vision or whatever he should call a conversation inside himself. At the immediate recognition of his surroundings, he snapped them shut just as quickly. The moment gave him only a partial image to take in, but he was used to getting an abundance of light all at once. The spirit told the truth. They had him in the central tower of the Theltus Nisdal, the same room he watched crumble before his eyes less than a week prior. They had recreated it perfectly. The high stone ceilings and windowless walls pretended they'd stood that way for ages. "What earthquake?" they seemed to tease back at him.

He needed more than the one quick look to determine how impossible his odds were. He hoped they weren't monitoring him too closely and cracked his eyelids open as slightly as he could. Even though his eyelashes still blocked out most of his view, he bent the light around them until the room took shape.

They had him flat on the stone table, which his conversation with the spirit revealed as an altar. Under his back was the mind-gripping emblem carved into the stone. How many years had that symbol haunted his dreams before he ever took the life that granted it? Was he really so destined to inherit it all along? He still had a thousand more questions for the spirit that could apparently communicate with him, but he couldn't imagine how to contact it. In this moment, he knew what he needed. That symbol meant certain death, and he could not hide safely behind his eyelids much longer.

Garen continued pulling in bits of light, slowly putting together the pieces of the puzzle around him until he saw the room clearly. Six others surrounded him but did not hover very closely. They seemed to have another issue preoccupying them at the moment. He recognized all but one, a nervous man in fine robes who fluttered around the room. He seemed dreadfully out of place among them. The way he fiddled with geonode trinkets and kept anxiously looking in Garen's direction led him to believe he was some kind of medicine man, probably responsible for what kept him unconscious.

He recognized the next two faces, but had seen them only the once, and not side by side like this. The first left his image seared into Garen's mind when they met at the waterfall. The gray specks in his short, jet-black hair were less obvious in the dim orange glow of the geonodes surrounding them. He remembered the same unyielding look of dominance in his eyes, barely visible beneath the shadows from his thick eyebrows. The dark cord of hair on his chin formed a point and only added to the eccentric aura of the man. If he'd smiled at any point, it would have sent chills up Garen's spine. But at the moment this man did not seem particularly pleased.

"Why hasn't the process started yet?"

A tall, slender woman hung on his arm and mimicked the same impatient scowl. Garen had seen her once before as well. But she hadn't been at the waterfall alongside the man she clung to. They'd met in the tunnels beneath Nhilim. She was the woman with the geonode whip. The one whose hand he severed.

"I don't know," the robed man said, wiping a layer of sweat from his forehead. "These worthless devices your mages gave me are registering all five spirits in the temple. If they've all come in contact with the altars, Valu's inscription tells me the process should start on its own."

What are they doing wrong? They should have all five. They had the Earth Rogue already, then they took my father and Drake and—they still think Morgan is Naia!

Indeed, among the other familiar faces in the room, Naia stood alongside Argus at the edge of the room, as empty and lifeless as he'd found them in the palace. He had to give credit to the clever use of these two in order to capture him. It was also bold and reckless. Mind control magic required an extreme amount of depth. The spell had to be shared among several mages, and even then most would crumble in a day or two, releasing the victim. It wasn't even very practical. A person under the spell had none of the resourcefulness or wit of their own faculties, only the ability to follow simple orders. "Crush Garen." "Stab Garen." If he had wised up to the danger even moments sooner, he might have held his own against both of them.

Of course, they had no idea the value of the lives they were gambling with, so the risks must have seemed fine. He couldn't be too harsh. Their plan got him here, after all.

The man with white and black hair turned to address the last familiar face in the room. Unlike addressing the medicine man, he spoke with a soft sternness, like a disappointed father talking down to his son. "Pyralis, you promised me these were the five. You gave me your word, and I trusted you enough to begin our next steps. I shouldn't have to tell you what kind of a problem we have if you've been less than thorough in your efforts."

"I swear by it, Sarkos, these are the five!" Garen couldn't

help but notice how shaken and defensive Pyralis became. He wondered what kind of person could hold that level of influence over a king, especially someone as obnoxiously defiant as Pyralis. Garen had watched the man he called Sarkos pull the strings and manipulate the Earth Rogue directly. Between the woman on his arm, the Earth Rogue at his service, and the king babbling in submission, Garen saw the reach of this puppeteer.

"You would do better to admit your mistakes before they are found by another. Isadora and I will check on the others. You will stay here and pray that I find what's wrong."

Again, Sarkos implied a threat to Pyralis, and again the fiery-tempered royalty took it apologetically. Or at least until Sarkos left the room.

"Alright, listen you idiot," Pyralis shouted at the already bewildered man. "When Sarkos returns, we find a way to start Project Theltus on our own, regardless of what your instruments say." Garen tried not to tense up as Pyralis glanced in his direction. "Is he properly sedated?"

"Of course. With the dose I gave him, he won't need another until dusk."

"Still, there's no reason to hold back at this stage. I feel like he's been twitching. Better give him some more."

"But too much of the toxin could…"

"Do I look like his caretaker? Keep him under, whatever it takes. We don't have Sarkos' earth pawn at our disposal right now, and I'd rather not take the place of one of our sacrifices just to put him back down."

"Understood. But if it kills him, your highness—"

"Then you will take his place, and your sacrifice will serve this world in an even greater way. But I guarantee if I have to handle him myself, one of us will make certain you die a far more gruesome death. Trust me, if you'd ever seen a fully attuned Light Spellsword, you'd triple his dose on the spot."

Thanks for the compliment. Sorry I can't return the kind words at this moment.

The additional dose coming his way meant that he had precious little time to uncover the spirit's riddle, that "truth will free them." Even assuming the medicine man would drop his tools and run, he still had Naia and Argus to worry about. Three-on-one did not sound like appealing odds. He needed to snap one of his friends out of the trance. With no offense to Argus, he'd much prefer a violently furious Water Spellsword. He pulled every bit of light he could from around her, but he had no idea what he was searching for. It wasn't like they had included a lever labeled "mind control off."

The medicine man tucked his head low and walked toward a shelf along the edge. He tapped nervously along the tops of jars until selecting one with a bright purple liquid. "If I may ask, in the name of good caution, why do you have those two here with us?" he said, tilting his head toward Argus and Naia.

"Relax, the imperial mages guaranteed them for at least another day, and I do hate to throw away perfectly good help. Especially when they're so quiet and obedient." Pyralis brushed the back of his hand along Naia's cheek. "I suppose afterward I'll have to dispose of them. It'll be a new world once I've saved it. And these would-be-saviors will have no place in it. Though I can think of a few celebratory uses for this one."

Garen hoped they wouldn't notice his fists clenching, but he couldn't exactly help it. *Please Naia, tell me you're still in there. Tell me that you can see this monster and you're as repulsed by him as I am.* Garen continued to pry into her vacant stare, to the point that he felt like a man pounding furiously on a door, screaming and begging to be let in.

Suddenly, he felt that door open. He hadn't moved from the cold slab of stone, but somehow, he was also inside another person's mind. He ventured deeper into the passageways. It was an experience different from walking or flying. He wasn't moving at all, and yet he continued searching every tunnel, bouncing from one to the next in search of what kept her captive. As he did, the memories poured into him. He saw visions of her family and their farm. He felt the carefree bliss of a young girl playing in the leaves. He felt the fear and grief crash over them. The waters receded, and every drop of that life was washed away. The passages grew darker.

Eventually, he found the source of the spell's control, or at least his best guess at its source. Garen could hardly explain his own existence at the moment, and trying to understand the blob-like wall in front of him was baffling. It was gray, it looked squishy, and it pressed against the walls and ceiling of this hall too completely to slide past. If this was the barrier, it was blocking her own flow of thoughts, sealing the memories that shaped her from her actions. He knew he needed to pierce it and let her personality through. But the "how" left him speechless. On impulse, he tried sending a thin beam of light into the barrier, but he realized that he couldn't. He wasn't physically there, and creating light without space turned out to be as impossible as it sounded.

Garen could hear the needle rattling against the inside of the jar as his captor swirled the drug around it. He had a matter of seconds to figure out how to use knowledge instead of light, and how to unleash truth like an explosion to break through this wall. He tried pressing against the gray blob with his strength, but only for lack of better ideas. He knew brute force wouldn't open the passage.

The spirit inside him warned that he needed to use something other than light. He didn't have time for philosophical wonderings, but if he couldn't answer the question "what is truth?" nothing else mattered. He conjured up a compelling image of Naia, shoving in as many defining traits as he could from the ocean of memories he travelled through. He felt the barrier recoil a little, but a caricature laced with stubbornness, sarcasm, and loyalty didn't have the force it needed. It was true, but it wasn't exactly pointed.

"Alright young one, time for another dose." The man took hold of his forearm.

Come on, Naia! What kind of truth would bring you back? Garen answered his own question immediately, and he had no problem crafting the lifelike image of Morgan laying on an altar the same as his own, knife to her chest. Pillars of light tore through the gray blob. Garen knew she had returned to herself

232

when the wave of disgust at his intrusion washed over them both. He pulled himself from her mind before she could find a way to kick him out on her own.

Garen had pressing matters to attend to in a more physical sense. He burst up from his reclined position on the table and knocked the man's arm away, sending the needle spinning out of his hand. As predicted, he backed away in terror and wasted no time finding the exit.

"I can't say I'm surprised, Garen. You won't seem to stay dead. I'm not sure why I expected you to stay asleep."

Garen slid off the altar and brushed the dirt from his clothes. "Don't beat yourself up over it. You were never very good at predicting what's ahead."

"Oh, and you are? Or did you forget I still have a particular influence on your friends?" Argus started his march toward Garen, and Naia tried her best to follow suit with the same mindless stride. "How do you feel about three-on-one?" Pyralis smirked.

Naia stopped between Argus and Pyralis. "In a moment, we'll feel great." She stretched out her hands and released two volatile jets of water into the sides of their faces. The forceful blast toppled Argus and slid him a few feet. But the much lighter Pyralis was sent tumbling through the air, stopped only by the far wall of the chamber.

"You free Argus. I'll take care of this creep," Naia said with a thankful grin. Garen couldn't explain how relieved he felt to have an honest ally at his back once again, but he had no time for a sentimental reunion. Argus was rising quickly, and if he could break the spell in even half the time it took before, he would have a lot of hammer swings to dodge.

He quickly found his access point into Argus' mind through the man's hollow stare. Traveling these passages had a much less coherent story to tell, mostly full of nights spent celebrating in the tavern and days of hard work alongside Garen's parents. He had been a Spellsword aide for nearly his entire life. Most of them were faded, coated in the dust of a man who lives for the present and doesn't dwell on such things. He found a hall that was very much the opposite. The faces were crisp and unclouded. This one had been replayed far too often for dust to ever settle.

A hilariously young, but still not-so-tiny Argus ran through the field chasing a girl his own age. He could not have recognized her from the vision, but the memory carried the identity with it. Layna, his mother, had been a childhood friend of his. Still, it was more than that. She had been the one to pull him into this life. In a city that wanted nothing more than to exploit his size and strength, she was his anchor and his guide. He loved her. And even when she chose Seth over him, he did not retreat. He carried on by her side and let it fade into an honest friendship, still filled with a gratitude that numbed the pains of rejection. He carried that love until the day he heard the news of her death, and Garen felt Argus' grief nearly equal to his own at the loss. Then he felt that same surge well up that day in the meeting room when he first saw her son, the living image of her.

Garen understood much of the softness beneath the giant's course skin. That softness, however, did not translate into reality at the moment. On the physical side of things, the incoming war hammer threatened to reduce Garen to a puddle of blood and finely crushed bone on the floor. He rolled to the side of the vertical swing and continued to multitask.

To further distract him, Pyralis had risen from his soaked corner. For all of his attempts to block it out, Garen would never be able to ignore that voice.

"Wretched mages," he cursed to himself. "There's no way you should have snapped free. Still, you're of no consequence to me, Morgan Talia. Just a delusional warrior, whose attempts to save her sister are about to get her killed."

"You know, the funny thing is," Naia shook her head. Garen had to turn and savor the moment of Pyralis' eyes widening. "Saying that wouldn't have pissed Morgan off half as much as it does me."

An outpouring of icy water cut off his ability to curse at her. She pinning him against the wall with the force of a waterfall. As exciting as it was to watch him thrash against it, Garen snapped his head back to the more pressing issue in front of him. He fell backward under the cross-swing of the hammer, but Argus did not swing it wildly. The hammer quickly changed direction and came crashing down at him as he lay on his back. Garen was far outmatched in strength, and had no choice but to rely on his wits against such brute tactics. With a gust of wind under him, he sprung to the side of the hammer's swing. Spinning his foot down, he kicked the shaft of the weapon, hoping to trap it against the ground and give him some leverage. Instead, the hammer fell out of Argus' hands, and the metal clattered against the stone. Garen certainly hadn't kicked it that hard. He didn't have the strength to rip the weapon out of his grip. Suddenly, Garen felt hands grip his throat, and he knew why Argus dropped the weapon.

Being choked was not an impossible situation to escape. He had a clear shot with any spell he chose at the unguarded strangler. But this wasn't some nameless enemy he could burn alive. He cringed at the question of how much pain he was willing to inflict on his friend to survive. What he did have was a point-blank stare into Argus' eyes, and he chose to pit his spell-breaking speed in a race against the air in his lungs. He was grateful to have already traveled most of the distance. In seconds he found the same blob-like barrier. He tried to imagine what kind of truth could shake his friend back to reality, but the crushing sensation was more than a little distracting.

Garen noticed the gray wall itself was already rippling. Something was doing the work for him. Through Argus' eyes he saw his own face turning red. Some part of that image was nearly enough to shatter the spell's control on its own. Thankfully, he had Argus' mind to point it out for him. He saw all the resembling features of his mother in him. Her eyes. Her nose. Garen shaped the image until Argus could see his own hands wrapped around Layna's throat. Those same shaking hands flung open as the vision tore through the barrier poisoning his mind. Garen watched the liveliness return to his eyes, followed quickly by tears.

Naia relented her icy stream to complete the taunt. "Now

what was it you said about being outnumbered? Find your own minions next time. And another thing. Don't you *ever* touch me again."

Pyralis had grown pale from the frigid soak, but he seized the opportunity to blast a hole in the wall behind him, quickly diving out. Garen stepped to follow after him, but Argus' held him back.

"Trust me," Argus said. "We'll take care of him later. Right now we got others to worry about." Garen's mind raced at the possibilities around him. Four sacrifices were in danger. One was his father. His own father. He was alive and waiting for him just below the tower. Unfortunately, he would be of little use in his current physical and mental state. Though it pained him to think so coldly, his father had to be their last concern. Garen considered the Earth Rogue as well. Pyralis did mention that they didn't have his services at the moment. Would he be drugged the same as the rest of them? Garen would have loved to deal with such a powerful enemy while he was helpless and not throwing mountains, but he knew that the three of them would not hold up against the army of guards surrounding the temple. They needed to free allies before they could take the offensive.

"Garen, can you wake any of the others up the same way you did for us?" Naia asked hurriedly.

"Uh, poisons are a bit different than spells, but I think I can." He reasoned that if the spirit in him did it, he should be able to do it too. "We'll free Morgan first then. She's in the most danger now that Pyralis knows who you are."

"No," Naia said sharply. He could tell the word pained her, but she held to it regardless. Her mind had evidently gone through a similar process. "We need support. If they kill Drake for his spirit, we're done for." They nodded in agreement.

Little thought was given to stealth as Argus smashed another hole through the wall. He wrapped an arm each around Naia and Garen and jumped out of the tower. His shield slid off his back and under his feet, controlling their speed and direction as they fell toward the swamp below. It didn't take long for Garen to remember why they all hated this place. The rain fell in heavy sheets with the intention of driving them into the ground, even while being tossed to the side by the bone-chilling wind. From their height, he could see random bursts of fire and the ground shift wherever it pleased. They all believed with good reason that this place was trying to kill them, and knew the importance of being slow and cautious. Unfortunately, he could see Western Kingdom soldiers posted around the perimeter of the Theltus Nisdal moving inward, reminding him how little time he had to save the others.

A few soldiers had already spread throughout the inner courtyards and rushed to meet them as they fell. Naia made use of the ammunition already in the air. Perhaps the men were smart enough to block incoming arrows and daggers falling from the sky, but arrows and daggers they could have seen. Pouring rain concealed the icy spears right until they punctured into them.

Argus glided down on the back of his shield, setting them down among the fallen soldiers. They did not have time to linger and mourn the brutality of their actions. Fighting against overwhelming numbers like an army gave them no opportunity for restraint or mercy. Another dozen men opposed them along the way, and Naia delivered them similar fates. The south-east courtyard came into view. They could only hope that the wind altar and Drake would be waiting inside.

CHAPTER
TWENTY-FIVE

"Alright, Garen, when we bust in there," Argus paused to suck in the air, winded from their run, "I want you to leave the skull smashing to us, do you hear? You find a way to wake Drake up like you did us."

"Gladly, but you're going to need to watch my back. I kind of go somewhere else in the moment."

Argus smashed through the wooden door and ran through the shrapnel without waiting for it to settle. Garen rushed in behind and quickly noticed a captive, but it wasn't Drake. Micah was gagged and strapped to a chair. His entire torso was covered in the rope that bound him to it. The sight was an unusual one, given the impossibility of restraining anyone that could cast the simplest of spells.

Garen wondered what kind of ropes these were to hold him captive, but his thoughts were only a curiosity. Even if he could determine their magic simply by looking at it, he would not have freed the creature they held. He focused instead on the other end of the room where Drake lay peacefully on an altar between four guards. His noble friend made even a drug-induced stupor look sophisticated. Garen wasted no more time admiring the refined presence. He tried to ignore the other actions in the room and get to work, taking some comfort as Naia and Argus rushed past him to handle the others.

Garen made his way into Drake's mind and started what felt like a race down the main hall. Once again, he had no idea what he was looking for, but he was certain he would be able to spot anything out of place in such a tidy bank of memories. Passing through the channels of Argus' and Naia's mind led Garen to believe that everyone's head was a cluttered mess, but Drake proved otherwise. Every memory and emotion clung to its rightfully organized corner. Even the darker offshoots were properly sorted.

"Sooner would be better than later," Naia's voice shook him from his concentrated search. She had dropped the last guard in the room and sounded anxious to move on.

"I'm sorry, are *you* looking in an imaginary space for something you've never seen that doesn't really exist?"

"Whatever, just hurry up," she said, rushing over to Micah's side. They pulled the gag from his mouth, and he did not waste a moment before shouting an order.

"No magic near me! Naia, use your dagger to cut the ropes."

"I was planning on it. Are you afraid I'm not accurate enough with my ice?"

She cut through the thick cords along the side of the chair, freeing him and revealing a large, thin geonode pressed against his chest.

"No, I was afraid you'd set this off. It's responsive to magic and particularly explosive I'm told. Assuming it works, I think they've found a way to take prisoners."

"I don't get it," Naia said. "Why didn't they just drug you?"

"Apparently there are some small risks with the toxin. And as much as they didn't want to let me go, they didn't want any chance of me dying either. At first I thought there might be some sentimentality at play, but I saw the look in his eyes. My brother wanted me dead. It seems more likely I was worth something to them. Possibly as a bartering tool in this 'new age' he kept rambling on about. I don't suppose any of you happen to know what he has in mind, would you?"

Garen heard the question, but he wasn't comfortable responding to that man just yet. Instead, he continued his search through Drake's mind. The deeper he went the more he understood why the memories were so neatly organized. They were all nearly the same. He attended the same banquets, the same ceremonies, the same dull festivals and holidays. Not only were the events a boring replica of each other, but in each memory Drake held the same purpose. He was royal decoration in the Ambersong guild and nothing more. His bloodline kept him in obligatory attendance, but every other faculty in his mind screamed for an escape. He saw siblings and cousins, all jockeying for position in the family hierarchy, but Drake made no effort.

Garen felt the disgust within Drake for the city of Kalyx, for his own country, and even his own people. Though the emotion was neatly compartmentalized, the raw darkness of it surprised Garen. He had no idea his friend was even capable of that realm of hatred and loathing. It reminded Garen a little of his own feelings for a few individuals, but that kind of grudge against an entire nation worried him.

Despite his unease, it was not the intruder he was looking for. Nothing looked out of place as far as he could tell, and finally, he reached what seemed to be the end of it all, connecting the conscious mind to the lower functions. He would have shrugged and left except for one small detail that caught his attention. The path ended in a simple wooden bridge trailing off into the distance. On that bridge, a single plank was missing. He stepped out onto it, and somehow the structure still held him. But as he peered down over the missing board, he understood how the drug kept him out. Just like the mind control spell, it disrupted the flow of his consciousness. Unfortunately, while Garen could break down a foreign substance blocking his way, he had no idea how to repair something missing, let alone stop the drug from just breaking the sequence again. Garen let his own presence slip back down the path he came in until he felt the disorienting jump to his own faculties. His legs wobbled for a moment, and he held his arms out to balance himself until he was sure he was back in control.

"I can't do it," Garen said. Argus had already stepped to Drake's side and slung him over a shoulder.

"Fine, then just get him out of here." Naia said, moving toward the door. "I'm taking Micah to get my sister. You and Argus go and rescue your father."

This time, Garen needed to insist with a painful no. "My father can't help us right now. If I'm taking Argus, we're paying the Earth Spirit a visit first. After we end his life and you save Morgan's, we'll meet in my father's chamber."

241

A group of Pyralis' soldiers burst into the room before anyone could acknowledge Garen's sacrifice. It was better this way. Now he didn't have to argue the point and risk admitting it was fear that kept him from wanting to charge in there. An entire season had passed since he'd seen his father. He had no idea what to expect behind that door.

"Let's find out if it was a ruse or not," Micah said to Naia, tossing the disc-shaped geonode at the intruders. The guard snatched it from the air and grinned with pride. Micah revealed a smirk of his own and launched a single, tiny fireball at them. The soldiers snickered at the pathetic display. The sputtering ball of flame crawled through the air, but as it came within a few feet of the geonode, its yellow glow intensified. The guard holding it panicked and tossed it upward. The stone let loose an explosion far larger than it seemed capable of. The ceiling collapsed around them, and Naia didn't wait around to check for survivors. She cut a hole into an adjacent wall and led them out into the swampy courtyard.

"They may be evil," Micah noted, "but at least we know they aren't liars."

They climbed over the rubble and parted ways. Garen was relieved to put off interacting with Micah. He did a fine job of ignoring the man at first, but he wasn't sure how long he could suppress his disgust. He had not forgiven him, not even a little. The revelation he found at Idrian's estate had nothing to do with forgiving a cowardly wretch for the death of his mother. For the sake of not turning into a lonely, isolated creature, Garen could ignore his feelings of contempt. He could not, however, give them up.

A column of flame ripped across the air in front of him. He looked for the source of out of instinct, but they were alone for the moment. Just another elemental spasm. He gladly pushed the dilemma aside and focused on his surroundings as they sprinted from one corner of the temple grounds to the other. The original Spellswords built this place just like the forces they inherited, and earth was opposite wind. This run took them through the bottom of the central tower, still dark and empty.

The etched lines in the walls hadn't lit up with their blue-green glow the way the outer chambers had. He suspected if they did, the whole grounds might start to collapse like they did before. He could hear the patronizing voice of Naia in his head screaming, *Don't touch anything.*

Garen kept his hands to his side as they ran through the base of the tower. They emerged back into the pouring rain, but this time not alone. Guards spotted their movement and raced to intercept them. Garen did not feel like stopping to cross swords with any more distractions, and he crumbled the stone pathway beneath them. He heard their shriek as they dropped unexpectedly into the murky water. One of the soldiers refused to be dismissed so easily. While treading along the murky pool, he focused on a fragment of the shattered pathway. The heavy slab of stone flung itself from the water toward Garen.

Garen took some insight from Naia's trick earlier. It was always easier to use the materials at his disposal than conjure up his own to block the incoming stone. It wasn't on scale with her storm of icicles, but he managed to form a substantially thick sheet of ice from the pouring rain and let it drop into the hefty chunk of rock coming their way. The two elements collided and dropped into the water while Garen and Argus continued their dash without interruption.

They arrived at the chamber, but the doors were already open for them. Garen hoped he'd find the same embarrassingly easy scenario as Drake presented, but time had worked against them. The brightly glowing turquoise room revealed three people he hoped he could avoid in general. Sarkos played with his strand of facial hair casually. He stood alongside his sickeningly pale mate Isadora. The chilling stare on her face told him that she hadn't quite forgiven him for the removal of her hand. He noticed the lifeless mold in place of the missing right hand and hoped she wasn't particularly ambidextrous with the whip she now carried by her left side.

Either of these faces, Garen could have done without, but none bothered him more than the sight of the Earth Rogue standing at the ready beside the other two. The only reason he insisted they come here first was because he assumed he would find the dangerous warrior lying unconscious on the appropriate altar. Even if the creepy mastermind, his eerie girlfriend, and the dozen-or-so guards surrounding them were complete push-overs, Garen didn't like his odds.

Argus did not share the same calculating sentiment. He rushed into the chamber in a screaming fury. The sight of a lifelong target would probably push Garen to the same ignorant battle cry. No matter how much he wanted to turn around and race to his father's chamber, his duty was to Argus. Garen let out the same wild scream and rushed in alongside his friend.

The first guard led with his sword before Garen could draw his own. Rather than amble backwards trying to gain the space to ready his weapon, Garen stepped toward his opponent. He drew the katana straight out, letting the half unsheathed sword block the cross-swing. Though he did not have the space to pull it clean, he was close enough to extend the pommel into the man's chin and stagger him backwards. Garen pulled his blade, spun the sword over his head, and brought it down sharply across the soldier's open side.

Garen immediately rolled to the side and barely missed the crack of Isadora's whip. It lacked some of the precision he'd seen before, but it was still deadly enough to worry him. He needed to sever the weapon short enough that it would become useless, but he couldn't do it while she was swinging it. No matter how sharp or fast his blade swung, the cord would wrap around the katana and likely fry him in the process. He needed the rope taut in order to slice through it.

Garen crouched low and waited for the next strike. As it came, he tumbled backward and let the whip strike the ground. In the tiny window of opportunity he had, Garen brought the stone floor to life. It swelled and enveloped the whip, trapping it into the ground. If the spell held, he had another brief moment to sprint forward and cut the cord down to size. An incoming spiked club reeled him backward. Garen hoped that the Earth Rogue would stay occupied with Argus while he took care of the scraps, but instead the ten other guards formed a mob trapping Argus against the wall where he set Drake's body. In order to protect the two of them, he was stuck slowly swatting the Western Kingdom soldiers away while hiding behind his shield.

Though he dreaded it, Garen knew it was time to settle the long overdue stalemate between earth and light. This battle, however, began in a curious new fashion. He had never seen the Earth Rogue fight with a weapon before. He seemed to rely on using the ground around him as his weapons of choice, and rightly so. The use of such a brutish, unimaginative club did not fit his talents. Stranger still, Garen hadn't dodged a single volley of stone shrapnel yet. The combination tipped him off. One quick look into the stocky warrior's eyes and two more dodges of his club gave the secret away entirely. In place of the usual grimace of regret, the muscles in his face were relaxed and his eyes were glazed over and empty. Sarkos had him under a more direct form of control.

Now why would you force your will onto someone already working for you? Garen grinned at the only logical answer. *Maybe because he's not anymore.*

The idea was farfetched, but the potential was worth investigating. With his powerful opponent reduced to a lumber-swinging chump, he could afford to split his focus between fighting back and searching for his answer. Garen found easy access to his mind. Once inside, he encountered a string of emotions and memories he never expected.

He saw life through a young man in love, covered in sweat and a smile as he tilled the field. He married that woman and became a family man when she gave birth to a beautiful girl. It seemed like every spare patch in his mind was covered with the memories of watching her grow up. He had soaked in every second. Garen turned a corner in his mind, and the lighthearted, tender emotion disappeared entirely. A man broke into their house one night. Garen felt the terror built into the memory and expected the worst. He was surprised to witness the brave father defending his family. His wife and daughter were unharmed. In the end, he killed the intruder. But he did not realize the power he inherited by doing so.

Garen thought the memories had grown their darkest, but they were still radiant compared to the stretch ahead. The memory's scar formed an arch leading into violent terrain: the night he met Sarkos. He appeared much younger as well, his hair a crisp black. Sarkos requested his cooperation, but this father would not leave his family. When Sarkos returned in the dead of night and stole his wife and daughter, the Earth Rogue's reservations crumbled. The terms were made clear. His family would be kept alive so long as he performed various, unpleasant tasks for them.

Such a gentle, loving man could not maim and murder other men without inflicting deep emotional wounds. Sarkos saw that his prized mercenary was cracking and taught him a simple way to fight the pain. Sarkos told him not to think of himself as doing these horrible things. After all, he was a good man, not even capable of murder. Sarkos was forcing him. In truth, Sarkos was doing them.

Garen wandered down several steep tunnels, but they all took the same odd shift. Suddenly Sarkos was doing all the horrible deeds asked of him. Even on the day he crushed Garen's father beneath the mountain of stone, a day Garen could personally attest to this man's presence, the memory showed Sarkos doing them. All the while the eerie mantra flowed through his head, surrounding Garen in the warping lens of the simple lie. *It's not me, it's him. It's not me, it's him. It's not me, it's him.*

Garen raced down the tunnels filled with distorting mirrors, showing only Sarkos in their reflection. This man had come to believe that he was someone other than himself. Unexpectedly, Garen emerged into an open passageway, as bright as the path he began on. The man found out about Project Theltus. They were going to sacrifice him. Shattered mirrors lay at his feet. He couldn't be Sarkos. Sarkos would not sacrifice himself.

The Earth Rogue gathered his courage and made his confrontation, demanding Sarkos set his family free. He was in control now, and he was prepared to use his spirit's gifts to fight, even kill this man if he must. But Sarkos was too close to his precious plan to leave anything to chance. The hidden soldiers with their venom-tipped darts eventually landed the one shot they needed and knocked him out. His trail ended there, blocked by the same pulsing mind-control barrier that he found in the others.

Garen had to reenter reality for long enough to sidestep the club once more. To add to his troubles, Isadora used the whip's geonodes to crack the stone holding it captive. The rocks exploded around it, and she had her trusted weapon back at her side.

He was torn. But with Little-Miss-Whips-a-Lot back in action, he didn't have much time to mull it over. Garen knew the very core of this man's mind. He was not the cold killer he once was. Still, helping him seemed unimaginable. This was the man who crushed the last thread of his father's sanity. Was he supposed to just hope in good faith that he would snap-to on their side? What if he came out of the trance believing he was Sarkos again? If Garen had learned a thing from Panther, he would have taken the fight as it stood without having to risk trusting another human being. But lately he'd fallen into league with a different sort of people. They'd brought a criminal into their fold with full confidence that he could be something more. He'd seen firsthand just how risky trust was. He'd also seen the rewards well enough to know it was worth it.

Garen sent a plain, unaltered vision of the man's daughter into the gray ooze that blocked his mind. The barrier disintegrated on contact, dispelled by a force stronger than anything he had ever seen before. This man's love for his daughter towered over any affection Garen had ever experienced. Even the childlike love and respect for his own father couldn't compare to the flow of compassion from the other perspective. The incredible sensation gave him goose bumps, just to imagine feeling that kind of selfless dedication to another person. Garen couldn't imagine the adventure of raising a child, but for a brief second, he experienced the unbreakable bond of a father's love. He found himself lost in the bottomless depth of it, so lost he never noticed the movement of the whip until he felt it wrap around his throat.

247

The whip tugged on his neck, pulling him off his feet and onto his back. The deadly flow of energy poured into his body. He had no comprehension of how long the torture lasted. The mind-numbing pain drowned out all of his senses. He writhed about on the ground until the agony numbed him enough that he could make out a clear image in front of him. The man whose mind he had just freed stood frozen in shock, staring at him with fear. Garen looked across the room to Argus, still fighting his way out of the cluster of soldiers. If Garen could have found the strength to voice a simple plea for help, he would have. But the spasms in his body took control again. Every sense began to blur. He could no longer feel the cold, hard floor his body shook against. The corners of his vision grew dark. He knew the feeling well. At any moment, he would have his peaceful rest and the pain would finally stop. And sure enough, it did.

But Garen was still conscious. His eyes adjusted and looked up to see how the cord had been severed. The whip was intact along the ground, leaving a winding trail to its dead owner, a massive shard of the stone floor protruding from her chest. She had fallen back against the empty stone altar like a rag doll, hunched over as blood dripped from the corner of her mouth.

Garen's eyes immediately turned to the Earth Rogue, who stood breathing heavily in the center of the room, and to Sarkos, who remained along the back wall as he had for the entire skirmish. Both stared at the corpse with the same blank shock. Sarkos snapped first, turning to her murderer, his body shaking with rage.

"Worthless puppet! I gave you everything and this is how you repay me? I should have killed you when I first met you, you and your family."

"Maybe you should have." He had the same somber veil that always accompanied him, but he stood tall and unyielding, no longer crippled with regret. His voice was deep and full of conviction. "I spent those years trying to protect my family, but how many families did I destroy?" His voice rose. "How many fathers and children did I separate permanently? You should have killed me. But more importantly, I'm done killing for you."

"You certainly are," Sarkos muttered. He pulled a handful of stones from a pouch at his side, each one pulsing yellow. Sarkos lobbed them at the Earth Rogue, and in the air Garen could see all five distinct stones. The Earth Rogue brought two layers of the stone floor up to swat the volley away, but one stone slipped between them. As it did, the geonode burst apart with a flash of light and a deafening roar.

Garen wanted to scream a warning, but he had no time and no name to address him by either. Even after searching the very depths of his mind, the only identity that came up was "Daddy." It wouldn't have mattered. As the smoke cleared, he saw what the explosion had done to the man. The splatter of blood was more than Garen wanted to see, though he seemed to be alive and desperately trying to crawl away.

The murderous assault had not consoled Sarkos. He carried a lust in his eyes for revenge. He stepped toward his victim, but Garen did not watch idly. He charged forward and stood between Sarkos and the man in his dying breaths.

"Argus, get here now," Garen shouted and released a blast of wind at Sarkos fierce enough to knock him back against the wall. "And you stay back."

"What do you care? This man was not your friend."

"Just stay away from him!" Garen released another depth-intensive gust, pressing the man against the wall and cutting tiny lacerations along his face. Garen looked down and watched the life fade from the Earth Rogue's dark eyes.

As the imprisoning wind relented, Sarkos wiped the blood from his face and strode toward him again. "You don't give me orders, rat. I'm in control now."

Garen turned to release another charge of air, but was met instead by an avalanche of rocks. The gale force of his spell provided a cushion against the stones, but their mass won out and sent Garen tumbling backward. He sprung to his feet for the next onslaught, but saw only the hole in the rear wall. Sarkos was nowhere to be found, taking his new toy, the Earth Spirit, with him.

Argus had crushed in the skulls of all but two remaining

guards, carefully circling around him. Garen took one from behind, leaving the other for a windmill slam from the war hammer. Argus picked up Drake and they quickly surveyed the empty room, or at least the room empty of living persons. Garen's eyes were drawn one last time to the brave and loving father who saved his life, and he wished he could thank him somehow. He had an idea, but it would have to wait. He had his own father to rescue now.

CHAPTER
TWENTY-SIX

This time Garen had the shorter distance to travel. But considering how long their failed mission took, he expected Naia and Micah to be waiting. Instead, Garen spotted them approaching the fire chamber as well from the opposite direction. He was glad to see Morgan slung over Naia's shoulder, but it struck him as odd that the petite girl was doing the heavy lifting. The scene made better sense when he witnessed Micah's injuries. He had a severe limp in his stride and the series of burns along his body were bordering on gruesome. Somehow, he wore a painless, determined expression on his face and managed to keep pace with Naia.

They exchanged urgent looks as they met, but there were no words to say. Without even a nod, they burst into the room.

Garen had envisioned this moment before, the triumphant act of kicking down the door where his father waited. That singular vision kept him going. It was the thread of hope that kept him from running from these Spellswords at first. It was the burning desire that pulled him back once he did. And despite every fear that someone other than his father would be laid out on that table, Garen's waiting and agonizing was over. It was him. Unconscious, but alive.

Each chamber had surprised them in some way, but this one held the strangest mystery. Garen's father was the only person in the room, strapped to the altar with metal clamps around the wrist of his remaining arm and both ankles. There were no dark corners for any ambushers to hide in the blue-green glow of the room, only the chained Fire Spellsword.

They quickly returned from their shocked state and rushed in beside the altar. Argus and Naia dropped their unconscious allies and, with a few simple spells, stretched the metal loose until they had freed him.

"So, did you take care of him?" Naia asked.

251

Argus carried an unusually dark expression on his face. But the scowl told more than just disappointment regarding the Earth Spirit. His eyes were locked on Garen's father, particularly the crudely bandaged wound where his arm had been torn off. Some of them had already seen his father in that state, but Argus was witnessing their brutality for the first time. Garen took it upon himself to answer Naia's question.

"We didn't. Sarkos did," Garen replied.

"Wait, is that the crazy-looking old guy? Are you telling me he's got the Earth Spirit now?"

"Seems that way."

"Who is he anyway?"

"I think he's behind all of this." Garen said. "He's got Pyralis answering to him, whatever that means."

"That's just called being polite. He is my mentor after all." Pyralis' haunting voice preceded the tall silhouette emerging into the chamber.

"No, the man you were about to sacrifice in this room was your mentor."

"Oh please, Seth was just another fool who bought into the lies of this age."

"Lies? What lies?" Garen asked in disbelief more than actual curiosity.

"Magic, you idiot. Haven't you figured it out yet? It's the curse of our time. You know the same as I do how power corrupts a man, and since the Dawn of Magic we've been rotting away from the inside. We were never meant to wield this kind of power. Without it, we will finally be free of this tyranny and east will no longer enslave west. Garen, we are putting an end to this dark era."

"No, you were about to end it, but now all your precious sacrifices are about to run away on you." Garen turned to blast a hole through the rear wall. He would like to settle this dispute with his old rival, but he had a more important task of getting his friends to safety. Unfortunately, the stone wall refused to budge to his contained explosion. The smoke cleared and left only a charred mark on the surface.

"Did I forget to mention?" Pyralis mocked, stepping to the side as another figure entered the room. Sarkos stood proudly beside his pupil. "We've got a pretty good grip on the surroundings."

"You're all crazy!" Garen shouted. "Do you have any idea what could happen if you actually succeeded in your sick little experiment? You could close the opening all the way. You could end life altogether in this realm."

"This world has already been given its death sentence, can't you see?" Sarkos matched the volume of Garen's plea, but with disturbing calmness. "At this rate, the corruption of power will only intensify. Men will murder each other until there are none left. Look around. Can you not see the horrors we unleash against ourselves? This world is broken, and it does not fear the risk of death. It sees only a chance to be reborn."

"Sarkos saved me from the escalating ruin men like you and your father were bringing upon the world," Pyralis echoed. "The more you fight magic with magic, the more it will grow and consume us all."

A connection clicked in Garen's mind as he heard Sarkos mention "this world is broken." This man had been influencing Pyralis even while he was a student. And he knew what that meant for Pyralis' involvement in his tragedies. "You helped organize the attack on our group, didn't you? The caravan ambush, the day my father lost his mind. You didn't just disappear. You were part of it." The realization quickly led to the infuriating conclusion. "You didn't just take him from me in the caves. You took him from me when I was a kid. I spent all this time blaming a sad puppet of a man, but you're the reason he lost his mind, and the sole reason he's here right now. Do you have any idea how much that makes me want to end you?"

"I'm happy to take the credit, but I wouldn't consider myself the *sole* cause of his madness. Would you like to know why he was tied up but the others weren't? I had to torture him to answer a few questions that bothered me." Garen looked back to his father as his friends lifted him off the table and set him beside Drake and Morgan. He had fresh wounds down his side and a noticeable gash across his face.

"You're just not helping your case." Garen said. "I'm already unsatisfied that I only get to kill you once."

"Don't you want to know what I found out, the secret that slowly ripped apart Seth Renyld's brain?" The words made their intended bite into Garen's resolve, but he would not reveal it. He had neither the time nor the place right now to dwell on that fear, the fear that he was destined to the same mad fate as his father.

"Maybe I'll just ask him myself when we're out of here. I won't need to torture him then, and I don't need a cheap exit now. I can go through you just as easily."

"Oh Garen, haven't you learned anything from our last encounter? When I say I have a secret, you really ought to listen. I'm telling you, it's a real monster." Pyralis wore his smirk with unshakable confidence.

"Save it. I'm still not a fan of your last revelation." Garen said with a confidence of his own, aided by his allies stepping beside him. "So, if you have something you'd like to throw at me other than lies, now would be the moment."

Sarkos wasted no time to answer the request. A dozen chunks of stone tore off from the walls and floor and flew across the room. Garen jumped over and quickly slid back under the two that came his way. The rest managed to dodge or deflect the stone volley in their own fashion, but their movements scattered them throughout the room. Pyralis, Sarkos, and the army of soldiers standing behind them wasted no time spilling in and dividing them. Pyralis made the unfortunate decision to strike at Naia in the chaos. His first shot of fire was doused from behind by a tidal wave of swamp water she pulled in from the courtyard. Similarly, Sarkos' rapid lances of stone had little effect other than to keep Garen bouncing around as he sliced up his soldiers. Pyralis and Sarkos both backed away and switched their opponents. Sarkos' voice rang over the clanging metal, "Tell him now!"

Pyralis skipped his customary fireballs and dove straight in to the melee, twirling both scimitars gracefully, slapping against the steel of Garen's katana.

"So, I found a very precious sword of yours recently." Pyralis said. His calm tone continued to give Garen chills. "You left your mother's wakizashi beside the dead body of Sustek Nash. Did you kill him?"

Garen tried to focus on the battle, but let a scimitar slip through their complex pattern of clashes. Thankfully, a loose chunk of stone lay at his feet, and he flung it up to knock the blade away. "I did. And since he killed my mother, I think he deserved it too."

The swing of momentum from the stone put Pyralis on the defensive, but he refused to let it interrupt his train of thought. "I thought you might say that. So, here's a funny development. No, he didn't."

Garen continued to press Pyralis back toward the wall. He focused his magic use on any soldier trying to strike at his back, tossing them aside with bursts of wind and water. It was an extravagant use of his depth, but he was in no mood to hold back. His focus remained in front of him. "I think you're slipping. Usually your lies at least make sense. I killed that man. Now I have the spirit. Do you see how hard it is to argue with that?" Garen's blows grew more intense. "Now will you please let me kill you in peace and quiet?"

"Just think back. Haven't you noticed you could always sense things, things you shouldn't be able to? I thought it was odd when we were kids. And you slipped out of my reach at times you never should have while running with your father. You've been manipulating light for a long time before you fell into leagues with these imbeciles. Am I right?"

A slight opening appeared, and Garen used the opportunity to knock one of the scimitars from Pyralis' hand. "If you had as many open stabs as you had ridiculous questions, I believe I'd be dead by now," Garen taunted. With his opponent far less of a threat at this point, he gave some consideration to the question. Despite the vagueness, his words were close enough to prod his curiosity. "Let me understand your mad theory. You think someone else killed my mother, and I killed him a long time ago?"

"Now what kind of secret would that be? Why would I even care? There's no poetry," Pyralis paused to give his customary grin. "No *sting*."

Unfortunate for him, the pause cost him the other sword in his hand. Pyralis now stood with his back against the wall, unarmed, and pinned by Garen's sword against his throat.

"Looks like you've only got a few seconds of life left. You might want to get to the point before I do." Garen mimicked the wicked smile. They shared the intense staring contest until the smirk faded from Garen's face, outmatched by the pure malice in his adversary. Garen's expression changed to horror as the words flowed from Pyralis' lips.

"You killed your mother."

"You've got a lot of nerve to even—"

"Don't believe me? My dear brother Micah was right there. I believe he would have seen the whole thing. Seems to me you've been poking around in people's heads lately, and I'd bet you're as nosy as your mother was with her gifts. I don't suppose it would be hard to confirm." Pyralis never broke from his smile, even with Garen's sword pressed against his neck.

Garen had no reason to believe the lie, but Pyralis had wisely thrown out the only person he trusted even less. He hated to take his eyes off the enemy he had hunted for so long, but these kinds of accusations deserved some solid answers, all of which Garen now had access to. Pyralis would have to wait against the edge of his sword for the time being. His eyes met with Micah's across the room, and although his lips never moved, Micah's eyes screamed "No!"

It was too late. Garen was in.

CHAPTER
TWENTY-SEVEN

Garen heard voices coming from the courtyard. He peeked around the corner to see what was happening.

"I'm not going to fight you, Mom!"

"Oh, come on! Don't tell me you're afraid."

I'm in Micah's head. This is the day...the day it all changed.

"Seriously, you'd kill me."

Micah heard his name and poked his head out. He nervously wiped the long, brown hair from his face and stumbled out into the open field.

"Well, I mean, I could," Micah stuttered.

I don't care about this part. I've seen it enough in my own mind. How do I skip to the end?

Micah dropped his things and ran over to them. "This I've gotta see," he muttered under his breath.

The memory sped up, and Garen watched the taunting and first pass rush by in a blur of incomplete memory.

"Garen, you're incredible!" Micah shouted with enthusiasm.

"He's fast, isn't he?" She smiled at him, and Garen wanted to pause the moment forever. But for once, the memory had a greater purpose than nostalgia. All he needed was to catch Sustek Nash in the act and set these wild fears to rest.

"But how are your reflexes?" Garen hated that those were his mother's last words. There was no hidden message of "I love you," just an overzealous mother and a fighter, hard at work on both fronts.

Garen dodged, deflected, and rolled through the next interchange. He knew the smirk of confidence that would soon take over his face, and he would have liked to wipe it off in that moment. Unfortunately, he could not see his own face nor his mother's in that moment. Micah was looking elsewhere.

He's doing his job. He's watching our surroundings. How did you get past him, Nash?

Micah snapped his head back to the fight and saw the punch. Thirteen-year-old Garen let out a gasping scream and tumbled backward. Micah raced alongside his mother to his body where the injured boy lay curled up in the grass.

No, Micah, leave me alone. I'm fine. Just keep your eyes on the horizon!

It didn't help. Garen had no control over the events four years past. He felt the surge of honest concern in Micah as he knelt beside Layna to help. She put her hand on Garen's shoulder, but he didn't move. She started to shake his body, but Micah's attention went to the clenched fists at Garen's side. A small red aura began to form around his knuckles, and by the time he realized its significance, Micah was too late to stop it. A defensive instinct triggered somewhere deep within the confines of Garen's soul. That much stored up power without any training on how to control it combined in a terrifying manner. Garen's back arched, and his arms shot forward. They released a burst of energy on an impossible scale. The spell drained the entire depth of his soul and left Micah's vision coated in white from the sheer intensity of the blast.

Then she screamed. Garen heard it, the same terrified cry that ended countless dreams before. He had always imagined her howling in pain as the killing shot tore into her body, but there was no physical pain, only emotional horror. When the blurry shapes reappeared, only an unconscious Garen and the scarce remains of his mother were left in the silent courtyard. The back door to their house swung open and Seth stepped out of it, witnessing the carnage at the hands of his son. Micah stood frozen in shock, staring at her. Garen could not bear another second of it.

* * * * *

Garen reemerged into the present moment, but carried the trembling with him. He felt his grip loosen and the sword fall from his hands. His gifts, his talents, even before meeting the Spellswords. That uncanny sense of "awareness." It wasn't something he'd achieved. It was hers, and he'd stolen it along with her life.

"How did it feel?" Pyralis whispered into his ear. His fist slammed into Garen's stomach as he crumpled to the ground. Even the harsh blow did not shake Garen from the traumatic visions playing in his mind. Pyralis gripped him by the back of his head and ground his face into the stone floor, dragging him by the hair. "I'm still not sure how you did it. But from what your father described, I wish I could trigger it again. I'd love to watch you kill your friends too. This works just as well, though. You get to watch me kill them."

Pyralis surveyed the rest of the battle, and Garen took in the scene through absent eyes. Sarkos had Naia backed against the wall. In a closed room of stone, he had an endless supply of his element to unleash at her. She had to conjure all of her watery strikes on her own. It didn't seem her defensive measures would hold out much longer. Argus had another mob surrounding him, and the badly wounded Micah could barely keep the three soldiers' swords at bay. The battle hung in a fragile balance, and Pyralis would tip the scales wherever he intruded.

"Where to start, where to start?" he mumbled to himself, dropping Garen's shell-shocked body to the ground. "Of course. What was I thinking? Family always comes first."

Having fought them both, Garen knew that Micah didn't have a chance. In his injured state, Pyralis needed only a moment to retrieve one of his scimitars, disarm his brother, and drag him back over to Garen.

"Any last words, you two? And speak slowly, Micah. He has a lot on his mind right now."

Garen lowered his head to the ground. He couldn't stand to look either of them in the face, not covered in this much shame.

"Garen, please, you have to forgive us. We never meant to hurt you. Your father and I, we kept it secret to protect you. No one should have to live with that kind of burden."

Micah didn't understand. Garen wasn't angry with them. He couldn't even imagine anyone beyond himself. The shame of his past drew his focus like a magnet. Nothing else existed but the horror and the disgust of what he'd done.

"Asking forgiveness from someone who murdered his own mother? As I understand it, killers of that degree aren't usually the forgiving type," Pyralis said. Garen stared at the floor without saying a word until Pyralis grabbed a fistful of hair and yanked his head upward. "Now I can't let you miss out on the good part. I'm about to kill the man you've wanted dead for, how long? You don't have to forgive him, but I'm going to expect a proper thank you in a moment."

Pyralis forced him to stare into Micah's eyes, and the shame grew so intense Garen thought he might throw up. The guilt and embarrassment multiplied until the burden's weight covered him entirely, consuming every sane faculty and driving him mad. He could feel the very insanity that crushed his father creeping in under the shroud of anguish. This was the feeling that drove his father mad, the nausea he had to live with for all those years. He must have felt it every time he looked at his son. Garen could not understand how his father stayed sane for an entire year after the incident. He could feel his sanity slipping right now only moments after learning the truth.

Garen shut his eyes to make the darkness disappear, but the thick fog of regret rolled in even faster, flashing images of the monster he truly was. He must have looked ridiculous wearing the mask of loyal friend or son. What had he done for his father but care for the very insanity he inflicted? And had he really taken up arms as the defender of the people? He tracked down Sustek Nash and killed him in cold blood. And why? To avenge his mother? No, because Garen Renyld was a murderer. Like a beast dressed in human clothing, they let him believe he was a person. Now, he could see himself clearly: nothing more than a self-deceived joke. An animal.

"Come on, I want you to look while he dies," Pyralis shouted and pulled Garen's eyelids open. The sight of the friend he betrayed should have sent him into convulsions, or else led him to pass out entirely. Instead, he saw Micah. Before that moment, he had seen only the judging creature his mind crafted with time. But right in front of his face was the real person, as broken with remorse as he was. A thin, narrow beam pierced the darkness of his mind and showed Micah in a new light. Here knelt the man who endured Garen's endless spite and deserved none of it. He did not have to pry into Micah's mind to find the truth behind it. The promise he made to his father was spelled out across his face. He would protect Garen, no matter what happened. He would stand up for him to his own dying breath.

But there was one problem. Garen had seen Micah's version of him, and it did not look like a beast dressed in human clothes. Micah put his faith in a person capable of love and integrity. The power of that faith shattered Garen's own perception of himself. He was no longer the monster pretending to be a man. His life had value, true value that Micah would give his life to prove. But this version of Garen would not sit by and let him.

"Goodbye, brother," Pyralis whispered. He lined his sword up with Micah's neck and pulled it back. The swing passed so smoothly through the target that Pyralis nearly fell over with the unexpected ease. He realized his mistake as the metal clashed against the ground. Micah knelt unharmed, and Pyralis noticed his blade-less sword. Someone had severed his weapon cleanly in two, slicing right above the crossbar.

Garen stood, his head still hung low, but revealing himself as the phenomenon's source.

"How did you even...?"

Pyralis dropped the worthless handle and launched a sweltering ball of fire at Garen to regain control. The shot passed directly through the false image. Before Pyralis could register the trick, Garen buried a fist into his side. He doubled over, and Garen brought his knee to Pyralis' chin to lay him out.

I can finish matters with him in a moment. Time to uneven these odds.

Garen picked up his katana and moved to help Argus. He did not, however, move in the traditional sense. With a single willing thought, he light-shifted directly beside an unsuspecting warrior and plunged his sword through the folds of his armor. The soldier nearest him witnessed the act and stepped in to attack. Garen did not even bother to leave the false image of him behind. His body took the form of light once more and shifted to his backside. Garen delivered a fatal thrust and pushed the guard's body off his blade and down beside his fallen friend. The extra help freed Argus to take more liberal swings with his hammer. A few dented breastplates later, the mob thinned into a winnable fight.

He stepped toward Sarkos, but something drew his focus to the other side of the room. The three unconscious bodies lay against the altar nearly begging to join the fight. He knew he couldn't repair that missing piece of their minds, but now he had a new theory to try. The truth of his own past cleared up a question he never received an answer to. How could he heal things like shattered bones so quickly? He now knew that he already had the Light Spirit when that occurred. Somehow, he had the power to accelerate his own body's functions. He didn't expect to re-grow limbs or anything, but "truth" affected more than just the mind. If his body was capable of something, he could teach it how to do it faster.

Garen looked to Drake and knew the solution. He did not probe into his mind, but rather his blood. The drug would naturally run its course, and Garen could make it run even faster. It took a moment for Garen to understand how to focus that kind of spell, but he knew he was on the right track when he felt Drake's pulse quicken. In a few seconds time, he wearily opened his eyes. He wished Drake would snap into action, but Garen reminded himself that Drake would have been under its effect for a much longer time than he had, and not to judge him for his sluggish response. He chose instead to wake Morgan from her sleep, which thankfully worked just as quickly. They took in their surroundings, eventually catching sight of each other. For the briefest moment, he saw Drake's face light up brighter than he'd ever seen it. The sounds of boots running toward the entrance drew their attention.

While Drake moved toward the new soldiers entering into the room, Morgan fell to a knee after a single stride. She clutched her side, and he could see the blood that had soaked through her bandages and stained her tunic. Garen remembered. They had cut the tracking geonode out of her. Apparently, they wanted her alive, but not for long. Garen thought he might be able to rush the healing to get her back on her feet. He quickly discovered the limits of that gift. The incisions were deep. She needed time, and this was not a safe place to be taking it. He found the spell that sped up her blood's natural rejuvenation and put a quick stop to it. The remaining toxin returned to its intended strength and left her unconscious once more. She might hate him for it later, but he could not split his focus looking out for a wounded warrior. He had another pressing matter to attend to.

His father lay in front of him, as still and peaceful as he'd ever seen. He knew it didn't justify the time at this moment to wake him up, but he had come too far to put it off any longer. With the same spell as before, he worked the drug out of his body. A scream caught Garen's attention in the process. He spun his head around but quickly realized the violent cry didn't come from the fighting behind him. It came from somewhere deep within his father. Garen would have expected all sorts of shouts if he had delved into the fractured mind of his dad, but strangely, he hadn't gone anywhere near his head. It wasn't his father's voice either. The scream came from somewhere else, and for all Garen's scanning, he could not find out where. It stretched his mind a little to imagine it, but he could only think of one part of a person that he couldn't find or observe in a physical sense. Worst of all, he had no idea how to look into a human soul.

Garen dove back in and tried to follow the screaming, but it seemed to come from everywhere at once. On the edge of giving up, he closed his eyes in frustration. But the loss of light did not stop his search. The scanning continued. He couldn't see a thing, but he could certainly feel it. A tremor of reverence swept over him as he entered what could only be the hallowed chamber itself. It did not take long to realize he was not alone. The being with him continued its shouts until Garen made sense of the chaos. The Fire Spirit was trapped there, stuck between two realms, and clearly in a great deal of pain by the sound of things.

He tried to ask what he could do, but he did not know how to use words in a place without substance. He had managed conversation with the Light Spirit, but that was in his own mind. In this setting, he didn't have the slightest clue how to express a thought. Thankfully, the spirit did. The screaming stopped and one overwhelming concept penetrated his thoughts: "empty." The word pointed to the exact source of his father's brokenness. Garen would not have known what to expect if the sacred chamber had been filled with a magical substance, but he knew what empty felt like.

His father had drained his soul completely, emptied it down to the last drop in the barrier spell to protect Garen. The spirit he possessed may have had a limitless connection to the source of fire, but all other spells had their price to pay. Garen was quite familiar with the penalty for draining the soul entirely. Without the smallest spark of life, the body becomes nothing more than a lifeless shell. Yet even with a soul as dry as the desert, his father continued to function, even if incoherently. The only explanation came from the spirit's presence, and in an odd way, it made sense. The spirit trapped between both realms wedged the door open. His father did not draw his life from any natural spark in his own soul. The only magic keeping him alive was a tortured spirit's connection to the Spirit Realm.

None of it was comforting, but a realization swept over Garen and took a tremendous burden off his shoulders. He now understood the source of his father's insanity. Seth Renyld did not lose his mind over the secret of his wife's murder. It didn't stem from the years spent looking her killer in the eye and calling him son. It was the price of his own sacrifice and nothing more.

Garen could barely stand to find another person that did not judge him for his mistakes. Both Micah and his father were ready to give their lives for a murderer like him. Their faith in him was magnetizing, pulling him toward expectations of greatness he would have never seen in himself. Once again, Garen was grateful for their sacrifice, but he was just as happy to keep them alive. His father was still breathing, still had his memories. Garen wouldn't have known how to fix a broken cup, but he could fill an empty one.

The drug was finally wearing off when he made the transfer. The process was wholly different than a typical spell. He would normally trade temporary depth for a powerful effect. Though he still spent a large chunk of his soul, Garen did not care about any effect. He was simply transferring that resource to someone that needed it far more. He felt their souls link, and he pushed the life-giving spark through just as his father opened his eyes.

"Son?"

Garen could hardly believe the look of sincere recognition in the tired man's eyes. This was no longer the statue of his father he looked after for years. This was the look of the loving parent from his childhood. Garen wanted to run closer and hug him, but the look in his father's eyes changed to a wide-eyed expression of horror.

Garen spun around to see two soldiers with swords mid-slice. Before he could react, a wall of flame rolled over both guards, tossing them helplessly back in the torrent of flame. Garen turned back to his father in stunned surprise, but the still-powerful Spellsword was already standing beside him.

"What have I told you about watching your back?"

Garen laughed, holding back tears at how quickly the years washed away. "I believe you told me it was your job."

"And don't you ever forget it." His father smiled and embraced him with the arm he had left, tears welling up in his own eyes. "I've missed you so much." Garen stood there holding his father with his back to the commotion of the room. Years upon years of jaded betrayals and letdowns meant nothing with the one man he trusted above all looking over his shoulder.

"Now, what kind of mess have we gotten ourselves into?" his father finally asked, looking around the room suspiciously. "Though, it's nice to see old friends."

Garen spun around and saw that the addition of Drake to

the fray made a world of difference. Argus continued to thin down the ranks of Western soldiers, no matter how many more entered, while Drake and Naia forced Sarkos into a defensive posture.

Argus was the first to notice the unexpected addition to their forces. "Seth, you goffing lunatic, tell me that's really you!"

The others snapped their heads back at the joyful news. Sarkos did not miss his opportunity to make his exit. Rolling the ground under his feet, he tore out of the chamber in a blur.

Garen's father had not grown rusty from the years trapped inside his own head. He understood the man fleeing was of importance, and decidedly took command. "Let's just say the Red Tiger is back. Now go after him, all of you. I think my son and I can handle these last few men and one sad, washed-up student of mine."

The others rushed out as he ordered, leaving the remaining three guards flustered over whether to chase after them or stay as commanded. Somehow, the words held sway over the soldiers.

"You can leave now," Seth offered. "Your king will be tried for his actions. But you don't need to share in his judgment. Leave him to us."

His father's calm tone did nothing to intimidate them. They charged the father and son in unison. Garen hated to see them throw away their lives, but a selfish part of him was happy to show off in front of his dad. The last time they'd fought side by side, he'd been a child, knowing nothing more than what he'd learned in a single year of training. Now he had a full arsenal of talents, and he wasn't about to hold them back. He looked over to give a confident nod, but found his father already focused ahead. He remembered the quiet intensity his dad brought to every skirmish, always at the ready. Just this once, for his father's sake, he would try not to run his mouth until all three had fallen.

Seth struck first, drawing a wall of flame up from the ground underneath the guard closest him. It consumed him entirely. Garen could not match the spell in size or intensity, but he could use the light for an equally devastating effect. Garen

266

imitated the blazing wall, sending the image directly into the second guard's eyes. The man saw the flames soar up under him and spun around in a panic. Garen knew the vision was entirely fabricated. He didn't hesitate to step through the inferno. The soldier's eyes grew wide in horror at the enemy who could walk through these towering flames without burning up. If he'd lasted another moment, he might have realized that he wasn't burning either. The only heat either of them could feel came from the true attack smoldering his ally next to him.

Garen gave him no time to make that connection. Garen found his opening easily in the flailing guard's armor. He landed the cut and turned to the other two. The first had crumpled up in the flames. The last stood behind the fallen bodies, eyes fixed on the columns of flame between them. Garen mistook the emotion for fear, but it was the soldier's resolve and focus on a spell that kept him still. He redirected the true wall of fire toward Garen. It was too wide to roll out of the way. And if Garen passed through it physically, it would torch every part of him. But if he could pass through it in a different state...

Garen knew he didn't have complete control over the movement, but he knew how to move into a state of light for just long enough to dodge something. He shifted behind the last soldier, retaking physical form with his sword in motion. Unlike the movements earlier, this light-shift had been a calculated one, not fueled by the rhythm of battle. Given his inexperience, Garen found himself farther away from his target than he intended. The cross-slice of his blade would have missed its mark entirely. But Garen was not the only one who could aid another's element. Moments ago, he had used the light from his father's attack to fuel his own. Now his father proved that the reverse was possible.

When Garen turned his body, armor, and weapons back to physical form, his father captured some of that transformation, specifically the blade of his sword. Instead of letting it return to its metal state, he brought the steel back as molten flame. Though Garen felt his sword grow lighter, the length stretched twice as long. What should have been an embarrassing miss became a devastating slice clean through the leather armor. He and his father shared a smile of respect. After a moment, Garen realized that he shouldn't be surprised. His father had a great deal of experience working alongside a Light Spellsword.

Morgan remained unconscious near the far wall. Aside from her, Garen and his father were alone in the room with the badly injured king. Pyralis stumbled to his feet, still dazed from the previous blows but moving nonetheless. "You idiot," He mumbled. "It wasn't supposed to happen like this."

Garen couldn't care less about empty threats at this point. Standing beside his father, an army of Pyralises would not have intimidated him. "Yeah, that's how it feels when someone stops your crazy scheme. We usually just call it losing."

"I'm not talking to you." Pyralis opened his grip, revealing a small geonode. Yellow light glowed from the stone's core. "Seth, I never wanted to take this from you personally."

Garen refused to be ignored. "I've seen that little trick of Sarkos' in action already. There's no way you're fast enough get one of those near us."

"No, I suppose I wouldn't be. But that's why I chose to get far more personal during the preparations."

Garen had no clue what the puzzle meant, but his father clearly did. He raised his arm to feel his nose, wincing in pain. Garen interpreted the meaning quick enough and carefully bent the light in to see the faint yellow glow inside. The geonode was deep into his nasal cavity, too small and embedded to remove it by force. None of that stopped Garen from trying, and he formed precise threads of wind to dislodge it. It didn't budge. His father's hand on his shoulder broke his concentration.

"Son, you can do this. You've grown into quite the man, and I'm sorry I've missed so much of it. There's not much to say, except that your mother and I...we loved you very much."

Garen tried to form the words in his own mouth, to echo his love back, but it felt too much like saying goodbye. It was too sudden. His entire focus had been on getting him back, and he had done just that. It never occurred to him that he could still lose him. "No, you can't just leave me again like that. You can't! Dad, I..."

A small pop echoed out. His father's body crumbled forward into Garen's arms. He saw the coldness in his eyes the way his friends looked under the mind control spell. Garen tried to jump into his father's head, to race through his mind until he found a way to fix the damage, but he stopped at the eyes. This time, the doors were locked. Garen pounded and pounded, screaming and pleading for his dad to let him in. It didn't matter. No one was home. And the doors would never open again.

CHAPTER
TWENTY-EIGHT

Left alone, the denial could have lasted for days spent trying to revive his father once more. Pyralis' voice, however, ripped him from that state.

"You did this to him. He was meant to be sacrificed to fix the world, not wasted like this."

Garen placed his father gently against the ground. His attention turned to Morgan's sleeping body. He pulled the stone around her into a shell, hoping to keep her safe from the rage he could feel brewing between them. Without words or warning, Garen light-shifted over and stood face to face with Pyralis. Garen's punch came just as quickly. Pyralis caught his fist head on and gripped it firmly. Flames erupted, covering both of their hands. The fire danced harmlessly along Pyralis' skin, but Garen could feel his flesh singe instantly. A wicked grin spread across Pyralis' face. "Well, maybe not a complete waste."

Garen kicked him back, breaking free from the scorching grip on his right hand. He immediately went to work on the spell that would hasten his hand's recovery, but the burns had scarred his tissue deeply. He knew he wouldn't be able to even grip his sword at the moment.

For once, Garen would have gladly entertained his rival's pompous ramblings. Coincidentally, for once, Pyralis did not seem interested in chatting. He charged at Garen, a shadow of flame trailing off his body as he ran. He shot one arm forward and released a thick column of fire. Garen rolled to the side of the blast. Pyralis followed up with another, this time expanding into a cone. Without space to naturally sidestep its path, Garen light-shifted across the room. The act of turning his entire body into light left him invulnerable to the wave of flame, but he still saw the blaze flow through him.

"You're pretty good at being two places at once. Let's see if you can be in none," Pyralis shouted, raising both hands in the air. A small orb of flame formed above him. The glowing sphere shrunk until it had nearly disappeared. Suddenly, an eruption of flames burst from the spot, sweeping the entire chamber. The fire spread quickly and left flames in its trail, filling the room from floor to ceiling. He had nowhere to dodge safety. Thankfully, from his distance Garen had time to put a wall of wind in front of him. The shield could not stop the blast head on, but the draft could channel the fire to either side of him. He felt an enormous gratitude for Micah's training with elements other than his own. Going from the simple diagram he'd learned, he could fight fire with its natural opposites, wind and water.

The flames cleared, and this time Garen took the initiative. He charged in, ready to use those advantages to exact his revenge. Pyralis stood his ground and met the assault with a fireball larger than them both. Garen conjured an impressive chunk of ice just as large and sent it in front of him as he ran. The fire and ice met, letting the ball of flame reveal its pulsing intensity as it melted clean through the glacier without shrinking or slowing. Garen hadn't put all his faith into the icy counter-attack, but he certainly didn't plan on it doing nothing. Garen had grown accustomed to the balanced power of fire in his training. Nothing had prepared him for magic like this.

The unstoppable force tore through the ice, and Garen sprung to his right to avoid meeting a similar fate. Pyralis shot a blazing disc to catch him in the air, but Garen was becoming increasingly proficient at changing states.

Pyralis was on the same learning curve. No sooner had Garen retaken his physical form than the next burning saucer launched toward him. If water was outmatched by the intense flames, he would have to make better use of wind and redirect the projectiles. Garen stirred a column of air until it formed visible shape in front of him. Based on any previous experience, the vortex of wind should have ripped the flames apart, or at least pushed it aside. Instead, Garen witnessed once again the unrivaled power of the fire at Pyralis' command. The current nudged the disc slightly, enough that it didn't tear him in two. Even without solid form, the fire's edge cut through the leather armor and carved a slice into Garen's side. He dropped to a knee, nearly overwhelmed by the sting of the cut mixed with the throbbing burn.

"And here I didn't think anything could be easier than killing your father. Are you trying to prove me wrong?"

The pain may as well have disappeared from his side. The bite of Pyralis' words became the focus of his senses. The wound it picked at swelled a rage he had managed to restrain. His side would take time to heal, but his hand was finally serviceable, albeit unsightly with its coating of blistered skin and pus. In the blink of an eye, he light-shifted across the room and retrieved his katana. He still had his most powerful, deceptive ability to employ. One false projection of light would give him the opening. One slice of his blade would make him pay for it all.

Garen rushed in again, on foot rather than by light for his trick to work.

"You just don't ever learn do you?" Pyralis said.

Good, let that confidence blind you.

The image of Garen charging forward continued in Pyralis' eyes, even after Garen changed course. The real Garen approached Pyralis from the side and drew back his katana for the killing blow. Oddly, Pyralis ignored the false projection and spun around to face what should have been a blind spot. Before Garen's blade could finish its arc, a crackling blast flung him backwards. His body tumbled over itself several times in the air and slid along the ground before slamming against the wall. The vicious tingling across his body nearly blocked out the explanation Pyralis felt he had to offer.

"It's amazing how attuned I am to the sources of heat in this room. I can feel your every movement, the way your heart is speeding up, the rising heat and exhaustion that is wearing you out. Sorry to say your little tricks won't work. Go ahead and play with all the light you want. I could kill you with my eyes closed."

"Care to really give that a try?" Garen choked out the response while stumbling to his feet.

"Honestly, I might. I'd try anything to make this a more appropriate challenge." Garen could feel that anger inside him reaching a point beyond his control. He wanted to lash out at the creature that could murder a man's father and heap insults at the grieving son. It felt so simple, as easy as letting go of the ledge and flying into the chaos. His instinct told him releasing that rage would make him stronger, but Micah demonstrated from under the shroud as Kiron that it only made him blinder. If he was going to find a way to get the better of Pyralis, he would need his full wits in both quality and quantity, not intensity.

Pyralis prattled on theatrically, playing up his own dominance while wearing that smug grin of self-satisfaction. "If getting rid of you is this easy, you don't leave me much hope for a tough fight down the road."

"That's a kindness on my part. I try not to get anyone's hopes up before they die."

Pyralis arched an eyebrow. "You think you still have a chance, do you? Let's see what happens if you get close enough to actually use that sword." He held up his arms, and a long pole of fire stretched out between his hands. Garen had seen the cutting potential of the fiery discs and imagined this weapon could do the same. If he had any chance, it would have to be fast. If he didn't rely on the false image, he might be able to bounce in quick enough to connect with his sword.

For lack of better options, he took a breath and shot across the room in his elemental state. Just as he tried to reform behind his opponent, Pyralis swept his blazing staff in a full arc around him. Garen quickly changed himself back to light. He felt the smoldering sensation cross through his chest. Unnerved by the intense heat, he continued his travel across the room to a safe distance.

"Careful, Garen. You're getting predictable."

He tried to calm himself down, but the exchange rattled him deeply. He could move across the chamber faster than the eye could follow, but needed to take physical form to actually strike him. What if next time he reformed while the staff went through him? If he thought the flames were hot in that state, how uncomfortable would he be skewered on them? He shook himself, trying to clear the image. He had to keep Pyralis from

274

getting inside his head.

In doing so, an epiphany struck Garen. If Pyralis could get inside his head, he was certain he could do the same on a much more devastating scale. Micah taught him how to deflect the mental and emotional blows of battle, but defense wasn't winning this fight. He sheathed his katana, ready to take the offensive.

Before Pyralis could stop him, not that he knew how, Garen plunged into the depths of his enemy's brain. The entrance was dark and twisted, but with a little work to pry deeper, he found the memory he was looking for.

A four-years-younger Pyralis returned to his father after the disappearance of Seth and Garen. The simultaneous return of the emperor's sons made it clear that the time to pass on the crown was near. Pyralis surprised his father one evening in his personal chambers with a bottle of wine and a request to talk about the kingdom's future. Emperor Tibalt politely accepted a glass, but told Pyralis that bribes would not get him very far. He was the youngest, the weakest, and the least responsible of his sons. When Pyralis tried to interrupt him, Tibalt screamed at his son for wasting time and money trying to negotiate his worth instead of proving it. Pyralis clenched his fists, aching with regret that those would be his father's last words. Tibalt was wrong. The wine was no bribe. It was poison.

Garen tried to scrape together what details he could about Sarkos, but panicked when he saw the image currently in Pyralis' eyes. He rushed toward Garen's position along the wall to take the opportune strike. Garen returned just in time to duck under the fire stream that blazed by his head. Pyralis did not waste his efforts on the nimble target. He screamed and let an explosion of flame emerge around him. Garen expected a more targeted blast that he could dodge, and the force caught Garen by surprise, throwing him back across the chamber once more. The amount of fighting in the room left the stone floor jagged, and he felt the shards scrape his open side as he slid. Still, he pushed through the pain and rose to his feet. He was already on the verge of collapsing, and he knew he couldn't keep taking these incidental blows for much longer. With his new strategy, he hoped he wouldn't have to.

"Must have been nice to meet someone like Sarkos," Garen said.

"Is that supposed to bother me? You don't know the first thing about him."

"I know he paid attention to you, even praised your skills, your ambition. Which, if your memory serves you, is more than your father ever did." Garen could feel the temperature rise in the room as the words found their mark.

"Steal my thoughts all you want. You have no way to know what that felt like."

"Which word stung the most? When he called you irresponsible? Weak? Short-sighted? He never paid you the respect you deserved, did he?"

Flames jutted behind him as he charged toward Garen recklessly. He launched a column of flame to silence him, but Garen had already light-shifted across the room.

"And when you couldn't feel more insignificant, he ships you and your brothers off to live with my family. You know, I think my father cared for you more than your own did."

Pyralis spun and released a wave of flame engulfing the entire chamber. Distance was Garen's friend, giving him time to anticipate and jump past the consuming fires. "Not that it mattered. Seems you're fine killing any father figure, whether they care for you or just despise you."

"Will you shut up!" Pyralis screamed, fully blinded by his rage, releasing a cone of flame at Garen with each word.

"Does Sarkos even know how far you went to speed things along and follow him?" Garen continued, dodging the last threatening blast. "You haven't offered him any wine lately, have you?"

With his own secrets out in the open, Pyralis' blasts became wildly uncontrolled. They were larger and more devastating, but carelessly aimed. Garen could dodge fireballs twice as large and fast from a distance, but moving in close was riskier than ever. He knew he had pushed his foe to the edge.

Sheer recklessness wasn't going to bring him down, though.

Garen had tried to use water and wind to his advantage, but fire was their natural opposite too, and Pyralis had a much stronger use of them. The amount of ice Garen would have to summon to compete would empty his soul completely. He had already used a heavy portion throughout the battle. Garen couldn't use the elemental relationships to his advantage, but another memory of that lesson popped into his head. Micah told him just how many young Spellswords met their fate by over-relying on their own element when it did not fit the response. So, if he could not play to his own strengths, perhaps he could play to his enemy's weakness.

Garen launched a jet of water at Pyralis, which he easily turned to steam. Garen shifted to the other side of the room and released a powerful gale wind. Garen could feel the spell tug at the bottom of his soul, and he knew he was nearly empty. The restoration of his father's soul and all his creative attempts caught up with him. If this final plan did not go accordingly, he would have no depth left to give. Garen clung to the last bit of life in his soul and watched to see how his enemy would respond. Pyralis fired his own salvo, overpowering the gust. Garen had already disappeared when it crashed onto the wall.

Pyralis could feel his prey's heat on the opposite wall again. He turned to release another wild shot of fire without looking to see what was coming for him. The blast was powerful enough to evaporate water or dissipate wind. It crashed into Garen and seared every inch of exposed flesh. Garen stepped into the blast with his arm raised, as if throwing a javelin. The overwhelming heat knocked him backward. It did not, however, slow the katana he released overhead. The heated blade spiraled through the flames. Pyralis saw the molten weapon approaching, and fury became fear. It pierced straight through his chest. The look of terror still covered his face as he fell flat against his side.

Garen rolled along the ground, extinguishing the smoldering parts of his tunic. Every part of him ached or burned, some both. He had no more than a moment to stare blankly at his deed before the footsteps from the courtyard forced him back to his feet. Instead of more soldiers, Drake stepped into the room, quickly followed by the others. They gasped at the sight of Garen covered from head to toe in blood and charred scraps. Moments later, they noticed both corpses. Each Spellsword was stunned beyond words. All except the last to file in.

"Seth? Seth, no!" Argus screamed, racing over to his friend's body. "I knew it. I knew I should have stayed with him." He sobbed angrily and pounded the ground beside him. Garen tried to speak, but Argus didn't stop pounding.

Garen stepped closer, avoiding looking at his father, and forced a word in. "It wouldn't have mattered," Garen said, still overcoming the shock himself. "They put some kind of explosive in him."

Drake's eyes widened at the fear he could have the same inside his own. Similarly, Naia began to search the room for the sister she could have sworn she left here. Garen noticed them both and responded to Drake first.

"No, I think the rest of us are safe," Garen reasoned. "It looks like he did it for his own purposes, since it went against their plans to sacrifice the spirits." Garen pulled back the shell of stone that covered Morgan, revealing her unharmed state. He resumed the spell in her bloodstream until the drug thinned and relinquished control.

The fight was over, and the calm demeanor that helped him survive it had no purpose anymore. He could feel his own shell cracking as his hands started to tremble. He turned to the only other person that he felt could share his pain. "He's gone, Argus. He's gone. I'd just got him back, and now he's gone again." Argus placed both hands on his shoulders and held him firmly, though the man himself was still shaking a little.

"No, you saved him. I figure you've always been his redemption. And now you got the spirit that lived inside of him. It's a part of you."

"Actually, not yet," Drake said, bending over Pyralis body. Garen looked over and saw the arm twitch, realizing he hadn't yet finished the job.

"Then I don't have to take the spirit, do I?" Garen asked,

rubbing his eyes to regain some composure. "You know, it could get a little crowded in here."

"It would, and I'm hoping to avoid that scenario in our lives. Now the person who has trained for this day can take it," Micah said.

"Well, Argus, I know you've been aching to become a full-fledged Spellsword for some time. Finish it quickly, will you? He's a bit of a nuisance to bring down."

"No, Garen, I'm not in line for the Fire Spirit. I've just trained to inherit the Earth Spirit."

"You're kidding, right? Then who is?"

"The only one of us—," Morgan coughed out, limping her way to his body, "—with a level enough head to control it." She reached for the katana sticking of the Pyralis' chest and yanked it to the side and out. His twitching arm fell flat against the charred stone beneath him. She took a moment and breathed in her own victory.

Garen wasn't ready for silence yet, and he chimed in, "Seriously? Like you two weren't opposites enough already?"

"I don't know," Argus said wiping his nose. "I think the 'fire and ice sisters' has a nice ring to it."

"Fire and ice?" Naia shot back. "She just matched my rank five seconds ago, why does her name come first?"

"Sorry, Naia, now it's stuck for sure," Garen said, barely able to force a smile. She stuck her tongue out at him, and he knew for certain that, amidst the grief, he'd survive it with them. One last question entered his mind.

"What happened to Sarkos?"

"He's long gone by now," Micah responded. "He tried to hold out against all of us, but he quickly realized his odds. He took his exit traveling underground like the coward he is. But I suspect with the Western Kingdom's leader dead, he won't stay hidden for long."

The room fell quiet for a moment. For the first time in their presence, Garen did not feel any awkwardness. The lull of the moment soothed him.

"Should we tear this place down?" Drake asked, ready as

everyone else to leave it for good.

"I think Garen is the man for that job. He has a bit of experience, I'm told," Micah added in with a smirk.

Garen followed them to the central tower. "If you have any tender good-byes to say, better do them now."

"May you rot in the soulless city, Theltus Nisdal," Morgan said, groaning in pain as she kicked a pile of dirt onto the outer wall.

The others nodded, feeling much the same about their surroundings. Garen placed his hand against the stone and felt the spirit inside him agree as well. The turquoise glow spread through the tower. He did not feel like waiting for the collapse to begin. Drake glided them out of the temple grounds, distantly watching the structures collapse below. He had a strong feeling they were all enjoying it much more the second time around.

CHAPTER
TWENTY-NINE

Garen had forgotten the thrill of Drake's wind chariot until they were soaring through the clouds again. When they touched down within the palace courtyard, he felt the journey went too quickly, but he knew it was not the last. Or at least it was not worth asking Drake to take him around the sky for a few more laps.

"I should probably inform the counsel their king is still alive," Micah said casually. "But after those matters are taken care of, I believe a celebration is in order, or perhaps a long nap. Which comes first?"

"I've think I've slept enough to last me through the year," Drake quickly replied.

"I'll second that," Morgan added. "I'm in the mood to feast."

"Alright, one banquet fit for a king and the men and women he owes his life to, coming up."

Drake and Morgan were only too thrilled after their extended hibernation, and Argus followed closely, as enthused as any other about the prospect of food. Naia fell to the back of the group alongside Garen, clearly wanting to say something. He knew he had a good portion of hero-worship on its way after saving them all, and he was ready to let that tide start rolling in.

"Listen, there's no need to say th—Ouch!" Garen recoiled in surprise as she buried her knuckles into his arm.

"That's for running off on us, you moron." They had stopped walking and let the group take off inside. She stared him down with her fierce blue eyes, brow furrowed in judgment. The piercing glare broke suddenly as she wrapped her arms around him. Garen was far too surprised to return the embrace, and stood awkwardly wondering if this was really happening.

"But Morgan wouldn't be here, none of us would, if you hadn't come back." She stepped away and looked Garen in the eyes once more, smiling this time. "So, thank you. Maybe you aren't just a presumptuous thug."

"Aw, and maybe you're not a complete ice queen."

"Ooh, you think you're the first person to come up with that?"

"I'm the first person to use it as a compliment, am I not?"

She snickered and punched him in the arm again. "You're a real pain, you know that?"

He did, and he enjoyed it.

* * * * *

The feast was beyond even Garen's expectations, and he expected quite a showing after what they'd survived. The meal centered around an exquisite Teochew braised duck, accompanied by a spread of imported grilled sea bream. Garen's tastes were not expansive enough to appreciate many of the exotic cheeses, pickled vegetables, and candied onions that surrounded him, but as he bit into a freshly ripened persimmon, he knew he would not go hungry tonight.

Surely the kitchen staff must have wondered what to think with the conflicting signs in front of them. Micah made his address, reassuring all of Vikar-Tola and its surrounding estates that they had nothing to worry about. "Inclement weather," as he put it, kept him from returning to deliver his timely update for the coming autumn season. The physicians did well to hide his injuries, but anyone close enough to see him in the palace knew that he'd been through some kind of torture. Adding to those rumors, now the chefs had been ordered to prepare a feast of unrivaled magnitude for their king and his equally war-torn Spellswords.

The gossip was certain to be rich, but none of the returning heroes cared in the slightest. The six of them sat around their dining table enclosed from the rest of the world and its worries. Drake sat across from Argus, one cutting and savoring dainty portions, and the other devouring figs by the fistful. Morgan made slow, careful movements as she reached for dishes, but grimaced every time she raised either arm. Naia tried to help her struggling sister, but she would have nothing of the sort. Garen and Micah couldn't help but laugh, but they both scaled the chuckle back as they noticed the other. There was no foul air between them, but something still felt strangely out of place. It probably had something to do with the unfamiliar face, for once not shadowed behind the draping hood. Still, the others carried on no different than before, which comforted Garen. They had known all along, keeping his orders to conceal his identity until the time was right. As such, the nature of their relationship with Micah was no different with or without the shroud, and he was grateful to have that bit of his new home hold true.

Micah's eyes caught Garen mid-thought, and seemed to ask a question. "Are you okay?" it probed silently. In the midst of everyone carrying on, Garen could see the worry in his eyes. Though they all felt the loss, Garen had been the only one whose entire purpose had been shattered beneath him. The group as a whole had labeled the day a victory, but did he feel that way personally?

Garen nodded, trying to dismiss his friend's concern. The response felt strangely out of place again, too casual for a response to the king. It would take some time to completely merge the sections of his mind on Kiron and Micah. Still, even in that moment he could remind himself that this was the person he had trained beside all spring and summer. This was the man that instilled value and purpose in him and nearly died for that belief, the same way his father had. Garen had to stop and honestly consider the implicit question. Was today a success? He failed to save his father. Avenging his murder was a poor substitute.

He thought back to the day he killed Sustek Nash and that feeling of setting things right. This was different. On that day Garen left with the sense of a new presence within him. Regardless of when he actually inherited the spirit and its gifts, it was the feeling from that day on that let him embrace it. Now he had actually, in full truth, set the crimes against his father to rest. But what did he have to show for it? He had not inherited any greater power. He knew in some part of his mind that he could take the credit for saving the world, but that was too distant a victory to latch on to. Years of life on the run taught him that no mission was worth its risk unless you made it back with bags in hand. So, what was his cut?

A loud coughing fit erupted from Argus and stole Garen's attention. Between short wheezes he motioned frantically to his throat. Naia raced from her seat to help him, wrapping her tiny arms around his gut and squeezing. Though the effort seemed pointless, Garen had to remind himself that the girl was deceptively strong. After the second heave, Argus flung his head forward, expelling the troublesome fig. In the commotion, Drake had stood from his chair, but had not yet raced around the table to help. The position left him directly in the line of fire of the soggy chunk of fruit. It caught him right between the eyes, and the mush and seeds began to drip down his nose. The room fell silent long enough for Drake to sit back down and stoically wipe the mess from his face.

"Go ahead. You can laugh," Drake sighed.

The room did not even wait for him to finish. From the first word, the howls of laughter echoed around them in a style each their own. Argus bellowed deep chuckles between his labored breathing. Naia squeaked with her shrill giggle. Morgan started to join in, but quickly reached for her side. Amidst the pain, she managed to laugh quietly through the frown. Micah wore a simple smile, a form of laughter in his own way. Garen put his hands behind his head and reveled in a smirk all his own.

This is your cut, right here.

Through the loss of his mother, he'd inherited an incredible power. That gift, however, seemed small compared to what his father left for him: community. True community, where everyone gets because everyone gives. It was no less a source of strength. The more he understood it, the more he would not hesitate to carry it into battle either.

* * * * *

"Garen," Micah called out, catching his attention before

he stepped into his room. With a full stomach, Garen was hoping to lay back and drift off as soon as possible. Still, he could postpone it for this inevitable encounter. He wasn't sure what to expect the man to say about the strange twists in their relationship over the past week. Even more so, Garen wasn't sure what *he* should say either. His hand left the doorknob, and he walked over to where Micah stood at the top of the stairs.

"I understand if you'd rather disappear right now. But if you have a moment, I'd really like to talk."

"I can talk," Garen responded quickly. He opened his mouth to go on, but it seemed too casual to simply ask, "What's on your mind?" Instead, after the awkward interchange, Micah went ahead.

"I know that there is no amount of 'I'm sorry's and 'Thank you's to make up for what I've done and what you've done for us. But before the shock of today settles, I needed you to know something." He paused briefly, both capturing Garen's full attention and worrying him slightly. "We've deceived you further than I ever should have let it go. Especially when it came to Nash. I can assure you that he was a loathsome man. If you knew the families he tore apart and the innocent people he shipped off in slavery, I don't believe you'd have acted any differently. But it wasn't right to send you to kill any man under false pretenses. I understand now just how wrong that was, and thus, I want to offer you an exit. If I've betrayed you beyond what's possible to forgive, you are welcome to take your talents and part ways. I know you'll still do justice for this kingdom even on your—"

"No thanks." Micah's eyes had trailed down as he spoke, but the unexpected interruption snapped his attention back up to a level view. Both waited for the other to say more, but neither had another word on their mind.

"Alright." Micah wore the same smile Garen imagined countless times under the hood. Now it hung in plain sight and with smiling eyes to match.

Garen turned back toward his chamber, but Micah's voice spun him around again.

"Before you go, there's just one more matter I could use

your help making sense of. You went to the Earth Rogue's chamber, right? Do you know what prompted Sarkos to kill his own servant?"

The memory of the man popped back into Garen's mind, buried underneath the avalanche of pain and victory that came after. He remembered his debt to the warrior along with the only way he could think to repay it.

Without a second thought, the familiar surroundings of the palace vanished. He felt weightless within the dark void. His body reformed in a dim chamber, staring into the prison cell of two women. Both were terrified by his sudden arrival and huddled to the corner. The older one stepped in front of the younger girl to protect her.

"It's okay," Garen whispered. "I'm here to set you free."

They kept their distance. "Why?" the older woman finally asked.

"Because your husband gave his life to save mine. Now it's time to get you out of here."

The younger woman stepped out from behind the other, and Garen just barely recognized her. She had grown so much from the distant memories inside her father's mind. Still, this was his daughter Elise, the unmistakable center of his world.

"You knew my dad?"

"Only briefly. But he was an incredible man."

She smiled through the grief. "Thank you."

Garen could get used to words like those. They were nearly addicting. But right now, he needed to focus on finding their exit. He had arrived here more by accident than anything. One day he hoped to understand why that kept happening, but in the meantime, he would have to settle for more natural methods of escape. Garen laid his hand against the simple metal lock and bent the tumblers into place. The door squeaked open and Garen motioned for the women to step outside the cage. He could tell from their reluctance just how long they'd been forced to survive in that cramped cell. The thought made him cringe, but he forced himself back to their current situation and needs.

"So, where are we?" he asked, starting to take in their

strange surroundings. The high stone walls had no windows, and a hundred small geonodes along the ceiling dimly lit the space. Their cell stood alone in the back of a massive storage facility. There were other freestanding chambers laid out in a grid, but they were much smaller, rounded, and covered entirely in red-iron. The structures confused Garen for a moment, unsure whether he was looking at Western ingenuity or the product of pure magic. Unlikely as it seemed, he had to guess a combination of both.

"It's horrible," the mother whispered in disgust.

Garen tried to search her expression for anything more helpful, but she turned her face to the ground. He walked over to the nearest container, and up close it just looked like a rounded metal tank. Strangely, the entire front was on a hinge.

"No, you can't look! It's too—" the young girl froze, unable to describe what she'd seen. "They're growing—" Again, the word either eluded her, or she could not force the truth out. Garen understood their concern, but he had to see what Sarkos was planning. Garen wanted to believe that Project Theltus was the end of it, that all these madmen wanted to do was strip the world of magic. But a facility like this told him otherwise. There was more to their plan.

The pod had a small window on the hinged portion. Garen cautiously approached it. It was hard to see anything with the dark liquid inside. He cupped his hands around the edge and peered closer. Something was suspended the water. He stared for a moment until the figure tossed about in its sleep, turning its face toward him.

"Really, you can't!" She screamed. "They're growing—"

People?

287

Garen returns in
SPELLSHIFT
(Spellsaga Book 2)

Details at AllenSnell.com

Made in the USA
Middletown, DE
21 November 2020